I0748365

A SERENADE FOR SELENE

Book one of

Memories from Oblivion

Atlas Hill

Rhapsody Books

This is a work of fiction. All the characters, organisations, and events portrayed in this novel are either products of the author's imagination or are used fictitiously.

First published by Rhapsody Books in 2018

Cover art by Zicuta
Map art by Shovel

ISBN 978-0-6482852-0-5

eBook ISBN 978-0-6482852-1-2

The Land of Skybed
Aizary
12
Cetal
3
Astilow
7
8
4
Sequiposa
Pichreuse
Vinawell
Saffron
Whitesand
1
2
Trubannis
5
Easterclem
Farella
Cellarsy
9
Noel
6
Strombolith
Zenith
11
Kraga
Seniblum
10
Fernusin
Busparen
13
1 Zorlia
2 Bastion City
3 Cetal City
4 Derellsdale
5 Frey
6 Dawnsdale
7 Poppaross
8 Aragon
Harper Springs
9 Millenzburg
10 Spheria
Illudia
11

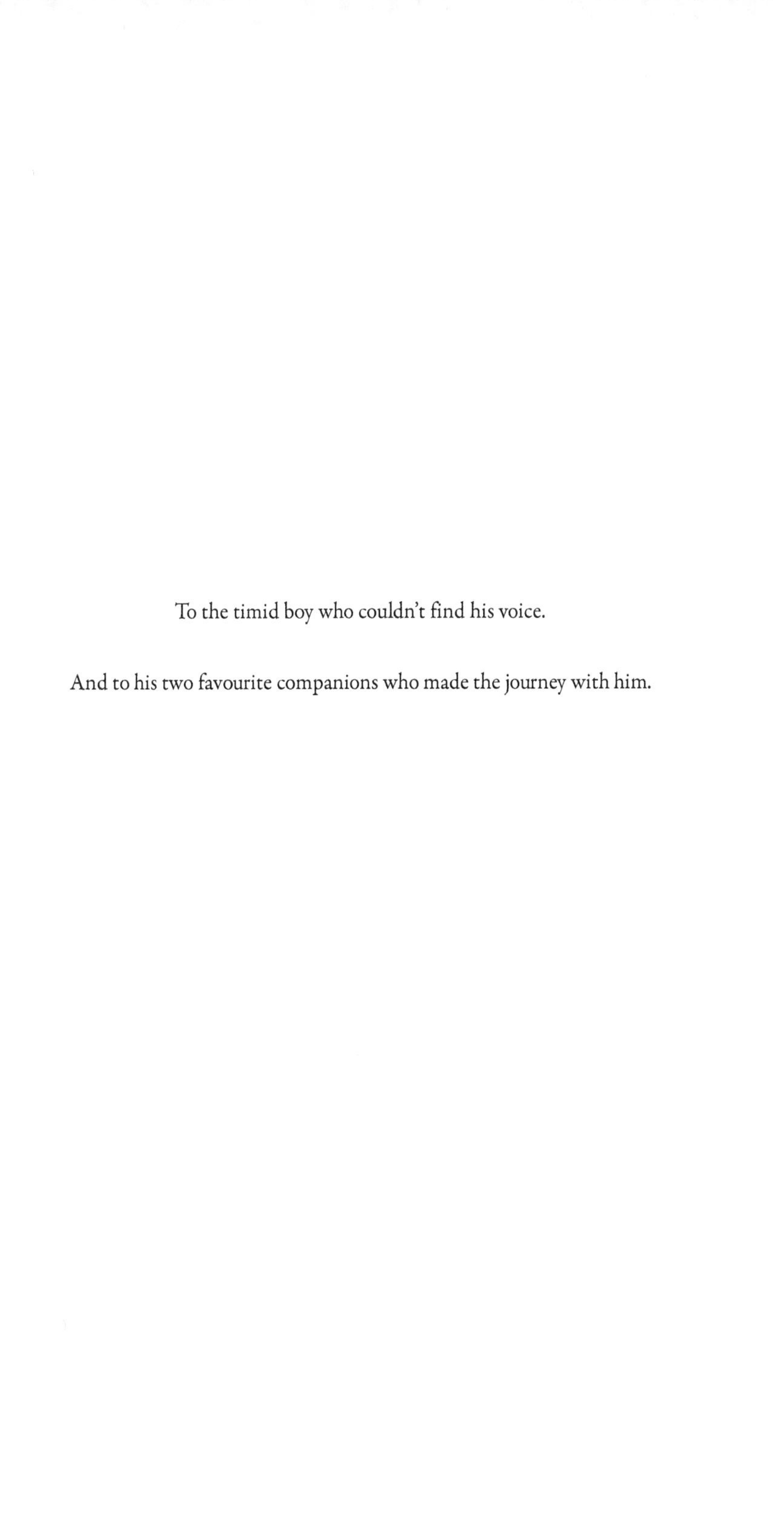

To the timid boy who couldn't find his voice.

And to his two favourite companions who made the journey with him.

Contents

PROLOGUE 1

PART I 3

PART II 121

EPILOGUE 267

ACKNOWLEDGEMENTS 274

FINAL WORD 275

PROLOGUE

Magic was no new concept. They had known magic since the beginning of time, always synonymous with good virtue and divinity, a power accessible only to the angels, the saints, and the Immortal himself. Because if this same power ever extended beneath the heavens and granted freely to the mortals, the admiration for it would diminish like withering flora enduring a merciless winter, and the balance of the land would tip forever toward discord and disorder.

But whether it was a blunder by the heavens or an experiment of grand design from some unknown source, the unimaginable had become a dreaded reality. Magic had managed to spill its way down to the land of men and was now granted to beings who could neither control nor understand these new powers.

Magic was now in the hands of fools who did not deserve it.

Everything could be traced back to that fateful day, barely a year after the end of a decade of war that had ended the lives of far more people than the history books would ever properly record. It was almost as if the heavens decided that humankind should be obliterated after all. If self-destruction failed, then divine judgement was surely in order. The survivors spoke of a pernicious storm that had swept violently across every corner of the land, a storm that many claimed to have originated in the northeast following days of blackened skies that grimly foreshadowed the end of all life. All the while, rain and wind crashed about as endless thunder tore forth from the skies. Had the storm lasted longer, the hundreds of fatalities might well have been the utter end to all human life.

But the storm finally cleared as mysteriously as it had appeared, and emerging from the fading clouds were Achelois and Selene—the moons, aligned one atop the other in the same way as depicted by the Ionian symbol of faith. As resplendent as the image had been, the moment was also marked as the awakening of magic users and the birth of a new, uncertain world.

Seven years had passed since then, but people were no closer to being able to explain the seemingly apocalyptic phenomenon. Had there been a purpose? A message? Philosophers and other great thinkers, including those hailing from the celebrated *Villa of Enlightenment*, began defining those who were bestowed with the ability to wield magic as the *chosen* minority. The faithful did not agree, especially those of the *Holy Church of the St. Bernard Order*, instead labelled these people as sinned, as cursed. And as faith had experienced a grand revival in recent years, widespread preaching resulted in mass disdain for magic users.

Some scholars defended magic users, however, asserting that they were no different from anyone else. These scholars argued that not only did the practitioners of magic look the same, but they thought in the same way as they previously had, too. The general consensus was that magic users were extremely rare. They had not 'risen' or threatened civilisation as some commentators had claimed. There had been no documents of harassment on any level by magic users, and there certainly was no evidence of anyone in possession of powers that could move mountains or break apart the seas.

But everything changed with the recent emergence of one such being who many believed possessed those very powers.

Not only was this being bold in his actions, but he was far from an ordinary magic user—if there was even a definition for that. Alleged witnesses were convinced that this thing with the shell of a man was not human. It was said that he believed that death was true liberation, and sure enough, he had the ability to easily arrange for it. No man survived a confrontation with him to describe their experience. And the number of the dead was now listed at more than three hundred.

They called him *The Apostle*.

PART I

ONE

The Apostle

The painting was coming to life.

Alpheus dabbed onto the palette, sliding toward the darker colours. He spun the brush forward, stroking again. He didn't care for the speckled paint that stained his snowy-white robe, or the fact that he was confined in the attic of a tower.

From the glowing pale skin to the long tresses of silvery hair sweeping down, the portrait was undoubtedly taking form. Alpheus continued to swab, using his thumb to slide up the platinum framed spectacles resting on the bridge of his nose, which reflected the imposing yet ominous diamond shape of his subject on the canvas. Moving up from the balbo beard, Alpheus stroked his brush harder on some finer details, gazing into a set of murderous eyes that seemed to stare back at him, causing him to tremble with great trepidation. Those hooded eyes of gleaming violet glistened toward him, spurring his heart to race more and more fervently... until the brush snapped in his hands.

He gasped for breath and took a step back from the canvas, dropping what remained of the broken brush.

His interpretation of the Apostle was now complete. Excitement spread across his face in the form of a proud smile. For someone who dreaded the mundanity of everyday life, a *messenger* with the potential to change the world was almost better than he could wish for.

A fierce light streamed into the attic suddenly, blinding Alpheus briefly into a cringe and then reducing his expression to a squint.

"Have you reflected on your misdirection?" a voice asked from behind.

Alpheus closed his eyes for a second and sighed. He didn't have to turn around to know that it was Yorke, and he was also sure that Yorke didn't realise that his arrival had caused everything to dull back into reality: the attic of a poorly lit tower, humble, and quiet as still water.

"I regularly reflect upon everything I do," Alpheus finally said in response, picking up the broken brush from the floor. "Misdirection is aplenty, but with this, I shall pave out a path."

Yorke huffed in annoyance. "Ornamental words," he said, his voice seeming to grow deeper now as it resounded in the confined space. "Pack your tools. You have been summoned."

The grizzled man, grave as always, was already on his way, his softening footsteps receding as he descended. Alpheus sighed again, then flapped a large cloth over his artwork. He carried it with him as he trotted down the narrow spiralling stairs, wary of the tap of his every step. He remembered the day he had first come here, and also why he had come. But he had done none of what had been expected of him, and for that, Yorke had every reason for being blunt. And if Yorke's attitude was a precursor of what was to come, Alpheus might be left to regret it soon enough.

Alpheus took a deep breath upon stepping out of the tower. No one appreciated daylight more than those from whom it had been withheld. Wisps of clouds sailed about wistfully in the otherwise clear sky. The sun seemed eager to emerge from those thin layers of white, but this shade might just be more agreeable to him on this fine autumn day. The tall canopies of red, orange, and yellow upon which the leaves rustled was another sight that Alpheus had missed. And beneath those trees were blooming anemones and a ground swept over with fallen leaves, some lifted gently by the breeze. The panorama was completed with a reflection cast in the rippling waters.

Now wasn't the time to appreciate the landscape, however. Not when Alpheus had already noted the gazebo further down the bay where the man summoning him was waiting. Alpheus recognised his figure even from a distance, the usual top hat he was fitted in, his darkly coloured dress shirt, and the trench coat that fell to the ground from his seated position. The refined man was of course Jeffery Reeling, the Lord Count of the Truban Empire, his gaze focused on the stand before him where the map of the land was clipped.

Alpheus paused just outside the small roofed structure as Yorke proceeded to join his liege. Alpheus winced without a sound, regarding Reeling's back, imagining the heavy burden the man often carried.

Reeling raised his cup of tea, taking a quiet sip. "You failed to recognise what I am asking of you," he said without turning.

Alpheus's lips turned down in a frown. "I was never the right person," he said. "You know I want to help... if only I knew how."

Reeling turned toward Alpheus. A dazzle shot from his right eye behind that distinctive handcrafted monocle, its wire ring dangling past his neat moustache, reaching down his equally well-groomed goatee. He grasped onto a noble mace, waving it along with a dismissive hand. "Perhaps you are not," he said regretfully. "Perhaps my efforts have become void of meaning."

Yorke gestured at Alpheus with a twitch of the brow, and though Alpheus met his eyes, he simply couldn't bring himself to say more. He was never sure what Reeling was looking for, only that it wasn't an apology. Alpheus cringed slightly then, unsure if he was succumbing to a guilt game that Reeling was playing. The man was a master in reading emotions, and sometimes there was pressure just being in his presence. Alpheus was a philosopher himself, a scholar of the Villa of Enlightenment, highly regarded by his peers despite his tender age. But compared to Reeling, his seasoned mentor, Alpheus often felt common, humble even.

Reeling shifted a curious gaze to the sky. And when the man frowned at what he saw, Alpheus glanced up, too. He widened his eyes as the sky grew darker and darker while the clouds thrashed about, thickening in haste. Those wisps of glaring white had expanded out into a furious overcast, and when a seething gust came crashing violently through the gardens, Alpheus realised a very real sensation. The fallen petals seared through the blades of grass and whirled at him like a maelstrom, tossing him to the ground and briefly blinding him.

The blast of air didn't last long, but its effect remained, as the garden was now shrouded in a deep mist. The bay was invisible behind the swirling grey.

Alpheus peered about as he urgently tried to collect his bearings. He eased slightly when he recognised the shape of the gazebo and Reeling's silhouette within it.

"Young master!" Yorke called out to Alpheus, next to Reeling. "Come!"

Alpheus was almost certain that this was some nebulous dream. But that didn't stop his heart from thumping as he raced up to join the pair. *Cannot see anything!* he thought, gritting his teeth. And indeed, vision alone barely allowed him to make out Yorke's face. Alpheus could only confirm it was him on the resolute alertness that he thought defined the man, and which was still apparent in the mist. Reeling, on the other hand, seemed calm enough as he didn't even bother to rise to his feet.

Alpheus shook his head and then peered back out across the field of mist. There was definitely something out there, in the direction from where he had trotted down only moments earlier. If only the thick fog would clear. What was the origin of the fog, anyway? The bay was notorious for misty mornings and evenings, but not even during those times was the air ever this thick.

"There!" Yorke cried, pointing out at the greyness.

A dark patch. Contours barely discernible. Despite that, a curious aura emanated from it, weaving out independently from the visible gloom. Alpheus stared hard as he leaned in. His arms tensed as his hands grasped into thin air. *Wait*, he thought, realising that his painting was missing. *Where is it?*

"Stay alert!" Yorke hollered.

That thing emerged from the greyness now as a pulsing luminance of blood red. As its intensity grew, a figure manifested. Was it... a person? It certainly *looked* human. Alpheus stared harder, then finally let out a gasp when he recognised an eerie resemblance to something only he knew.

"Impossible," he uttered, almost stumbling back in disbelief.

Reeling glanced to Alpheus, noting his awe. But he opted to say nothing as he finally peered out himself.

The creature was stepping forward, gradually revealing a form that appeared more and more human. The brightness pulsing from his core almost made it seem like he was a man engulfed in flames, particularly because of a rippling red cape that flapped ferociously behind him.

"It's him," Reeling said, a nervous grin creeping across his face.

Yorke eyed his liege with a frown. "Must we retreat?" he asked, trembling slightly.

"I do not believe we have that option," Reeling said, finally rising to his feet now.

Alpheus raised a hand slightly as if to urge his mentor from moving directly toward a creature they couldn't even define.

Reeling took only a couple of steps forward until he stopped, but only in response to the intruder who had paused in his approach. The intruder lifted his head slowly as the illumination of striking red continued to pulse. Beneath that hat and the crown creasing up toward the top of his head, a pair of eyes, glistening and violet, glared out toward where the three of them were watching. The swirls of grey began to clear, and the intruder became more defined with identifiable human features. Still, only his eyes were visible, the rest of his face enshrouded behind a puffy shawl that extended out as a ragged cape now riffling more gently.

He didn't remain passive for long, sweeping out an arm that cast away some of the fading mist. With that same arm, he flapped the cape forward, appearing to vanish altogether. Alpheus peered wildly for traces of the disappeared man, but Reeling seemed to know better than to trust only his vision. Either way, they could both agree that the intruder was still around. They needed no further clue than the atmosphere growing more and more tense by the second. That invisible weight forcing down on them inched closer and closer, pouring forth as a sudden heatwave. They turned, and there it was—the creature kindled in a golden radiance, burning within an aura of intense agony, face scrunched up in rage.

It's really him! Alpheus realised, freezing over in horror.

Reeling snatched Alpheus up in haste and leaped out of the gazebo, which had caught onto the golden flame and spreading dangerously. "Yorke!" he cried. "Get out of there!"

Even as Alpheus was being carried away, his eyes were still on the burning small roofed building. He noted Yorke rolling out to safety from the crackling blaze, but the intruder was the one he was watching intently behind his hazing vision. Alpheus was shaking as he clenched tightly at his *double crescent* pendant, which symbolised his faith. *Father of Heaven, what is this?!*

"Watch him," Alpheus heard Reeling say, as he was handed over to Yorke. When Alpheus managed to peer up from Yorke's arm again, Reeling had darted away and lured the intruder and a wall of golden blaze to chase. With the mists almost cleared, it was no longer possible to brush off this spectacle as an illusion.

* * *

Reeling came to a screeching stop at the edge of the bay, achieving the advantage of surprise even against his deity-like foe. *Now!* he thought, swinging his arm out and shooting a stone-sized item from his fingers. He managed to knock off his chaser's hat, extinguishing a fair amount of the golden flames along with it. And as if in reward, the intruder came to a pause, giving Reeling a good look at him. Long tresses of his silver hair undulated under the breeze.

The intruder peered down at the projectile that had sent his hat away with the winds. A pebble. He then looked up again, meeting Reeling's eyes.

A young man, Reeling noted. *And of Aizar descent. Those eyes...*, he thought, looking into the hooded contours whose violet irises seemed infinitely deep, perhaps enabling him to gaze into impossible distances. Reeling jumped then as the pupils dilated suddenly, the phantasm of an *endless knot* billowing out.

Reeling blinked and shook off the gloss. When he was alert again, the intruder was already revolving his arms in a silky motion, bringing fallen leaves and flower petals into the air to encircle him along with that golden radiance in another display of his miraculous abilities. Reeling grunted and then began racing away a second time. His chaser traced him with only his eyes until a sweep of an arm directed those leaves and petals to dart toward Reeling, flitting up like a ribbon and then raining down lethally, like blazing golden arrows.

Reeling dove behind one of the largest trees, a sycamore. He considered himself fortunate that those blazing leaves hadn't homed in on him. Even so, they thundered into the trunk on the other side like hundreds of swords, every foray shaking the sycamore, more and more leaves sprinkling down.

Reeling eyed the nuts that fell, snatching up a few of them into his hands. The flurry had ended, but idleness wasn't an option. He poked his head out carefully, noting that the mists had all but cleared. Resolute, he sprinted away from the sycamore and back into the open—racing directly toward the intruder. But just as the pair was to clash, Reeling sprung high up into the air.

The intruder groaned as he looked up with a squint, obviously bothered by the glaring sun. He was eyeing Reeling's flapping of his trench coat until the soporific motion induced a mirage of silhouettes that had him shutting his eyes altogether. Perhaps he sensed it in other ways, but the intruder seemed unable to do anything as Reeling flicked down the sycamore nuts with acuity and strength, striking the critical ligaments and knocking his foe to the ground, snuffing out the last of the golden flames.

Reeling himself landed with a heavy momentum that forced him to kick off to a roll. But he was quick to find his feet, pulling out a thin string from his coat as he raced once more at his opponent. He would allow the intruder no opportunity to recover, flicking out another nut, hitting an ankle that kept him down. Reeling allowed himself a brief smile as he then proceeded to bind the man's hands together, circling him and pulling that string tight.

Yorke, who had been watching from a distance, ran to his liege now, who seemed to have achieved the impossible. The intruder was contained and forced to lie face down, though still trying to writhe his way out from the confines of the bindings. To further restrain him, Reeling spun his mace and then blasted him, causing the intruder to spurt out a heap of blood from his mouth. The scene merited triumph, but Reeling instead withdrew his grip and turned a surprise frown as he noted that his foe's insides were already in shambles.

"I did not realise your handicap," Reeling confessed as he stepped away. "But this is the least you deserve," he continued with a snort. "For all those you murdered."

The intruder grinned as he continued lying lamed on the grass, though he had managed to turn his head to the side, some of his long silver hair falling over his face. "Numbers are meaningless," he said in a thin voice that didn't reflect his fearful abilities. "In a world where the physical is but imperfect, life fails."

Reeling lifted his chin, musing on the remark. "Do you intend to tell me your purpose?"

"My purpose is no longer relevant," the intruder said, staring out into the field of green from his angle. "Perhaps I never had one. And now that falsehood would wane away with me."

"You might not have to die just yet," Reeling said. "If my sources serve me right, there is a physician who—"

"With or without this temporal existence," the intruder cut in, "nothing will change our collective fate. Our time has come to an end. As always, he was right from the beginning."

"He? Who?"

The intruder finally afforded a glance up now. "I see you are no ordinary man. It is best that you learn the truth on your own. And once you do, remember that I warned you that resistance is futile."

"I have not a clue what you are saying," Reeling said, shaking his head.

The intruder laughed. He pushed himself up with his elbows and then hopped up to a precarious footing. He eyed the yarn that bound his hands together, snapping them free with a simple thrust, only for his arms to hang limp from his shoulders. Reeling stepped further away, gesturing for Yorke to do the same.

The intruder raised his head now, looking heavenward with eyes that had grown suddenly hollow. "Doom is imminent," he whispered, his voice growing weaker. He murmured some words that were unintelligible to Reeling and Yorke, which then became a bloodcurdling scream that resounded into a terrible vibration that shook the ground and riffled the bay. His hair and cape fluttered out under a sudden gust that seemed to have formed from his feet, while the earlier pulsing luminance of blood red returned.

Yorke hissed, but Reeling simply watched on with quiet curiosity. Reeling believed the intruder had had no intention to fight from the beginning, though what he was attempting now was anyone's guess.

"We are an experiment," the intruder said, laying his eyes on Reeling again, his thin voice returning to strength. "We were necessary. But our time has ended. Mark my words, as they shall do you good."

He smiled somewhat peacefully as his eyelids fell. That golden radiance ignited again, roaring out from his body. But this time, the flames flared into his body, burning him with a soft crackling.

"No!" Reeling cried, reaching a futile arm out, only to be held back by Yorke.

Saving the man was impossible, and now it was too late as the golden flames caught momentum, blasting out a stronger second round, engulfing the intruder's entire figure.

It was barely seconds later when the flames died off as swiftly as they had emerged. The intruder lay dead in the middle of an incinerated patch of grass, the corpse covered in dust but otherwise remaining inexplicably unscathed, including the strange clothing he wore. Reeling cleared his throat and stepped ahead while Yorke followed with a hesitant step. Reeling crouched down and ran a hand softly over the dead man's eyes, brushing off some of the ash.

"Lord Count," Yorke said, crouching down too at the corpse's hand. "Look at this."

There on the open palm of the hand was a ring that gleamed brilliantly, a sapphire solitaire mounted on top of a silver band. Reeling picked up the ring, regarding it with a slight frown.

Yorke groaned. "Was he... human?"

"He was," Reeling said, closing his hands. *But he was more than that*, he thought. Reeling looked up then, turning to the tree where Yorke had left Alpheus. Alpheus was still there, and still trembling, sitting against the trunk with his legs extended out as his hand clutched onto his religious pendant.

"Are you all right?" Reeling asked, concerned for the young scholar as he trotted toward him.

Alpheus glanced up at him, breathless. He then gestured at Reeling with a sideways turn of his eyes. It was his painting, lying on the grass, its protective cloth having been swept away long ago. Reeling held his breath as he regarded the painting, his eyes widening as he realised the source of Alpheus's horror.

The portrait was that of the intruder—*the Apostle*, someone Alpheus had never met until today.

Reeling turned a nervous smile, rising again and flapping out his trench coat. "Yorke, let us head to the court. Zorlia is in for a big day."

TWO
The Truban Empire

The year was *Advent 8*, which marked the eighth year of the *Advent Era* following the forty-year reign of the *Anaphora Era*. Perched on the most enviable throne in the land was Kasimir de Spartamon, who had renamed the obsolete *Sargon Monarchy* to the *Truban Empire*. After leading the largest rebellion army in history to fend off foreign enemies, he had been hailed as the leader of Trubannis, pronounced the Lord Emperor. And in the eight years under his leadership, the country had seen an impressive resurgence to power. The Empire had reformed into a feudal system and was arguably the greatest authority across the land.

Spartamon had aged some years since the war, but he hadn't lost his charisma. He had been called *the wolf* for as long as one could remember, that name highlighting his sharp intelligence and his appetite to free others, as well as his frightening ability to pounce at his enemies. And with those qualities, he had continued to lead with efficiency, arranging restoration work across what had been a war-torn country when he had won his crown.

The phenomenal efforts had since translated to conditions that already bettered the pre-war times, especially in the major cities. A renewed focus on the Ionian religious doctrine had resulted in a major resurgence of churches, and the vital spread of the faith had proved to be instrumental in the efforts to rebuild. Education reforms had seen numerous academies established across the country where, in some cases, even commoners were given opportunities to learn. Perhaps the most radical change had been the prohibition of slavery and prostitution, which the emperor had described as one of the greatest barriers to uniting the people.

It was also credit to the extraordinary collective effort of the people—which, in turn, was a product of the infectious promotion of patriotism by the Empire that edged close to chauvinism. It all seemed merry on the outside, but unfortunately, there was an uglier truth beneath. And anyone who attended the court could attest to that.

During this last year, rumours had suggested that a number of people were vying for the throne. And while most of those names could be laughed off simply because they could never pose a threat to the great Emperor Spartamon, one name in particular stood out as someone who could actually usurp his power. And that man was the Lord Chancellor Schim, who, in his years of trekking across every part of the country as a regent for the emperor, had won himself enough favour and support to rival his liege.

The prospect had initially been met with indifference. After all, Schim had been the emperor's most loyal supporter for longer than anyone could remember. The man adored the emperor and had done far more than anyone else for his cause. Schim had been known as someone who would defend the emperor with his life, not someone who would turn on him.

But recent incidents from only a little over a year prior might suggest otherwise. Sure, it had been only another rumour, quickly quashed as a falsehood fabricated with the most malicious of intent. But when the incident had involved the near murder of the Lord Chancellor, tingled curiosities had been inevitable. It had been said that Schim was the target of a failed assassination attempt. The assassin had managed to escape, but the evidence had pointed to the emperor as the source of the attempt at the Lord Chancellor's life.

The rift in the relationship between the two most powerful men of the country wasn't obvious, at least not to the unknowing civilians. Even the two men themselves had time and again brushed off any differences between them in public settings. And yet, the more they had appealed that there was nothing to suspect, the more suspicious people close to them had become. And whether they had any intentions for it, the court had effectively been divided between those who supported the emperor, and these others who supported the chancellor—and worse yet, the minority that planned their own bid for the throne.

This current deadlock had been previously unthinkable in the earlier years of the new era. Spartamon had been the unanimous leader that the country had wanted. And this predicament could only be blamed on a massive blunder three years prior that had caused his reputation to plummet. The Empire had published chronicles that detailed their much-adored leader's rise to power, with the intention to further unite the people. But a chapter in the book entitled *The Proud Conqueror* had been less inviting to acclaim, alluding to the emperor's love of killing and his alleged mass execution of the men who had fought for him. And this excerpt had quickly become a folk tale that spread like wildfire from Zorlia to the rest of the country. The *wolf* label had somehow been defiled to stand now for his wicked schemes and the terrorisation of the common people.

The chronicles were no longer accessible, however, and the folk-tale was no longer told anywhere. And that was only after the Empire had responded with the brutal persecution of anyone who referenced it, an action that further dented Spartamon's reputation.

No one found this growing tension in the court merry. The rest of the country, even in the outskirts, was in unrest without knowing exactly why. The stalemate had begun to take effect, and the ones to suffer were the civilians who were regularly bombarded with new, contradicting laws. The emperor had lost the grip on the people's trust. He was no longer able to unify the people.

* * *

It hadn't been so for a while, but the court of *Vondra Dawn* was a lively place today. After months of deliberation and planning, all of those three dignified members of the Empire who had been based outside the capital state had finally arrived. From here on, they were to be a part of the court's everyday line-up.

One of those newcomers was a burly military man named Breunor. "I hear there's a madman running rampant here in Zorlia," he said with his gravelly voice. "The Apostle, they call him. It seems like no one can catch him. But if I were put to the task, he would be contained within a week."

Victor Breunor was of state *Zenith*. He was widely known as the man who had sensationally abandoned the falling Sargon Monarchy before forming the *Golden Dragon Knights Army* in the aid of the Clan of Light. After the war, he had retired as a golden knight, taking on his new role as State Minister of Zenith.

In Zorlia now, however, he was to function as the *Margrave*, responsible for spearheading military forces across the country. He had grown bald since the war, but his iconic, friendly mutton chops were still recognisable by many. He appeared stronger than ever with his burly physique, and that was despite him closing in at nearly fifty years of age. It was a strange sight to realise that Breunor no longer donned golden armour, but he made sure people knew who he was with the high-quality woven woollen garments attached with strips of golden velvet. It was stranger yet that he no longer held a sword. Instead, his right hand grasped onto a bludgeon of obsidian black.

"There is no need to contain anyone," Reeling announced as he treaded onto the court, spinning his mace with one hand as his momentum lifted his long coat.

Every man turned to him, some with inimical gazes. The emperor looked up, too, wearing a grin. "Lord Count," he said, meeting Reeling's eyes. "I trust that there is good reason for your late arrival."

"There is, My Lord," Reeling said as he tipped off his top hat, following with a bow. He then turned slightly to his butler behind him. "Yorke, please bring him in."

Yorke nodded from the double door and clicked for a pair of servants to bring in a body on a stretcher of tough linen. Some of the men wore frowns while others raised their brows, suspicious about what Reeling was conjuring this time. As the silver hair and the pale skin of the body became apparent though, the men exchanged confused looks as mutters and low rumblings suddenly filled the court.

"It's been a while, Reeling," Breunor called out without the honorific, speaking over the others. "Cannot say I expected you to welcome me with a dead body."

Reeling glanced over at the military man. "And you, Lord Breunor," he said, "are as candid as I remember. But please hold off our reunion for now. An urgent task awaits us."

Reeling peered across the room, ignoring Breunor's dissatisfaction while making eye contact with several of the men at court. "This is not just anyone," he said, gesturing at the corpse, "but the most wanted criminal in the country." He paused for a moment, adding to the suspense. "He is... the Apostle."

Gasps filled the court then as everyone glanced about for reactions. There were murmurs, and then mumbling. Soon, loud chatter filled the air. For a being who had been described as a deity—or at least with the powers to be one—it all seemed too easy, too sudden, to now have his lifeless body on a stretcher. The truth is that even Reeling himself had hardly digested the Apostle's death.

"Lord Count," the emperor said now, with a squint that hushed the court. "What is this about? How can you verify his identity?"

"There are witnesses," Reeling said. "It happened earlier this morning, in the gardens across the bay. I believe his grand entrance of thick billowing mists was seen by more than a few men from the towers of Vondra Dawn."

"And you managed to kill him?" Breunor asked, clearly unconvinced.

"I managed not to *be* killed," Reeling replied with a simper. "But no, I am not his murderer. The man killed himself."

That claim had knitted several more brows. As some of them looked askance at the corpse of a rather lean man, it was apparent that their doubts grew. The emperor, however, seemed more trusting.

"Was he...," the emperor said, his words echoing in the court that had turned silent, "a magic user?"

Reeling grinned in affirmation. "Precisely, My Lord."

"And? What else did you learn? Who was he?"

"I learned nothing, except that he was as strong as the rumours suggested," Reeling claimed. "I know nothing more than anyone else. It was by chance that I happened by him."

The emperor's eyes glinted down now, perhaps suspecting that Reeling was hiding something. Other men on the court probably shared similar suspicions. The implication that the Apostle was a magic user was a frightening prospect that could change the world as it was known. If magic users could muster that kind of power, one could only imagine what a group of them could achieve. While the Empire had avoided speaking of the occult and had yet to declare their stance on any matter that involved magic users, people were already growing afraid. The emperor knew it, and so did the rest of the court. Indeed, some of them probably dared to dream about building their own army of magic users, if only they knew how.

The fact that this court was located at the highest point of Vondra Dawn suddenly became distinct again. From the outside, the primarily grey citadel was an imposing cluster of steeples that seemed to reach up to the skies. The citadel sat on the *Dunn Bay* where mists formed on colder days—mists that crept their way up the side of the steeples, but never reached the top. It made any man recognise how small and insignificant he was.

And from the inside, particularly upon this court inside the tallest steeple, the atmosphere was stately, yet harsh. It was where the most powerful men of the country gathered to discuss the business of the day. The ample floor space complementing a high ceiling accommodated a hundred men. The throne was installed on a platform ascending a modest two steps. Above and behind the throne was a sizeable rectangular window of lightly tinted glass from where natural light shone generously through. The vast dimensions of this glass window and its quality craftsmanship attested to the continued improvements in glazing techniques among many other advances seen in recent years. Hanging down from both sides of the window were giant banners of primarily grey and white that depicted the *Fenrir* emblem that the Truban Empire had inherited from the Clan of Light.

Multiple hand-sized windows facing east and west were installed on the top edges of the walls. Like the rest of the citadel, the court had been stripped of its marble walls and beams, those luxuries having been distributed to other parts of the country where they were needed. The current court was constructed humbly, with floors and walls of light grey granite.

Unlike in other ruling governments in the past and present, the emperor wasn't the only one seated. He didn't have an empress, and his many concubines had no place at the court. Standing next to Spartamon was his most able servant, Golden Knight Sir Lionel Lachman, who was hailed as the *Defender of Saffron* and arguably the strongest knight in the country. On either side of the throne were five seats, making a total of ten, but with only half of them occupied.

Schim, the rumoured challenger to the throne of recent years, sat on the right, and standing behind him were the *Raiders*, three of his most able men who had fought bravely alongside him during the war. The people seated next to him were Breunor and one of the other newcomers. Reeling had found his seat on the left, opposite them.

"The man's identity is unimportant," Schim said. "A messenger, a spy, a shaman—to me, he was but a blind murderer. This matter is closed. So for the sake of Zorlia, let us rejoice."

Some of the noblemen were quick to join Schim's chorus, and they, too, would invite others to focus on the positives—that the much-feared Apostle was gone forever. And soon, most of the court went on to share a brief moment of joy. Even Breunor afforded a laugh, rueing in good spirits his missed opportunity to cleanse the city with his own hands.

The next point on the agenda was ironically the mourning of a death and the smiles all faded at the introduction of this subject. The veteran golden knight, Kay Wallace, who had served as the Defender of the state of *Noel* for over three decades, had passed away. With a celebrated career that spanned to the current era, Wallace had a hand in helping the previous monarchy to become arguably the mightiest the land had seen. And yet the man was also distinctly remembered for being one of four golden knights to turn against the Sargon Monarchy for their authoritarian ways, before offering his skills to Spartamon and the Clan of Light, helping the rebellion army to achieve ultimate victory.

"At seventy-one years of age, Sir Wallace left us with his head held high," Breunor said, reading his eulogy. "As a warrior, his only regret may be that he didn't die on the battlefield. He was a brother to me and a hero of our country.

I have been told that he passed away peacefully in the company of his family. Let us smile as we say our final goodbye to him. Let us see his death as salvation from the six years during which he battled his ailments day and night. Let the great man rest in peace."

Breunor stroked his mutton chops, and then raised a hand to click. One of his men stepped forward, holding a bulky item covered with a cloak. Breunor gazed down at it, brushing a hand over it before flapping it open, creating a brief blast of air and revealing a gleaming golden breastplate.

"Lord Emperor," Breunor said with a bow. "Allow us to pay our honours to Sir Wallace."

The emperor nodded. Breunor then grasped onto the tray that held the breastplate. He swung toward the giant tinted glass behind the emperor, saluting earnestly. Everyone else rose to their feet and saluted in the same manner.

They all stood frozen for a minute, glaring out of the glass window as if seeing the late Wallace floating into the clouds as a saint. When it came time to relax, the *real* discussion was to begin. The men returned to their places as they readied themselves to the task of finding Wallace's replacement. Of the eight states of Trubannis, Noel was the only without its *Defender*, without its golden knight. And while the sole purpose in filling this void without delay should be the safeguarding of the country, it was likely that many people had other ideas on how the potential replacement and solution would personally benefit them.

"Sir Wallace certainly did his time," Reeling said, speaking before some others who looked like they were itching to take the initiative. "He was a man of moral excellence. And to honour him, we must do our best to fill the void he left behind. Let us not replace him with a single soldier, but instead, let us call for many soldiers to compete for the honour."

"What are you getting at?" Breunor grumbled quietly, likely offended that Reeling was proposing something before him, especially after everything he had said and done just then.

Reeling eyed the military man for a second, and then turned back to everyone else seated there. "We need fresh blood, a whole lot of new soldiers, young men if possible, to enlist their services to our armies. Despite the peaceful times we live in now, we must ready ourselves for potential aggression from foreign countries. Allow me to say that our ability to nurture soldiers is lacking far behind Vinawell and Kraga. It all starts with us, the Empire, presenting our people with the opportunity to become warriors who we can be proud of. Since the war ended seven years ago, the number of soldiers we have at our disposal has diminished at a frightening rate. Apart from the Defence Army, led by the great Sir Sagramore, our armies are small in both numbers and quality. We are in desperate need of soldiers—not only a single replacement for Sir Wallace."

"What is your suggestion?" Forredan asked with a friendly grin. "How do you propose the recruitment? Our resources are being stretched thin as it is."

Quinlan Forredan was from the affluent state of *Whitesand*. He was also a newcomer, who, with his unparalleled sense of gathering and managing resources, was to function as treasurer, and pronounced to be *Duke*. Although he had never stepped foot upon the battlefield, Forredan was heavily credited for the part he played in the war, injecting the mercenaries with the necessary funds crucial to maintain the armies.

He had also made a name for himself as the founder of the once-powerful army known as the *Scorching Salamander Knights*. Forredan's hedonistic nature had made him into a large, portly man, equal to the weight of about three average men. He was several years older than the next oldest person on the court, but he had spent a fair amount of money in an effort to look youthful. Unlike Breunor, who rarely smiled, the wealthy man of Whitesand appeared jolly and well cared for.

Reeling shook his head, returning the smile. "We will organise a warrior's tournament—invite anyone with the potential to become able soldiers to a stage where they can show us what they can bring to the Empire. Let it be known as the *Golden Knight Exchange*. The ultimate prize is the honour to be just that—a golden knight. Any others who show their worth shall be selected to join our armies. I do not believe funding for this will be a problem."

The idea certainly sounded viable, and it had some men already murmuring about how it would actually work out. Reeling glanced over toward a few different men, some of them nodding back in response. Schim was one of these.

"I object," Breunor inserted with a sneer. "It is absurd that you would think to select some random man to replace Sir Wallace. And it is disparaging to every man trained with the sword to know that their fate might depend on a *festival*—a mere show."

Reeling hardly raised a brow. He had expected objections and was prepared to answer to every one of them.

"Tell me, Lord Breunor," Schim said, speaking before Reeling, and apparently *for* him. "How long did it take you to become a golden knight?"

"Lord Chancellor," Breunor responded with a slight bow. "I became a member of the former monarchy at twenty years of age. Within three years of my submission, I was recognised as Golden Knight. But that was *me*. Not your average man."

Schim smiled, folding his arms. "And that is my point," he said. "How long must we wait for another golden knight to become as strong as you? *Or*, did you have some other idea?"

Reeling held in a grin, watching Breunor's face redden, the man silenced. According to his resources, Breunor did in fact have other ideas, which was to promote a silver knight loyal to him and to him only. But even the military man, as candid as he was, likely realised it was imprudent at this stage of the conversation to make that suggestion.

"I believe it's worth a try," Morlan said, nodding at Reeling. "And I will see that commoners be invited—always surprises there, of course!"

Pierre Morlan was of the state of *Cetal*, the latest of the three newcomers to arrive in the capital. He sat on the left, next to Reeling. The man had been proclaimed as King in his native north-western sovereign state. His primary function as the adored leader he was would be that of mediation. He was to converge divided opinions across the country toward a stronger sense of patriotism. His first task was the amalgamation of Cetal, to merge the third most populous state of Trubannis back under the ruling of the Empire. The man was firm and unrelenting on the outside, but many who knew better trusted him as a leader who cared for the people.

"Excellent, Lord Morlan," Reeling said. "That was exactly what I had in mind."

Breunor grunted, glaring at Reeling. "So in this *Exchange* of yours, how do we proceed? Don't tell me that *you* are the one to pick out the future Golden Knight of Noel."

Reeling simpered. "Me?" he said, bemused. "I wouldn't dream of it. There are countless others on this court more suited to the task. And you, Lord Breunor, are one of them."

The former golden knight finally afforded a conceited grin, lifting his chin at some of the men before him. "The onus is always on me, I suppose," Breunor said brashly.

"Well, not only you," Reeling continued, and this remark drew quick ire from Breunor again. "Every man on this court shall be involved witnesses to the dawn of the Empire's new soldiers. Sir Sagramore of the Defence Army would be one of the first to consult. As would the Lord Chancellor, who has proven his eye for talent as well as his ability to draw great men to help fight for his cause."

Reeling then turned to the emperor, who had waited for this address. "And of course, we have our Lord Emperor whose feats in assembling the greatest rebellion army in history speak for itself." Reeling bowed despite his seated position. "I trust that our Lord Emperor will not overlook any soldier who shows promise," he finished.

The emperor raised a hand. "Lord Count, I'll entrust you to run the Golden Knight Exchange. All men on this court shall support you."

Breunor swung an arm in protest, together with the bludgeon. "Your Majesty! *Do* rescind your words. I urge you! Reeling is just a scholar. He knows nothing about knighthood—let alone what it takes to be a golden knight. Me, on the other hand—I fought on the battlefield... for decades—*as* a golden knight!"

The emperor narrowed his eyes. Anyone else saw how foolish it was of Breunor to lash out like that, to question the single most powerful man of the country. He wouldn't want to be the end of the emperor's wrath, and especially not on his inauguration day as part of this court.

"I certainly remember your status and contributions," Reeling inserted without raising his voice, regarding the burly military man again. "However, fighting on the battlefield *alone* does not warrant an eye for talent. To you, I may be *just* a scholar. And to me, Lord Breunor, you were *just* a golden knight."

Breunor gritted his teeth this time, tightening his grip on his bludgeon, apparently restraining himself from acting rashly. Reeling shivered briefly in response, appreciating he had effectively and completely drawn on the military man's wrath. It was a shiver of excitement, however. Moments such as this one now reminded Reeling of how far he had come.

During the war, he had been but a mere pageboy, coordinating nursing tents for wounded soldiers. He had been popular even then, and he was often lauded for his efficiency to supply the armies with revitalised soldiers. Some had even gone on to say that his management of those treatment camps was invaluable to the morale and eventual victory of the emperor's then-army. But despite all that, he had still only been just that—a pageboy, a mere number who was both powerless and unrecognisable to the masses.

Breunor clearly didn't realise how drastically different a person Reeling had become. No one could appreciate the mighty struggle Reeling had had to live through in order to get to this stage, to not only hold his own on the court, but also demand a level of respect and attention second only to the emperor and the chancellor.

"We have an extraordinary group of people here on this court," Reeling continued, turning back to the rest of the room. "We are the envy of every other country. Even so, we could be so much more. And to steer ourselves to the right trajectory, I see us turning to the youth.

"In the past, we have dismissed young people as inexperienced and unworldly—believing that they know nothing about war, that they have been pampered in this time of peace that we all fought so hard for. We have been reluctant to entrust *boys* to do what we believe only men could. But, despite that, those boys *are* our future. Indeed, I believe there is no better time to call for their services than now. After years of basking in the peaceful times, they might just be the ones who know best how to preserve it.

"This Golden Knight Exchange shall welcome soldiers of all ages. And while seasoned soldiers are expected to stand out, I wish to encourage our young people to seize the opportunity—to prove that we have dismissed them too soon."

Reeling's elaboration would take a moment to digest. While objections on the court were traditionally viewed as healthy, as well as a sign of power, no one had yet come up with any words of protest.

And one of the reasons behind this had to do with how the Empire had been established, and how the emperor needed to show the people that he wasn't another dictator like the former king. Since rising to the throne, Spartamon had found himself nod reluctantly at suggestions he didn't agree with. One of those he most regretted was the court's disfavour for allowing 'unproven' people to offer their services. And yet, the emperor was also the one at the end of all the criticism when the court was questioned for its benighted ways.

The emperor grinned now as he regarded Reeling, perhaps noting that Reeling might have saved him from an enduring predicament.

Seeing no objection, Reeling continued. "Within a year's time, the court will be boosted by a wave of talented young people. On the soldiers' front, we have the Golden Knight Exchange. And on the scholar front, we have The Villa of Enlightenment. I have word from Yusuf Seer that there are a few State Scholars ready to join us here in Vondra Dawn."

Forredan coughed in interruption. "It would be best if the court had more people like you, Lord Count," he said, finally adding his voice to the discussion. "Surely, we'd benefit from having one or two more scholars around. But may you specify which State Scholars we are dealing with? I'm sure some of us would know their names."

"You are well-informed, Lord Forredan," Reeling said. "But I do not believe you would know them for they are not yet recognised as State Scholars."

Forredan chuckled. "Oh, Lord Count, you strike a good joke!"

Reeling simpered. "I *do* enjoy the occasional joke. But this is not one of them. A symposium has been announced for this year. It is to be held in two months' time. That is where they will shine brightest and earn their badge of recognition."

"You make it sound easy," Forredan responded with a grin. "I think, Lord Count, it's better to take back what you said. I wouldn't want to see you eat your words come December."

"I appreciate the concern, Lord Forredan," Reeling said. "Let my reputation be the gamble, if you would like to see it that way."

Forredan sat back and folded his arms, looking quite pleased with himself. "Let us move on to another matter—an announcement, if you like," the stout statesman said. "Now, ever since the Lord Emperor gratefully granted my company here at Vondra Dawn, I have thought about housing issues."

Forredan looked over to Morlan and Breunor. "Zorlia will be our permanent home. And while this magnificent citadel can comfortably accommodate us, I have instead constructed humble dwellings for each of us just outside, in *Phantom Pond*."

"Humble dwellings?" Morlan said with a glowing smile. "Lord Forredan, *you* are the humble one. By the time I realised you were building manors for us, it was too late to refuse. It was an incredible gesture and gift."

"Gift...?" Forredan said, shaking his head. "There's no gift. I don't want people to think there's any bribery going on. Your servants shall be receiving the account soon."

Morlan fell silent, awkward, exchanging a glance with Breunor who looked as confused.

"I jest!" Forredan then said, followed by a laugh joined by the other two. "I love money. But it's the least I can do for my fellow lords."

It was all very strange for the rest of the court. The newcomers had somehow directed the attention to themselves. To be fair, they needed to impose themselves early on if they were to be taken seriously. Even so, they were getting on the nerves of at least a few people there who whispered among themselves while wearing subtle scowls.

"Lord Count," Schim cut in. "I hear that your acquaintances from the academy have discovered something interesting. Would you care to share the information?"

Reeling nodded. "Indeed. Scholars of The Villa have located a natural mining site in Noel—not too far, actually, from Sir Wallace's home."

"Limestone again?" Forredan asked with a raised brow. "Trivial work *does* pay off at times. Well done, scholars."

"No, not limestone," Reeling replied. "The academy has reported significant deposits of *osmium*. For those who don't know, this is a rare, valuable metal, a part of the platinum group."

Forredan turned silent, gaping suddenly.

"The densest element in the world," Morlan remarked. "Extracted deposits could perhaps be used for weapon forging."

"Preposterous!" Forredan snapped, returning to his senses. "Pardon me, Lord Morlan. But allow me to worry about how to use the country's resources. That is *my* role, after all."

"Actually, this osmium site is not yours to control," Reeling said.

"'I'm sorry?" Forredan responded, leaning in, clearly baffled.

It had been less than a month prior when a limestone mine had been discovered near the emperor's hometown of *Dawnsdale*. And at that time, Reeling had argued, with the geographic location as his main point, that the emperor himself would best utilise the mine to its maximum. That argument wouldn't apply this time, however, because this new osmium mine was in Noel, and no men of power, after Wallace's death, called Noel home.

"Osmium is rare," Reeling said. "It can produce equipment of extreme sturdiness and durability, but its extraction is no easy matter. We'd need someone knowledgeable about nature and the elements to oversee every step of the process—that is, we would need scholars. The mine itself was discovered by scholars of The Villa. Naturally, the Grandmaster has been informed."

The mention of the Grandmaster—the ninety-four-year-old Isaiah Felipe regarded as "the man who knows all," or simply the one who had reached *omniscience*—was rare, and came with a great deal of implication. Despite the man's detachment from worldly matters, and despite his apparent seclusion from even the scholarly academy he had founded, the Grandmaster was arguably the most revered man in the land. His seclusion for the past fifteen years meant that few had had the pleasure to meet him, and while one would wonder whether the man would show himself once more for a mere osmium mine, they could only take Reeling's word for it. After all, Reeling had once been lauded as the Grandmaster's favourite student by the great man himself.

"The Grandmaster has spoken," Reeling continued. "He has said that proceeds would be for the benefit of the Empire. But there is no one better than scholars to utilise this metal. In other words, allow me to humbly accept the responsibility of overseeing all activity in this osmium mine."

If Forredan's disquieted expression was an indicator, then the statesman was as stunned as Breunor—and so they should be. Perhaps no one could make sense of how Reeling had managed to grapple onto so much power so quickly. Reeling himself realised it was unfathomable for the newcomers to imagine that even the emperor and the chancellor, the two men in conflict with one another now, were similarly torn on what to do with him. Reeling was sure that both the emperor and the chancellor wanted him to submit his allegiance to them personally in a precarious test of patience where everyone involved was forced to act with extreme caution.

In this way, Reeling was the balancing act between the emperor and the chancellor—or more simply—the one preventing a civil war from breaking out. And yet, by claiming the valuable osmium site today, he had invited great menace.

* * *

The Lord Count's chambers—the man's second home—were situated in one of the tallest steeples on the western front of Vondra Dawn. Rarely did he have guests these days—not after inimically dismissing a host of visitors in the past who had wanted to form alliances with him. It was a long walk, too, to get to the chambers. One had to ascend a long set of spiral stairs before having to race along an even longer corridor. The journey was uneventful, and the destination wasn't merry, as Reeling had a reputation of turning visitors away without any stated reason.

The one to visit him today, however, wasn't an average guest. He was Kasimir de Spartamon, the emperor, the most dignified man in the country, perhaps in the land. It was the emperor's first visit, and possibly his last. He had made the journey alone, a twenty-minute walk from the court. Standing guard at the large wooden door was Xander Yorke, who saluted him.

"Inform the Lord Count of my arrival," Spartamon said.

Yorke hesitated. "Your Majesty, I'm afraid the Lord Count didn't return with me."

"And where might he be?" the emperor asked, staring down at Yorke.

"Apologises, Your Majesty," he said with a self-controlling frown. "The Lord Count didn't indicate to me where he was off to."

Spartamon recognised that look of obstinacy—of loyalty. It was futile to press any further. In fact, he considered Yorke's dedication to Reeling praiseworthy. Either way, it didn't matter. It was only a matter of time before he would learn about any secrets Yorke might be hiding—or, for that matter, what Reeling might be hiding.

Later that evening, the emperor sat alone on his throne. With no oil lamps lighted, the only source of light was the moon shining from above him through the giant window.

He waited and waited until a short message was delivered to him, a parchment sent from one of his espionage experts. And according to the message, Reeling had paid Schim a visit shortly after court, and presented the chancellor with a glass tube of greyish powder. It was a brief message of two sentences, but the emperor stared at the note for a long while, reading into the blankness and discerning the discourse that had taken place at Schim's chambers.

"Reeling," he uttered, closing his eyes and crushing the parchment in his fist. "Have you finally chosen?"

THREE

Lonely Soldier

The encounter with the Apostle had changed everything for Alpheus. He was no longer confined in a tower. But for days, he had locked himself inside the Lord Count's estate which housed many papers either written by or collected by Reeling. Prying through a heap of records, Alpheus was collating all of the information he could find about magic users. It was the first time he had read up on *Yesod the Marvel Mage* and *Zip the Disbeliever*. Before this, he had refused to read accounts based on legends, believing them to be fantasy.

Some accounts spoke of an ancient race, allegedly the *chosen children*, who had been born with an energy source called *grace*, a pool from which magic users drew their power. But other texts described the entire concept as the work of the damned, and its application—if any—was in dissonance with the divine. It was one of those rare cases where the more he learned, the more he realised he didn't know, and hence the more he wanted to know.

He had been flipping and skimming through thousands and thousands of pages from loose papers, taking down notes to connect the dots to the best of his ability. Unfortunately, after days of research where every mention of magic was poorly referenced, Alpheus was no closer to learning how magic was even possible. What was grace? How would one cultivate it? In the grand scheme of things, what did it mean to the land of the mortals? If there were a purpose for everything that happened, what was the purpose here? Why did the Immortal allow the power of magic to sprinkle down to the land, when surely there were a host of men who couldn't be trusted with the power?

These questions seemed impossible to answer.

And yet, Alpheus felt no frustration. Instead, a smile was painted on his cheeks now as he turned away the paper that couldn't offer any more information for him.

There was finally something to be curious about again. There was hope again for his artwork—his beloved creative venture that had suffered so much recently from a lack of inspiration, from the fact that nothing interested him anymore. Alpheus himself confessed that his recent work had been lacklustre.

But that would be no more, he thought with a grin that was nudged ever wider by his growing curiosity. *Magic would enchant for a long while.*

He brushed a hand from his front hairline, sliding his fingers softly along his hair tied in a braided ponytail. And then stretching out both arms, he pushed open the door. The early evening sky was adorned by the crescents of Achelois and Selene, the satellites almost at the same positions as depicted on his double crescent pendant of translucent blue and red—the symbol of faith. *I'm so blessed,* Alpheus thought as he grasped onto the palladium adornment hanging out on top of his cultured white robe. Alpheus looked up to the stone path ahead, fixing up his spectacles with a light touch of his index finger, the platinum frame also tinged by the moonlight.

Even at this hour, there were quite a number of people out roaming the streets. The smell of terracotta that wafted through the thoroughfare was distinctly Zorlian, the fired clay and its brownish—sometimes orange—colour that filled nearly every part of the precinct, accentuating the heritage of the city and the fact that it had flourished for hundreds of years. Unlike many other cities and towns that had turned to building structures of primarily timber and stone, Zorlia had managed to preserve its historic flavour as the people continued to favour the ancient building material even today. On a summer day, the sun-baked cooked-earth would be even stronger, particularly as it mingled with blooming wisteria vines that crept onto homes and other structures, which were planted generously across the city.

For a moment there, Alpheus wondered if the ancient tone of Zorlia could attract more magic users to come to the city. As he strolled past the Luxuriant Gardens then, the memory of the fantastic battle between Reeling and the Apostle came rushing back in vivid detail. Alpheus didn't waver before the gardens, however, instead looking ahead to the main street that was floored with light grey stone and illuminated by plenty of lanterns hanging off of buildings. There must be more magic users out there.

Vondra Dawn was just ahead, the citadel's dark cluster of stone steeples one of the few buildings not constructed with terracotta. He doubted there was anything that could interest him among or within those steeples that towered over the rest of the city. At the same time, he appreciated that it was too idealistic to think he could run into magic users by chance simply by wandering around the city. There was hope, however, in that it wasn't improbable that he might find clues on how to locate these curious beings.

Continuing along the stone path, and crossing one of the three main bridges of the city, Alpheus decided to settle into *King's Parlour*, a social venue for knights and noblemen. The architecture of the building was a subject of admiration, with its part forest glass ceiling where moonlight shone down generously, adding a charm to the ambience in the rising arcades and balconies. With hundreds of people there, however, the grand parlour of four floors was much more crowded and rowdier than Alpheus cared for.

Alpheus soon realised that the parlour was hosting a function to welcome the newcomers of the court, which included a former golden knight, an esteemed statesman, and the King of sovereign state Cetal. Despite his indifference to anything concerning the Empire, it was close to impossible to remain ignorant of this new arrangement that had been consistently publicised all over the city for at least the last few months. As a matter of contrast, Alpheus doubted that anyone in the building would recognise him, either as a member of the academy or his mentor-disciple type of relationship with the Lord Count. It was better that no one attended to him, however, especially among the noblemen present who were experts at the art of adulation.

Still, Alpheus proceeded to the first floor and found a seat on the balcony that overlooked the open ground floor, which was swarmed with men.

Magic users, he thought with a brief sigh as he peered down. *Just how do I find them?* Alpheus perked up then as he noted a cluster of bodies moving toward the entrance, apparently to welcome an honoured guest. And indeed, stepping in from the wide entrance was a brawny man in white garb embroidered garishly by strips of golden velvet. The man was middle-aged and bald with thick mutton chops that could nest bugs. Immediately behind him was a giant of a man both bigger and wider than his bald leader, wearing armour of gleaming gold.

They must be Victor Breunor and Walford Bors, Alpheus assumed, remembering that Bors had recently succeeded as a Golden Knight and the *Defender of State Zenith* from none other than Breunor himself. It didn't make sense that Bors had travelled with Breunor, and in turn left Zenith vulnerable.

The first to greet the two veteran knights was a younger man in silver armour, Percival Pole, who was perhaps the king of the fawners. He was a member of the powerful *Defence Army*, the largest army of the Empire. Even Alpheus was aware of Pole's popularity, that the knight had befriended almost every nobleman in recent years. However, it was not Pole's esteemed rank to which his popularity level could be attributed. Apparently, members of the court favoured him for his conformity. At the same time, they suspected that his combat ability was only sub-par.

Pole was said to carry a rapier at all times, but he had never been seen wielding it. He had neither the height nor the build of other knights of his class, standing at barely six feet. Despite being a student of Golden Knight Sir Sagramore—who was also the Chieftain of the Defence Army—Pole's ability on the battlefield was a dubious matter at best. Traditional knighthood valued friendly duels between fellow knights, but Pole had never taken part in that tradition, and the doubters had conveniently assumed that he was simply afraid to lose.

Right this moment, Pole was already drinking away with Breunor and Bors. Breunor, in particular, was hopping around with a drink in his hand, demanding that people applaud him.

Alpheus shook his head and then turned his attention to the left corner of the parlour floor where another large group of men gathered. At the centre was an exceedingly portly man whose shoulder-to-shoulder width equated to at least two regular men. Among the group was another golden knight, Claude Lucan, the *Defender of State Whitesand* who had also travelled with his liege. But unlike Zenith, Whitesand was favourably located in the northeast, far away from potential foreign enemies.

Alpheus had seen enough already and was ready to depart. But as he peered about once more, he met a pair of soulless eyes glancing out briefly among the soldiers—a young man, about the same age as Alpheus, hardly playing a role in the festivities. His dark, messy hair shrouded parts of his eyes, which glared out to Alpheus, as if calling to him.

What is this sensation? Alpheus wondered, feeling a cool tingle pulsing up the spine.

The curiosities took a new level when a glass of wine was suddenly flung across the room and landed directly at the feet of the soldier who had been glaring at Alpheus, the spatter from the wine tainting his armour. Breunor was cushioned at the centre of the group from which the beverage originated. Although the veteran knight was quite a dancer, his style and rhythm suffered as the evening grew darker, which happened to coincide with more and more liquor poured into his glass. He had likely lost grip of his wine glass after a few spins and a couple of hops. All that, however, and his mutton chops were still neat as a pin.

The soldier drenched in wine displayed little frustration, and yet, as if to test his patience, Breunor treaded toward him, mocking him and inviting others to add to the humiliation with their own jeers. When Breunor finally settled down, he asked the soldier to tell him his name and post.

"The name's Julian Roland," the soldier replied with a hint of disdain, the likes of which only the sober would have noticed. "A patrol soldier."

"A *what*?" Breunor said with a hiccup. "Bah! Forget it. Why don't you just clean yourself up?"

"I shall," Julian said. He took one step, perhaps toward the lavatory, before Breunor stopped him again.

"Hang on," the military man said, pointing down at the floor. "Clean up the mess first. *Lick* up that spilled wine for me."

Julian glared at him, but seemed careful about not acting on impulse.

Breunor hiccupped again, and then slowed down to study Julian. "Oh, I see, I see. You see all this festivity and you think I'm playing with you. I'm not. I *command* you to lick the floor clean!"

"Lick! Lick!" the men chanted, throwing their hands in the air.

Julian cringed and apparently whispered a few words, possibly a disparaging remark given that Breunor stiffened suddenly while all the other men in the vicinity hushed. Alpheus leaned down a little, squinting for more detail, jumping slightly then as the burly physique bolted forward. Julian was suddenly being held by the neck, a position that illustrated Breunor's complete dominance over the young soldier whose whimper was the only sound left behind amid a heavy silence.

Breunor exhaled his reeking breath into the poor soldier's face. "What did you say just now...?" He didn't wait for an answer, slamming Julian against a wall with a forceful impact that seemed to shake the entire building. And Julian lay on the floor without a flinch—dead, perhaps?

"Get up!" Breunor demanded.

It took a moment, but Julian pushed himself up to his knees, cringing as blood dribbled from his mouth. Alpheus stared, feeling his eyes water up as he sympathised with the soldier whose back must be throbbing.

Breunor held a thick book up into the air then, apparently a book he had taken from Julian in the brief exchange.

Alpheus squinted harder to make out the title of the book. It was written in a runic script unintelligible even to him, who knew the basics of a few ancient languages.

"What have we here?" Breunor said, studying the worn-out tome. He held it up to his face and shook his intoxication away. It took him a moment, and when he finally appeared to have made it out, he began to tremble. "A magic user?!" he said with a gasp.

The other men gaped. Alpheus perked up as well, suddenly hopeful, curiosities returning.

"You're mistaken," Julian said. "The book is simply for pleasure."

Breunor glanced at the tome with suspicion, and then back at Julian. "Where did you learn to read the words?"

Julian hesitated, offering no further explanation.

Please let him be a magic user, Alpheus wished. Suddenly, something resembling a phantom flashed above the men before crashing down into Julian, forcing the soldier to his knees.

It turned out to be silver knight Pole, who had also snatched Julian's hands together and now brutally twisted his arms, causing Julian to cry in pain.

"This is no place for a lowly soldier," Pole said.

Breunor regarded Pole with a grin, possibly scheming something, and perhaps also surprised by Pole's show of agility. "Hold it now, Sir Pole," Breunor said. "Take it easy. I still have questions to ask."

"Of course," Pole responded with a subservient bow, before pulling Julian up again for interrogation.

Julian gritted his teeth, scowling at Breunor. He stood no chance. Perhaps the only people who could help him were the other newcomers to Vondra Dawn, Morlan and Forredan. But it was unlikely that they would openly challenge Breunor for a soldier they didn't even know.

Alpheus inhaled deeply and then stood from his seat, trotting down the stairs. "Good evening, my lords," he began with a loud voice in a gleeful tone as he was descending, prompting many to raise their eyebrows. "Allow me to say a few words."

"Who are you?" Golden Knight Sir Bors asked.

"My name is Alpheus, a member of the academy."

More raised brows. "What business do you have here?" Bors said.

"That book," Alpheus said, referring to the tome Breunor held. "I'm here to retrieve that. It belongs to the academy. The soldier... Julian, was it? Allow me to hand him to Master Seer."

Breunor cocked his head, stroking his beard. "You're Yusuf Seer's student?"

"Actually, we're all students of the academy," Alpheus said. "Him included."

"All right, boy," Breunor said as he handed the tome to Alpheus. "Give my regards to Seer."

Alpheus bowed slightly and then was quick to trot over to Julian as soon as Breunor gestured for his release. Julian appeared more confused than grateful, however, when he looked up at Alpheus. Still, Alpheus acknowledged him then with a brief nod before throwing the soldier's arm over his own shoulder to support him as they both rose to their feet.

"Lord Breunor," Bors said quietly. "Are you sure about this? He might be..."

"What? A magic user?" Breunor responded with a smirk, looking askance at Julian. "If he were, he would have put up a fight worth my time."

He then chuckled, his laugh a deep howl. Pole joined him, sharing his joy. And soon, all of them were laughing. Alpheus turned away after a brief smile and then walked out into the night with Julian.

It was a short distance later when Julian pulled his arm back with a hiss. "Who are you?" the soldier demanded.

Alpheus grinned in surprise, noting that Julian didn't seem as hurt as he had imagined. "Is that your way of thanking me?"

"My book," Julian said, peering down to Alpheus's hand that held the tome. "Are you going to hand it back to me?"

"Now, look, I'm not your enemy," Alpheus assured, not ready to return the unidentified tome just yet. "As I was saying before, I'm Alpheus. You may not know me, but you might have heard of my sister, Charlotte Hindlow."

Julian acknowledged the name with a twitch. No one in Zorlia was unfamiliar with that name. Despite having relocated to the island-country of Aizary six years prior, Charlotte Hindlow had long established herself as the finest scholar in the land second only to the Grandmaster.

"I know what you're thinking," Alpheus said, looking down at his own lean frame, aware that he was both shorter and smaller than Julian who was already relatively thin by soldier standards. "You think you can snatch the book back by force. I'm sure you can. But if you were to do that, you'd be making more enemies you can do without. All I want is a brief skim inside."

Julian said nothing yet. It might have been subtle, but the religious pendant hanging at Alpheus's chest was the only thing the soldier responded to, which was in the form of a wince.

"I've been honest about who I am," Alpheus continued, hoping for more of a response. "Maybe you can tell me a little about yourself. You can start with—"

"There's something about you," Julian inserted, finally speaking then. "I don't know what it is, but it's not that you have a famous sister."

Alpheus frowned slightly with a shrug. "Well, that's more recognition than I've received from a few others. Could it be that you have some curiosity for me? Listen, let us have a change of scenery. I know a place."

Julian hesitated for a moment, but then finally nodded.

* * *

They eventually arrived at *Rogers*, a tavern almost as crowded as the parlour, but not nearly as rowdy. The patrons there were made up of commoners and soldiers who had been exhausted from another day of forced labour and untold frustrations about the social structure. Tending the bar was the master, Jonathan "Dock" Rogers himself. He was a portly middle-aged man, always jolly on the outside.

"Who's your friend?" Dock asked, grinning at Alpheus since he had entered.

"I'm not sure he's a friend just yet," Alpheus said, finding a seat on a stool. "But his name is Julian."

Julian simply rolled his eyes as he sat himself down two stools from Alpheus.

"Just came from the parlour," Alpheus said as Dock poured him a frothy beer. "The people there afford only the luxury problems."

Dock chortled. "Who whined about getting his robe stained with a wine mark last time?"

Alpheus simpered. "That was one time."

"You're born noble. Maybe you ought to act like one every so often."

"But I can't stand those people," Alpheus said before downing a mouthful of beer. "Actually...," he continued in a more solemn tone, "I pity them. They're the principal victims of the system. They're subject to intense struggles every day just to remain in their positions. It's all about survival. In that respect, it's not so different from how the peasants live."

He sighed when a bang sounded suddenly from the kitchen, the rattling of utensils falling to the ground. Then a child came rushing out, knocking over a servant who then soaked his customers in liquor from the tray he had been carrying. The boy was in rags, frantically searching for a place to hide.

"Stop, you little thief!" cried a bearded man who emerged from the same kitchen. The man held onto a wooden club, chasing the boy who skipped about like an animal. The boy, about ten years of age, was agile. But he was never going to escape when he was being cornered by several men more than twice his size.

The child was being cornered now as the bearded man looked to beat him. The boy apologised, begging for a chance to explain, but no one wanted to listen.

"You people talk about an imperfect system," Julian said quietly as he stood from his stool. "But little by little, if we all play our part, things just might get better."

Just when the bearded man was ready to use his wooden club, Julian jumped in, shielding the boy and then parrying off the attack.

"A soldier…?!" the bearded man said with contempt. "And you're helping a thief?"

"He's just a child."

"A child thief!"

Julian frowned. "What did he take?"

"Ask him," the bearded man said, growing impatient. "He's still holding onto it."

Julian looked down at the frightened boy. He forced his hands open, and indeed, the boy was holding onto two gold coins.

"We let him work here," the man said in protest. "And how does he repay us? By stealing!"

Dock nodded to confirm that this was true.

Julian sighed then, seizing the coins from the boy and then tossing them to the bearded man. Then, reaching into his sachet, he picked out another coin.

"Take this as compensation."

Content with the incentive, the bearded man growled quietly before returning to the kitchen with his crew. The customers returned to where they were. The boy pouted at Julian, saying nothing, looking rather upset to have been forced to return what he had stolen.

"You're not the only one who needs to eat," Julian said to the boy, who merely snorted in response before bolting off to the rear exit.

Clearly, Julian wasn't very good with children. Despite being a scholar, Alpheus wasn't sure he could manage any better in convincing anyone of anything. It was still amusing to see others fail, though, especially with children.

"This isn't the first time," Dock said as Julian returned to his stool. "And he'll continue to steal."

"Then… why do you keep him?" Alpheus asked.

"He's an orphan… still learning to survive on his own. I hope he'll come to realise that there are good people in this world."

Julian narrowed his eyes, looking both nostalgic and sympathetic. Had he once been a helpless boy, too?

But the apparent nostalgia ended suddenly as he stood up abruptly from the stool, checking his pockets for something, probably his coin sachet. "That brat," Julian cursed quietly, clenching a fist.

Alpheus put a fist over his mouth to hold back laughter, realising that Julian had been thieved by the boy. It was almost too funny when Julian turned to Alpheus wearing an expression of both embarrassment and anger, hesitating to ask what Alpheus could guess was on the tip of his tongue.

"I'll come with you," Alpheus offered, letting slip a brief chuckle as he snatched up the thick book and stood from the stool.

Julian groaned softly and then stormed out through that same rear exit as the boy had fled through. Alpheus waved goodbye to Dock and then trailed Julian, watching from behind as Julian peered across the evening street that was tinged by satellites of stunning red and blue. Among the fair amount of people still roaming the streets at this hour, there were no traces of the boy. Visibly frustrated, Julian dashed toward one of the passing civilians.

"Have you seen a boy in rags?" he asked.

"I see many," the unknowing man said with a shrug. "This is Zorlia. We have urchins everywhere."

Julian frowned, grabbing the man by the collar. "Don't play with me," he warned.

"All right, all right," the man said, nearly choking. "I saw one just now—headed that way." He pointed straight ahead, and with that, Julian released his grip.

It turned out that this first man was the only one who dared to throw in a caustic remark, but it could also be Julian's more forceful tone when he asked the next people he came across. In any case, Julian and Alpheus were soon led to the outer-eastern neighbourhood of *Ramsgate*, and specifically in front of a run-down chapel. It was one of the many small places of worship, barely larger than the crude hovels commonly found in the city. It looked abandoned, with no illumination inside, and parts of the fences and roof had been torn open. Julian couldn't be sure if this was where the boy lived, but if it was, he looked determined not to be taken in by sympathy again.

Julian prowled in through one of the ripped-out openings in the fence. Alpheus, meanwhile, took a moment for a prayer as he clasped onto his religious pendant. Julian glanced back at him with quiet dissent, only for Alpheus to return another smile that showed his excitement.

Julian rolled his eyes, and was about to breathe a resigned sigh before he suddenly perked up in alert. Alpheus could hear the sound too. Murmurs. Voices of men. *And the wailing of a child*, he realised.

Rather than heading directly into the humble chapel, Julian led the way, circling out to the right of the building, which they now saw was covered in cobwebs. They almost missed a window that was enshrouded in the plentiful spider silk. Alpheus cringed when Julian brushed away the web, still doing so quietly. They peeked inside now, squinting their way through the tainted window.

The boy—the child thief—was pinned up against a wall, apparently forced there by the men inside. They were... knights? And there were three of them. One donned a glowing silver breastplate.

"That's all I have!" the boy cried. "I'm sorry I stole from you, but I don't have any more!"

Alpheus glanced over to Julian who wore a grimace, perhaps thinking that the boy deserved it. His expression changed, however, when one of those knights pulled out a sword, holding it like a club, without drawing the blade from its sheath.

"No more running," the knight said.

"Please, no," the boy begged, his voice weak.

But the knight battered the hapless boy, aiming for his legs. The boy screamed as the aggressor pounded him repeatedly without mercy. Alpheus winced at the horror, turning his gaze back at Julian, hoping that he would do something. Julian, however, simply shook his head as he continued to watch. The knight stopped soon enough, perhaps having been appeased as the boy was now reduced to a whimper.

Unfortunately, the knight wasn't done. He held the half-dead boy up by one of his legs, which was likely broken. A sudden gleam of bright orange pulsed from beneath the boy's rags, causing the knight to raise an eyebrow. The knight then picked out the glowing item, and snatching it away as if by instinct.

"My God!" the knight remarked, moving his fingers from the gemstone to the chain. "This thing's hot."

"I bet it's worth more than a few coins," one of his allies replied with a smirk.

"Take anything you want," the boy pleaded, his arm outstretched. "But not that! It's the family treasure!"

"It's *our* treasure now," the knight said with a grunt, now swinging the boy by the leg from side to side.

Alpheus clenched a fist, ready to jump in. But crashing in through the window just at that moment was Julian, achieving surprise before dealing a fiery blow to the knight that sent him flying into the wall. In the process, Julian caught onto both the boy and his gleaming pendant.

The boy widened his eyes in fright, but the astonishment he would have experienced must have been a whole lot merrier than the knight who had collapsed with his damaged area still burning.

A magic user indeed! Alpheus thought, watching in awe. *Father of Heaven, thank you.*

The knight smothered the flames in desperation before getting back on his feet and skipping toward his allies who still had yet to act. Indeed, the silver knight spared only a brief glance over his shoulder. In response, their other ally unsheathed his weapon.

"Be careful," that first knight said, stepping behind his ally.

The second knight frowned, eyeing Julian. "You're a soldier?" he asked, grinding his teeth.

Julian ignored him, turning away to lay the boy down. As he presented his back to the enemy, the second knight began to charge forward.

"Watch out!" Alpheus cried from the window.

In his crouching position and with his back facing the enemy, Julian murmured some strange words. A roaring flame that had seemingly sparked from his broad shoulders hurtled out in a spectacular display that lighted up the shack—and, at the same time, engulfing the knight in a great red flame.

The silver knight peered over to the action this time, his youthfulness highlighted by the blaze for a few seconds. He was possibly younger than Julian. It was remarkable for anyone at that age to don that armour of silver, and even now as he stood, the silver knight retained his calm. He regarded his vassals with caution as the first knight slapped a collection of rags in an effort to relieve his ally. And he smiled when the flames were put out in mere seconds.

The strength of the flames didn't reflect its impressive display, Alpheus noted.

"Acting like a hero won't get you anywhere," the silver knight said, regarding Julian. "Your reliance on heresy deems you unworthy as a warrior. I won't draw my sword on the likes of you. I'll let you go. You can continue to live your life in shame."

"Let me go...?" Julian asked, almost rhetorically.

"I was interested in the Apostle, who was said to be a magic user. But judging from your limited skills, I doubt you and he are part of the same caste."

The silver knight glanced over to Alpheus, shooting him a smirk, causing Alpheus to jump. He then turned and began to walk away. His men seemed irked that he was turning away from the confrontation, but they soon raced off from the shack behind their liege.

Alpheus rounded out to the front door and entered from there. The boy was barely conscious. His legs were badly bruised, particularly the knees and the ankles.

"We need to get him to a healer," Alpheus said, already trotting away to lead the way.

Julian nodded and then threw the boy on his back, trailing closely behind.

"The treasure...," the boy uttered before falling unconscious, not realising that Julian had already looped the pendant back around his neck.

The glow has faded, Alpheus noted as he sped up to a sprint, certain that Julian could keep up despite carrying a child on his back. He glanced down to his side then, catching a glimpse of the tome he was still holding in his right hand.

This has been a field day, he thought with a grin.

* * *

The healer was reluctant to receive an urchin as a patient, especially at the late hour, agreeing to treat the boy only when Alpheus presented him with three gold coins. Julian acknowledged the favour with a quiet nod. While the healer treated the boy, Alpheus simply sat waiting on the side next to Julian who said no word. He glanced over to the young soldier-magic user every once in a while, holding in his curiosities, until Julian finally turned to him.

"Go ahead," Julian said, voice tired. "Have a skim through."

"Really?" Alpheus asked, grin widening, already tightening his grip on the tome.

Julian nodded before closing his eyes for a doze. He had looked weary since they arrived at the shop that attended to the sick and injured, a place that was also the healer's private dwelling. Was Julian drained of energy after the fight? Or had he simply had a long day? If magic users were indeed the *chosen children* of the Immortal, one would assume they were blessed with greater vitality.

It didn't matter anymore when Alpheus flipped open the tome, flicking through its pages. *A spell book*, he realised with joy. *A magic user's manual.* He didn't understand a word of what was written, but the accompanying illustrations convinced him that this was something else indeed.

It was a while later when the healer allowed the boy to be discharged despite still being unconscious. "I don't think the child has a home," the healer said, his words carrying some obvious scorn.

"He can stay with me," Julian said, awake but seemingly still weary.

The healer groaned as he wiped his hands clean of blood and grime. "Don't bring him here again."

"I hope I won't have to."

Julian glanced at Alpheus and then threw the unconscious boy on his back again, pacing out of the building. Alpheus followed urgently, hardly noticing that dawn was upon them—the empty streets was a sign of that. He had eyes only on Julian, staring at him, almost studying him with an inquisitive set of eyes until Julian stopped suddenly in his tracks.

"Will you quit it?!" Julian snapped.

"I'm sorry," Alpheus said, trying his best to look away. "I'm just curious about magic. And I was hoping you could show me more."

"Why should I show you anything?" Julian responded, annoyed.

"Because we're friends."

Julian returned a stare that turned into a squint after a moment. "I suppose I do want to learn more about you," he said. "I thought I sensed something in you back at the parlour."

"You *did*?" Alpheus responded, pleasantly surprised. "It was probably my curiosity."

"You're a strange one," Julian said quietly, in submission.

"No stranger than you."

The two of them shared a brief chuckle.

FOUR
The Sail Band

Marvin sat beneath the darkening sky, under thick forest canopies that were blowing wildly. He kept his eyes on the rampart, watching the soldiers carefully from afar to confirm that they were following the same routine every day. He had been camping outside the castle for days now with his small crew, hiding among the abundant bushes and each day edging closer to the grand castle wall. It was now the fourth day.

Ash had just re-joined the group after disappearing for hours. He had come back with four sets of armour to help them replicate the castle guards once they get inside. Even now as Marvin took one last glance up at the towering southern wall of the magnificent castle and across the never-ending rampart, he thought not of the dangers that might lie ahead, but the tediousness of having to probe the *Monarchal Castle*, home to *The Legion*, which was the second largest army in the country.

There was no better time to raid the place, however. Cetal was now in a state of confusion, in the midst of an identity crisis. Morale was low while uncertainty was high as the *Kingdom of Cetal* was soon to be restored as a state of Trubannis. The *Cetallers*, as they liked to call themselves, had believed none of it until King Morlan left for Zorlia earlier in the month. The latest update from the capital had verified their fears: Morlan had given up his kingship and, apparently, he was in Zorlia to stay. Marvin's sources told him that the soldiers weren't sure who they fought for anymore, and that the kingdom itself were at their most vulnerable since their move to independence.

Apparently, Morlan had worked to persuade his people long before he had left for the capital. He had promised that it was for the best, contrasting the reigning Truban Empire with the former Sargon Monarchy, and pointing out the economic benefits that Cetal would enjoy by being restored as a part of what he labelled as the greatest country in the land. The people probably believed that Trubannis was indeed a much better country than it had been.

But, having lived for over half a century with their own laws and customs, it was only natural that the people were unsure.

The army, on the other hand, while boasting an impressive number of enlisted soldiers, had been disparaged and condemned across the country for decades, with their most infamous action—or lack of it—being their reluctance to support the country during the war. That decision apparently had nothing to do with Morlan, however, who hadn't succeeded the throne until seven years ago when his predecessor—his grandfather, Henry Morlan—had died of old age. Henry Morlan had elected to stand as a neutral to the war, and was also responsible for instigating the state to its independence from Trubannis before his self-acclamation as the King of Cetal.

In any case, Marvin was aware that there was an addition of fifty thousand men still stationed at or near the castle. Capturing the fortification was certainly a task for the greatest generals in the land together with tens of thousands of their bravest soldiers. But Marvin had no intention to seize the castle. The plan was to bypass the soldiers altogether, if possible. After all, the crew had only one agenda: to capture the *Mirage Ring*, an ancient artefact thought to have the power to draw illusions to one's liking.

There was no need to provoke, and there was certainly no need for bloodshed. Marvin led a thieving crew of only five men, all of whom were equipped with extraordinary skills that could shake even armies.

Marvin himself had once been a prominent member of the former rebellion army led by Kasimir de Spartamon, who had of course since become the Lord Emperor. The first to join Marvin's venture had been Rover Watts, also a former mercenary, who had been called the *Lone Eye Vulture* for his blinded right eye and his tendency to sit idly until the moment he struck. Ashley Addenlocke, a self-proclaimed geologist, lent to the crew his fine intellect and crafty ability to pick locks. Leonardo Edward Bassing, a man of Vinan descent, was the expert of transportation, responsible for sending the crew to where they needed to be—and perhaps most importantly, to arrange quick getaways. Finally, there was Carolos "Karl" Mindsz, a man of Kragan descent, an impressive cartographer with the ability to map out the anatomy of any place.

The evening blue of Achelois emerged now as a full moon from behind the clouded night sky. This was the signal for their mission to begin. The thieves—save Leo, who was out preparing for the escape later on—formed a huddle for a final briefing.

"Check that you each have the blue and red missiles," Marvin said quietly. "Fire the blue one when you capture the treasure. And the red when—well, we won't need it—but, just in case, fire the red missile as a signal to retreat."

The others nodded rather indifferently. They didn't share Marvin's enthusiasm, at least not outwardly, especially Rover, who had always hated huddles.

"Make use of the disguise," Marvin added, referring to the guard's suits of armour they were now fitted in. "It may be ugly, but we want to avoid attention. We're not here to hurt anyone."

"And yet you told us to use a servant for navigation just now," Ash said sarcastically. "It's not easy to take someone hostage without hurting them."

Marvin shook his head in response, though he maintained his grin. "Karl, you go south. Ash, east. Rover, west. Let's move."

Marvin circled toward the north gate with only a pair of daggers. As he had said, he didn't plan to harm anyone. He hoped he didn't have to. And with the way he was moving now, climbing up the northern tower like a stealthy arachnid, he might not have to confront anyone at all.

The rampart was only several feet away now but the footman there wasn't going away. Despite his ability, Marvin wasn't going to hold onto the wall forever. He rolled his eyes and then flung a dagger up, not *at* the innocent footman, but over and behind him, only so that he would turn away.

The footman spun as Marvin had intended him to, only to then be promptly knocked down unconscious with a subtle blow to the neck. "My apologies," Marvin whispered, trotting away to retrieve his weapon.

He dragged the unconscious man and laid him away from view. Then he headed to the stairs and paced his way down.

When he arrived in the tremendously long hallway that led all the way to the southern tower, he looked up and wondered for a moment if Karl had penetrated from the other end yet. Sometimes, he felt truly blessed to have a crew that was comprised of such incredible people. And while every individual crew member offered unique abilities and were—in his mind—irreplaceable, Karl still stood out as an exceptional addition to the group. The big Kragan, despite his reserved character, was unbelievably good at playing his role as the cartographer. No one knew exactly how he managed, but just like every other time when they had broken into supposedly impenetrable structures, he had drawn out a map of the place, detailing the exact anatomy of the entire castle, missing nothing but labels and a legend.

Marvin and the others had since engrained a less than perfect representation of that map in their minds. They had also marked several places in which they believed the Mirage Ring might be kept. From the northern tower where he had started, Marvin had to survey only three rooms in the otherwise enormous castle with nearly two hundred rooms.

In any case, as Marvin paced carefully along the hallway, he was glad to note that it was difficult for anyone to detect him. The sparsely installed oil lamps on the walls were barely practical as a light source. The dabs of moonlight that shone through the small windows hardly helped the cause. The armour he had changed into was the same as most of the guards there were also wearing. Marvin lowered his helmet, too, to help himself blend in.

The camouflage worked, but that was only the beginning. The real challenge was to get to and pry through the three rooms he was allocated to. As he traced back to his mental map, Marvin followed the route toward his first point of interest, one of the largest rooms of the castle. He treaded slowly on firm steps as he looked to avoid attention, walking past nearly ten guards who couldn't see through his disguise. He sighed softly after passing each of them, noting that the longer his crew was there, the less likely they would succeed. Barely minutes had passed so far, but he was already growing anxious.

He sighed again when he reached the first room that he was to survey. It was behind a double door constructed of a glazed red wood with strips of valuable metal. Two men stood guard at the front.

There's no avoiding this, Marvin thought.

The men perked up as Marvin paced closer. It was probably unusual for any soldier to enter the room.

"Halt!" one of the guards cried, pointing a sheathed sword forward. "Who goes there?"

Marvin lifted his helmet slightly, revealing only his cheeky grin, before hurling the headgear forward, striking the head of the guard on the right, then bouncing at the head of the other guard with enough momentum to stun them both. Marvin then jumped forward, landing soft blows at their necks in the same way he had knocked down the footman from before. Then he retrieved the now dented helmet, fitting it back on.

He palmed the right door open, pushing it carefully, making sure it didn't creak. The generous light from inside glistened out toward him and into the hall. He gripped the two men on their back collars and then slipped inside to a carpeted chamber in a hue of maroon, dragging them along, then closing the door shut behind him.

It was a massive space, as large as Marvin had remembered from the map—enough for a challenging game of skittles. He peered past the furniture to the far corner where he noticed a door. If he had remembered correctly, it led to another room within the room he was already in.

Should I start there? Marvin wondered. His eyes then fell to the lavish couch in front of him woven in a fleece of gold with plenty of space beneath it. He looked back at the unconscious men he had dragged in with him, and then promptly started sliding the them under the ample seating.

"Who's there?!" called a voice.

Marvin poked his head up from the couch, and there, stepping out from that door in the far corner, was a young lady. She looked to be in her late teens, dressed in a white gown that hung loosely around her body. She was slim, edging closer to skinny. Her fair auburn hair was tied back to a pair of simple pigtails, which made her look younger than she probably was. She was quite pretty, but her grimace which looked like a mix of bemusement and annoyance discarded any sense of attraction.

Don't want to hurt her, Marvin thought, staying still and waiting for any other people who might appear behind the young lady. *Looks like she's been fooled to think I'm a guard.*

She didn't seem to be a regular servant, at least not a friendly one. She paced over now in her bare feet. She lifted her chin, staring down at Marvin in condescension. She widened her eyes with anger as she inhaled, perhaps ready to reprimand. All that would come out from her mouth, however, was a gasp—for Marvin had slid out a blade, inched up to her neck.

"Keep it down," Marvin warned in a whisper, getting back to his feet now as he pressed the flat end of the blade softly onto the side of her neck.

The young lady shivered. "What... what do you think you're doing?" she asked, clearly confused.

"Do as I say, and I promise it will end well."

"What...?!" she asked again. "Are you... *not* a soldier?"

"No."

"Then... you're an intruder?" she then guessed. "A thief?!"

Marvin chortled, withdrawing his dagger. "I'll remember this," he said. "Insult from a domestic servant."

"A domestic servant?" the young lady said, looking baffled. She hesitated a little then. "I may only be a servant but does that mean I cannot cry thief?"

"I'm a *Treasure Hunter*!" Marvin snapped.

The young lady gulped. "And what do you want?" she asked carefully.

"A ring," Marvin said. "I doubt you'd know anything about it. So why don't you let *me* ask the questions? Tell me now, what is this fancy chamber?"

"It's... the princess's room," she responded. "This is where I work."

"Who would have guessed?" Marvin said, peering out at the chamber again. "And they kept her room tidy." He turned back to the young lady. "What's your name?" he asked.

She opened her mouth, but uttered nothing, hesitating again. "Tavie," she then finally said.

"You'll help me navigate," Marvin said. "Play any tricks, and you'll come to regret it."

She sighed in short breaths and then impressively calmed herself down. "I'll do what you say."

Marvin kept an eye on her as he stooped down and reached his arm under the couch. He pulled out one of the unconscious men and then expertly stripped him of his armour.

"Put this on," he demanded the servant, who abided immediately, though she was clumsy in fitting on the suit of armour over her own clothing. She had to roll up her sleeves so that the gown would be hidden from view.

"There are a lot of rings here, actually, in this very chamber," Tavie said after she finally got dressed in the same disguise, tucking away even her pigtails under the helmet. "Ruby, sapphire, diamond—anything you can imagine."

"Show me," Marvin said.

Tavie led him to the door from which she had come out—the princess's own private room, where she would have spent most of her time. A bed complete with an extravagant canopy of silk was the main feature of the sparsely furnished room. The bed itself could accommodate perhaps four people, so unless the princess was a giant, it signified the affluence of the kingdom. In any case, Marvin couldn't care less about the bed, and had already spotted a dressing table which was every part as extravagant as the rest of the furniture—wide, polished, and with a large rectangular mirror engraved into a frame of salmon-pink cushions.

Tavie pulled open the top drawer, revealing an organised case that displayed more than fifty different rings, all boxed separately with transparent tops. Marvin's eyes glistened at the jewellery, which in turn, sparkled back at him. He skimmed the collection for dabs of blue, finding only one—which was *the* one. He picked it out, the ring of blue diamond.

"This is it," he said softly, holding it up to his eyes. "The Mirage Ring."

It's been a while since I last beat Ash and the others to the prize, he thought with a faint smile. *We might be a team, but the competition can sometimes be ferocious... of course, unless I win.*

While the diamond itself wasn't particularly large, the clarity and colour were impressive. Even on a closer examination, Marvin saw no imperfections. The hue of cobalt blue was thought to be rare, and that meant that it was also extremely valuable. But its beauty was secondary to Marvin's purposes as he had hoped to acquire the gem because of the legend that it had the power to draw illusions upon resonating with the blue of Achelois.

Tavie raised an eyebrow. "The *Mirage* Ring?" she asked. "It has a name? I didn't even know. It's not the most precious ring here, though."

Marvin shot her a wry smile, and then slipped the ring beneath his brigandine. "Let's go," he said.

"That's it?" Tavie asked with surprise. "Just one shabby ring?"

Marvin thought her reaction strange, but refrained from commenting. Instead, he reached behind his back where the two small missiles were clutched—smaller even than his daggers. He picked out the blue one, which was to signal success to his crew. He then sauntered to the only window in the room with a finger on the sling, ready to fire it away. Before he reached the window, however, a luminous red missile rocketed up into the skies—the emergency signal to flee.

"Intruders!" yelled men from afar.

Tavie raced to the window, poking her head out, looking more distressed than she should. "How did they know you were here?" she said in protest. "How careless *were* you?"

The low rumbling of horns began to fill the air outside. The castle had declared a state of emergency. Clusters of men appeared from every corner, marching—trampling out with urgency.

"Are they heading here?" Tavie asked, growing more agitated. "Are they—"

She trailed off as Marvin snatched her at her wrist, bolting out of the private room and dragging her with him. Just as Tavie had assumed, a group of five or six soldiers had stormed into the chamber, looking more startled then they probably should, drawing their swords and pointing them at Marvin and Tavie as soon as they noted them.

"Hold tight," Marvin said quietly, clutching harder onto Tavie's wrist.

He then dashed forward, taking one giant leap to reach the group who were only starting to gape before being knocked out with Marvin's simple swipe of his arm. Two swipes, perhaps.

Need to get back to the northern tower, Marvin thought, not sparing another glance at the defeated soldiers. Instead, he turned a glance to Tavie, whose widened eyes showed her astonishment at what had just happened.

"Come!" Marvin said, dashing out to the hall, still dragging Tavie along behind him. He picked up velocity after several steps, now racing at a speed that rivalled the mightiest of stallions. He had taken what he had wanted. The mission was complete. There was no longer any reason to prowl.

"Heeeeeey!" he heard Tavie cry as they burst up the set of stairs then, her futile hollers reverberating behind her.

Marvin finally released his grip when they reached the top of the tower, only for Tavie to collapse immediately to the ground, probably because of vertigo. The strong winds that continued to blow in the open air would help her overcome her blur, as would the brilliant blue of Achelois.

Marvin dashed to the wall of the rampart, whose height reached his chest. He peered down from there, noting hundreds of soldiers rushing away to the central courtyard where two men from his crew, Ash and Rover, were surrounded. There was no rush if Rover was there, not for their crew anyway. Marvin turned back to Tavie, who still seemed lightheaded. He stepped over to her and removed her helmet, which then allowed the winds to lift her auburn hair to blow about wildly.

"Be my hostage," he said, his words probably an indistinct mutter to her.

Without any further warning, he wrapped an arm around her waist, throwing her up over his shoulder. Tavie gasped, but then soon lost her voice as Marvin dove down from the tower, at which time Tavie screamed as they began tumbling down together in a free fall. Although he had expected it, Marvin thought the sharp cry was extravagant, especially as the fall was completely under his control. He had whipped out a dagger, which he now thrust into the tremendous wall, tearing out a screeching scar trailed with a dangerous spark of tangerine, slowing the fall considerably.

He stepped on the ground unscathed and took only a brief glance at the worn-out blade before discarding it. He didn't bother assuring Tavie that they were safe. She was still shivering, and her eyes were shut tight with a few beads of tears gushed out. He carried her on his back now and raced away, heading to the courtyard, betting on the soldiers to recognise Tavie as one of the princess's servants, which would potentially make her a valuable hostage—all that effort only for minimising the damage his crew would potentially deal to the innocent soldiers.

He reached the courtyard in barely a few blinks. He made quite an entrance, too, leaping over the hundreds of soldiers as if flying, and then landing next to his allies with a strong whirl that shot out gusts in every direction. He finally let go of Tavie, who knelt on the floor, trembling.

"Showing off again," Ash said with a grin.

Both he and Rover were unharmed, as expected.

"What happened?" Marvin asked with a grin of his own.

Ash shrugged. "Don't know. It wasn't me who fired it."

Marvin glanced over to Rover who shook his head. "Karl, then?"

The soldiers, hundreds of them, found themselves backing off. They had seemed to finally realise how dangerous the intruders were. Many of them had also seemed to recognise Tavie whose long auburn hair was exposed.

"Hold it!" a commanding voice echoed from within the sea of men.

The soldiers made way as a man strode out, looking stately and confident. The man, despite his white hair that gave away his old age, sported armour of gold. His frown, however, showed that he was less than pleased. He regarded Marvin with a squint.

"I assume you are the Sail Band?" the knight said with a grunt.

Marvin winked back. "And you are Sir Tristan?" he said.

"Indeed, I am John Tristan of the Kingdom of Cetal."

"Look, Sir Tristan," Marvin said. "I'm done here. I'm just looking to leave now. I suggest you let us go."

"Release her," he demanded, nodding to Tavie, who was still trying to shake off the fuzz. "Don't even think about—"

The golden knight stopped mid-sentence as Marvin knocked Tavie out with tap at her neck. "She shall return when we get out," he said.

Tristan growled quietly, glaring at Marvin. He then turned to his men and ordered them to clear the path. The soldiers paved the way toward the south gate. It was only a short walk from the courtyard, but everyone moved slowly, holding their breath, with the exception of course of the thieving trio.

They eventually reached the gate, which was already opened ahead of time. Leo was on the other side, leaning forward at the deck of the horse-drawn wagon he drove, and wearing a wry smile. Marvin nodded at him, and then turned around, eyeing Tristan and the soldiers one last time.

"Goodbye," Marvin said.

"Don't you *dare* go back on your word," Tristan warned. "And don't—"

The golden knight obviously had more to say, but he trailed off again when bunches of tiny metal balls showered in from the outside—by Leo, who had grinned at them while holding onto the reins that he had used for catapulting.

"Look out!" Tristan cried, directing his men to hack away the projectiles.

The soldiers did just that, and effectively, too, destroying the stone-sized objects heaving in. Unfortunately for them, however, the metal balls were filled with solid fuel and sulphur, which triggered a dangerous black flame and smoke on forceful contact. The soldiers became enwrapped in thick smog almost immediately. They coughed and waved their arms with their best efforts to clear the air. Marvin and the crew didn't know much more than that, for they were already rolling away into the woodlands.

"Go! Go!" Leo cried in excitement, urging the pair of horses to race harder for what was a jolting ride. When the mares picked up some momentum, he glanced back to the rest of the crew. "Now, that was close. I guess it's Leonardo to the rescue once again."

"It wasn't just *close*!" Ash complained. "You got me with one of those smoke bombs!"

"Hey now, we got out," Leo responded, still wearing his grin.

"We got what we wanted, too," Marvin said with a chuckle as he slipped out the Mirage Ring that suddenly illuminated the wagon in a glittering blue.

"Wow...," Leo said, looking over his shoulder again to the spectacle. "Now, *that's* something to hunt for."

"It's striking enough," Ash said. "But does it really work? The illusions, I mean."

Marvin brushed open the drapes on the right of the wagon, and then held the ring outside the window. "Let's try it," he said, directing the ring at the full moon of Achelois, which it was thought to resonate with. He held his breath, waiting for a reaction. The others naturally leaned in, too.

But there was no reaction, at least not for the minute Marvin held it out.

"Maybe only magic users know how to use it," Ash joked.

Marvin frowned, and then withdrew the ring, slipping it back beneath the soldier's armour that he was still wearing. "Anyway... hope Karl is all right. He fired the distress missile. Did he perhaps run into that golden knight?"

"Probably," Ash said with a shrug. "But I doubt he's in any trouble. Knowing him, he's probably ahead of us."

* * *

Winds were blowing outside with an eerie sibilance. The breeze that managed to stream in was crisp, rushing gloriously over Tavie. The scent of wild grass wasn't the same as she had been accustomed to. It wasn't as pleasant, but it was far more refreshing. The sound of trotting hooves and squeaking wheels were evidence that she was in a wheeled-vehicle of sort, moving at a slow pace, probably far away from the castle. But she didn't dare to open her eyes just yet to confirm any of her assumptions, wary that it would startle the intruders who had kidnapped her. Instead, Tavie pretended that she was still out as she listened in on what her kidnappers were saying.

"...but it was still a hell of an experience," one of the men was saying. "I'd do it again and again for the thrill alone."

"It *was* fun," another man said, his voice familiar—likely the madman who had dragged her away from the chamber and then jumped down from the tower. "But I wouldn't do it again for the sake of it. I think we're past that."

"You know," a third man inserted with a hint of sarcasm, "you'd be more convincing if you weren't wearing that smug grin. Don't try to act all noble now."

They all shared a laugh then. The tone of their voices and their occasional chuckles were all that Tavie could rely on to help her analyse who her kidnappers really were. The madman—whose name was apparently Marvin—sounded cynical in everything he was saying, at least superficially. It was too early to appraise their characters, but while she thought that she should be feeling threatened or at least anxious by them, she instead felt an air of refuge sweeping over her along with the gentle breeze.

It was more important to her that she was indeed within the heart of the woodlands, a place that she had always only been allowed to view from afar. She had pictured herself there for as long as she could remember, wishing that she could one day step foot upon that great patch of trees and shrubs. Who could foretell the irony that her wish was finally granted in such circumstances?

It was a secret that no one was interested in: Tavie hated her life. For as far as she could remember, she had been given everything one could wish for—every material possession, anyway. She had never been given much freedom, however, neither of how she wanted to live her life, nor who she was allowed to acquaint with. She had never even stepped outside the castle, and the explanation she had received was that it was for her own good. Perhaps it was her fate. Born as Octavia Morlan, the hereditary princess of the Kingdom of Cetal, her life had been predetermined to correspond with what was best for the kingdom—which, incidentally, seemed to always disagree with what she had personally wanted.

Her mother, the Queen, had died a couple of years earlier, and that had left her relationship with her father further estranged. She had since spent her days engaged in daft soliloquy, alienating every servant who probably pitied and envied her all at the same time. She wasn't actually ill, mentally or physically. She *had* contemplated a move to Zorlia, but she had decided that it would change nothing, that she would be constrained again, albeit in a new environment. And since her father's departure to Zorlia, she had decided that she must *escape* her fate. She didn't care for the epicurean life of a princess, and particularly not under the stringent watch of her father who she was sure regretted that she wasn't a boy. Indeed, it was probably ironic to her father that she—a *girl*—was his only child recognised as part of the royal family. After all, she could only assume that her father's many lovers meant that she had countless illegitimate siblings—some of whom must be male.

Perhaps that was why the scents, the wind, and even her kidnappers, were altogether liberating to her—for she recognised now that she had finally escaped that dreaded fate. Her kidnappers wouldn't have predicted that she was the princess, that she had remained at the castle when her father, King Morlan, had left for Zorlia. They would never learn who she was. To ensure that her identity wouldn't be taken advantage of and to give herself the best chance to lead a new life without the burden that was tied with her royal line, she wouldn't allow them or anyone else to ever learn the truth.

"What are we going to do with her?" one of the men said then, which had Tavie's heart suddenly thumping.

Although the winds were still roaring outside, Tavie recognised that she was no longer in motion. They had probably arrived at a den in which the thieves used as a hiding place.

"I suppose she stays with us for the night," said Marvin, his voice fading off into the winds, evidently stepping out from the wheeled-vehicle.

"So, we pay for her?" asked the other man who had been sitting closest to her, also stepping out.

Some indistinct mumbling followed. Tavie tried to listen in, but even the murmurs soon ceased behind the strident winds.

Were they gone? Had they left her alone?

It seemed like a golden opportunity to escape, but could it be a trap? After all, she had no idea where they had taken her. What could she possibly achieve on her own even if she had the chance to flee? Tavie certainly didn't think herself naïve or incapable of surviving by herself, but having read many stories from the outside world, which included some tragic narratives, she recognised it was imprudent to roam the land by herself. She needed support, someone or something to depend on, at least in the beginning.

She finally snapped open her eyes then to a small, dull enclosure. Staying still and maintaining her position where she was lying to her left, she peered about, recognising the hardwood construction of what appeared to be a modest wagon, which had thick drapes sheltering the illumination from the outside save a tinge of blue that was likely given off by Achelois.

Tavie waited for a moment longer before finally sitting up. She was still in the suit of armour the madman had forced her to wear, which had indeed provided her with much more warmth than her evening gown alone could manage. She inhaled deeply and then crawled quietly to the front of the simple carriage, gently brushing aside the drapes to a pair of horses' behinds, but also a strip of humble buildings whose entrances were dimly lighted by some meek-looking lanterns.

It wasn't a dream. Without a measure of doubt, she had departed the castle. And despite the circumstances, it was truly liberating. As she continued to gape, she found herself crawling out further from the carriage, and closer to freedom. She was finally free to live a life she could choose, free to journey away to any unchartered territory she wished, free to—

"It's late now," a voice said, causing Tavie to jump. "We're staying the night here."

She turned to her left. Stepping into view from the side of the carriage was the man who had kidnapped her—*Marvin*, they called him. His imposing physique was indeed similar to the greatest knights she had known, such as Sir Tristan and Sir Ormond. But this man looked much younger than them, and yet he had managed to break in and out of the castle with apparent ease, which implied that he was potentially even stronger—or at least more cunning—than the knights.

The man was still wearing the guard's suit of armour, but without the helmet, which exposed his short hair and a wide headband tied at an angle on his forehead. He was holding onto a leather wine flask, which he now plugged its cap back on.

"Don't worry," he said. "You won't have to share with anyone. Ash is reserving an extra room for you. It's been a long night. You can return to the castle tomorrow morning with one of the horses."

Tavie peered back to the building in front of her. It was an inn, a lodging place for travellers, a kind of establishment which she had never thought she would see, let alone stay in. She then regarded Marvin with curiosity, not saying a word.

"What?" Marvin asked, looking annoyed. "Do you *not* know how to ride a horse...?"

Tavie flushed. "I can ride a horse!" she asserted. "I can do *so* much more than you can imagine!"

Marvin smiled back.

Tavie frowned then. "But are you actually letting me go?" she asked in a more amiable tone. "You could use me against the soldiers."

"Are you *offering* to be used...?" Marvin responded in bemusement.

"I... I just... they're going to take me to Zorlia. And that means... it means..."

"That you'll serve the princess again?" Marvin said, finishing her sentence. "I sympathise, but that's your problem. Plus, I don't need a girl to journey with."

"It wouldn't just be a girl to journey with," she said, surprising herself. "I'm no burden. I'll join you in your guild of thieves."

Marvin shook his head. "All right, this is just getting ridiculous now. You've got it all wrong. I'm not—"

"My mistake," Tavie cut in, her words slipping out now. "I'll join your treasure hunting team."

Marvin raised an eyebrow this time, clearly taken aback.

"I want to live," Tavie continued. "I want freedom. I want to see the world. Now that I have escaped the castle, I can finally pursue... *life*."

The man regarded her with suspicion for a moment longer. "All right, I see," he finally said. "But what do you know about treasure hunting? How do you plan to contribute?"

"I'm no thief," she admitted. "But I've had training with a variety of weapons. I'm particularly confident with my archery skills."

"That means nothing to me," Marvin said with a snicker.

Tavie groaned. "I've been living in the castle all my life," she said, her eyebrows knitted. "I know how castles operate. If you were ever to raid a castle again, I can be your guide. Just... don't make this castle your target again, though."

Marvin lifted his chin. "But still... you're a girl."

"Now, come on," Tavie said, still trying to make her case. "I'm very capable despite my gender."

"No, I mean you're just a child," Marvin said, waving out a dismissive hand and seemingly eyeing beneath her chin. "Hardly a woman."

Tavie blushed slightly and then glanced down at her chest, which was admittedly, rather flat. "Pervert!" she snapped, flinching as she crossed her arms to cover her chest. "I'm twenty-one years old!"

Marvin rolled his eyes. "And I don't need that attitude, either."

Tavie forced a grin. "Marvin," she said. "I'm going to follow you wherever you go. So... let the land remember this moment where I... Tavie, become one of the treasure hunting team."

"When did I agree to that?" Marvin asked, bemused once again. "You have no idea what you're even in for. Did you know that we kill for money? Have you considered that we might kill you if the price was right?"

"If you wanted that, you would have done so by now," she said. "We're staying the night, are we?"

She didn't wait for an answer, instead hopping away to the closed entrance of the inn, pausing when she gripped the door knob. She took a deep breath then.

Goodbye, Octavia, she thought as she turned the knob and entered.

FIVE

Back to the drawing board

The community of scholars had regarded Alpheus as a genius. They had prematurely tagged him to succeed in his brilliant sister's footsteps, to whom Alpheus owed his fantastic reputation. Those lofty expectations, though, had seen a gradual decline throughout the past six years, incidentally the time when Alpheus had begun to distance himself from the academy, indulging himself instead in the arts, particularly in painting.

Reeling would be the first to acknowledge that it was unfair to Alpheus to have lived with so much pressure to succeed even before his admission into the academy. Charlotte Hindlow's standing as arguably the Grandmaster's finest pupil meant that Alpheus had been subject to immense scrutiny by the community, in an unforgiving environment in which he had few friends.

Even so, Alpheus had managed to earn his worth during his active years there, and was even nominated once as a designated speaker at the symposium. That particular experience had been forgettable, however—his first taste of failure, his ideas rejected outright as impractical and far too romanticised. Alpheus had blamed the inconsistencies in his presentation on the irregularity of the symposiums, which were held every two to three years, citing the limited preparation time he had been given between nomination for the part and the actual event. He had then failed to qualify for the two symposiums since then, offering less than the bare minimum required for the abstract.

"This again?" Alpheus said in protest, regretting now that he had gone to Reeling's estate again. "I thought we were over it."

"I thought so, too," Reeling said. "But things have changed."

"I don't pride myself as a scholar. You know that. Weren't you the one who said I should choose how to live? I want to paint. That's my choice."

"I made a mistake," Reeling said, shaking his head. "And now I need to make amends. This is not only about you."

Alpheus simpered. "Then is it about *you*?"

"The Grandmaster has faith in you. Are you going to ignore that? Your sister expects you to have landed a position within the Empire by now. What are you going to say to her?"

"I'll say: *that's your wish, not mine*."

Reeling smiled, shaking his head. "I'd be the first to applaud you if you dared to say that."

Alpheus fell quiet. He dreaded the thought of working for the Empire, but he dreaded the potential consequences of upsetting his sister even more. He respected her. In fact, he admired her. But that didn't mean she was easy to be siblings with.

Reeling sighed. "In any case, the next symposium, the twenty-fifth, has been announced. I need you to make a mark, to become a State Scholar. Things will come easier then."

"And what next? The Empire? Are you setting me up on a path?"

Reeling looked him in the eyes. "I have no intention to force you into anything... perhaps besides this. Once you are there, I am sure you will be digging into the thick of everything you thought you wanted nothing to do with."

Alpheus smirked, knowing there was no way of that happening.

"Anyway, Seer tells me that a scholar from the Far East is coming to Zorlia to take part in the fun."

Alpheus said nothing, but his musing frown showed his curiosity.

"It is to improve relations between Trubannis and Aizary. A lady, I have heard. She is not quite an envoy, but certainly an important guest for the Empire. Rumour has it that she is blessed with talent, as are most scholars from the island-country. And if you are looking into magic, you should know that Aizary embraces its use. You may even learn a few things about magic from her."

"When is she arriving?" Alpheus asked, pondering the idea.

"Early December, about two weeks prior to the symposium. Use this time to revise your studies. That way, you might have a chance to measure up."

Alpheus wanted to laugh off the challenge. But before he could, Reeling tossed him a ring, which he was quick to catch. The solitaire sitting on the silver band was a round sapphire the size of a pebble, but with the quality of the most valuable of gemstones. Alpheus held it to his eye, noting the gem's excellent clarity as he looked around to see a clear blue world.

"A gift of encouragement," Reeling said.

"Wow, thank you," said Alpheus. "But I don't wear jewellery."

Reeling said nothing, only gazing down at Alpheus's double crescent pendant.

"What! This?" Alpheus said, clutching his pendant. "My faith."

"Promise to keep it with you."

Alpheus nodded and then looped the ring into the same chain, together with the double crescent. He tucked them all underneath his white robe.

"There," he said.

* * *

The next morning, Alpheus went to the *Church of the St. Bernard Order*, the most prominent worship house of Ionianism in the country, and a place that he frequented as a devout adherent. It had been more than a month since his last visit, however, due to his new-found curiosity about magic—a subject generally regarded by Ionians as the workings of *The Eternally Damned*.

The cathedral was in Arcadia, a high-elevation neighbourhood in the northwest, bisected from Vondra Dawn by the Dunn Bay and the longer *Dunn River*, which ran all the way to the sea. The closest bridge was far from a direct route, which meant it was quite a stroll to get there by foot. But that didn't stop Alpheus and many others from making regular visits, and neither did it stop many of the most faithful from competing for residence in the area since long ago. On top of its reputation for being home to the most devout adherents of Ionianism, Arcadia had also been the most affluent neighbourhood of Zorlia until Phantom Pond had later taken over that honour at the turn of the new era. With its proximity to Vondra Dawn and hence the city centre, Phantom Pond was simply more conveniently located.

Although it was over a century old, the cathedral itself was a miracle of a structure that sat on the beautiful ravine section of the river, erected from the river-bank with its highest point towering five floors above land. The entrance was a short bridge that extended over the ravine, offering some of the most spectacular views of Zorlia. Constructed primarily from a grey-hued stone, the building was grand in both size and design with the nave accommodating hundreds of people. Twin towers of black roofs framed the façade. Between them was a sizeable ornate sculpture of the faith's central symbol: the double crescent, carved from a light-coloured limestone. Although the symbol was commonly seen in Trubannis, Vinawell, and Aizary, only the more educated or devout fully understood what it depicted.

The crescent on the top, waxing from left to right, was the red moon Selene. The crescent on the bottom, waning in the same direction, was the blue moon Achelois. The symbol was simple in its depiction of the natural phenomena that occurred once every two months, days before the moons lined up together in an eclipse. It represented the central teachings of the Immortal, which were based on the philosophy that everything followed a predetermined cycle and, specifically, that the death of one entity was the birth of another.

For Alpheus, it was his faith and his admiration for the Immortal that had helped steer him toward a contented life since the passing of his parents when he was only three years old. Every time he came to the cathedral, he would worship and meditate for over an hour before he confessed his sins to Father Abraham, the fourth and current head of the church. Today, he had many confessions involving the improbable series of events that had taken place recently. And, as always, Father Abraham was most amiable in pacifying him.

Alpheus was at peace after the session, and things only got better when he happened by a friendly face among the followers, Agnes Gardner, a devout young lady three years younger than him. She was his childhood friend and a fellow scholar at the academy who had only just returned to Zorlia after an expedition with her peers. Like many Trubans, Agnes was born into the Ionian faith, but she had grown ever more attached to her faith since being orphaned when she was eight years of age. Like Alpheus, she wore a pendant of the double crescent, which she would clasp onto when she said her prayers.

Alpheus beamed at her, gesturing for her to retire to the atrium with him. They stepped outside into the fine day and settled next to a large, rectangular fountain where water was cascading harmoniously from beneath life-sized sculptures of the angels Raziel and Jeremiel.

"How was it?" Alpheus asked.

"Very worthwhile," Agnes said with her distinctive voice, which was hoarse yet sweet and innocent. "We were certain to learn with Lady Willow as our mentor. Anyway, Alfie, I haven't seen you for a while. The last time I tried to visit you, the Lord Count said you went to Carrington."

Alpheus looked askance at the calmer floor of the fountain, twitching slightly at the turquoise tinge of the water on the ivory-shaded tiles. *Yes, Carrington,* he thought. *I was hiding from him... the Lord Count. Didn't realise he knew.* "A month," he said instead. "It's been that long?"

Agnes nodded. "There's so much I have to tell you."

"I have things to tell you too," Alpheus said with a grin, regarding her again.

Agnes cocked her head slightly, waiting.

"Magic," Alpheus said. "I've met some magic users—well, two of them, anyway. One of them is dead. The other one's become a friend."

Agnes fell silent for a second. "What...?" she then finally said.

"Magic," Alpheus said again. "Are you *not* interested? And I thought it was something we could share."

"I'm interested," Agnes inserted with a pout. "I just—"

Alpheus shook his head. "I'll tell you more when I know more. I'm sure you'll share my passion then. Anyway, on a less exciting note, I should probably update you on this... I'm working for the symposium."

Her eyes glowed this time. "Really?!" she asked. "I didn't want to say," she continued, shying away slightly, "but I am, too."

"What? But... are you ready?"

"I don't know, but Master Seer said I should try."

Master Seer said that? Alpheus thought with a raised brow.

"They really didn't give us much time, though," Agnes said with a sigh.

"No, they didn't. But I do like the open theme. *Imagination, Beliefs, and Action*. It has to be one of the more general themes in symposium history. I don't think anyone would have much trouble finding a suitable topic."

Agnes groaned. "Still... there's no less preparation."

"You'll be fine!" Alpheus assured her, resting a hand lightly on her shoulder. "If Master Seer says you're ready, then you're more than ready."

Agnes regarded him with surprise, as if she wouldn't have expected those words to come out of his mouth. She then finally blinked away her surprise and acknowledged the praise with a firm nod.

* * *

It was barely past midday. After parting ways with Agnes, who had a few chores on hand, Alpheus headed to the academy. It would mark his first visit there in three years.

He held his breath as he stood outside the grand entrance consisting of curved marble steps that led to the great mahogany double-door sandwiched by giant sturdy pillars. It was a magnificent building of six floors, coated primarily in a creamy white—not so different from Alpheus's preferred colour of dress. He took a deep breath and stepped into the expansive antechamber. Alpheus looked up at the walkways of the multiple floors, in addition to the wide-arcing spiral stairs that led there. As always, it was a sight to behold. It was a privilege to be there. And this was in spite of the fact that he was only there now after being badgered by Reeling.

The atmosphere, though, was different from what he remembered. As

Alpheus passed other scholars, he realised that not everyone seemed to recognise him. And the ones who did recognise him didn't seem intimidated, instead acknowledging him like anyone else. It was strange because he had once been a scholar of celebrity status. Perhaps the expectations his peers had for him had changed after three years. Perhaps he would no longer be scrutinised for his every action. And perhaps, it was really time to revisit his identity as a scholar. After all, it was arguably the most important aspect of who he was.

Alpheus allowed himself a few grins here and there as he headed toward the main library. He recognised some faces, but also noted that there was a generation of younger scholars loitering about, people he had never met.

They didn't know him. Or so he thought, at least.

Alpheus headed to the library, picked out an addition of ten tomes, and then settled at a secluded corner enclosed behind a section that was rarely visited. He piled the texts onto the only desk there, hoping to study without distraction. He flipped open the first tome, which was about two of the four subjects that made up the quadrivium. He sighed, picturing the Grandmaster who had spent most of the past fifteen years in seclusion on the top floor of the academy for one purpose alone: to push the boundaries of what people could know and experience. Alpheus didn't think he could survive a year in isolation, let alone fifteen. But if he was to make a mark on this upcoming symposium, he might have to endure some time alone.

It had barely been two minutes when someone stepped into his insulation. Alpheus didn't expect anyone. He didn't want to see anyone, either. He looked up now with a frown, meeting the eyes of two young boys who watched him from the end of the bookshelf, their twinkling eyes showing visible admiration. The boys were barely in their adolescence, and yet they sported the same garb as Alpheus, holding onto thick books that looked too heavy for them to carry.

"We're sorry," one of them said. "But can we ask you a few questions?"

Alpheus simpered as he cocked his head. "About what?"

"We're studying the stars for the first time," the second boy said. "We heard that you could help us."

"Really? From who?"

The boys exchanged a look. "From everyone," they said.

Alpheus gestured them toward his desk and the boys flipped open one of the books they had brought.

Astronomy basics, Alpheus noted as he scanned the text and the accompanying diagrams. *Why are they asking me?*

But..., he thought, peering up at the boys again. *This feels... better than I'd imagine.*

Other than the peers he had mocked inadvertently in his younger years as he had worked to prove his points, the only person Alpheus had taught was Agnes. He was never sure if he was a good teacher, but if the boys' comments were anything to go by, Alpheus was at least better than their instructors.

It took five minutes to explain what the boys had believed to be a complicated concept. Their delight in overcoming what had stalled them for a while resonated with Alpheus, who found himself smiling as he waved them goodbye.

It was several minutes later when another visitor came—a girl, younger than even the boys from before. She was biting her lips and looking more hesitant than the boys. She then slipped out a tome of her own.

"Can you help me, please?" she asked.

Alpheus sighed, but then waved her over.

Her question was about geometry. Alpheus managed to help her understand the question in hand fairly soon, and even went on to advise the girl on how to progress from there. When she finally left, though, Alpheus groaned to himself. *I'm not here for them. I'm here for...*, that thought trailing off as an image of Reeling sparked inside his head. "I need to do this," he whispered to himself, shaking his head.

But sure enough, people kept showing up. And Alpheus had no choice but to turn them away. It soon got out of hand, though, as more and more came. Word must have gone out with the first young scholars he had helped. The next one to step into his vicinity, the thirtieth or so, would have the worst: Alpheus shouted at her to go away, a child who jumped in fright before running off in tears.

No one came back after that, and he was finally left in peace to absorb the abundance of knowledge in front of him. At his level, there were no instructors or set assignments. The only way to progress was to read up on what had been written and carefully choose what to believe and what to challenge.

Scholars were expected to know everything about wide-ranging topics from philosophy to the sciences, to political theory, and almost everything in between. A great scholar was distinguished from an average one not only by how much they knew, but more so by how they applied that knowledge to solving real problems.

During his childhood, Alpheus had been lauded as a genius for that reason: he had come up with plenty of creative solutions for problems that had troubled even the greatest government authorities. Of course, none of his ideas had ever been applied to practice, when even established scholars found it difficult to reach the authorities, who often dismissed their caste as idealistic and naive. Kings and noblemen often said that they embraced scholars, and it was true that they trusted scholars with all the menial tasks, but rarely for anything beyond that. Reeling was a rare example of a scholar who held an important position in the Empire.

Alpheus realised that he wasn't nearly as capable as his mentor, and for that, he wanted nothing to do with the Empire. During these years away from the academy, he had tried to convince himself that nothing good would come of advancing his way through the ranks of the scholars.

A waste of time, really, he thought, as he squinted his eyes at the text.

He jumped slightly then, as the ground seemed to shake. *Footsteps?*

He looked over to his pocket watch that he had opened and leaned against the books in front of him. It was late. There were no windows nearby, but it must be completely dark outside.

The ground wasn't actually shaking, but someone was approaching. In fact, every approaching step of this newest stranger almost seemed to knock off particles of the thoughts he had just now been contemplating.

Alpheus groaned quietly, grasping the thickest book from the desk. He waited and waited until a set of heavy boots stepped into his field of vision behind the end of the bookshelf.

A man, Alpheus noted. *Could it be...?*

He breathed a sigh of relief when he realised it wasn't the man he most dreaded to see, Yusuf Seer—the man entrusted by the Grandmaster to oversee everything in the academy—who was like a meaner, sterner Jeffery Reeling. Instead, it was Christopher Hartland, an established scholar his age who he knew all too well.

"Why are you here?" Hartland questioned, face scrunched up more than Seer would have managed. "Why did you come back?"

Alpheus grinned. "Now, *that's* the academy I remember. That attitude—that very unwelcoming attitude."

"I'm not joking, Alpheus," Hartland said.

Alpheus fell back into the chair. "I'm working for the symposium. I need to make a mark."

"You sound confident."

"Not right now, I'm not," he said with a shrug. "Ask me again in a week, and I should be."

Hartland snorted this time. "A week?" he said. "That is an insult to all our peers."

"Look, Chris," Alpheus said, rolling his eyes. "I believe in hard work and I applaud anyone who works hard for what they believe in. But as thinkers, as philosophers—as anything you want to label us as, talent is everything."

"And yet your talent failed you in the only time you spoke at a symposium," Hartland said.

"I hear the same thing happened to you," Alpheus said, glancing back down to the book before him, flipping to the next page. "You made no impression on anyone when you went a few years ago."

Hartland narrowed his eyes. "Is that a challenge, Alpheus?"

"If you want it to be."

SIX

The potential of sorcery

Since the incident at King's Parlour a couple weeks ago, Julian had been arranged to patrol the eastern edge of the city where there were fewer people. And that was only so that he would avoid running into more trouble. Julian didn't think to thank his colleagues, however. He considered them well-meaning, but he also saw them as cowards.

In any case, this neighbourhood was rather uneventful. It was peaceful—a patrolling soldier's dream, even. But Julian wasn't just any patrolling soldier. He was a magic user in disguise. And he secretly hoped for trouble. The best and only way to grow stronger was to face real enemies.

As much as Julian wanted conflict, he had been bothered by something he wouldn't usually fuss about. And that was his meeting with Alpheus. He thought he could never befriend someone of the noble class, least of all a scholar. But he had enjoyed the scholar's company on the few times Alpheus had sought him out.

And then there was that orphan boy. An ungrateful child. After saving him that evening and taking him in, the boy had since disappeared, leaving only a note behind: *No one asked for your help*.

Julian shook his head, trying to forget the boy. It was dusk now, and he was ready to report back at Vondra Dawn, which was a little over an hour away. Ahead of this last crop of houses was an isolated low-lying wetland with thickets of bushes. It was a dab of nature that Julian had come to admire since being assigned here. With only a narrow walking path that led to the city centre, things in the marshes here felt truly quiet. It was a break from the bustle of the Zorlia he knew.

Julian didn't let his guard down, though. This passage was the most prone to bandit attacks. He hadn't encountered any for two weeks, but he remained hopeful that something exciting would happen.

He paused suddenly, perking up. Footsteps—more than one set of feet, more than two, even. His heart was racing as he imagined facing a group of bandits. It had been a while since he last drew his sword.

The group emerging from behind the thickets was indeed hostile. But they were no bandits. They were knights—and there were five of them, forming a barricade, adamant not to allow Julian to proceed further.

"What is this about?" Julian asked, not sure whether to be excited or not.

"Punishment," one of those knights said, his voice coarse and demanding. "You dared insult Lord Breunor. Now you shall pay."

Julian twitched a brow, surprised that Breunor had actually marked him out for what should have been a petty incident in his eyes. He then realised that he recognised one of those knights before him—two of them, in fact. They were the ones he had assaulted to save the orphan boy.

So much for being reassigned here, he thought.

"I don't want to hurt you," Julian said. "And I don't want trouble."

The knights looked at one another, and then burst into laughter.

"You must be mistaken, Roland," said one of the knights, reaching for his sword at his waist. "You're the one getting hurt."

The rest of them followed suit. Five knights, five swords, pressing up on a mere soldier.

Fine, he thought with a frown, drawing his own sword buckled onto his back—a chunk of iron far heavier and sturdier than the sabres he was up against. He swept the iron sword out in a flurry, drawing up a gust that slapped at the knights. Julian then darted right into them, sloppily whipping out his weapon to break their formation. The knights managed to block his attacks and even managed to strike back, only for Julian to parry them off.

It went back and forth like that for a while, and it felt to Julian more like sparring than like a real fight. Julian was hardly holding back, however, and he suspected his opponents who were crying out orders to one another weren't either. The clanging of metal and the sparks ignited from each exchange had Julian feel alive—at least that was until those knights got used to him and started adapting to his tendencies. It turned out that the numerical advantage the knights had was too much to overcome. After barely blocking off several more slashes, Julian suffered a kick on his back, followed by a slice on his sword wielding arm.

This is real, Julian reminded himself, pressing over the wound on his arm from where blood dribbled out. It was as real as it ever had been when those knights hacked at him still, cutting him again—this time on the knee. He hissed as he widened his eyes at the sight of the fresh wound.

But it wasn't the time to be sorry for his injuries when his opponents looked to make him suffer further. In a desperate response, Julian waved his good arm in a zigzag motion, catching a red flame that blazed in his hand. The knights paused, cringing slightly, a lazy effort that wouldn't save them from what was coming. Julian withdrew the blazing hand and held a fist, quenching away the flame in the process. But he then followed by swinging that very arm back out while also unleashing a scorching flame that roared toward the knights, setting them ablaze in a viciously dazzling spectacle.

Screams filled the air among billows of smoke. The knights squirmed on the ground, some rushing to the shallow water of the marshes, trying their best to extinguish the flames.

Julian himself grunted as he pressed harder on the wound that stung the most—the one on his right arm that gushed out even more blood when he swung his sword. One or two of the knights were already standing again, but their throbbing burns had them reluctant to try anything more. Julian winced, but then suddenly realised that he was strangely left wide open for an attack.

He looked up to see arrows showering down toward him. He gritted his teeth and scrambled to slap away a few of the arrows before rolling away to dodge several more. Then he was hit in his left thigh, and it stung badly—worse than the sword wounds.

The knights were all back on their feet now, standing their ground with caution. None of them had carried a bow. Julian peered down to where the arrow was rooted. It was deep, and the blood streaming out wasn't a pretty sight. He restrained himself from rubbing on it, instead wincing as he looked up over the thickets to see a man in silver armour—the same one he had met that fateful night whose youth was noteworthy. He was the archer, matching his shimmering armour with a shining composite bow.

"I didn't want to do this," the young silver knight said as he lowered his weapon. "But you have crossed Lord Breunor, and he demands your punishment."

Julian peered back down at his wound, grasping tightly at the end of the arrow. He took a deep breath and then groaned as he pulled it out. Blood gushed out, and he was prompt in tearing off the fabric from his sleeve and swaddling tight at the wound.

Julian finally turned his glare back at the silver knight. "Come at me," he said, struggling to his feet.

"You can barely stand," the silver knight said with a frown.

"Worry not for me," Julian said with a grin. "But for yourself."

He clasped his arms on his chest in a criss-cross, murmuring some words. Within a moment, the air around him tinted to a pigment of crimson red, reminiscent of his flames. Julian dropped his arms then, and immediately the tinted atmosphere seeped into his body. He now emitted a soft scarlet glow, illuminating the ambience around him that had otherwise returned to its usual clearness.

"Don't let that scare you," the silver knight said to his men, who were all standing around in stupefaction.

But he had spoken too soon, for he was the next to be stupefied. He had glanced away only for a moment, and Julian had darted away from his field of vision, dashing to the knight's far left. The silver knight growled, swinging a jab out, only for Julian to bolt off again, this time to his immediate right. His change of pace and direction wasn't humanly possible, particularly behind an aura of red splashing into the air. Because indeed, Julian wasn't a regular man.

To ensure that the silver knight would eat his words, Julian finally threw a blur of punches at him, piercing the sturdy silver armour with only his bare hands—albeit flame-enhanced hands. And with a final thrust at the sternum, Julian knocked him into the shrubs.

The other knights who had recovered from their burns were left gaping.

The silver knight wasn't to fall just yet, however, climbing back to his feet now. In fact, the knight didn't seem as bothered or pained as his crushed armour suggested, looking more like he had trouble appreciating what had just happened. All the while, Julian panted heavily. Not only was he pestered by the deep arrow wound, but the magic he had drawn just now was a little more than he could comfortably manage.

"Your reliance on heresy shames the knighthood," the silver knight condemned. "But heretic or not, Julian Roland, you have proved a worthy opponent. I never expected to be beat to the ground like that."

"Sir Kite," one of the other knights cried. "Fight him already! Show him what it means to cross Lord Breunor."

The silver knight turned an annoyed glare at his man, silencing him without uttering a word. "I'll let you lead the way, Sir Spade," he then said, crossing his arms.

The knight nodded with visible reluctance. He led the other four into an organised formation, pressing up against Julian, surrounding him.

Amid the danger, Julian flipped open his pocket watch and glanced searchingly at the hands. His vision was blurred from fatigue, and when he noted the time, a drop of sweat or blood spattered over the watch. He flipped it closed and then looked up to his enemies again, which were all a smudge to him.

He heard a signal for attack, and those smudges grew larger. Julian squinted hard in response, waving his arm in that same zigzag motion as before, swinging his arm as he spun. The silver knight was quick to leap away, but his men were less vigilant. A blast of intense heat and multiple explosions scattered across them, blasting and burning them viciously. Julian didn't hold back this time. It had been a mistake on the part of the knights to underestimate his power as a magic user, and with this attack, the knights were left brutally wounded, if not dead.

Julian blinked away some of the blur, looking up again to note that the silver knight was indeed still standing, watching him with an analysing eye. The man then finally turned, apparently looking to leave.

"Orel Kite," he said. "Remember my name. Prepare yourself... because next time, you will fight me. If you hadn't resisted, things would have been settled. You are creating your own misdeeds."

Julian snorted. "If I kill you now, there won't be a next time."

The silver knight said nothing, only maintained his glare. He then turned away for good, setting off and leaving his defeated men behind. Julian stood his ground still, watching him recede, praying that this last enemy didn't realise that he was about to pass out. When the knight finally disappeared from view, Julian relaxed, collapsing to the ground as everything turned blank.

* * *

Julian woke to daylight shimmering through a ruptured roof. He eventually realised that he was on a bed of hay at the abandoned chapel in Ramsgate where he had first met Orel Kite, a safe distance away from Vondra Dawn and the eastern marshes.

No one was around, and yet his injuries had been delicately bandaged with what smelled like herbal medicine. His sword was next to him, and his armour was washed and hanged to dry.

He didn't wonder why he was there, but felt instead an urge to leave. He sat up, feeling aching pains all over. He eyed his armour, which was hanging on the wall next to him, ready to take it and leave.

"What are you doing?!" a voice demanded, the voice of a child. "Your wounds haven't healed yet!"

Julian peered over to the door, noting with surprise that it was the orphan boy sauntering in, the same boy he had saved at this same building not too long ago. The boy was annoyed about something, but he only stared at

Julian instead of telling him anything about why he was there.

"I'm all right," Julian said, throwing on his brigandine without another glance at the boy. "Give my thanks to the person who helped me."

"Well, that was me," the boy said. "*I* saved you. *I* picked you out from the marshes. *I* transported you back on my wheelbarrow and bandaged you up. And *I* was the one who gave up my chance to work at the tavern for two days to make sure you didn't die from your wounds."

I've been out for that long? Julian wondered now with suspicion, peering out to the modest courtyard to where a worn-out wheelbarrow was parked.

He eyed the boy now, finding it difficult to believe that someone at that tender age could apply such delicate and efficient bandaging. "What's your name?" he asked as he sat back down on the bed of hay.

The boy's name was Oscar. He was from the state of *Farella*, which bordered two foreign countries of great power in Vinawell and Kraga. He was only nine years old, with an elder sister still in his home state. He had travelled to Zorlia on his own, apparently to earn money for his family. And whether that was true or not, Julian realised that he had the boy to thank, or perhaps it was the boy simply returning the favour.

Just then, he heard a rumble on the ground. It was the clanging of metal gauntlets and the stamping of heavy sabatons, all part of a knight's suit of armour. As Julian held his breath with sweat running down from his hair, he stared toward the entry of the abandoned chapel. Then he noted the tip of a sabaton, armour covering the feet, and knew for sure that it was that of a silver knight. But just as he feared for the worst, their eyes wandered up to the scabbard of a rapier, which Julian recognised immediately, allowing him to breathe a sigh of relief.

"Finally found you," Pole said, treading in with a big smile.

Despite his size, it was Oscar who bravely snatched his wooden sword before standing in front of Julian to defend him.

"He's no enemy," Julian said, nudging the boy aside.

Pole grinned at Oscar and then turned to Julian with a frown. "The men you fought are in critical condition. Breunor wants you dead."

Julian cleared his throat, and then puffed out a sigh. "Do you know Orel Kite?"

Pole raised an eyebrow. "I know *of* him," he said. "The kid's built a reputation as one of the strongest young knights of the country."

"Do you think I can beat him?"

Pole didn't seem to expect this question, but he crossed his arms and mused over it. He then suddenly whipped out his rapier, its tip at Julian's throat.

Oscar gasped as the two men froze before him.

Julian had lifted his chin slightly and sweating from the inside. He had noted the skill in Pole's quick draw, but he didn't understand his point just yet.

"The kid might be stronger than me," Pole then finally said, withdrawing his weapon and returning it to its sheath. "So no, I don't think you can beat him."

All right, Julian thought, relieving himself from the fright. *But was that necessary?*

"I say Julian could beat anyone!" announced a second visitor.

The three of them spun to see a young man enter rather clumsily, sidestepping the rubble scattered on the ground. His cultured white robe was a symbol of his noble status, but his thin build intimidated no one.

"I brought you something," Alpheus said, holding up an old runic book similar to the one Julian already had. "You could defeat even the golden knights if you knew how to better use sorcery."

It was no surprise that Alpheus had found out about Julian's impasse, for he had sought him out every second day since their first meeting. Alpheus didn't care for Pole, however, who he seemed to have recognised from the parlour. But he didn't seem to mind him, either, for he showed no discretion when flaunting out what he claimed to be a book of spells.

"Percival is an ally," Julian assured, just in case.

"All right," Alpheus said, shooting a cautious grin at Pole, who rolled his eyes in response.

"What were you saying just now?" Julian asked. "About sorcery."

"Right," Alpheus said. "So first of all, *sorcery* is the correct term for magic. Magic users, meanwhile, should be called *sorcerers*. I feel that we need some context here, so let me start with some history."

Pole simpered, his smug expression carrying more than a hint of belittlement for the scholar.

Alpheus shot a confused frown back at him, but then proceeded with his explanation. "Now, before the mark of this Advent Era, sorcery was generally treated as myths. There were only two accounts of successful magic practice: *Zip the Disbeliever* and *Marvel Mage Yesod*. It's been over a decade since either of them were last sighted. Closer to our time, specifically in August of Advent 1, we all remember *the* giant storm that swept over the land, taking the lives of tens of thousands. While most people remember it as a disaster, some scholars have coined it *The Awakening*, the moment when sorcerers were reborn. Certain people were bestowed with a power known as *grace*, and *that* was the source that enabled them to practise magic."

"Interesting," Pole remarked, still not paying due respect for the scholar.

"Anyway," Alpheus continued, slightly annoyed, "scholars haven't worked out a way to identify whether someone had grace or not. And that means even the most unsuspecting person could be a sorcerer. What we *do* know is that magic ability occurs in less than one in ten thousand of the population. Scholars from Aizary have further suggested that the ability to practise magic is hereditary. They claim to have traced certain lineages to support their hypothesis—the idea that sorcerers occur in family clusters, and that grace was blocked by some unknown force in pre-Awakening times."

"So... what is this *grace*?" Pole asked. "An organ? Blood? Or just something that glosses and blesses over the sorcerer?"

"Grace is understood to be a highly mobile energy pulse," Alpheus said, furrowing his brow in annoyance. "It is harvested to perform sorcery."

"I feel this pulse inside of me," Julian finally said.

Julian had learned about the concept of grace from his father, the man who had trained him. His father had told him that grace could be harvested from any moving object, not only from one's grace pool. The difference was that the grace drawn from nature was often very limited, and that meant that the power of sorcery was kept in check by nature itself.

"Grace to a sorcerer is like blood to a regular person," Alpheus said. "It replenishes, and it is a vital source of one's life. But if used up all at once, one will die."

Julian grimaced at the idea, reluctant to accept that the encounter in the marshes had almost killed him.

"Perhaps magic..., no, sorcery is worth a look at," Pole said now. "But that's a story for another day." The silver knight turned to Julian. "You're on Breunor's tails. Sorcery provides no immediate solution to *that*."

"And what do you suggest I do?" Julian asked.

"Submit to someone."

Julian winced. "What do you mean?"

"Victor Breunor is a powerful man in both stature and physical strength," Pole said. "But he is by no means the only one with power. If you're willing to do the bidding of another man—that is, if you can prove your ability to another man of great power, Breunor would have to give up his incessant pursuit.

"There'll be plenty of suitors for you, Julian. Believe me."

Julian said nothing as he pondered the implications of this idea.

"The man holding supreme power is the Lord Emperor," Pole then added in elaboration. "Despite some of the negative rumours circling the emperor, the man is undoubtedly a master tactician in war. His charisma attracted many incredible talents to fight for him, and he has a reputation for lifting great people to even greater heights."

Alpheus snorted quietly. "Unfortunately, his leadership on the battlefield didn't translate to his ruling of the country," he said. "A lot of those men who fought for him have been executed... Marvin Sailanson has long disappeared, and Nine Arms was killed by the Kragans. Regardless of how much he has achieved, the emperor's methods reflect the tyrant archetype."

"What you believe you know may or may not be true," Pole responded. "After all, the court is full of lies.

"In any case, we also have the Lord Chancellor. He stands as the second most powerful man in Trubannis, and with arguably more supporters than even the emperor. The trio of mighty warriors loyal to him are the *Raiders*, whose names all start with R: Raphael, Raven, and Roth."

The caveat for submitting loyalty to either the emperor or the chancellor, however, was the possible risk of crossing the opposite man, which might result in a predicament far worse than Julian's current situation.

"Pierre Morlan of state Cetal is the next best choice," Pole went on. "He's gravely concerned for the wellbeing of the people. A mighty warrior loyal to him is Golden Knight and *Defender of State Cetal*, Sir John Tristan, who didn't travel with him to Zorlia.

"Quinlan Forredan is another man with great political power. He was the State Minister of Whitesand, and the founder of the once-powerful army known as the Scorching Salamander Knights. He is an expert in allocating and building various resources.

"And, finally, there is Sir Paltiel Sagramore, my master," Pole added with a smile. "He is, of course, the most powerful man in the country in terms of military control, the leader of all the golden knights—the *Defender of Trubannis*."

Julian said nothing yet. If he could choose, Sir Sagramore and the Defence Army was the wisest of choices. But it wasn't an option. The Defence Army never allowed anyone a second chance, and unfortunately, Julian had used up his only opportunity to trial as part of the army when he had first arrived in Zorlia with little skill to offer. Perhaps the only gain from that experience had been his meeting with Percival Pole, who had been a friend of sorts through the years.

* * *

Julian was in training again as soon as his visitors left, wielding his iron sword with his good arm in the courtyard. He spared Oscar little attention initially, but in realising that the boy was peeking out at him from inside, he stopped and turned to the boy who was indeed holding onto a twig, perhaps imitating his strokes.

"Do you want to wield a sword?" Julian asked. "I can teach you to defend yourself. Consider it gratitude... or rent. I'll be staying here for a while."

"I can defend myself just fine!" Oscar claimed with a pout.

Julian regarded the boy carefully from afar, and then strode slowly toward him. "Is that your weapon?" he asked, referring to the twig.

"No," said Oscar in protest. "It's just a toy."

"Actually, it *could* be a weapon," Julian said.

He then snatched the twig from the boy, catching it on fire in that same motion. Julian waved the blazing weapon at the dark of the far wall, sending out a small wave of fire crashing forward. The boy gaped at the burning wall, watching as the brief flame dissolved away to reveal a burnt mark—a five-sided star with perfect proportions.

Oscar then turned his head slightly. "Well, you *do* have to pay rent."

* * *

Two days later, Julian found himself in *Soma*, a southern neighbourhood of Zorlia often referred to as *the slums*, home to the poorest people, its streets lined with urchins and paupers. Today, those same streets would be blessed with a visit of one of the wealthiest men in the country, Quinlan Forredan.

Julian had come here on Pole's word. According to the silver knight, Forredan had claimed that he wished to uplift the miserable neighbourhood from their normal lives of poverty. But Julian wasn't so sure, instead suspecting that the statesman was there to win the support of those men who might do anything to survive. After all, these were the best people to exploit.

Forredan was as powerful as Breunor in terms of court presence, and more than substantial to protect him from the military man. An alternative to Forredan would have been Pierre Morlan, the former king of Cetal, who Pole had lauded as a great leader. Unfortunately, Morlan had departed from Zorlia for what the man had promised as a brief return to Cetal City, from where his daughter had allegedly been kidnapped.

It hardly mattered to Julian because he didn't know either of them. Soma, however, was indeed a wretched neighbourhood that had even Julian cringing as he walked the streets. It was drenched in poverty, with clusters of people in rags cuddled up together for warmth at the corners of old ruined buildings much worse than the one Julian was now staying at. The homes here—or hovels for that matter—were constructed with terracotta like the rest of the city, but the common sight of debris of fired clay next to cracked façades was a stark contrast to the well-maintained buildings closer to the city centre.

It was easy to locate Forredan and his retinue handing out soup for charity outside the Soma worship house. The line for soup was long and disorderly, with a large crowd part of the frenzy. But Julian wasn't going to wait in line. Instead, he tried his best to march his way past the sea of hungry men. He pushed and pushed until he finally caught a glimpse of the stout statesman who was perched at an open-elevated platform with his retinue that included a knight in golden armour.

The statesman's neat moustache upward of his double chin was the same as Julian remembered from nearly a month ago at King's Parlour. Julian didn't see the man's waistline that time, but it wasn't something he could miss today. It was enormous, with flabs forming layers over his pelvis, especially drawn out from that upward angle where he sat, glancing down at the people with apparent boredom. The lofty statesman was conspicuous with servants holding up velvet parasols for him while he lazed on what looked like a luxurious lounge, with strips of precious metal stitching the ends.

Unable to push his way any further through the tight clusters, Julian instead leaped into the air, landing on the table where the soup was served, shaking the table and causing the bowls to rattle.

"Get down, you hungry dog!" bellowed one of the men serving the soup, waving a ladle angrily at him.

The men serving the soup, only four of them, were clearly overworked. The last thing they needed was disorder. And yet Julian could hardly worry about them when a horde of angry paupers behind him shouted abusive remarks that even included threats to *eat* him.

And this is supposed to be the most prosperous city in the land? Julian wondered as a chill ran through him. He squinted at the paupers and then snatched the heavy chunk of iron off his back, sweeping it across in the air, drawing a brief gust that almost immediately silenced the crowd.

Julian spun back and looked up at Forredan, who raised an eyebrow in return. The stout statesman was even larger at this proximity, with a width of more than two regular men, and the weight of at least five.

"My Lord," Julian said, bowing slightly. "I am Julian Roland. We have met once before, at the Parlour."

Forredan pinched his moustache and then his lips formed a kindly grin as he looked down at Julian. "Ah, you're the child who was tangled up with Lord Breunor. Now, you're not here to give me trouble, are you?"

"I'm here to offer my skills," Julian said. "I've heard about the Golden Knight Exchange, and I wish to represent you on that stage."

There was a thin line between confidence and delusion, and unfortunately for Julian, no one there considered him to be particularly confident, at least according to their unimpressed expressions. His soldier outfit had given away his status as the lowest class of warriors. It was probably laughable to his audience that he dared to speak of reaching the pinnacle of knighthood.

Claude Lucan, the golden knight, stepped forward with a frown. The man carried a huge sword not so different from Julian's iron sword, also clipped onto his back.

"Be gone" he said, looking down at Julian with disdain. "Lord Forredan has no time for this."

The stout statesman, however, held out a hand. "Not yet," he said. "If I remember correctly, Lord Breunor called this man a magic user. If that is true, he can perhaps back up his words. Now, Julian Roland, perhaps you could show me a trick or two?"

Julian nodded and then swept his sword from left to right. The paupers shuffled a couple steps back in response even though Julian wasn't about to slash his blade in their direction. He instead eyed the velvet parasols held over Forredan. He brushed his iron sword forward in a flash, drawing only air, but throwing out a violent blaze of red that seared straight toward the stout statesman.

Lucan groaned, jumping forward and slamming out a gauntlet-fitted fist to smother the flames.

Forredan leaned forward, almost wobbling out of his seat. "Bravo," he remarked as he applauded by putting his hands together.

"But, Lord Forredan," Lucan urged.

Forredan turned to him with a smirk. "If you couldn't defend that, you wouldn't be a golden knight."

Lucan stepped back, restraining himself from challenging his liege, who had now turned back to Julian.

"Why are you submitting to me?" Forredan asked.

Julian slipped his iron sword away. "Lord Breunor has a problem with me," he said. "I need someone to fend him away—and I chose you."

Forredan fell back into the backrest of the lounge, his eyes clouding over with boredom once again. "That is how the world works, I suppose," he said. "You offer your magic for my protection—all in all a fair trade. Very well, your safety is warranted as of now, *but*... Julian Roland, if you want to represent me in the Exchange, you would have to impress me further."

"Need I set this place ablaze?" Julian asked, cocking his head.

Forredan grinned. "Not necessary. Go to my camp in Carrington tomorrow and you shall be organised with some work. Be patient, and you shall be rewarded."

Julian managed a half-smile. "Thank you," he finally said. "But, for now, I'm still expected to report in as a patrol soldier. I might need to—"

"They can surely survive without you," Forredan cut in with a dismissive hand. "But rules are rules. It'd be taken care of. You just worry about how to earn my trust. Go now."

Julian glanced over to Lucan, and then back to Forredan. "Very well then, Lord Forredan. Let this be a new beginning for the both of us."

Julian turned to leave, hopping off the serving table finally, and then shuffling past the crowd.

* * *

Lucan leaned his head next to his liege as the charity soup service resumed. "My Lord," he said quietly. "The boy may have potential, but I don't believe he's worth the risk of making an enemy out of Victor Breunor, who might see it as a challenge."

"And I thought you would know better, Sir Lucan," the statesman said, hardly raising a brow.

"I'm sorry?"

Forredan grinned, raising his rounded cheeks as he turned to the golden knight. "I would never use the boy. Have you not heard that Julian Roland was once part of the Defence Army, but was later thrown out? If he's not good enough for Sir Sagramore, then surely, he's not good enough for me."

"But... that was a long time ago. He'd have been a child."

"Tell me, Sir Lucan," Forredan said with a wink, "how old were you when you first downed a man?"

"I was eleven. But to compare with me—"

"He wants to be part of the Exchange," Forredan cut in, this time raising his voice. "He wants to be a golden knight—why *not* compare him?" The statesman shook his head. "He has a negative return yield. I'll lose more than I gain."

"Then… why did you tell him to go to Carrington?"

Forredan shrugged, his lips turning into a smirk. "Maybe I was too nice to turn him away to his face."

SEVEN
The silver-haired scholar

Alpheus perched on the right of the three-walled quarters, reclining on a large pillowed couch, with Agnes also leaning against it. The quarters were designed for no more than twenty-five people, which meant that some of the other scholars were left standing. But no one seemed to mind. It was a privilege just to be there in the only room on this floor of the academy, private and exclusive, accessible only via the long hallway that ended at the magnificent set of spiral stairs.

Alpheus wasn't going to miss his first encounter with a native of what he had since regarded as the most progressive country in the land. He had arrived early at the academy, waiting now in the *Thinker's Quarters* on the fifth floor, a room reserved for important events. The symposium was to take place there, but not for another three weeks. Today, the quarters were reserved for a special presentation of the foreign scholar. Although attendance wasn't mandatory, more than half of the forty scholars working for a place in the symposium shared the room with him now. They all wanted to meet the newcomer, who was rumoured to be one of the many great thinkers of Aizary.

The academy had long been waiting for this day. The exchange had been anticipated for six years, ever since the departure of Charlotte Hindlow, who was undeniably the academy's finest. It was no accident that her move to Aizary had marked the natural shift of balance that favoured the ever-rising talents of the Far East. And now, finally, Aizary would return the favour with one of their own brilliant thinkers moving the other way. Her name was Trulips, a savant who promised to grace the Villa, if not to lift it from the stagnation of recent years.

Even Alpheus had marked the date on his calendar. The foreigner's reputation as a scholar was certainly intriguing, but it was the fact that she hailed from the icy island-country that had Alpheus thinking. It had been said that the Far East had the largest proportion of sorcerers in the land at nearly one in two thousand, which was almost five times as much as other countries.

They had chosen to embrace sorcerers and their supernatural abilities, as implied by the apparent fact that the *Valhalla* court saw sorcerers in everyday attendance.

"I'm thrilled," Alpheus said, sitting up to regard Agnes. "I really am. This scholar—she could tell me everything I've wanted to know about sorcery. It's something every scholar should look into. For better or for worse, I'm certain it will change the land as we know it."

"You know, Alfie," Agnes said. "She might not know much about it, if anything."

"Don't say that," Alpheus said with a slight pout. "She *has* to know. And depending on what she says, our perspective of the world might change altogether—into a world where sorcerers rule."

"And that would be chaos," Agnes said with a giggle.

"She's here!" one of the scholars exclaimed loudly.

Everyone turned to the stairs, as did Alpheus. *That's Lady Willow,* he thought with a wry smile, recognising the woman who had been Agnes's mentor in recent years. *Of course, Lady Willow may well be wiser than this scholar from Aizary.*

As an established member of the academy and one of the few recognised as a State Scholar, Nola Willow edged close to fifty years old. The woman continued to be celebrated for her refined presentation as well as her esteemed status as an elite scholar.

"No, the woman behind her," another said, much more quietly than the initial exclamation.

Another woman indeed trailed behind Willow, a woman of fair skin and long silver hair. She sported the standard academy mantle, and yet her striking beauty outshined even Willow, especially with youth on her side. Age had never been a focus within the scholar community, but the foreigner had been expected to be in her middle years, so it was certainly a surprise to see long tresses of hair dangling behind a slender figure of a young woman. The hair was a splendid silver, which was apparently a rarity even for Aizars. Her fair skin, meanwhile, was at least a few shades lighter than any Truban—not unlike the Apostle.

The pleasing upturned shape of her eyes agreed with the crisp contours of her eyelids. Her eyelashes were long and beautifully rounded, lining up so orderly that one could make out each individual lash. The sparkling purple irises of her eyes—also demonstrating her exoticness—gleamed out as if to melt even the iciest of hearts.

As every other scholar gaped down the hallway, Alpheus felt that he was washed away in that same allurement that had the others in awe. To him, she was an embodiment of an angel.

She's... pretty, Alpheus thought as his lips curled into a smile. *But... there's something more.*

A tingle. Just like that time...

A third person appeared from the stairs now, a man donning a flaxen-golden mantle that glinted in the light, forcing Alpheus to blink away. But it wasn't just the colour of his dress that made the man shine. It was the stern face beneath his kausia that demanded attention. He was the brilliant Yusuf Seer, the man tasked by the Grandmaster to run the academy in his place.

The man often drew comparisons with Reeling, as they had been admitted into the academy at roughly the same time and separated by only one year in age. It was thought that the two had once shared an intense rivalry, until Charlotte Hindlow had later eclipsed both of them. In any case, Seer was regarded as reserved and earnest in his ways. The deep creases under his eyes attested to the number of sleepless nights he had endured in his illustrious career. His calm demeanour and relatively lean build, meanwhile, was deceptive, in that it was said that in addition to his intelligence and wisdom, he also had the ability to hold his own in a battle ring against some of the strongest knights.

Alpheus wasn't interested in fistfights or sword clashes, however, and so he had no interest in learning whether any of it were true. The only thing that could tingle his curiosities would be if Seer had the ability to wield magic, which was unlikely—absurd, in fact.

Willow and the foreigner waited for Seer to lead the way toward the quarters. He shared no word with them as he paced forward with his hands clasped behind him. They stopped when they reached the open end of the quarters, distinguished by its marble walls as opposed to the stone walls of the hallway.

"I see that you have made yourselves comfortable," Seer said, regarding a few of the scholars who had not yet risen from the comfort of the pillowed couches. Sure enough, the scholars scrambled to their feet and bowed as an apology. Alpheus paid them no heed, as he instead maintained his gaze on the foreigner, still admiring her exotic beauty.

"The symposium is upon us once again," Seer said. "And we are glad to have invited a guest from Aizary to take part." He paused there, turning his eyes to the foreigner. "I ask you to welcome Lady Kathryn Trulips of Illudia."

The scholars applauded as Trulips stepped out for a bow. "I am glad to be here," she said in a confident pitch. "I have been told that the Villa is an academy that strives for excellence and constant improvement. I look forward to the symposium where we can share our ideas and wisdom, of which I trust there shall be plenty."

The scholars put their hands together again in a rather solemn manner. Seer's presence had that effect on others, but the youthful newcomer seemed to emanate that same air of sedateness. She probably wasn't the easiest person to be around.

Willow was next to speak. Her disposition to smile was a welcome deviation from the other two. Indeed, Willow had been widely known for her friendliness, especially among established scholars who usually had little time for others.

"Lady Trulips is well-versed in various fields of study," Willow began. "But she specialises in the study of action—that is, ethics. She has written a number of dialogues on the topic, some of which are highly regarded among our peers. In particular, her third title, *Accession*, which depicts a small but fruitful society, has been compared to the works of some of the greatest figures in the field."

Trulips nodded with modesty, though at the same time showing a hint of pride that seemed well-warranted. "The journey of a scholar can be a lonely one," she said then. "But I believe it more worthwhile to journey in unison. Let us progress together. That is the reason I am here."

Another round of applause followed as Trulips turned to Seer, gesturing for something. Seer returned a glance, nodding, and then turned his gaze back to the other scholars.

"Lady Trulips wishes for transparency," Seer said, his tone grim. "And to show that determination, she wishes to advise that she carries an added identity that is less ostensible." He trailed off there, as his audience perked up. Alpheus in particular yearned to hear what would come next.

"Lady Trulips is a sorcerer by nature," Seer said as the foreigner grinned for the first time to acknowledge her identity.

The audience widened their eyes at this claim, and for a moment no one could swallow the assertion, despite recognising the principled source of the information that was Yusuf Seer.

"I expected this reaction," Seer said, expression unchanged. "And it is all but natural. However, as enlightened members of society, I expect you to brush aside any preconceptions you have. Observation and reason are the tools with which we see. I urge you to apply them, and in turn regard Lady Trulips as a fellow member of the academy."

Most of the scholars nodded, trying their best to hide their ambivalence toward the newcomer. Seer was likely aware of their concerns, of course, but he went on to dismiss the scholars anyway, instead reminding everyone the deadline in which they had to submit their abstracts for the symposium. He spun and headed back down the hallway, excusing himself first.

As soon as he disappeared from view, the scholars started shuffling down the hallway, too. Alpheus eyed Trulips who was pacing away next to Willow.

"Lady Trulips," Alpheus called out after her. "Can we... have a word?"

"And you are?" she asked after a brief glance over to Willow.

"Alpheus," he said, reaching out for a handshake. "Alpheus Hindlow."

Trulips eyed his hand for a moment before receiving it. "You are the brother," she remarked with a smile.

A tingle suddenly pulsed up along his arm toward his shoulders. "*Or...*," Alpheus said with a simper, hiding the sensation, "she is the sister."

A subtle squint and her withdrawal from the handshake demonstrated that Trulips was unamused. "A pleasure," she said with a flat tone. "You are but one of the people I most anticipated meeting."

"The pleasure's all mine," Alpheus said, unable to hide his joy. "You know, I am *fond* of sorcery. I cannot speak for others, but I have absolutely nothing against you... or your identity, for that matter. In fact, I admire you for honesty—*that's* ethics."

Trulips pursed her lips now. "I appreciate it," she said, turning back to Willow. "If I did not have other matters to attend to, I would certainly see to prolong our conversation. Let us speak at length the next time we meet."

"Let us, indeed," Alpheus said with a wide grin, waving her goodbye, then watching her as she receded.

"What was that about?" Agnes asked with a slight frown. "Are you interested in sorcery, or the person?"

Alpheus turned back to note that he and Agnes were the only scholars left in the quarters. "Well, both," he said. "Sorcery is first, of course. But you cannot deny her beauty." He paused there for a moment. "Wait, are you jealous?"

"What?" she exclaimed, almost laughing. "Why would I be? I just didn't want you looking silly in front of our guest. Some have already billed this coming symposium as a contest between Trubannis and Aizary. I don't want one of our more promising representatives—*you*—to be on the wrong end."

"You're being silly," Alpheus said, waving a dismissive hand. "The symposium was never intended as a competition. The aim, as Lady Trulips has said, is to support one another. You know, a journey done in unison."

Agnes sighed. "I just hope you put your mind to it."

"Oh, I will."

* * *

Alpheus spent the next week reading up on all the texts about ethics that he managed to get his hands on. It wasn't easy to land a copy of *Accession*, penned by Kathryn Trulips, but Alpheus had managed that as well. The text was about a twenty-person society in which each individual was crucial to the whole. Everyone contributed for the benefit of all by doing *good* under the guidance of a central figure who wished for nothing but harmony for the collective. While the basis of the work was simple, the underlying discussion involved in the extensive dialogues proved fascinating to Alpheus. It discussed the role of individuals, self-interest, and the harmony of interests, all of which were dependent on rational thinking. It also alluded to the value—and, therefore, the purpose—of man as individuals and mankind as a whole, delving into other branches of philosophy. Its lyrical prose added to the reading pleasure.

Alpheus recommended it to Agnes, and while she welcomed the recommendation, she wasn't sure Alpheus was doing enough to prepare for the symposium. He had been the one to suggest her company, but he had done little to necessitate the arrangement, which was intended to be an opportunity to note down ideas and finalise their abstracts, which were to be submitted to Yusuf Seer in order to ensure a place at the symposium. While Agnes was almost ready to submit hers, Alpheus had yet to write a single word. And every time he had attempted to share some of his 'insights' on the texts that they looked at, he later realised he had been naively patronising, presenting his ideas in a way to imply he knew much more than her.

"Come on, Alpheus," Agnes said, trying her best to display her annoyance. "You haven't even told me your topic yet. All I can assume is it's about ethics. I don't even—"

"It's *not* about ethics," Alpheus said with a shrug, dismissing the urgency. "Well, maybe a little. But it's not the main idea."

"Then what *is* the main idea?"

Alpheus cocked his head with a grin. "A secret," he said. "I'd rather surprise you on the day."

"I don't see why we're working together, then," Agnes said.

"I didn't think you would. But it's been a week now. I suppose it's all right to say."

"*What* is all right to say, Alpheus?" she said. "You might not have realised, but I have worked extremely hard to get to this point. I'm only one step away from my first symposium. It means a lot to me—for any scholar. I have to make an impression. I'm under enough pressure already, so can you please—"

"There it is!" Alpheus exclaimed.

Agnes winced at the sudden outburst. "What are you talking about?"

"Pressure," Alpheus said. "My first and only symposium was a disaster. And the reason? *Pressure.* I need you to ease up a little. Listen, pressure is necessary. But we need to moderate it to a level where we are the ones in control, or else there will be the danger of being devoured."

Agnes pursed her lips, saying nothing. Alpheus smiled at her, remembering how he had taken her under his wings when she had first been admitted into the academy as an oblivious eight-year-old girl. Alpheus had fostered her talents in her initial years, and while she had been late to blossom, his influence had become a fundamental part of all her ideas.

Agnes sighed then. "Thank you," she said, holding a hand to her chest, "for always being there. Perhaps it *is* worthwhile to read up on ethics."

That's not the only reason, Alpheus thought, maintaining his smile.

That evening, Alpheus stepped into the atelier of his mansion of a home. It was the room where he had spent countless hours dabbing away, brushing up works of art that even some of the greatest artists would be proud of. He trudged through those paintings now, however, some of them stacked aside while others lay among a scatter of brushes, palettes, and quill pens. Alpheus had eyes on only one painting which was resting on the stand in the left corner. He hesitated as he grasped onto the large cloth draped over it. He then breathed in deeply and flapped it away, only to be awed once again.

It was the portrait of the Apostle that he had painted from physiognomy that he had dreamed up. He pushed his spectacles up the bridge of his nose for the clearest view of those hooded, murderous eyes that jumped out at him. This was only the second time he had seen the completed painting himself, after he had hidden it away after the fright of meeting the man in person.

You were the first one, Alpheus thought, hovering a hand over the painting as he gazed into the pair of violet eyes that seemed to glint out from the canvas.

Alpheus groaned, pulling out a block of blank canvas, setting it upon an empty stand. He picked out a few oils, wedging out sloshes onto a palette. He snatched up a couple of brushes, and then there he was, already stroking away. Alpheus started with the outline of the head, first applying thin strokes and light colours. The hair was next. Getting the fringe right was imperative to how the rest of it would fall. Colour was a challenge for later. Alpheus then stroked an extended neck for the head to sit upon, adding the shoulders and the thorax for more support.

She's a sorcerer, Alpheus thought, his heart beating faster now as he worked his way up to the eyes. *Just like him, the Apostle.*

And then there's Julian, also of the same caste.

Why?

What is this connection I have with them?

By the time his wandering thoughts caught up with him, the portrait was done—the outline, anyway. The subject of the work was none other than the Aizar scholar, Kathryn Trulips. She had confessed that she was a sorcerer, a being with the potential to wield the same power as the Apostle. And she was from the Far East, from the same place as that fearful man. But other than the colour of their skin and eyes, which Alpheus had yet to apply to his newest work, there were no obvious similarities between the two. He had never thought to paint Julian, and now he didn't think he would have to. One's appearance offered no clue about whether or not one was a sorcerer.

Twice, it's happened, Alpheus thought, squinting at the canvas. *That quiver. Three times if I count the Apostle. When I met Julian and then when I met her.*

Why? And they didn't seem to feel a thing.

Could it really be...? He groaned again and shook his head, dropping the brush and palette to the floor in a rattle.

No! I refuse to believe it.

Alpheus stormed out of the atelier, trotting into the study. He pored through the bookshelf, finally picking out the tome that he was safekeeping for Julian. He riffed madly through the pages, turning to one he had marked a while back—entitled *Latent Grace,* with a set of instructions that he had learned to translate, but remained reluctant to do so. The potential revelation that might change his world had been too daunting.

He stared blankly at the page for a while. And finally, he began skimming over the runic script, deciphering it with care, but also with tremendous anxiety.

Grace is the source of life, it roughly translated, *and the constant that runs in all of us. It seems to serve no purpose, then, that grace can be dormant. I can only dare to assume it is a mistake made by the heavens. I extend my deepest condolences for those who are plagued. Only if there was a way to ignite that life stream.*

And there is.

Alpheus held his breath, growing impatient of the witty prose.

Pain, the next part translated. *Unbearable pain. Survive it and grace shall burn bright.*

"What?" Alpheus said aloud, still squinting at the script. *What counts as unbearable? I could die?*

And if I was never a sorcerer in the first place?

I die an idiot.

He scoffed, despite himself, and skimmed over to the smaller print at the bottom corner of the page. He was reluctant to translate more, feeling as if he had been mocked enough. At the end, though, the curiosity was too much to resist, and he started interpreting again.

More than anything, I am beset by those plagued with cowardice, it went on, the sentence drawing a wince from Alpheus. *But I suppose if I am writing this, I should mention an alternative. Be warned that this cannot bring out one's full potential. Then, of course, even a speck is preferred to complete dormancy. Now, thrust a thumb into the centre of the sternum and apply a rotating force until a heat diffuses over you.*

Alpheus traced that last word with his finger, surprised that it ended there. He flipped over to the opposite page, but noted that it discussed another topic.

He sat back then, forcing a grin, wondering whether he should try it.

He breathed in deeply and held out his right thumb. *Here goes*, he decided, thrusting that thumb into his chest. *Now spin.*

Once. Twice. Three times. Nothing.

He pressed harder. Four times. Five. Six.

All right, starting to feel silly now, he thought, though he kept spinning his thumb. *Perhaps after a hundred times? Or... perhaps I've played the fool. Should I—*

It came, then—a surge of heat exploding from within, jerking Alpheus forward altogether. As he sought to calm himself, he realised a sensation he couldn't deny. It was... pleasant. As if cradled by a fantastic warmth in the midst of a blizzard.

And what of the implication?

Alpheus regarded his hands now, his face darkening with fear. "I'm… a sorcerer."

EIGHT

A stage on which to shine

Reeling had been reluctant to visit the academy recently. Although he didn't expect it, he dreaded the mere possibility that Alpheus would go back on his word. And today, on his brief sojourn, his fears were half-way realised. Not only had Alpheus been absent for two days, but he had yet to even submit his abstract for a place in the symposium.

Reeling did his best to remain calm, however. He wasn't about to be angered, not before he got to the root of the problem. He tried to get an answer from Yusuf Seer, but his old rival offered nothing. It was a pity, but the two of them had never been fond of one another.

In any case, Reeling was left with no other choice than to seek out Alpheus himself. He tasked Yorke to other chores as he rode away on his gentle mare to Phantom Pond, the most affluent neighbourhood of Zorlia, which was also where Alpheus lived.

Unlike most of the city that had preserved its historic flavour of terracotta constructed homes among other buildings, Phantom Pond was distinguishable with edifices made from dark shades of timber, stone, and brick. Almost all the great manors of the neighbourhood were usually ornamented by woody climbing wisteria vines popular in Zorlia—many also with spectacular pergolas of the flowering plant used as entrance paths to the estates. But the plant had shed its leaves since the beginning of the winter season. Leafless wisteria vines indeed filled almost every corner of the city in this rigid season, dulling Zorlia into a rather drab shade of colour.

Reeling was no stranger to Phantom Pond, having lived there too for most of his life, until his move to his current estate on the other side of the bay.

It's been a while, he thought, hopping off the horse and pacing toward one of the great houses there, each of which occupied extensive plots of land. Reeling knocked hard on the front door. A response came soon, the left of the heavy double door opening in slowly. Daylight streamed into what appeared to be a gloomy interior. The head that poked out behind the door wore a dismal expression to match.

"I was expecting you," Alpheus said in a tired voice, his eyes drooping, dark circles around them.

Reeling stepped in with his usual confident stride, treading through the antechamber and into the great hall which was just as dark as the previous room. The chandeliers and the hearth were left unlighted—rather wastefully, he thought, in a room of such grandeur.

"And can you guess why I am here?" Reeling asked, pacing toward the windows.

Reeling flapped open the drapes of a sizeable window then, the daylight that poured in reduced Alpheus to a squint.

"You cannot afford to idle any longer," Reeling said, turning back.

Alpheus sighed as he adjusted to the light. "Something has come up. I'm just a little lost."

"Enough of the excuses!" Reeling exclaimed. "There is *always* something. First, there was painting and then—"

"I'm a sorcerer," Alpheus said, cutting Reeling short.

The assertion followed a long silence, the emptiness of the room intensifying the quiescence, Reeling finding himself at a rare loss for words.

"You knew all along, didn't you?" Alpheus said then, gazing out toward Reeling.

Reeling cocked his head slightly. "Knew... what?"

"This ring," Alpheus said, clasping onto the silver band looped into his necklace, together with the double crescent. "You gave it to me. It wouldn't have worked otherwise. I don't know where you got it, but surely you knew what it could do."

"I *did* suspect a few things, yes," Reeling admitted.

"Then why didn't you say something?!" Alpheus asked with a rising volume, almost shouting the last word. "I was curious about sorcerers, but I didn't think to be one myself."

Reeling regarded him without a word, noting the tears in Alpheus's eyes that had gushed out suddenly. The truth was harder to swallow for Alpheus than he had assumed. "I am sorry," he said. *And I understand why it is hard*, he thought, regarding the silver band and the symbol of faith hanging from the necklace in tandem.

"That's it?" Alpheus asked with a snort, suddenly suspicious. "You don't have anything else to say? I thought you could justify everything you do."

"Not this time," Reeling conceded with a sigh. "The ring belonged to him... to the Apostle. He was the mightiest of them all. You were always going to make better use of it than I could."

"So when did you suspect it?" Alpheus asked. "That I am... what I am."

Reeling huffed out another sigh and tapped up his monocle. "For years," he said. "Three, or perhaps four years. Reports from Aizary suggested that Charlotte Hindlow identified as a sorcerer. And while I cannot confirm the validity of those reports, it is easy to believe it. Sorcery is hereditary. It is only logical that you have inherited the same ability."

Alpheus said nothing as he glanced elsewhere, apparently musing over it.

"That's my side of the story," Reeling said. "Now tell me, Alpheus, how did it happen? Over the years, I have made more than a few attempts to spark the grace that I believed was in you. But with every passing day, it seemed less likely that you were a sorcerer."

"You seem pleased," Alpheus said. "Almost as if you wanted this."

"I am," Reeling admitted. "I wanted you to be ahead, to wield a power that others can only dream of. But it was a mistake on my part that I only considered it from a rational standpoint."

Alpheus narrowed his eyes. "So you didn't exactly *expect* this to happen?"

"No. Contrary to popular belief, I am not omniscient."

Alpheus nodded, with no intention to respond to that poor attempt of a joke. "It was a couple months ago when we met him... the Apostle," he began. "That was the first time I felt the curious tingle sweep over me. I had no idea what it was then. But I've since met others. Sorcerers, that is. One of them is Julian Roland. I'm sure you've heard about him... a patrol soldier who is also a sorcerer."

Reeling nodded.

"The other one is Kathryn Trulips," Alpheus continued. "I felt that same curious tingle on meeting both of them. It turns out that that tingle was grace. Although hiding in dormancy, my grace resonated with theirs. It wanted to respond. It wanted to awaken. But it couldn't, not by itself." He paused there and tapped the ring with a finger in a tinkle. "None of this would have been possible if not for this silver band... and, of course, the tome from Julian."

"What tome?" Reeling asked.

Alpheus squinted. "I suppose you couldn't have planned it after all," he said. "I have a text penned by a nameless sorcerer from long ago, written in the ancient script of *Babili*. It seems to imply that sorcerers were once the norm. But in a land ruled by sorcerers were individuals with latent abilities. I am one of those people. A short chapter in the text is dedicated to how one of these *plagued ones* could ignite his powers."

Alpheus paused again, holding out a thumb before thrusting it onto his sternum. "They probably didn't know what the thymus was at the time," he continued. "Instead, they speak of a *cauldron* between the throat and the chest that holds one's grace. Strong stimulation stirs that cauldron... and that strength I needed I would *not* have gathered if not for the ring lending me power."

Reeling eyed the silver band and the sapphire solitaire at its centre. "The ring amplifies grace?" he said musingly. "If you could—"

"I have no intention to learn sorcery," Alpheus cut in, his firm tone demonstrating his resolve. "And no one is to know about this."

"So... you plan to hide forever?"

"I just want to be who I have always been. Sure, I marvel at the power of grace—as anyone would. But I don't need that power. It's not me."

Reeling shook his head. "You are still you," he said. "Regardless of what this new power could bring, I am convinced that your beliefs, and your values, will remain intact. But... if it is your wish to forfeit that power, then so be it. Be warned, however, that certain people may be attracted to your power even when you have no wish to use it."

"I did my research," Alpheus said, looking up. "I'm sure I can live without anyone ever knowing about it. Besides, it was but a speck of grace that ignited. I doubt anyone would even notice it."

Reeling nodded with a contented grin. "Now back to why I am here," he said. "The symposium. There are ten days left."

"A promise is a promise," Alpheus said with a sigh. "And I apologise for having you worry. But I assure you that I still have every intention to impress. The abstract is done. I just have to pass it on to Master Seer. I'll be ready."

"I trust that you will," Reeling said. "It is a shame that I cannot be there, however, as I have been tasked for an errand in Cellarsy. I am due for departure tomorrow and will miss the symposium by a day."

"Well then, you take care," Alpheus said, looking glad.

Reeling turned away, wincing despite himself. *One day when you learn to cultivate the power, you would have to use it. Until then, you will continue to mature. The symposium shall steer your path suitably.*

* * *

No one seemed to have realised that he had been absent from the academy.

Everyone preparing for a place at the symposium were too self-involved to worry about where Alpheus was. Perhaps the only exception was Agnes, who had likely spared Alpheus more than a few thoughts each day. Knowing her, she had probably prayed for him at every opportunity, praying first that he would take the symposium seriously, and then that he would earn his badge as a State Scholar.

Alpheus reminded himself to remain focused on that goal, too—at least as a distraction to the shocking revelation of his newly discovered identity. He had said that he hoped to hide his powers and continue to live his life as he always had. It was difficult, however, when he could barely suppress his own curiosities about who he really was. If magic users were part of an experiment by the heavens, then was he a mere part of that same experiment?

"You are late," Seer said, regarding the loose paper in his hand—the abstract to Alpheus's proposed presentation.

"I don't recall you setting a date," Alpheus said.

"There was no date," Seer admitted. "But it was certainly implied, given that the participant list is to be published on the fourteenth—three days from now."

"I'm not sure implications are what the academy should rely on. Interpretations of the same idea can come in many forms and the end result can vary drastically depending on—"

Seer raised a hand, palm open. "Are you done?" he said.

"I am when you confirm my place."

"I will confirm nothing until the fourteenth. I do not believe that there are other ways to interpret that."

Alpheus glanced away from the glint of Seer's flaxen-golden mantle. Seer had never been one to jest with, and his eyes—though brimming with wisdom—always sent chills down the spines of those he encountered.

"Now, if you will," Seer said, gesturing to the door.

Alpheus nodded and bowed. "Please excuse me."

Seer's chambers weren't a place anyone visited often. He lived on the top floor of the six-storey building, and it sat as the first room from the wide-arcing spiral stairs. One visited only when one was summoned, and Seer rarely summoned anyone, as he preferred to speak with academy members in more genuine situations, particularly during his observations on his regular tours of the building.

Still, his chambers were still frequented more than any other room on the floor, which also included the Grandmaster's private quarters. Few had met the Grandmaster, who was also the founder of the academy, and who had secluded himself away from worldly affairs for more than fifteen years. He was thought to have achieved 'omniscience' during this time, generally defined by scholars as a level of consciousness where one had the ability to know anything that one chose to know, as well as the ability to solve any problem that one could encounter.

Alpheus couldn't confirm whether any of it were true. He had only met the man once, at the symposium which had been held almost seven years ago. And his memory of the man was only vague, since all he had been concerned about at the time had been his presentation.

Assuming he attends the next one, I'll be seeing him soon enough, he thought, taking a glance down that hallway accessible to only a handful people. Alpheus then trotted down the stairs, making his way to the ground floor.

He recognised several faces as he turned into the main library, mostly those he had seen at the Thinker's Quarters a little over a week ago. Many of them seemed to be discussing the ideas that they hoped to present in less than two weeks' time. They sat on long desks, some of them working in groups, perhaps sharing thoughts about how they should deliver their speeches. It was a shame that some of them would miss out on the symposium altogether.

"Alpheus," a voice called. "Over here."

The voice belonged to Agnes, the only other scholar Alpheus could call a friend. She wore her usual cheerful smile, but it was apparent from her pale face that she had been deprived of sleep. A few other scholars close to her looked up, annoyed. One of them was Christopher Hartland, who had never cared for Alpheus. He spared half a glance up before turning back to his text with a scoff.

"I don't know if I want to stay," Alpheus said softly, crouching down to Agnes.

"This is the best place to prepare," Agnes urged, gripping his arm. "Where else can you access so many resources?"

"I suppose."

"Stay. I won't bother you. No one will."

Hartland snorted without looking up. "You make it sound as if the rest of us will drag him down," he said, the remark causing a few others to scowl.

"That's not what I meant at all," Agnes maintained. "I was just—"

Alpheus rose to his feet, staring Hartland down. "I hope your childish bickering will not be reflected in your presentation at the symposium. I don't want to see you fail to make a mark again."

Harland looked up. He did his best to calm himself, doing so promptly. "I look forward to the challenge," he then said. "That is, if you manage to earn a place."

Alpheus regarded him for a moment longer. "Agnes," he said, turning back to her, "have you seen Lady Trulips?"

Agnes seemed surprised by the question, or perhaps the sudden change of topic. "She's been around," she said. "I think with Lady Willow. Why do you ask?"

"There's something I need to ask her about."

* * *

The list was announced three days later. A total of twenty-one people were confirmed places at the symposium. While that seemed generous, nearly half of that number was made up of the panel which included five aristocrats and five State Scholars whose primary function was to oversee the event, rather than to put forward any ideas. Simply put, aristocrats didn't have the knowledge and skill to contribute to what was often seen as an esoteric circle. State Scholars, meanwhile, were too well-equipped to be seen competing with their juniors. This was especially true for the Grandmaster and Yusuf Seer, who were among the State Scholars confirmed to administer the event.

In effect, only eleven of the forty scholars who had applied for a place were successful. Although Alpheus had been confident that his abstract warranted a place, he had quietly worried that his late submission would cost him a place altogether. Instead, as he gathered now in the crowded antechamber around one of the giant pillars that hung off a large banner listing the participants, he let out a sigh of relief.

His name was listed as one of three primary speakers, alongside Kathryn Trulips and Christopher Hartland. The Aizar scholar was nowhere to be seen, but Hartland was elated for the opportunity, unable to hide his joy as he received words of congratulations from his peers. It was his second symposium, and his first time as a primary speaker.

Agnes, Alpheus thought, peering back to the banner for the name. His cheeks soon tensed up into a wide grin. The topic of *Common Volition* by Agnes Gardner had won a place as one of two secondary speakers. She was sure to be thrilled. And to think she had been too anxious to come.

Alpheus turned now, dashing away toward the exit of the building. He had to bring the good news to Agnes, and he didn't have to go far. She was sitting just outside on the curved marble steps, praying with her eyes closed, hands clasped onto her pendant of faith.

"It's there," Alpheus said, causing her to jump.

"Alfie!" she exclaimed, turning.

Alpheus pursed his lips, teasing her to succumb into asking. But she didn't ask. Instead, she looked away as tears began to build in her eyes.

"No, no!" Alpheus assured. "Don't cry. I was just teasing you. You made it, Agnes. You're a secondary speaker!"

"I *am*?" she asked, perking up.

"You are," Alpheus said with a smile.

She swung herself toward him and held him in an embrace. "That means the world to me!" she said in her mumbled speech against Alpheus's chest.

"Well, now I suppose you can afford at least some sleep," he said.

"What about you?" Agnes asked, shaking her head after digging herself back out.

"A primary speaker."

She beamed at him. "It was expected. But still, I'm so proud of you."

"Mister Hindlow," a voice called.

Both Alpheus and Agnes turned to the mahogany double door. There stood Kathryn Trulips, who regarded them with a buoyant gaze. This was only Alpheus's second time seeing the foreigner, and the allurement with which he had previously regarded her hadn't diminished even slightly. She donned a neat mantle like any other scholar, but her fair skin and long silver hair always made her shine above anyone else, at least in terms of beauty.

"You seem startled," Trulips said, descending the marble steps. "I am here to tender my congratulations. I am very much looking forward to your presentation... the compatibility of philosophy and faith. It is one of the most daring topics one could choose to present."

Agnes regarded Alpheus with surprise. Indeed, it was a surprise for everyone. This was a topic every scholar wanted to avoid. The awkward balance and conspicuous conflict between philosophy and faith had challenged the brightest minds since the beginning of civilisation.

Alpheus stood up, with Agnes following his lead. "It needs to be discussed," Alpheus said. "And, mind you, as the first one to bring it up in a forum of public significance, I do not dream of offering anything conclusive."

"There is no need to be humble," Trulips said, impressed. "Master Seer would not have made you a primary speaker if not for a strong abstract that managed to convince him."

"The same goes for you then, I suppose," Alpheus said.

NINE

An evening of philosophy

The theme of the symposium was perhaps the most open of the last decade, entitled *Imagination, Beliefs, and Action*. The apparent challenge was the lack of preparation time, barely two months from the announcement date to the actual event. Scholars who had failed to earn a place cited not only the limited time given to prepare, but also the lack of guidance on aligning a topic of choice to what they had thought to be an open theme. More than half of the abstracts submitted had been rejected on the simple basis that the theme of the symposium wasn't carefully considered in the topic. Of course, even if they had satisfied the criteria, they might have simply been short of the quality expected at the symposium.

None of that mattered anymore, though, for the day had come. *The Twenty Fifth Symposium* of the Villa of Enlightenment was scheduled for a twilight session on this twenty-first day of December, Advent 8.

The sun had yet to set, but all eleven presenters had made sure to arrive early to the Thinker's Quarters. The centre seats of the three-walled quarters were assigned to the primary, secondary, and tertiary speakers. Seats against the left wall were for the quaternary speakers and the aristocrats, and finally, seats on the right wall were reserved for the State Scholars—which included the Grandmaster and Yusuf Seer—all of whom had yet to arrive. The pillowed couches of each seat were intended to ease pressure, but judging from the solemn faces that filled the quarters, hardly anyone could afford to relax.

Agnes found it almost hard to breathe, especially after learning earlier that she was to be the first presenter of the evening. How the symposium was sequenced had always been somewhat of a mystery, and while being the first to talk had its advantages, it was rare to have a debut speaker start things off. Agnes glanced about now, trying to distract herself.

She turned to the window, a wide panel behind the centre seats from where the last glimmers of daylight shone through from a tangerine sky. The imposing steeples of Vondra Dawn were visible from there, as were most of the brown shade of terracotta buildings that sat along the bay. Agnes peered east along the river that extended from the bay, across the stream, and into a small hill where a chapel-sized building sat. She remembered that same building from the last time she had looked out this window.

"I never knew what that is," she said quietly.

Though she didn't care for a response, Alpheus looked out next to her. "Don't know," he said, apparently mulling over it. "Never seen it before. Maybe it's—"

"A prison," Hartland said, cutting in. "That building on the hill. It has only been there for a year or so. Cannot accuse anyone of ignorance for not knowing. What you see is the entrance. Inside is a stairway leading to an underground prison that houses criminals destined for execution... and that is where it earns its name as the *Stop before hell*."

"You seem to know it well," Alpheus said. "Were you a dweller?"

Hartland rolled his eyes. He was clearly unamused, and to his credit, he didn't look like he was about to bicker over it. He was one of the most relaxed people around, perhaps second only to Kathryn Trulips, who perched deep into her cushioned seat, cross-legged, with her eyes closed as if in meditation.

Agnes glanced over at her now. Trulips *was* beautiful. Even Agnes thought so. But that wasn't what she was thinking now, however. Instead, she wore a slight frown, remembering how Alpheus had been strangely reserved that last time they had met her at the main entrance of the academy, only a week ago. It had bothered her. And she knew too well that she would continue to be bothered until she learned why.

Alpheus is hiding something, she thought. *But what?*

Alpheus turned to her now, wearing a warm smile that brushed away some of her suspicions. "You'll do great," he said. "Just be yourself. Let the conversation flow naturally."

"I'll... try," Agnes said, huffing out another long breath. "Alpheus," she then said in a solemn tone. "Can you promise me something? If I manage to make an impression today, can you promise to share something with me?"

"What's with the gravity? You know I'd tell you anything."

"It's a promise then."

* * *

All eyes turned to the long hallway now, and specifically to the set of spiral stairs. Yusuf Seer was the first to appear, donning his usual flaxen-golden mantle, holding on a lighted lantern, leading a host of aristocrats who were part of the panel. Every presenter was prompt in rising to their feet from the comfort of their cushioned pillow seats, knowing well that the men pacing in now would help decide whether their ideas were worth any merit—and, for some, whether they were worthy to be recognised as State Scholars. That, in particular, was all Alpheus wanted, perhaps only in order to please Reeling.

Seer didn't look like the most genial host. Other than the fact that he was leading the way, he seemed reluctant to share any word with the aristocrats, wearing that same stern face that other scholars had often dreaded.

Members of the Empire, Alpheus thought as he regarded the approaching nobles, all of them immaculately presented and well groomed. *Members of the court too, perhaps? Do they know enough to be our judges?* None of the faces were familiar to him. There was no reason for them to be. Reeling, who wasn't to make an appearance today, perhaps knew all of them. But Alpheus had no envy for Reeling. If he had a choice, he would wish he never had to see those faces, in the academy or elsewhere.

The other part of the panel, the State Scholars, strode in only a few steps behind. Leading them was an elderly man with white hair, one of the most respected men in the land—Isaiah Felipe, the Grandmaster, the founder of the academy and the lone mortal thought to have achieved omniscience.

The Grandmaster had long brows that dangled from the edges of his eyes, with a pair of glasses not dissimilar to Alpheus's. He also wore a neat beard that fell to his chest, and a wide forehead complemented by hair pulled straight back from his scalp. He sported the same glamorous mantle as Seer, adding a spruce shawl of ivory white to illustrate his more esteemed standing. He seemed to have shrunk with age, standing out as the shortest among the disciples who walked with him. But despite his old age and despite the long hallway from where he gazed out, the man's eyes gleamed ever so brilliantly—the one thing that Alpheus remembered with vivid detail in an otherwise hazy memory of the man.

When the Grandmaster's lips curled up into a smile, Alpheus blinked away his haze and realised that all his peers had dropped down to one knee. Even Kathryn Trulips, who had earlier perched comfortably inside her allocated cushioned seat, bowed down to welcome the old man. Alpheus followed suit, and as his knee hit the ground, he wondered if he had ever bowed down to any man for any reason.

The panel members were standing before them when he looked up again. There were ten of them—and only eleven presenters. "Please rise," the Grandmaster said, his voice nasal. The creases under his eyes and around his cheeks were evident now at this proximity. "Please return to your allocated seats."

The presenters nodded and did just that. Many of them had grown suddenly cautious, leaning against the edge of their cushioned seats despite the deep space on offer. The Grandmaster then regarded the aristocrats and the other State Scholars, who then made their way to their seats, too, doing so quietly but looking much more comfortable than the presenters. Seer, meanwhile, strode to all four corners of the open quarters to light the lanterns already installed there. They would soon be needed.

Seer returned to the Grandmaster's side, the old man now peering out to his disciples and guests, meeting the eyes of every one of them. "Welcome, all," he began, brushing his white beard, "to the Twenty Fifth Symposium of the academy, a place where inspired ideas are conferred among curious souls. As a group, we crave for a deeper understanding of everything around us and our place within it. This forum continues to delight me over the years, for this is where some of the greatest thinkers of the present and past began their path to omniscience, the ultimate destination. Nothing in this world gives me greater joy than walking this path with you."

He paused then, his smile deepening. "I look forward to being inspired."

He gestured at Seer to take over from him as he made his way to one of the vacant seats on the right wall. The Grandmaster was unlikely to say much more this evening. Alpheus remembered that his sister once said that the Grandmaster reserved any comments he might have for the *House of Sages*, a select group of extraordinary scholars the old man himself handpicked, of which his sister was a member. Reeling, Seer, and Willow were also members, but there weren't many others since even State Scholars weren't ensured of a place. It didn't seem to matter, though, as the group rarely met—the last time had been six years ago.

Alpheus had tried to rationalise the Grandmaster's apparent disinterest in unproven scholars, but even now he could only see it as condescension. In any case, the Grandmaster was widely considered to be the wisest man in the land—a true sage. If the old man had such ambitions, one could imagine the man reigning as emperor, holding the power to reshape the land altogether. He had no worldly desires, however. Status and fame meant little to him. He never boasted of his achievements, and had wanted nothing to do with any ruling authority since leaving his post as the chief advisor to King Paillard of the Canon Era, over sixty years ago.

Seer bowed to the Grandmaster and then regarded the presenters.

"Before we begin, let me introduce you to the panel."

He pointed their attention to the right wall first, where the State Scholars sat. Perched alongside the Grandmaster were Nola Willow and two middle-aged scholars who rarely appeared in public: Dante Black and Jerome Reginald.

Unlike Willow, who would readily lend a helping hand to other scholars, Black and Reginald weren't nearly as approachable. Indeed, rumours suggested that they were rather arrogant, often dismissing others as fools, as people who only got in their way. Their achievements and reputation paled in comparison to Seer, but were more than sufficient in commanding wide respect in the community of scholars. No one seemed to know precisely how old they were, but both of them were thought to be in their forties now, and thus at least a few years older than Seer. However, age had never been a reliable indicator of success.

Seer now turned to the aristocrats. Of the five, only one was female, a middle-aged woman. None of the presenters seemed to know who she was, but surely she had tingled curiosities since appearing with the aristocrats. She was a beautiful brunette noblewoman who wore no headdress, instead letting her long hair drape down behind her spectacular velvet gown of midnight blue, tied with a jewelled girdle at the waist. But while her garb was certainly ornate, it was her physiognomy that had people thinking. She didn't look Truban.

"It is our pleasure to welcome Lady Winter as part of our panel," Seer said, nodding at the woman.

Winter. That name reduced nearly all the presenters to silent gapes. It was a name of the West, a Vinan name. The woman must have had origins from Vinawell. And yet she was known as the most benevolent member of the Empire, known for her active and timely involvement in responding to different crises across the country for the past eight years since the Empire had first been established.

She was known to be a faithful follower of the Ionian doctrine and a strong advocate for peace, usually preaching in the name of the Immortal. And for anyone who didn't care much for faith or good deeds, Winter was also the wife of the Lord Chancellor, Yeremia Schim. If the rumours that Schim was challenging for the throne were true, Lady Winter could well be an Empress in the near future.

She grinned now, nodding to the presenters. "I am not here to intimidate," she said, although she seemed to have done just that to even the aristocrats she sat with. "But anyone who is unnerved by my presence may not deserve a place here."

Some of the presenters, including Alpheus and Agnes, perked up, turning suddenly lively. Seer gave a subtle smile in response. "Now," he said, pacing to his seat on the right wall, "without further ado, let us begin the symposium. The first presenter of the evening is Lady Agnes Gardner. Her topic title is *Common Volition*."

Agnes stepped up from her seat as gentle applause filled the quarters. Alpheus held his breath for her, sharing her anxiety despite his belief that she would do well.

"People," she said with a loud, confident pitch as she paced away from her seat, "are gifted with the wonderful ability to reason, and it is this gift that most defines who we are as a species, and what we can expect in the future that eagerly awaits us. As a learned people, it is but a matter of course that this ability is used in every aspect of our lives, and in all situations. It is unfortunate, however, that learned people make up only a very small proportion of the human population.

"While it is not viable for everyone to be scholars, it certainly *is* viable for everyone to make conscious decisions, to reason for oneself, at least at times, and not depend on another to set one's path.

"History suggests that our kind has done well in the relatively short time we have been walking the land. But I disagree… for I believe that the gift of reasoning should have allowed us to accomplish much more. Indeed, I argue that we are in a period of stagnation, and it will be a struggle to reach that next critical point in our advancement if we do not turn to our collective potential. We need everyone to play a part.

"I call it Common Volition—a challenge and proposal for every individual to *focus*, to see the change they can make to the world by simply realising the power of reasoning. Let us all benefit."

It was a solid start, both for Agnes and the symposium. Her topic fell right in place with the theme of the symposium, and her surprisingly confident delivery thus far boded well for the other presenters. More than a few sharing the quarters smiled for Agnes, but the real challenge was to begin now.

"Well then, Lady Gardner," said Antony, a presenter three seats from Alpheus. "How do you suppose the less fortunate can learn to focus? How do these people even access education?"

Ennis Antony was his full name, a scholar twenty-nine years of age who had been named as one of three tertiary speakers this evening. It was unlikely that he held any grudge against Agnes, who had won a more prominent role than him this evening. This was simply how the symposium functioned: ideas were conferred in the form of conversations, which were, in turn, accommodated with questions and challenges to assertions. One's ideas could be as important as one's critiques. Antony's comments might have come earlier than expected, but if Agnes had no answer for it, she had no chance when the State Scholars were to query her.

"It's simple," Agnes said, her eyes twinkling, almost as if welcoming the question. "We guide them. Me and you, alongside all our peers. Let us be the teachers. We guide them until they are well-learned, at which time they can extend the benefit to others. Knowledge belongs to no one. And while we have the duty to share, knowledge is *not* the item to advocate. It is beyond us to share our entire wealth of knowledge. Instead, we are to advocate action. And *focus*. Thinking is natural for scholars. But it is not an automatic process. The aim is to kindle that latent ability to reason—the ability to focus, to think deeply."

"Focus, you say," Antony said. "Define that for us, will you?"

"Gladly," Agnes said without a glance over to him. "In the realm of ideas, focus is key. Our choices of thought are stringed from our knowledge base and memories. The more we learn and experience, the more prone it is for the mind to wander from topic to topic. Focus is crucial to stay on topic, for reasoning deeply."

Well done, Alpheus thought, noting that Antony had been reduced to a silent grin. *You're doing well. If this keeps up—*

"Have you considered the intricacies of that idea of yours?" Reginald said, his remark turning attention to the right wall. His early comment was a surprise, and it had Agnes quivering slightly. "Focus is certainly important to logical reasoning, but it is a skill that some of the greatest scholars in history have spent a lifetime in mastering. Can we really expect even fools to think? What value might it add?"

Agnes cleared her throat. "I was getting to that," she said, looking a little anxious as she peered away toward the aristocrats. "*Evasion*... it is called. Just as we can choose to think, we can also choose not to think—or not to focus. People are prone to taking the easier option when confronted with alternatives. And by doing so, it is likely that one would choose to avoid the task of understanding. It is easy to be ignorant, and in comparison, it is demanding to ruminate. But has anything worthwhile ever been easy? I think not."

She paused there and spun around to face the State Scholars. "As for the value of more thinkers... now, why do you think the Grandmaster established the academy? If he had thought we were all fools, no one would be standing here today."

The Grandmaster nodded at her, while Reginald simply grinned in response. Agnes might have conjured up a structured answer, but Alpheus noted that her confidence had waned from earlier, a visible weakness that the panel members would surely pick up on. That hint of hesitation carried on now as she elaborated on her ideas. Several other presenters were ruthless in critiquing her, and while she couldn't fend off every query, Agnes seemed conscious of the time she was given and she managed to conclude strongly.

She finally breathed a sigh of relief when the others applauded her at the end of her presentation. She was the youngest presenter this evening at only seventeen years of age, and while no one expected her ideas to merit the badge of a State Scholar, it was encouraging for her to know that she had made an impression.

* * *

Seer welcomed the second presenter of the evening, a female scholar named Imelda Dew. She was thirty-three years of age, and had also been granted a place as a secondary speaker. Her experience showed in her relatively more mature age, responding to queries with solid composure from even the more established scholars.

Dew's topic title was *Imagination precedes reasoning*, which discussed the field of aesthetics and its importance in opening up unique forms of thinking. Her ideas and assertions resonated with Alpheus, who wished he could speak about something along the same lines. While few people—presenters or from the panel—objected to Dew's points, it also seemed that no one was particularly interested in the subject matter of art. Unfortunately for her, aesthetics wasn't considered central to deeper philosophical discussions.

A brave attempt, Alpheus thought. *But those ideas have been discussed many times over. Unless you have something new, there's no chance anyone would listen.*

It had grown dark outside by now. The night sky was tinged with the blue of Achelois, some of it filtering into the quarters. Alpheus was growing impatient. He was scheduled to be one of the final presenters of the evening. He glanced over at Kathryn Trulips, who continued to effuse that air of equanimity. Nothing ever seemed to concern her. One could only wonder what she was thinking.

A tertiary speaker was next, followed by a quaternary speaker who barely managed five minutes of presentation time before he was asked for a premature conclusion. Stepping up next was Christopher Hartland, hailed as one of the three primary speakers this evening. He was young, at only twenty-three years of age, but this was already his second symposium. And if the rumours could be trusted, many established scholars expected him to make a real impression today. His topic was entitled *One step and you are half-way there.*

"Many thinkers of the past and present," Hartland began, "have an obsession with debating about science, philosophy, and theology. But for the most part, such discussions are meaningless."

A bold statement, the kind that was needed in order to make a lasting impression. That daring opening, however, only allowed for the smallest margin of error for the rest of his presentation. Nearly everyone cringed for him already—some of them *at* him.

"Make no mistake," Hartland followed. "I am a scholar. I engage in rigorous research to answer some of the grimmest questions our predecessors failed to answer. But I have discovered a new approach, which I am here to share with you.

"Consider a lighted lantern," he then said, gesturing toward the lantern closest to him in the left corner. "The flame inside offers light, but it also has the potential to burn us. That flame can spread to offer even more light, but the danger it poses also grows accordingly. Now let us suppose that the flame is actually harmless. Like an animal, it prickles us only when it feels threatened—when it is touched. As absurd as this may sound, I assure you there is no way to disprove this supposition. *And yet...* there is no meaning to the theory of a harmless flame. What we sense defines our world, and it is this definition that people should live by."

Pragmatism, Alpheus noted with a nod of approval. *A contemporary concept... and one that defines him. Good choice.*

Many others nodded along, and even the State Scholars seemed impressed as Hartland carried on. He was careful not to offend anyone or inadvertently label others as impractical.

"Knowledge is the truth," he continued. "The truth is what we act on. But the truth is not necessarily a fact. As long as we believe in something, it is true to us. This belief is useful because we act in its accordance.

"To illustrate the idea, consider a man deserted on an uninhabitable island. It is important that he believes that there is a way to escape the island, for if he is to survive, he must act—perhaps by building a raft to conquer the waves. By doing so, he will have at least a glimmer of hope. The opposite is also true. If he believes there is no escape, he will do nothing, and will be left to die. Either way, his initial belief—whatever it may be—can be *made* true by purposeful action."

Hartland seemed to be gaining more momentum as he spoke. His ideas were comprehensive, providing little opportunity for others to find faults.

Reginald scratched his beard. "You give me the impression that any belief, even a peculiar one, can be made true by acting upon it."

"The supposition was based on the subject being a reasonable man," Hartland said, maintaining his composure. "In any case, the initial belief must be justifiable in accordance to the available evidence. The aim is to look away from principles and toward consequences."

"Abandon our principles, you say," Black inserted with a smirk, his first comment of the evening. "We are to forget everything that we have learned, abandon the research we have done... because the debates we have are meaningless. Is that what you are saying?"

Hartland regarded the middle-aged man whose achievements bettered even Reginald. "Largely, it is," he replied, still wearing a grin. "I dare not claim that every debate is meaningless, but may I remind everyone here that the path we walk as scholars is not a path taken in solitude. Ultimately, we are here to educate, to enlighten, in order for the world to be a better place. And to do so, we must engage the people some of our peers regard as fools."

He paused, glancing over to Agnes, who had said something similar in her presentation. "As we busy ourselves with debate," Hartland continued, turning back to the State Scholars, "people are dying in the outside world. As a group, we are noble in our constant search for the solutions that could improve life as we know it for the world at large. Our approach, however, has never been timely. But the approach I advocate for is many times more practical. It is what the land needs.

"As for the reluctance that some of us may have to rely on unproven beliefs, I ask you to consider faith. Now, without debating the existence of a god or accusing anyone of blasphemy, it is difficult to argue that belief in a god is not useful to its believer, since it allows him to live a more fulfilled life. In the same manner as I have described earlier, this belief—a more fulfilled life—can be made true if one is faithful enough."

Neither Reginald nor Black said any more, which perhaps signalled their approval. "Logical," Seer said in their stead. "And fitting to the theme of the evening."

Hartland nodded in response, and then continued to elaborate his ideas. Without a doubt, his arguments and theories were stronger than the four scholars who had spoken before him. He had done more than enough to earn his merit as a primary speaker. He had the State Scholars impressed as well, and yet it was as if his theory was tailored for the equally impressed nobles who always preferred the practical side of things. In any case, Hartland had set a high standard for the rest of the evening.

An intermission followed, with light meals of exquisite detail and flavour being brought into the room. The event itself was sponsored by the nobles—it had been this way for decades. It was no secret that the academy also received funding in areas such as maintenance expenses and offers in scholarships to promising scholars who couldn't afford the tuition.

Despite this, however, the Grandmaster—and, in more recent years, Yusuf Seer—had managed to exercise almost complete control over the everyday functioning of the academy. One of the only compromises was the aristocrats' demand for the academy to nominate at least two disciples as State Scholars every five years. State Scholars were constitutionally recognised, and had been sought after by all forms of authorities.

In Trubannis, the recognition was almost an invitation to join the Empire. Reeling was one of those who had accepted the invitation, but there were those like Reginald and Black who preferred to have nothing to do with the Empire, perhaps to avoid meaningless political games.

* * *

The symposium eventually resumed, with the sixth presenter taking centre stage. He was a tertiary speaker named Nicholas. He was the second youngest presenter of the evening as well, at only nineteen years of age.

His topic of *Man is inclusive of women* discussed political philosophy with an emphasis on the gender divide, asserting that women need not be the subordinates to men—that women in fact could acquire all the knowledge men managed to acquire if given the same experience and education. It was refreshing to see a man, a young man at that, speaking about his feminist views. His words resonated with more than a few people sharing the quarters, particularly—and unsurprisingly—the women. His was a radical idea, however.

Outside of the community of scholars, women were rarely given opportunities to succeed—and, if the hearsay were true, even in cases where they had managed to climb the ruthless social hierarchy, their accomplishments had often been understated and undermined by the men in power.

Still, it was a start for Nicholas and the feminist perspective, but unfortunately for them, the dream for women to take on more prominent roles was unlikely to happen any time soon.

Nicholas received some well-earned applause upon his conclusion, and the young scholar seemed pleased with himself. But the attention shifted hastily away from him when the next presenter rose from her seat—Kathryn Trulips of Aizary, a young woman whose poise might just strengthen the case for women to be bestowed with greater responsibilities.

TEN

A conversation with the unknown

Every person sharing the quarters, including even the aristocrats, had long anticipated this moment. Some of them had been waiting for years. The foreigner was to finally make her mark. Having made her intention clear from the beginning that she was here in Zorlia for the long term, the question was only whether she would prove to be an asset or a burden to the city.

Trulips had won credentials as a top scholar. The dialogues she had written on ethics were highly regarded by established scholars. In her home country of Aizary, she was already recognised as a *Sage*, a title equivalent to a State Scholar. But in Trubannis, she would have to prove herself all over again.

She was resplendent as usual as she prepared for her presentation. From the silver hair that dangled behind her to the purple irises that seemed to gleam out, and to the fair skin that almost blended in with the snowy white mantle she donned, she possessed a beauty that was both conspicuous and exotic. But appearance alone meant nothing this evening. The symposium was a stage where the harshest criticisms were expected if one was unable to convince. Trulips had been rather quiet thus far this evening, reserving herself to only a few brief comments, but they had always prompted more meaningful discussion.

"Good evening to all," Trulips began, regarding her audience with those alluring upturned eyes. "My topic title is self-explanatory: *Circumstances precedes character*. In its most basic form, one's character—and, hence, one's behaviour—is the circumstance of what one is given—one's resources. We can predict, often with great accuracy, how certain people will behave in certain situations from the experiences they have had, the resources that are within their reach, or a combination of both. The case I would like to discuss is what it means to be bad—or *evil*, as some call it. To me, anyone has the potential to be evil if the rewards are tempting enough, or if circumstances encourage it.

"Consider the depravities of soldiers at war," she continued, pacing toward the aristocrats. "On the battlefield, in the war camp, people often demonstrate a complete disregard for human life, a wickedness they might not otherwise exhibit. Human lives are considered next to worthless. Even the lives of one's comrades are an afterthought in the midst of a baneful battle of survival. The number of casualties is merely that... a number. A statistic. What one could potentially do to an enemy if given the chance... is unspeakable. And without elaboration, I am sure that you can imagine what it might involve.

"The horrors of war, however, are justified on the principle that the enemy deserves it. And on the virtue of that notion alone, one could slaughter legions without any feelings of guilt. The circumstances have moralised an action that is normally thought of as immoral. Morality, and hence our judgement of good and evil, depends on perspective. It is all relative."

Trulips paused there, peering out at her audience who had found nothing to fault her on just yet. She had barely finished her introduction, but she had the people reduced to grim frowns. Some of those, particularly the noblemen who had been attracted by her beauty, seemed to realise now that the foreigner was a deeper person than her looks suggested.

"To further illustrate my point," Trulips then continued, now pacing the other way toward the State Scholars, "consider two friends enjoying a fine afternoon of hunting in a forest. Behind the dense trees, they are ignorant of what they are firing at. The instinct is to fire at any signs of prey. The first friend fires and kills a boar. He laughs as he snatches up his prey. It is something to boast about for weeks. The second friend fires in the opposite direction but ends up killing a man. There is nothing to boast about there. He would instead have his conscience to answer to, perhaps for the rest of his life, and perhaps on top of having to answer to the ruling authority that may have him prosecuted. The first friend can be hailed as a great hunter, but the second friend, unfortunately, might be now considered an awful human being.

"Luck is a factor that shapes one's circumstances, and circumstances are what we base our judgements of good and evil on. A war general spearheading into an enemy camp may be regarded as brave and heroic, but that same general, in the eyes of the opposition, would surely be regarded as cruel and barbaric. Both sides are equally valid in their judgement. And whether this war general will be remembered in history as hero or villain depends on whether his side ends up victorious."

Trulips paused again, now turning to the centre seats where most of the presenters sat. Antony and Nicholas cleared their throats when Trulips met their eyes. Agnes glanced elsewhere to avoid eye contact altogether. Alpheus was the only one who welcomed it, acknowledging her with a nod.

"Well then, Lady Trulips," Alpheus said. "What do you make of the Lord Emperor and the *barbaric* southerners he fended away? Our Lord Emperor Kasimir de Spartamon is widely regarded as the greatest war strategist in the land, but his title has come at the cost of much bloodshed."

Alpheus knew that if this had been the court, more than a few gasps would have sounded at what would have been deemed to be inept and disparaging comments to both the Lord Emperor and his Empire. But this was the Villa of Enlightenment, where sensitive topics were encouraged if it helped to challenge or prove an argument. Any word spoken at the symposium this evening wasn't to be leaked outside the quarters.

Still, it was never wise to prompt someone into defaming the most powerful man in the country, especially after what the Empire had done to suppress any person who referenced the book entitled *The Proud Conqueror* that only a few years ago had alluded to the emperor's love of killing. It was even less wise to do so with aristocrats present, a group that included Lady Winter, who now narrowed her eyes in response.

An air of silence followed. The noblemen grew visibly worried while the State Scholars, besides the Grandmaster, exchanged grave looks.

Trulips glared at Alpheus and kept hold of her poise. She wouldn't have expected this—that anyone would impel her into the precarious territory of potentially maligning the Lord Emperor.

Go on, Lady Trulips, Alpheus thought, looking into the foreigner's eyes. *Impress me.*

Trulips scoffed. "Your query was a long one," she said, prepared to respond. "Let me begin with what you have termed as the *barbaric* southerners. I assume you are referring to the Kragans. In accordance to what I have said, *barbaric* is merely a mark they are associated with. And who brands them as such? People outside of Kraga.

"There is no argument against what some of them have done to your fellow countrymen here in Trubannis. But were these Kragan *murderers* not compelled into doing what they did? Was it not their circumstances that led them to commit unspeakable horrors? It is understood that some are more prone to be bad than others. But whether they are innately barbarous is a different matter.

"The same principle applies to the Lord Emperor of Trubannis, an incredible man I have not yet had the pleasure to meet—a man I adore for the many remarkable feats he has made possible. He was the leader of a mighty clan at a time when the country was torn by war. He was in a position of power, of responsibility. His ambition to take the country's fate in his own hands was necessary—even if it meant killing hordes along the way. If not for him, Trubannis would not be the prosperous country it is now. Neither you nor I would be standing here discussing philosophy."

Alpheus nodded in response as his sign of approval, even though Trulips wasn't speaking to him in particular. *You didn't mention that he hails from an Aizar heritage*, he thought.

Several others then queried Trulips. Nola Willow was one of them, posing the question of whether it was bad to be unlucky or unlucky to be bad, if only to further flesh out the idea. It was nearly an hour later when Trulips presented her conclusion, which was responded by the same gentle applause that everyone else had received. The impression she had made, however, was deeper than anyone else's—bettering even Hartland. The implication was welcoming. Kathryn Trulips was here in Zorlia for the long term, and her audience today learned that she was indeed a gem who could prove to be a vital part of the Villa, or even the Empire if she chose to take that path.

* * *

A second intermission eased the tension. Another round of light meals was on offer, as presenters and the panel judging them were able to mingle without any added restraints. Trulips was proving to be popular, her wisdom proving to be far more than her looks. She had more than matched the lofty expectations others had placed on her. Nearly every State Scholar approached her to commend her on her presentation. Most of the aristocrats did the same. Trulips seemed to find the attention and praise quite natural, likely having grown used to it long ago.

The third and final part of the symposium was next, with four remaining presenters. Alpheus realised that no one among the four could possibly be under more pressure than him, but he didn't allow himself to be fazed. Instead, he had put his mind elsewhere, clinging onto Agnes, and still praising her for her earlier performance. Agnes was clearly grateful for his compliments, but she was likely thinking that his compliments were at least in part an attempt to ease up before his own presentation.

The symposium resumed for its final presentations. The eighth speaker was another tertiary speaker, and following her was a quaternary speaker. Alpheus was scheduled as the tenth presenter, the second to last.

Don't do this, Alpheus urged himself with a fist over his mouth. *Show your respect. Listen to the presenter.* He looked up then to the young lady, a peer who was speaking. Alpheus didn't know her name. He hardly recognised the face.

I don't want to, he thought, glancing away again to meet Hartland's eyes. Alpheus quickly turned the other way. *Did he see... that I was trembling? I cannot help it, but. The opportunity for redemption—this feeling—it's overwhelming!* He sighed. *I suppose I am still a dedicated scholar at heart.*

His inner monologue ended when his name was announced as the tenth presenter of the evening. Alpheus cleared his throat and clasped onto the double crescent pendant over his chest. His heart was thumping beneath his hand. It was from exhilaration, a feeling not so different from the excitement that burned inside him when he was working on some of his best paintings.

"My topic title is *A conversation with the unknown*," Alpheus said, rising to his feet with a slight tremble. "The *unknown* in this discussion is who I, along with many faithfuls, refer to as the Immortal. I intend to explore the age old debate of the compatibility between philosophy and faith. To me, and to many others, the written word in the Holy Scriptures is undeniably true. But some parts of it are demonstrably false, especially under the scrutiny of a scholar.

"One does not walk on water. Animals do not talk. The dead cannot be resurrected. Such phenomena are implausible, and as learned people, we can only reject them as utter nonsense."

Alpheus paused then, peering out to the audience, all of them ready to challenge him on any inconsistencies. "So it seems," he then added, squinting at the upturned faces listening to him speak. "As a follower of the Ionian doctrine, I contend that everything written in the scriptures is true. Parts of it, however, should not be read literally. Its poetic verse was a requisite for the uneducated majority to absorb and adhere to its lessons. Indeed, as learned people, it is our task to interpret the written word with philosophical reasoning."

Alpheus glanced over to Hartland then, expecting him to be the first to query him on what had only been an introduction. Hartland said nothing, however, seemingly musing over the assertions, and perhaps conjuring up something to fire at him later on.

Surprisingly, Willow was the first to react. "I applaud your courage in conferring what has been a controversial subject matter," she said. "My question is simple. Should we believe in miracles?"

Alpheus nodded at her. It *wasn't* a simple question. Not when asked at the symposium.

"Miracles are the work of the angels and the saints, or the Immortal himself," Alpheus said. "The Immortal is God. And God is omniscient, omnipotent, and omnibenevolent. On the topic of miracles, let us first consider the attribute of omnipotence. God is able to do anything that is logically possible to do. That means God *can* perform miracles. And with God's third attribute of omnibenevolence, one would be inclined to think that God would impart miracles onto the humble beings that are *us*. And it is here where we are confronted with our first contradiction. Because if God is performing miracles on an everyday basis for our benefit, then why are we not seeing these wonderful occurrences with the same frequency?

"There could be many reasons for this, and the main line of argument is dependent on God's first attribute: omniscience. God knows everything that it is logically possible to know. Even as learned people, there is only so much we can grasp. It is absurd to think that we could ever surpass God, let alone match God in his knowledge."

Alpheus paused again, this time glancing over to the Grandmaster who was said to have achieved omniscience himself. The definition of the word as it applied to mortals was different, and perhaps because of that, the old man maintained a slight grin and didn't look offended in any way.

"We can never truly understand the Immortal's divine plan," Alpheus continued, "but a good guess is that God considers us his children, or even an extension of himself, not dissimilar to the angels and saints. God cannot lend a helping hand in every situation, for it will only hinder our development, our progress, and our ability to evolve into self-sufficient beings.

"Before I digress further, allow me to answer the initial question," Alpheus then said, regarding Willow again. "I consider it necessary for us to believe in miracles. But in saying so, miracles need not be phenomena such as walking on water or animals developing the ability to speak. Miracles are cultivated. They are dependent on persistency, but also on luck—or what I prefer to call *chance*.

"With one's determination, one can perform miracles, but still with the aid of the Immortal, or under his guidance. A few centuries ago, our kind did not and could not imagine the applied science we enjoy today. Whether it is the comfort of the wonderfully sheltered homes that resist the worst of weather, or the elixirs we brew that prevent us from falling ill to the many ailments that were once considered lethal, we, as mankind, have performed many miracles.

"Another interpretation of miracles is how their circumstances differ from the norm. Anything that is odd could be considered to be a miracle. Consider the mass migration of certain animals, for example. From the great distances covered to the sheer size of the flocks, and finally to the fact that they *know* where to find sanctuary… to me, it is all a miracle."

Alpheus looked to Trulips then. "And if I may mention this," he said, "the latest miracle that I have come to know is a phenomenon called sorcery."

The foreigner raised her chin slightly, as if to acknowledge the comment. Many others exchanged grave looks, meanwhile, noting that Alpheus had perhaps heedlessly raised another controversial subject matter.

"I have been fascinated with sorcery ever since I discovered what it was," Alpheus said. "But I have been back and forth with it."

"Why is that?" Trulips asked with a squint.

"Because it contradicts the teachings of Ionianism. Although not referenced specifically, magic is implied as taboo. It is only ever associated with The Eternally Damned."

Trulips looked askance at the supposition. "How one interprets the messages from the Immortal is but the most subjective," she said. "The obscure is always feared. By this logic, sorcery is regarded by some faithfuls as malign *because* it is obscure. Faith, meanwhile, is looked upon as benign because it is considered to be certain and absolute. But is faith really all that definite? Sadly, most people simply believe what they are told. That is not to say people shouldn't have faith, however.

"Indeed, faith is possibly the most important thing for anyone if cultivated correctly. The opposite is true as well, however. Faith can destroy those who are constantly held back by it."

Alpheus agreed, but he did not make this known vocally. Everyone else remained tight-lipped. Most of the people in the quarters, if not all, likely shared some level of devotion for the Immortal, if not for the angels and saints. But it was still a sensitive issue when discussed alongside philosophy.

"Having faith is to believe in miracles," Trulips went on. "As scholars, we do not rely on miracles—at least, we do not wait for them to happen on their own. We help to create those miracles with our craft."

Alpheus hesitated, feeling his forehead heat up, as he ideated the radical view of what he believed was the foreigner's standard of faith—a delicate level of devotion. While Trulips had avoided quoting it directly, her words implied that she adhered to a doctrine where the Immortal was less than perfect—that one shouldn't rely too heavily on something that was immeasurable.

But this is what I wanted, Alpheus thought. *To start a debate on the contradictions that no one wants to discuss. And I might have achieved just that.*

"Sadly," Alpheus said now, "it is in our nature to classify everything as either good or evil. People see only black and white. Faith is good and sorcery is evil. As a follower of the faith, I adhere to those teachings. But I also believe in magic—sorcery. It is unfortunate that the world is so stubborn in its quest to justify the stance of one thing and to invalidate the stance of another. Coexistence has always been a problem for people, and it will continue to be if we resist change.

"In the end, much of what we believe in depends on perspective. But as humble beings who are unable to demonstrate the miracles only God could manage, or are unable to grasp what only God would know, we must accept that we could be wrong, regardless of how certain we are in what we believe.

"There are infinite potential perspectives about a single problem, and further to that, there are various levels of interpretation from within the same perspectives, or the same line of reasoning. We may never attain the base of knowledge exclusive to the heavens, but be assured that we could come close. And to begin, we must stringently apply the deeper levels of interpretation that we are capable of in order to first realise that philosophy and faith were never at odds."

* * *

It was midnight when the symposium ended. The final presenter had been a secondary speaker, and while her discussion on another perspective of epistemology was by no means negligible, Alpheus had left the people in contemplation with perhaps the most thought-provoking topic of the evening. Regardless of whether Alpheus had presented the best idea, every presenter and guest this evening was sure to ponder on his contentions, possibly for a long time. Even Agnes had regarded Alpheus with widened eyes upon his conclusion. And almost everyone else had peered over to him every now and then, perhaps without even realising it.

The Grandmaster rose now to address his disciples and guests about what he called another insightful evening of philosophy. "I can only urge you all not to believe everything you are told," he said, concluding his brief speech. "Inquire. It is always worth your while."

The old man acknowledged his audience with a simple nod. He then turned to retreat away toward the spiral stairs as the people bowed to him. When he might present himself again was anyone's guess. It could well be at the next symposium, which would not take place for at least a couple more years.

Seer paced now toward the aristocrats, who each yielded a sheet of paper to him. These were their appraisals, and together with the ones Seer had already collected from the State Scholars—including the Grandmaster—he now held the result of each presenter's performance. A more in-depth evaluation would be saved for later, perhaps in the following week. But arguably the most important result was to be announced now: anyone who might win the badge as a State Scholar. It was the only reason why the nobles had yet to depart.

All eyes were on Seer as he flipped through the pages, wearing that same stern face, as if adding to the suspense. At the last symposium, no one had been awarded with the prestigious honour. But that was unlikely to occur again tonight. At the very least, Kathryn Trulips was expected to win the honour. It was expected to be a mere formality, especially as she was already recognised with an equivalent title in the Far East.

"Lady Kathryn Trulips," Seer said, glinting up.

The people applauded as Trulips accepted the approval with a reserved smile. It was never easy to tell what she was thinking.

"And...," Seer uttered, quieting the group, "Lord Alpheus Hindlow."

Silence.

And shock.

Alpheus began to shake, plunging into an invisible tempest of mixed emotions. He was finally there. Finally recognised as an elite scholar, independent of his brilliant sister. He shook away his daze then to realise that he was now at the end of some gentle applause. Agnes, though, was beaming at him, looking ecstatic.

"And...," Seer said again to the same effect, "Lord Christopher Hartland."

Attention turned to Hartland immediately, who looked nearly as surprised as Alpheus had been a moment ago. The people put their hands together for him, perhaps believing that he deserved it more than Alpheus. Hartland quivered as tears drowned his eyes. If there was anyone who could be commended for relentless effort, it was him. But the greatest surprise was neither Alpheus nor Hartland. It was the fact that three different scholars were recognised as State Scholars at the same symposium.

The last time that had happened was when Yusuf Seer himself managed it, alongside Jeffery Reeling and Charlotte Hindlow. Those three were often referred to as the *Golden Generation* of the academy.

The formal recognition of their status was bestowed now, with chrome-plated pocket watches given to all three of them, a token recognised by the Empire that demanded a level of authority that most noblemen enjoyed. The pocket watch itself was handcrafted to the highest quality and with a considerable weight, about three times heavier than Alpheus's original pocket watch. The inside replicated the great astronomical clocks which indicated the positions of certain celestial objects, while the cover was chiselled with the symbol of the academy. Finally, the back was to be engraved with the scholar's name, as Reginald would do now with his delicate carving skills.

The evening ended there but as the people dispersed, Alpheus eyed Trulips. He had a few things he wanted to say to her. He nodded at Agnes first, as a sign of goodbye, before pacing toward the foreigner who noticed his measured approach.

"Congratulations, *Lord* Hindlow," she said. "I believe you will soon find it natural to be addressed with the new honorific."

"Thank you, Lady Trulips," Alpheus said. "I…," he uttered hesitantly, glancing away, struggling to bring up the topic of sorcery. "May I ask what's next for you?" he asked instead. "What are your plans?"

"The Empire," she answered succinctly. "More precisely, the military."

Alpheus pursed his lips. "I have thought, as scholars, we are learning to avoid that—to avoid war."

Trulips shrugged. "I do not support war, but despite the supposed peaceful era in which we live, it is effective military power that could finally bring true balance to the land."

"I'm sorry. But that seems to defeat the purpose of what we do as scholars."

"This is new," Trulips said with a snort. "You sound as if you are wholly against the idea."

"I am."

"Then what of the combat practices we study?"

"I'm not sure who you mean by *we*, but personally, I have avoided studying the art of killing in any form. A scholar doesn't need to fight—at least not physically."

Trulips frowned slightly. "Then how would you fend yourself off physical hostility?"

"With intelligence. With reasoning."

"It is an imperfect world we live in. Reason does not always prevail."

"And that's exactly what we're here for—to guide the ignorant to see reason."

"And if reasoning fails?"

"I will try again, perhaps in another way."

"And if you fail again?"

"My dear Lady Trulips, I will try until I succeed."

The foreigner smiled. Alluring as always. "In any case," she then said, "it is unprecedented for a foreigner to possess authority over Truban armies. But I have more confidence to make that happen than to earn a place in the House of Sages. If possible, Bastion City is where I hope to be based. Indeed, I have already submitted an application. I assume, from what you have just said, that we cannot expect to walk down similar paths?"

Alpheus hesitated for a moment. "No, we cannot," he said. "The Empire was never in my plans. And despite my elation just now, I don't plan to walk the scholar's path much further, either. The academy is a special place to me, but my dream lies elsewhere."

Trulips regarded him with a squint, as if preparing to be disappointed.

"I may not have mentioned it before," Alpheus continued. "But I'm an artist, more so than a scholar. My dream is to paint the future with my brush."

Trulips turned away slightly, closing her eyes as she shook her head. "A pity," she said.

It was only two words, but it was never easy hearing it. "I've realised what I want," Alpheus claimed fervently. "I'm more fortunate than many who may *never* realise their purpose in life. You say you want to join the Empire, but does that have *anything* to do with your personal desires?"

The foreigner turned to him with a glare this time that carried a bitterness that seemed to leap out at him. "I ask that you never again speak of my purposes, together with your low standards of what you call a dream."

She turned away then, receding along that same hallway everyone had already departed through. The exchange was worse than Alpheus had expected, but he was adamant to stand by his beliefs, saying nothing as he watched her leave. Until now, he hadn't realised that anger was even an emotion that Kathryn Trulips was capable of feeling, let alone expressing. For all her equanimity and angelic looks that propelled her above others—all worldly beings—it turned out that she had her delicate moments, too.

As for all the questions he had wanted to ask about sorcery, Alpheus could only blame his own insecurities he had for his new identity. Until he could accept that he, too, was a sorcerer, it was meaningless to learn anything more about the topic.

* * *

The night had not yet ended for Yusuf Seer. He sat now in his chambers, collating the appraisals he had collected, thinking back to how each presenter had performed. On his left was a list of the eleven participants of the symposium, of which his eyes now inadvertently narrowed to only one name.

"You needn't be overly concerned," spoke a voice that startled him briefly.

The unlatched door in front of him was pushed in now with a gentle squeak. It was Jeffery Reeling, holding onto his top hat rather than wearing it. From what Seer remembered, the scholar-turned-nobleman only started wearing the hat upon joining the Empire.

"And what might you be suspecting that concerns me?" Seer asked.

"The future of the academy. I suppose it is the only thing that adds to your grey hair."

In his younger days, Seer might have pointed out that Reeling had more grey hair than him. But it was a different time now. "How long has it been?" Seer said instead. "Since you last spoke with the Grandmaster?"

Reeling breathed out an uncharacteristic sigh. "Five years," he said. "It was then when he asked me to consider leaving the Empire."

"And why have you not?"

"There are things needed to be done. It may be beyond me, but no one can blame a man for trying."

The atmosphere in the room grew heavy with the utterance of those words, and a long silence filled the air. "Now," Reeling said, trying to break the tension, "you know I am not here for small talk."

"I know. But do you really think he is ready to submit to the Empire? And I am not referring to his reluctance."

"You worry for his simple-minded black and white reality," Reeling said. "You worry that he cannot hope to survive within the court, which is always muddled with intriguing schemes. But I shall take him under my direct tutelage. His real training begins now."

PART II

ELEVEN

Playing by the rules

It had been nearly two months since Julian submitted his loyalty to Quinlan Forredan. He had been patient. He had been waiting for a chance to prove his ability. Even upon learning that his commute to the mining town of Carrington—a daily four-hour return journey—was to be a regular part of his everyday schedule, and even upon learning that he supposedly had to further prove his allegiance by doing his part as an actual miner, Julian had convinced himself that it was all going to be worth it in the end.

But it certainly hadn't been so far.

He had been relieved of his duties as a patrol soldier, but this was effectively a demotion from the bottom of the warrior class to the even more unceremonious peasant class. Within the peasant class, miners were actually at the upper end of the hierarchy, but the occupation itself was certainly dreary. Their world was lit by torches more often than by sunlight, with working days that often began before the first glimmers of sunrise. By the time they returned to the surface of the living world, it was dawn.

The fact was that no one in the mining town seemed to care about him or his abilities.

Stability was what many people wished for, and this was the life that could provide it. Julian realised that. But accepting it for himself was something else. The mundane lifestyle of running routine errands wasn't a luxury he could afford. He didn't know what the future held, but there was no way he could convince himself to abide by the 'rules' of society and live as an ordinary civilian.

The only positive about all of this was that the former golden knight, Victor Breunor, had stopped pestering him. But how was he supposed to grow stronger when all he did was dig? How was what he was doing now going to prepare him for the Golden Knight Exchange?

It was ironic that there *was* indeed a person sharing the mine who could prepare him—one of the supervisors, a man in his forties named Tannon Gale. According to what the other peasants had told Julian, Gale was a former silver knight—a national 'hero' who had once led his own army, and had once been regarded as one of the most charming young knights in the country.

The hearsay was that Gale was then later left scarred for life following a crushing defeat at the hands of a *Primal Soldier* of Kraga. Gale *did* have the brawn to be a celebrated warrior, but so did many of the peasants sharing the mine who worked tirelessly day in and day out. In any case, the man's time as a knight was but a story from the past. Today, he was no hero. He was a miserable man, and he rarely uttered a word. The other peasants preferred it when he was quiet, anyway, for when Gale *did* speak, it was often accompanied by his maniacal bouts of rage.

Julian had already considered talking to him, but it was obvious that Gale hated to bring up the past. If the man was nagged about it, things would very quickly turn ugly.

Julian peered over to the former knight now, who was sitting a good distance away, not working. The man was wearing that same bleak look that he always wore. His half-closed eyes were dispiriting, and the long hair that dangled in messy strips over his face, coupled with his thick, bushy beard, made him look more like a beggar than anything else.

Julian then turned to the peasants, dozens of them repeating the same procedures over and over again. They were hard-working, but... spiritless.

It was a bottomless pit.

"I quit," Julian said suddenly, dropping his pickaxe.

Not everyone had heard him, but the ones who did perked up.

"I *quit*," he said again, this time much louder.

The peasants paused, looking over to him now.

Gale, too, looked up. "What did you say?" he asked.

"I said I've had enough of this. I don't want to be like *you*," Julian said, nodding in Gale's direction as he said the final word.

Gale snapped his eyes wide in visible annoyance. He rose from his simple stool, clenching a fist that cracked.

Julian smirked at him. "Let's not do this," he said. "I wouldn't want to hurt you."

Gale growled, treading slowly now toward Julian. His thick beard had puffed out, and even his dangled hair had bristled up. The man was furious.

Julian stood his ground, wondering for a brief moment why he had provoked a disgraced warrior. By the time he shook away the untimely thought, he realised that Gale had stepped in front of him, glaring at him at level height.

A long silence followed. The peasants gawked, perhaps torn on whether to be excited or to call one of the other supervisors from the next section. But it was too late for that now as Gale threw out a punch, which brought about gasps that immediately filled the cavern, resonating throughout.

Julian had been hit square on the jaw, but he managed to keep his feet firmly planted on the ground. His left eye, however, was already half-shut. He gently brushed the fist aside, revealing his bruised face. He winced a little, but instead of rubbing where it throbbed, he started patting his garments off the dust and grime collected on this work day.

His apathy provoked Gale to throw a second punch.

But this time as he was ready for it, Julian caught the man's fist in his hand. "That's enough," he said, glinting out with his right eye.

Gale gnashed his teeth and then swung out yet another punch that Julian barely managed to block, the contact leaving his forearm shaking, albeit slightly. No one else would have noticed, but this third blow of the fist was at least several times stronger than the previous attempts.

And Gale didn't stop there. As if possessed, the man threw jab after jab, and in turn, forcing Julian into a dogfight that the peasants had now started cheering for.

He's rusty, Julian thought, trying to free himself from the scramble, reluctant to admit even to himself that Gale was moving well. By the time Julian realised that the former knight's attacks were indeed growing more and more purposeful, he found that he was struck again, this time a thump at the chest.

Almost as if by reflex, Julian responded immediately with flame-enhanced knuckles that seared the former knight, sending him crashing into the wall and onto the ground.

The cavern fell silent, everyone clearly shocked to learn that Julian was a sorcerer. Julian smothered his flames, recognising that the battle was over. He recognised also that look of despair on Gale's face that spelled one's resignation. It was both pitiful and familiar.

"Never thought you a magic user," Gale said in despondency, scrambling into a sitting position, his hair dangling over most of his face. "But regardless of that, you are still only a peasant, just like the rest of us. And I lost to you."

He seemed to be soaking in more of the self-pity that had become part of his identity in the mines.

"No," Julian said. "You didn't lose to me. You lost to yourself."

These words seemed to trigger a memory of Gale's as the former knight jerked forward, pupils dilated. Julian found the expression disturbing. To him, it was a look of despair, a realisation and perhaps acceptance of having been overwhelmed.

Gale looked down again, staring blankly into the ground. "I had enormous confidence in my ability," he said with apparent nostalgia. "But that man was incredible, a man of colossal strength. I thought I was a golden knight prospect, but he made me realise how utterly weak I was. I was a silver knight, the best of my generation. I commanded my own army, the *Salamanders*."

Julian cringed, noting the army name, which was remembered as one of the most powerful in the country in the last decade.

"I was the only silver knight to ever command an army," Gale continued. "I was *that* good, and so was my army. Lord Forredan owes his success to us. By providing the resources to maintain the army, he went from being a mere merchant to a State Minister. You could say we enjoyed some great times together. We lifted one another to heights we never thought were possible."

Gale then shook his head with a grunt. "But everything ended when we met *him*—that Primal Soldier. It was my army's first and only defeat, an even battle between my men and his men. The only way to settle the stalemate was a personal duel between the commanders."

Gale paused, puffing out a long breath. "He crushed me. He crushed my camp's morale. He didn't think I was even worth killing."

A man of colossal strength, Julian thought musingly. *I, too, am chasing after such a man.*

He jumped slightly then as a glimmer of gold flashed across the mine. He turned, and there among them stood a man that exactly fit the description of colossal strength: Golden Knight Claude Lucan.

The man carried an enormous sword on his back. It didn't look like he was about to use it, however, as he instead held onto a metal pole with blunt ends attached to a thick red fabric. His gleaming golden armour reflected off the torches, in turn blinding the peasants who bowed down to him as if he was a deity. Compared to Gale, who rolled his eyes now with a snort, Lucan was certainly well-groomed and finely presented. His neat facial hair was a welcome contrast to Gale's crumpled hair and thick beard.

"What do *you* want?" Gale said, disgruntled.

Lucan said nothing, treading forward still. The golden knight seemed more irritable than Julian remembered. Lucan stopped when he reached Gale, stamping the metal pole down before shooting a cold stare at the disgraced former knight from above. Gale simply grimaced back.

"Get it together," the golden knight said.

"I don't need your pity."

Lucan scowled in turn. He raised an arm and then crashed a fist down upon Gale, sending him smashing into the rocky wall. The ground seemed to shake, and the peasants were left trembling, wondering what would happen next.

"You want another chance! You know it!" Lucan goaded. "We all want to see you fight again!"

Gale slowly picked himself up. He wiped off some blood dribbling from his mouth with his thumb. "Is that all you wanted to do?" he said, and then gestured to the exit. "Please."

Lucan shook his head. "I've been forever proud that I once worked on your command," he said. "You taught me well. The Defender of Whitesand... that title should have been yours. You could have been one of the greatest."

"Shut up," Gale said, turning away, drivel soaking his thick beard. "Shut up!"

Lucan grasped onto the metal pole and then swung it out forcefully, flapping out a great war-flag of blood red. There was hardly enough air in the mine, let alone wind, but the flag wavered briefly, long enough for people to see the imprinted reptilian creature. It was the emblem of the now obsolete *Scorching Salamander Knights*, usually shortened simply to the Salamanders.

Gale seemed moved for a moment, but shame soon overtook his face again. "No!" he cried, smashing the rocky ground repeatedly, stopping finally when his fists were soaked in his own blood. Then he hung his head in shame. "Let me be," he said quietly. "Just let me be."

Lucan grumbled and then grabbed Gale by the back of his collar, hurtling him with great might against the rocks. Julian thought that he heard breaking bones. He didn't have to guess that Gale was in pain when the man was now spewing out a heap of blood. Lucan was furious, and he didn't seem to be holding back even a little. Indeed, the golden knight held Gale by the neck now, forcing him against the wall. He beat him at the torso again and again, each strike with a resounding dull thump, smashing him further into the rocks that were crushing open.

The peasants didn't utter a sound, and though Julian wanted nothing to do with the confrontation either, he found that he was growing annoyed.

"Fight back!" the golden knight prodded. "How much more do you want to be humiliated?!"

Lucan finally slowed down, but not because Gale was coughing up dangerous spatters of blood, but because of the sudden wave of heat that he must have felt behind him. Julian, standing only a few steps from them, had raised a hand entrenched in brilliant flames that lighted up the mine to the colour of a blazing tangerine.

"What do you think you're doing?" the golden knight questioned, turning only slightly, but still not letting go of Gale.

"Let him be," Julian said, echoing Gale's own words.

"You have some nerve," Lucan chided, reaching for his massive broad sword.

It was a blink later that he had the tip of weapon at Julian's neck—his quick draw was invisible. Julian gulped, fearing an unwarranted death, holding a fist to quash his flames. The peasants, meanwhile, backed off further.

"He's the only one who can help himself," Julian said. "There's no use beating him."

Gale snorted as blood continued to dribble out of his mouth, snorting perhaps at Julian's comment, at his pity. Despite still being strangled, Gale now snapped his eyes wide open and then finally forced away the rough grip.

Lucan lurched back and slowly slid his weapon away.

Gale grunted and then spat out a dab of blood mixed with saliva. He was bruised all over and covered in grime, and yet he looked suddenly vigorous, especially considering that he had just been beaten hard. Lucan seemed to know something no one else did, and he grinned now as well, looking quite pleased.

Gale turned to the peasants with a set of dark eyes and knitted brows that showed something that Julian had never seen in the man: grit. "Get back to work!" he instructed with plenty of volume.

The peasants were quick to abide, likely glad that they could finally excuse themselves. They might have been wondering how Gale appeared to have shaken off his pain, but they opted to mind their own business.

"This is the last time you'd have to put up with me," Gale said quietly to the peasants who wouldn't have heard him. "I'll make sure you have a better supervisor from tomorrow on." He turned to Lucan. "Claude," he called him.

"Don't ever do that again."

The golden knight smirked. "I hope I won't have to."

"And you," Gale said, turning to Julian. "Don't you dare pity me again."

Julian winced, not quite sure what to say.

"How did you land here, anyway?" Gale asked. "I don't know much about magic users, but I'd expect you to be doing more with your ability."

"I agree he could be something of a force," Lucan said. "But Lord Forredan doesn't see his value."

I thought as much, Julian noted, tensing up. *I'm just wasting my time*.

"What about the Exchange?" Gale asked. "I've heard about it. Couldn't he try that out?"

"Only knights can participate," Lucan said. "That is, unless he is granted an exemption."

"Forget it," Julian said, already on his way.

"Now, come on," Gale prodded. "Where's that audacity from before?"

"No," he assured without turning back. "I'll participate. But with my own rules. If need be, I'll burn every last contestant to show my ability."

* * *

Julian had been born to a wealthy family of clockmakers in the state of *Cellarsy*. His father, in particular, had been a great man—respected, admired, and even deified by many. Although he had never been close to his father, Julian had been given the best of everything as a child, which included opportunities to be trained by the finest masters in any field or area of study that he had liked. He had been used to adulation, and spoiled for choice.

He didn't know that old life anymore. He had even changed his name to avoid anyone finding out who he was, or who he had been. He had turned away from his past. Of the few people who had asked him, his answer had always been that he *had* no past. He *had* no family. And he *needed* no family.

It had been ten years since he had first arrived in Zorlia as a boy, barely in his teenage years. And although he hadn't achieved a whole lot, he had, at the very least, survived. He had arrived as a lost soul, and had since matured into a man. That, in itself, was an achievement to be proud of. Perhaps he was now on course to blossom into something of real value—and it was that much merrier knowing that he had reached this stage all on his own. The next step, though, was something else. Even if it was only a nudge, Julian needed someone to support him. Quinlan Forredan could have been that someone, the man to open the door for him to the world he thought he deserved.

But it was not to be.

He was almost back in Zorlia now, having treaded his way through a hazy path blinded by frustration. There were probably several people sharing the same road, but Julian wasn't sure—he didn't care.

What to do now? Julian thought, growing impatient as he hiked. *Am I just a discard?*

"Hey," Julian thought he heard. "Hey," someone said again.

He looked up, but before he could make out who was there, a blade came slashing directly toward him. He gushed out a mush of grace in that fraction of a second in order to whip out his iron sword, narrowly blocking the attack which sparked a brilliant clash of metals.

The few people along the road flocked away immediately.

Julian forced away the aggressor's weapon, which he now realised was a rapier. The aggressor, once he was able to make him out, turned out to be none other than Percival Pole.

"What the hell are you doing?!" Julian cried.

Pole grinned at him and then slipped away the rapier. "I *did* kill off that negative energy on you just now, did I not?" he said.

Julian, too, tucked away his sword. "What do you want, Percival?"

"Now, now," Pole said. "What's with the tone? I came all this way to bring you some good news, after all."

Julian huffed out audibly, raising a brow.

"I've found the token for you to enter the Exchange," Pole said with a deeper grin. "My master has agreed to help."

Julian brightened up almost immediately. He said nothing, though, as he waited for Pole to elaborate.

"He needs to meet you first," Pole said. "Just to see if you really do have the skills to compete. And, of course, I've already arranged for it."

Julian stared at Pole for a moment, regarding the silver knight with quiet gratitude. He hadn't expected this at all, not when the Defence Army never allowed anyone a second chance. It didn't matter how Pole managed to convince Sagramore, though, as long as he could be given one last chance to work his way toward the attention of the men in power.

"Thank you," he said finally.

TWELVE

Confrontation at the Parlour

Alpheus wasn't sure how he had arrived at the front gate of Vondra Dawn, but his ambivalence was forgotten when he pulled out the chrome-plated pocket watch hanging off his belt. His new status as a State Scholar was his pass to enter the imposing citadel.

He tried his best to keep a straight face when the guards bowed to him as they permitted his entry. It wasn't the first time he had stepped into the citadel, but while he wasn't fond of the place, it was a good feeling to enter on his own merits. The stupendous grey structure itself, however, was less inviting. The clusters of steeples that shot upwards were striking, but as Alpheus looked up now, he likened them to a heap of giant tombstones. The hue of dull colours didn't help to lighten the aesthetic.

He turned to the western front. Reeling was the only person he wanted to see. For once, it was Alpheus seeking *him* out, and not the other way around.

In his first week as a State Scholar, Alpheus had maintained a low profile. He had locked himself in his atelier again and spent his time working on his latest painting. He often became lost in his own creativity, into a world only he knew, where time was at a standstill. And that tendency had grown worse in recent years—or better, depending on how one preferred to perceive what it meant to create.

The new painting had a tangerine background. With dimensions that roughly matched a large book, it was one of his smaller paintings. A horde of men swarmed the background of the painting, defined by only dark outlines and forming a trail behind a glaring sun. One of those men stood out because of a mishap, hanging by the head from a single leafless tree that had grown from the hilly ground.

In the foreground, meanwhile, stood a child—of Aizar descent, perhaps, as implied by the subject's silvery-bluish hair. The child faced the silhouettes of the seemingly doomed men in the background. He or she wore no clothing, and was covered only sparingly in a blanket-sized cloth that revealed part of his or her buttocks. The overall theme was bleak, though some of that impression might owe to it being incomplete. Still, the allure was otherworldly.

You criticised me, Alpheus thought with a wince, still pacing toward the western towers. *Kathryn Trulips... you criticised my dream. Just who do you think you are?*

He frowned then, glancing down at the necklace that looped together both the symbol of faith and the silver band that amplified grace. *I still cannot believe it*, he thought, holding a fist. *This new identity. What do I do with it?*

Although it had been years since his last visit, Alpheus remembered with vivid detail the tedious walk he had taken in order to get to the Reeling's chambers. Alpheus was at the set of spiral stairs now that ascended about seven stories high. And when he reached the top, there was an even longer corridor ahead of him. One might wonder if it was by purposeful design that the Lord Count was stationed so far from the court and everything else that was important in the citadel.

When Alpheus finally reached the end of the drab corridor, Yorke was there to welcome him. The man called himself Reeling's butler, but Alpheus knew that he had once been a military man. His brawn still showed that he was a force to be reckoned with. Alpheus had also known the man as Reeling's closest confidant, someone who had first met Reeling during the war. Yorke was also a mentor of sort for Alpheus. He never said much, but Alpheus thought him wise and believed him to be a man he could trust.

"The Lord Count's been expecting you," Yorke said, eyeing Alpheus's new pocket watch with a smile, his way of offering congratulations.

Yorke then pushed open the heavy door behind him. Alpheus nodded and stepped into the chambers to see the man who he couldn't imagine ever winning praise from. Even without his usual top hat, which was hung on the coat stand to his left along with his mace, Jeffery Reeling was always the refined gentleman that others wished they could be. He sat behind a desk piled with a mountain of documents, and he was prying through them with quiet diligence.

"Jeffery, I—"

"I've been waiting," Reeling said, finally sparing a glance at Alpheus behind the glint of his monocle. "And please get used to addressing me as Lord Count."

Alpheus frowned slightly at Reeling's curtness.

"We are pressed for time," Reeling said. "Compared to you, the other two are already at work."

"What do you mean? What other two?"

"Christopher Hartland has submitted his loyalty to Pierre Morlan. And Kathryn Trulips has tried her luck with the Defence Army."

Alpheus shrugged. "And...? How did it go?"

Reeling threshed another document away to the 'completed' pile. He then regarded Alpheus carefully, raising a hand to his chin. "The Defence Army does not accept women for any roles, regardless of who they are or what they have achieved," Reeling said. "Kathryn Trulips has since asked to work with me."

Alpheus pondered this over for a moment. "That's wonderful," he finally said. "What did you say?"

"I said no, for I already have you."

"Me?" Alpheus asked, bemused. "What's this about? I believe you said you wouldn't force me into anything."

"And I am *not* forcing you," Reeling maintained, "but merely inviting you to see things in a new perspective. You need inspiration for your art, do you not? I could show you a world vastly different from what you think you know. Indeed, it is much more intriguing than you could ever imagine.

"I am a man of my word, Alpheus. I assure you that you are not chained. You can leave at any time."

Alpheus sighed. "If you care enough to make that speech, I suppose I can spare a little time." He paused. "How about two weeks?"

Reeling smiled, standing from his chair. "I am glad," he said. "And you should be glad too that we're going on a field trip of sorts today."

The courtly man snatched his gear from the coat stand, throwing on his top hat and trench coat as he led the way out of the chambers. Coming from him, 'field trip' could mean anything. Alpheus remembered a time when Reeling had invited him on a 'fishing trip,' but had instead been taken to a cave full of bats where the only thing remotely related to fishing was the meagre amount of groundwater. There was another time when Reeling promised to find him a serene environment to work on his paintings but instead had him sent to a remote cottage at the centre of a graveyard.

Shortly after trotting out of Vondra Dawn, however, Alpheus realised that their destination was King's Parlour, an opulent structure of rising arcades and balconies designed for the rich. Alpheus stepped into the building behind Reeling, not knowing what to expect. They advanced directly to the fourth floor, the highest point of the building and also the best vantage point from which to oversee everything that transpired there. Alpheus didn't care for watching noblemen mingle, but he did like sitting just beneath the forest glass ceiling of the building where daylight shone brightly through.

Reeling shot him a wry smile before sipping his cup of tea. "Our first guest has arrived," he said.

Alpheus looked down to the ground floor entrance where a group of knights had entered. The leader of the group sported gleaming golden armour, with a brawny build that rivalled that of Victor Breunor. He looked about the same age as the military man, with a receding hairline and neatly trimmed stubble. The man's weapon of choice was a golden partisan that glistened along with the rest of his outfit.

"That is Sir Sagramore," Reeling said, "the Chieftain of the Defence Army, honoured as the leader of all golden knights. He is the most powerful man in the country when it comes to military power."

Alpheus glanced at Reeling, saying nothing. He didn't want to make it seem like he cared. He had of course heard of the name, but it was the first time he had seen the man. And this man, Paltiel Sagramore, despite his less than gentle dispositions—he looked like... a good person.

Alpheus also recognised Percival Pole in company, and in turn remembered that the silver knight had once mentioned that he was a disciple of Sir Sagramore.

The golden knight settled down at a small table while all of his men, including Pole, stood behind him. Alpheus didn't want to guess how often Sagramore came to Zorlia. He wondered instead why Pole was always in the capital when the Defence Army was based in Bastion City, typically a three-hour horse ride southeast of Zorlia.

Reeling gestured toward the entrance again.

Julian! Alpheus noted, growing visibly excited. The last he had heard of Julian was the story of his miserable times in Carrington. Alpheus had thought to seek him out, but he had been preoccupied with his own demanding schedule.

Julian had arrived in his regular soldier outfit. He proceeded to the golden knight's table, going down on one knee and bowing down to Sagramore.

Alpheus couldn't hear what they were saying, though it appeared that whatever they were discussing, it was going well for Julian. *Did Sir Pole arrange this?* he wondered with a smile. *I sure hope Julian can finally put his skills to use.*

"Another one has arrived," Reeling said then, as he took another sip of his tea.

Treading in was an imposing group of about twenty men led by a burly man sporting a polished head of baldness and exuberant mutton chops—former Golden Knight Victor Breunor, marching in donning a large coat of black and white fleece, flashier than even Sagramore's gleaming golden armour. Even Walford Bors, Breunor's golden knight vassal, sported golden armour that stood out more than what Sagramore wore, with horn-like shapes forking out from the shoulders, elbows, and knees. Alpheus recognised a third man within the group, the young silver knight he had met once on the same evening when he had first met Julian.

Together, they sauntered toward Sagramore.

"Here," Reeling said, offering Alpheus a paper cone. Alpheus accepted it, and then eyed the long string trailing from it that disappeared off into the wall.

"It's connected to the ground floor," Reeling said.

Alpheus squinted off to the distance, and there, next to Sagramore's table, was indeed another paper cone hanging out from the wall. It wasn't particularly well-hidden, though no one else seemed to have noticed it.

It was almost shocking to see that Reeling would use something as unsophisticated as this. Around the courtly man, one had to expect the unexpected. In any case, Alpheus held the paper cone to his ear and turned his attention back to the two veterans of war engaged now in an embrace.

Sagramore and Breunor shared a long history. They had served as golden knights since the previous era under the Sargon Monarchy. Sagramore in particular was the only Second Generation Golden Knight left standing after the death of Kay Wallace earlier in the year. And he was standing strong. It was said that Paltiel Sagramore was still the strongest of all the golden knights, perhaps with the exception of the relatively youthful Lionel Lachman, who had emerged as an extremely skilled warrior in recent years.

Breunor wasn't fond of Sagramore—at least that was what the rumours suggested. And the reason for that was apparently because everyone seemed to consider Sagramore to be the greatest warrior of the class in strength, leadership, and morality. Breunor was probably mad that people seemed to forget that it had been *him* leading the famous Golden Dragon Knights Army during the war.

Alpheus listened through the cone as Breunor greeted Sagramore warmly. "Aye, my old comrade! What brings you to Zorlia today?"

"This boy," Sagramore said with a grin, referring to Julian. "My idiot pupil, Percival Pole, promised me that there was a talented warrior in the capital waiting to be discovered."

"Is that so?" Breunor responded with a chuckle, glancing at both Julian and Pole.

Sagramore leaned into his old comrade. "He's a magic user," he said in a softer volume, these words causing Alpheus to jump slightly.

Does everyone know? Alpheus wondered, worrying for Julian. *But Sir Sagramore... it doesn't sound like he shares the same negative impression as the others.*

"He could well entertain at the upcoming Exchange," Sagramore finished.

"Forgive me for spoiling the mood," Breunor said, his tone suddenly bitter. "But the Roland boy has neither the discipline nor the honour to be a knight. He dared defy my commands and followed this up by refusing to accept punishment. I turned a blind eye to it all, but not only was he ungrateful—he repaid my generosity with enmity by ambushing my men, leaving them fatally injured. He has no honour. He is not worthy to contest."

Sagramore turned to Julian, who had held a closed fist at his side, regarding Breunor with a quiet scowl. The veteran golden knight then turned back to Breunor. "And what did you ask of him when he defied you?" Sagramore asked, almost as if to challenge Breunor. "I never knew how generous you were in laying down punishment, but if he can leave your men fatally injured, he can definitely compete on this level."

Breunor shook his head with a smirk. He gestured for one of his men to step forward. "Sir Kite is my youngest knight," Breunor said. "He wields the sabre. He didn't carry one today, but even then, the Roland boy wouldn't be able to lay a scratch on him."

"What are you saying?" Sagramore said with a snort. "You want them to fight *here*?"

"I want you to see how weak the boy is—how he relies on heresy—that he has no physical strength to speak of—and that he is unworthy of the Exchange."

"And the way to do that is to send out your strongest man in Orel Kite?" Sagramore said with a scoff. "Do you think me a fool?"

"This is the *Golden* Knight Exchange," Breunor responded, tone growing more and more conceited. "As the organiser of the event, I'm here to assure that all potential contestants are the best of the best."

"Victor Breunor, you—"

"Sir Sagramore, please," Julian cut in, stepping forward. "Let me." Julian unbuckled his heavy iron sword, letting it drop to the ground with a clang. He then glanced at Breunor and perhaps at Kite. "I accept your challenge," he said.

Julian..., Alpheus thought, growing more worried as he watched his friend move out to a relatively open space between the tables. Julian wasn't one to shy away from a challenge, but if what Pole had said about Orel Kite's reputation were true, then Julian might be set up for complete humiliation.

"Make way!" Breunor demanded, to which his men began to shift away some tables to make more space.

Kite soon stepped out into the open space to join Julian. The other patrons of the parlour invited themselves to watch as people gathered to form a sizeable circle.

"Whenever you're ready," Breunor said, speaking to Julian.

Julian made no reply, instead gazing at his opponent until he suddenly swung out an elbow to ignite a spark, catching a blazing flame that enveloped his arm. Gasps and incessant mumbling filled the air in response to the sorcery, but Julian didn't seem to care for any of it. He then brushed that blazing arm onto the other, effectively creating a dual weapon of burning knuckles.

Julian bolted forward now, running at his opponent in a zigzag pattern. He threw out a couple of jabs in quick succession, attacks that were made more spectacular by the red flames that roared behind their wake. Kite wasn't to be caught out, however, evading those early jabs with relative ease. His slick steps showed that he wasn't to be intimidated by the ostentatious sorcery that had the rest of the spectators in awe.

Spectacular, Alpheus thought, holding a fist in a tremble. *And Julian... he seems so comfortable with his identity as a sorcerer.*

"Is he a friend?" Reeling asked suddenly, causing Alpheus to look away from the fight.

"I... I think so," he said, before turning his attention back to the ground, where Julian had stopped to clasp his arms in a criss-cross, a gesture that immediately prodded Kite to launch himself forward as if to prevent Julian from achieving something.

The silver knight grappled Julian by his shoulder, twisting the joint until a crack sounded, the impact causing Julian to cry out in pain.

But Julian wasn't to lose the fight just yet. He responded impressively by setting his entire arm on fire to ward off Kite's grasp. Though reckless, the desperate move that injured him as well also bought Julian the space he seemed to be looking for. The silver knight had hopped away, now flapping his arms frantically to quench the fire that had overcome him.

Julian growled and murmured some words under his breath. The air around him immediately tinted to a hue of crimson red. He grunted then, seemingly his signal for that tinted atmosphere to then seep into his body.

What's this...?! Alpheus wondered, eyes widening as he watched Julian emanating a scarlet glow. He blinked away to Reeling, noting that even the courtly man wore a surprised expression.

Back on the ground, even Sagramore and Breunor leaned in at least slightly. Kite, who had smothered out the flames on his arm, simply stood his ground now, but more than a hint of concern had already crept up his face under the red glow. All eyes were on Julian... until he suddenly disappeared into thin air.

Just then, to Kite's immediate left, a fire-enhanced fist appeared and crashed into his face. Kite, rather impressively, managed to maintain his footing, even drawing on the impetus to counter, only for Julian to flash away once again. Kite then turned to his right, perhaps expecting Julian to go there next, which Julian did, but only to blur from view almost as soon as he had appeared. Julian flashed in for a third time soon—this time from above, striking Kite on the crown of his head—which sent the silver knight collapsing to his knees, in turn cracking open a crevice in the marble floor.

The initial idea was a fair battle without weapons. But now that Julian had called on sorcery to his aid, as well as the blessing of superhuman speeds, the battle wasn't exactly fair anymore. No one should be expected to be able to follow Julian's movements with their eyes alone. For Kite, it would have been almost as if he was fighting with blindfolds. Indeed, Kite was forced to attempt to predict where Julian would strike next, seemingly striking out at random.

Julian maintained the pressure and the intensity, flashing about everywhere, causing headaches in more than just the skull of his opponent but also to many of those who were watching from the sidelines. He goaded the silver knight to run, as he himself dashed about at amazing speeds that left only specks of the scarlet glow visible to the naked eye. He stopped for a moment, finally manifesting as a whole, before charging at Kite head on. Kite threw out a rare punch finally, which Julian avoided by spurting off at the last moment, before flashing behind the silver knight, allowing him no chance to block or retaliate.

This time, Kite was sent scraping across the marble floor. Breunor nearly fell out of his chair, flustered as he was by the battle taking place before him.

It was likely the first time that most of the onlookers there had seen magic. They should be frowning upon it, but many were instead marvelling now at the phenomenon before them. The already divided opinions about sorcery were surely to intensify after today.

Unbelievable, Alpheus thought, feeling his heart thumping in excitement. *Is that... something I could manage too? Do I want that?*

Back on the ground, everything was silent. Sagramore and Breunor exchanged a look, likely both in awe. Kite was still down, but Julian's heavy breathing showed that he didn't have it easy, either. Julian probably wished that his opponent was finished, but Kite responded with a groan and a twitch now, sitting up slowly but surely. He glared furiously at Julian as he rose to his feet, blood dribbling from his mouth.

This couldn't be good, Alpheus thought, watching Julian put a hand over his chest, looking exhausted.

Breunor tossed a sabre over to Kite, who snatched it from the air. The silver knight slashed out the sword from its sheath in a heartbeat, drawing a puff of visible dust in the air as he did so. Sagramore shook his head, but his disciple, Pole, responded by hurling Julian's iron sword to Julian.

Both men wielded swords now, and were already slashing away at one another. Alpheus rose to his feet then with urgency, realising with grave concern the danger that was inching closer to Julian. Some of the spectators might have been thinking how unfair it was for Orel Kite to have to face off against a sorcerer, but no one seemed to realise the price Julian had to pay—that his body was close to shutting down, that his bones were imploding, his nerves swelling.

Julian whacked out the giant chunk of iron, but his opponent parried off the dangerous blade. Kite then followed with a slash of his own, but which drew nothing but air, as Julian had once again flashed off to a distance—appearing suddenly to Kite's immediate right and connecting with an elbow to the face.

While everyone else still seemed to be marvelling at Julian's skill, Alpheus noted that his friend's scarlet glow was evaporating, and it was far too dangerous to expend any more grace. Kite might have suffered a few injuries, but if the battle was to continue, Julian was certain to lose.

"What a crowd we have here," a voice announced from the entrance.

The spectators turned at once, and there under the wide arc of the grand entrance was a group of men led by Quinlan Forredan, who stomped in with his enormous bulk the size of more than two regular men. Golden Knight Claude Lucan accompanied the portly statesman, as usual.

"Lord Breunor," Forredan greeted in delight, shuffling in through the crowd. "And Sir Sagramore. What's the occasion? And why was I not invited?"

His jolly demeanour evaporated the tense tone from before, but if anything, Alpheus was glad for the intermission—glad for Julian.

Sagramore lifted his chin at Forredan, staring down the statesman. "And what brings you here, Lord Forredan?"

The statesman glared at Julian then. "That boy," he said. "I am here to arrest him."

"What crime did he commit?" Breunor asked, sounding hopeful.

"Treason," Forredan said, clicking his men to surround Julian. "Roland has infiltrated a mining site in Carrington. He instigated the peasants for a rebellion."

Ludicrous! Alpheus thought, eyeing Julian, who seemed to be as baffled as anyone. He was ready to crash down upon the scene to ensure Julian's safety. And he would have if Reeling hadn't held him by his sleeves, shaking his head forcibly as if imploring him to be patient for just another moment longer.

"Get out of the way!" Kite said in protest, surprising everyone by shoving aside one of Forredan's men, seemingly still looking to continue his fight with Julian. "Roland is mine!"

Whether it was a persistence to prove his strength or to end a battle that he had started, Alpheus thought Kite an honourable man. The young knight might well be one of the most promising young knights of the country, but he hadn't quite been able to show his ability today, not against Julian who had surprised him with every single move. Alpheus didn't think he knew much about combat arts, but he was inclined to believe that Kite would fare much better against Julian the next time the two met.

Breunor was having none of it, however. There was no way the military man would risk crossing Forredan for something so trivial. At the end, Breunor gestured to the towering Walford Bors, who, after a sigh, forcefully led Kite out of the building.

Julian was on his own again. The five knights up against him were perhaps a lesser threat than Orel Kite, in the end, but Julian was handicapped with severe fatigue and, most likely, barely a hint of grace left.

Sagramore stood up suddenly, thumping the end of his partisan on the floor, before inviting himself into the middle of it all. "No one will take his life today," he said, stepping next to Julian. "Regardless of the crimes he is accused of, the boy is undoubtedly a warrior." He then turned to Breunor. "I believe you saw what I saw. The boy isn't only a magic user. He is a user of Time-Shifting."

The proclamation was a shock. Time-Shifting was a power described only in legends, capable of greatly speeding up or slowing down movement. The legend was so popular that even Alpheus had heard about it, and that the Longinus family of Mt. Pinnacle were known to use the power. The family was also known as famous clock makers who rivalled the Roland family of the same region. Roland was of course a common name, but Alpheus—and perhaps everyone else—started to make the connection anyway, suspecting that Julian *was* a Roland descendant who might have thieved his rival family of their most valuable secret.

"That *was* Time-Shifting," Breunor admitted with a frown. "No ordinary man could catch such speed."

The people gazed at Julian for answers, but he offered nothing. Still, the crowd had seemingly grown excited at the prospect, and Julian, in turn, seemed to enjoy the positive reaction.

"Heretics," Breunor inserted with disdain, shaking his head. "To think you were related to them, and to think that you may have pilfered your way into learning their heresy."

"Absurdity!" Sagramore snapped back. "Time-Shifting is the skill every warrior wishes to learn. You will *not* speak ill of it."

Breunor sneered at the remark. He stroked his mutton chops again. "Were the Longinus not massacred by mere outlaws?"

The atmosphere suddenly turned downcast. Julian, too, closed his eyes in response, neither admitting nor denying the claim. There were many stories about what happened to the once powerful Longinus family, and the story told most often was that the family had been incompetent to begin with, and that the power of Time-Shifting was greatly exaggerated.

"What is the greatest skill in the land?" Breunor said, presenting the question rather than asking it. "For decades, every warrior in the land acknowledged that it is the *Seraphic Aura*, an energy skill recorded in the *Humboldtianum Manual*. Though the tome itself has been lost for years, many people—including myself—are in the firm belief that it exists, and without question the highest level of combat arts. And second to the Seraphic Aura…?"

Breunor paused there, his grin growing deeper, adding to a sinister undertone. "It is said to be Time-Shifting," he continued. "Unfortunately, it was but a big conspiracy—an ironic one at that—for Time-Shifting was unable to stand the test of time," he continued. "Through the years, there were a great many people desiring to challenge the Longinus, but no one did because they were all afraid to lose. But on the one account where the family *was* challenged, they were reduced to shreds. That was the *Mt. Pinnacle Massacre*. Their keeper, Royston Longinus, once thought to be a powerful mage—fled like a coward and is probably still in hiding today."

Breunor now turned to Julian. "Tell me, boy, are you proud to learn the skills of that cowardly family?"

Julian snarled at the military man in response. But Breunor wasn't the only unfriendly face around. All around Julian were faces of contempt, contempt directed at the Longinus family and their sensational fall from power to the pitiful reputation people now ascribed to them.

"What's that look?" Breunor questioned, staring down Julian. "You're not asking for a fight, are you?"

"One day," Julian finally said. "One day, when I grow stronger. Don't expect me to forget this."

"One day…? A true warrior fights his battles in the now."

"You sure talk a lot," Julian said, clenching his fists.

Breunor simpered. "What, are you thinking to challenge me?! Let me tell you: even if Time-Shifting *was* a real thing, it stands no chance against me. Given that you rely on this magic act to fight your battles, you clearly don't understand what it means to be a true warrior. Magic is mere trickery. It lacks substance. It will never prevail over physical strength. A real knight will never lose to a heretic."

The people in the crowd had turned against Julian, and perhaps more so against the Longinus family. The air of animosity overwhelmed Julian, who now managed only a snide smile, which Alpheus was sure only he could see.

"Since it's come to this," Julian said, spinning to address the crowd, "there's no longer a reason to hide. I never snuck anywhere to learn. My teacher *was* Royston Longinus. The man is… my father." He then paused to make sure his audience was ready for the final revelation. "My real name is Julian Longinus."

Just when the people thought nothing could surprise them anymore, this heavy claim sparked a chain of reactions—mostly of disbelief, of doubt. At the same time, many of those same people looked like they wished it *were* true. A connection of any capacity with Royston Longinus—who had been, and perhaps still was a deified figure—was probably a fantasy come true. In the end, it seemed like the people couldn't overcome the ambivalence they had for the Longinus family.

"Who you are makes no difference!" Breunor roared, before peering out at the crowd. "The boy's a criminal, a heretic! And if he *were* the son of Royston Longinus, he'd be the son of a coward. Don't fall into the fairy tale. There's nothing to be excited about here." Breunor turned then to the stout statesman. "Lord Forredan, please. You were here to seize him, were you not?"

"Yes, Lord Breunor, but this has become quite a revelation," Forredan said. "Why don't we give it some pause?"

Breunor said no more, but instead gestured at Bors, who would do his bidding: a sneaky, full-throttled thrust of his giant maul shot suddenly forward at Julian.

Alpheus gasped, realising the suddenness of this new threat of death. His soft cry would do nothing to save his friend. No one could save Julian at that range, not from a golden knight.

And yet, Julian would survive again. A speck of light came crashing down from the skies to deflect away the heavy maul—which then spun dangerously in the air before falling with a loud clang to the marble floor.

The people lifted their heads, and only then did Alpheus realise that the person who had intervened was Reeling—the Lord Count—still sitting across him. Reeling stood, gazing down at everyone, wearing a smug expression. "Quite a scene we have here," he said.

Reeling then dove down with a spectacular entrance, his trench coat floating behind him like the wings of a vulture, landing gracefully in the middle of the action. He brushed a hand over the marble floor to retrieve the item he had shot out, hiding it away before anyone but Alpheus realised it had happened. The courtly man had used the same power that had helped him overcome the Apostle. And today, he had used it to deflect away a giant maul.

THIRTEEN

The amazing Lord Count

Alpheus peered about, looking for a quick way to get down. Having watched everything pan out from the start, he didn't want to miss what was next. In the end, he resorted to taking the stairs, racing down as fast as he could.

When he finally reached the ground, he was panting, but he was glad to realise that everyone was still at a standstill. Breunor had tensed up, cringing slightly even. Forredan winced. It was apparent that they didn't like Reeling. But it also looked like they feared Reeling, who seemed to be radiating an air that melted others—an air that oozed confidence and fearlessness—a quality Alpheus had never really paid much heed to in the past.

Walford Bors had retrieved his maul. He looked shocked, probably still wondering how it had happened. He wouldn't want it to be the focus, though. Indeed, the giant man said no word as he returned behind Breunor.

"Lord Count," Breunor finally greeted, wearing a forced smile. "That was quite an entrance. You're not here only to surprise us, are you?"

Reeling grinned at him. "That would depend on what you're doing."

"Lord Breunor was here to see Sir Sagramore," Forredan answered for the military man. "And I'm here to take Julian Roland... or was it Longinus? I don't know. Either way, the boy is mine."

Julian was still shivering from his near-death experience. Alpheus trotted toward him, helping him to his feet, and helping appease his terror.

"Who in God's name are you?" Forredan questioned, wincing at Alpheus, but pausing soon after his own question. The stout statesman seemed to have noted the chrome-plated pocket watch dangling at his girdle, which was the token that proved he was a State Scholar.

"You again," Breunor said, apparently recognising Alpheus from their single encounter in this very building. "You damned scholar... how *dare* you poke your head in our affairs!"

Alpheus pouted, still panting. "I have not the slightest interest in your affairs. But if you were to torment him, you'd have me to ask."

Julian glanced up at Alpheus in spite of his exhaustion.

Reeling clapped his hands in applause, regarding Alpheus with pride.

"Lord Count," Breunor said with a huff. "I have duties to perform, and I would appreciate it if you didn't interfere."

"And I am here to perform my duties as Count," Reeling claimed. "I am surveying potential candidates for the Golden Knight Exchange. And with the Empire's blessing, I'm delighted to say that I have found one today." Reeling regarded Julian now, who gawked back. "I want to see Julian Longinus at the Exchange."

The crowd exchanged stupefied looks. Even Julian himself was taken aback.

"Not so fast!" Breunor cried, raising a hand. "The boy's guilty of treason."

"I do not believe he is," Reeling said, shaking his head. "Ask your advisor. I believe his name was Nelson."

Breunor grunted and then turned to his retinue, eyeing the only man who wasn't of the fighter class. The aged Nelson was probably an advisor to Breunor for on-court matters. But this aged man didn't look his best now. Not only was he trembling visibly, but his eyes were drifting about with unease, peering everywhere but at Reeling.

"Nelson's your vassal," Reeling said. "He holds the evidence to prove Julian Longinus's innocence. Did he not update you?"

Breunor huffed again, regarding Nelson with knitted brows. The old man leaned in to the military man's ear and whispered something. Breunor flinched upon hearing it, almost stumbling, finding his feet again only after shaking his head. He said nothing to Nelson, but he was visibly stunned.

Breunor turned back slowly to Reeling, looking away just before their eyes met.

"So," Reeling said, "am I correct to say that Julian Longinus is cleared of all crimes? May I grant him entry to the Exchange?"

"You may," Breunor answered reluctantly, to gasps from the crowd.

"What is this about?" Forredan inserted with a curious grin.

"Nothing, really," Breunor offered with a wave of his hands. "But allow me to apologise, Lord Forredan. The ones who instigated those peasants in Carrington were some of... *my* men—inadvertently, of course! But no, it wasn't the Roland boy at all. I assure all present that I'll see the situation corrected."

Forredan raised a brow, regarding Reeling, perhaps suspecting that

Reeling had some handle on Breunor. Alpheus suspected the same thing.

"Lord Count," Forredan then said, "I have no intention to challenge you. But the boy works for me. If anyone is to grant him entry, it should be me."

Reeling grinned at him. "I beg to differ."

"The boy has worked for me for months," Forredan claimed with a snort. "Will you take him from my grip?"

"With all due respect, Lord Forredan, you made Julian Longinus a peasant. You may have changed your mind about him in light of the revelation just now, but you are a tad late. Thanks to the Lord Emperor, one of the first laws laid down in this Advent Era was the ordinance for people with power to cultivate those who show special talents. Reports tell me that it was a conscious decision to send Julian Longinus to a career as a miner—and that it was in spite of the talent he showed. For your mistake, you have forfeited the right to be his liege."

The statesman grimaced as the flaps beneath his cheeks formed distinct stacks.

"Please don't look at me like that, Lord Forredan," Reeling said with a snicker. "I actually have a present for you. I stopped by Carrington only a few days ago, and I did you a favour."

Forredan forced a grin, wearing that jolly mask to hide his confusion and anger. "How kind of you, Lord Count. And what might this present be?"

"I convinced a retired warrior to take part in the Exchange," Reeling said. "Someone to represent you."

Golden Knight Lucan flinched behind the statesman.

"The name's Tannon Gale," Reeling announced now, surprising more than just Forredan and Lucan. The veterans in the building—including Sagramore, Breunor, and Bors—all seemed to be familiar with that name.

"He might not at his best right now," Reeling continued, "but I am sure that with your guidance, Lord Forredan, we shall see another exciting participant at the Exchange."

The statesman exchanged a look with Lucan, which seemed to ask if they should simply take Reeling's word for it. Their suspicions—if any—were forgotten, however, when Reeling then gestured to the wide arcing entrance from where many distinguished guests had passed through in the last hour. Stepping in was an imposing man, armoured in dark red with the embossment of a blazing salamander on the breastplate. His eyes were rolled wide open, exuding an air of vigour. His hair was tied into a neat ponytail, while his beard was trimmed to a stubble. The men who knew him recognised him immediately—even Julian gawked at the newcomer, who he also seemed to know.

"You're finally back!" Lucan cried, lurching forward for an embrace, clasping the other man in his arms. "This is a dream no more."

"Claude," the newcomer addressed him. "Let us fight together once more." He then turned to the stout statesman from afar, sparing no glance elsewhere as he then treaded to the stately man. "I have returned," he said as he bent down on one knee. "I owe everything to you for not giving up on me."

Forredan beamed at him, seemingly at a loss for words. "Good, good," was all he could utter.

The stately man then stood, peering out to the people. He wasn't tall, but his tremendous waistline—along with his esteemed status—attracted all the attention he wanted. "I ask the men here to note that I have, from this moment, terminated all ties with Julian Longinus. But I'd like to add that I, Quinlan Forredan, would also want to see the boy appear at the Exchange."

Forredan regarded Reeling now, nodding at him. "If you would excuse me," the portly man then said, "I have other chores to attend to."

The newcomer afforded a slight nod at Reeling too before joining the others. As the group marched out, Breunor stood, looking to depart as well.

"Before you go," Reeling said, without turning to him.

The military man paused with a quiet sigh. "Yes…?" he asked, also reluctant to turn.

"The Exchange will be great," Reeling said. "And for that to happen, let Orel Kite be part of it."

Breunor nodded and then headed swiftly out of the building, taking with him the approximately twenty men who he had come with. Reeling simply shrugged, turning back to meet the eyes of Sagramore, the only other man of great authority who remained in the building.

"I look forward to the Exchange," Sagramore said, rising to his feet. He glanced over to Julian and then laid his eyes once more upon Reeling. "Prior to this, I have thought this upcoming Exchange to be something of a joke. But with Julian Longinus at the centre of it, it has become quite intriguing indeed. Tannon Gale has committed to be a part of it, and intuition tells me Orel Kite will partake too." The veteran golden knight paused then, glancing at his famed pupil. "Percival shall partake as well. And I ask of you, Lord Count, to support him while he's here in Zorlia."

Pole shook his head in confusion. "Master… but you didn't want me to…"

"It's time," Sagramore said. "It's time that you showed the Empire just what you're capable of."

* * *

The day had been admittedly interesting so far for Alpheus. And now as he was lined up next to Julian and Pole who had both been invited back to Reeling's chambers in Vondra Dawn, Alpheus was hopeful that the courtly man was going to offer something more to Julian, perhaps help make him a silver knight. He didn't know if Reeling had the power to arrange for that, but it was certainly exciting to see Reeling take Julian under his wings.

Reeling regarded Pole first, who stood on the far right. "I've been watching you for some time," he said. "You have a unique reputation here in Vondra Dawn. It is a shame we did not acquaint earlier."

Pole bowed down slightly, and sombrely too, in a manner rather different from his usual flamboyant flattery of men with power. "Your words are too generous, Lord Count. I owe you my gratitude for your involvement today."

Alpheus winced at the exchange. Initially, he had thought that Reeling was merely doing a favour for the great Paltiel Sagramore, but it was looking more and more like Reeling was actually fond of Pole. He glanced over to Julian who seemed similarly clueless about the vibe between Reeling and Pole. Julian *did* seem surprised by Alpheus's relationship with Reeling, however—perhaps even upset that Alpheus had never brought it up.

Reeling eyed Julian then. "Longinus," he began with a pleasurable sigh. "I can hardly believe I am speaking to a descendant of the family famed for Time-Shifting. It is truly an honour."

Julian nodded politely. "The past is the past," he said with a slight shrug. "But thank you, Lord Count. Thank you for helping me. Please allow me to make it up to you."

Reeling shook his head with a smile. "No, I have no need for your services. Quinlan Forredan might not be the man to follow, but neither am I."

Julian frowned slightly. "But—"

"I am well-served as it is already," Reeling cut in.

Julian sighed, trying his best to make peace with it. He hesitated then. "I... do have a request, though," he said. "Something that might pique your interest."

"Oh?" Reeling said with a wry grin.

"There's a man I seek," Julian continued in a grave tone, swallowing the excessive saliva in his mouth as he spoke. "I believe he holds the key to my past, and everything that has to do with the Longinus family."

"Are you speaking of *Yesod*, the *Marvel Mage*?"

The enunciation of that name had Julian trembling suddenly. "How did you—?! Do you—?!"

"It was but a wild guess."

Julian's brows knitted with suspicion. "So, can you help me?" he said.

Reeling regarded him gravely. He stood up from his chair and then turned to the window. "Let us hear the story."

Julian cleared his throat. "We were a family from the famed Mt. Pinnacle, one of the *Four Holy Peaks*. We were makers of hourglasses. We used only natural quartz sand, a type of sand whose angular shape usually flows poorly through glass. But we made it work—the Longinus hourglasses were produced to excellent quality, and their accuracy in timekeeping was unmatched."

He paused there, looking at one of the bookshelves left of Reeling's desk where an hourglass of the Longinus brand sat. "But I'm not here to boast about that," he continued. "Let me first say that my skill in Time-Shifting is barely a glimmer of my father's ability. I'm no longer bothered by the speculation of what happened. The truth is: I don't know. But the one thing I can be sure of is that no one could even land a scratch on my father... other than *him*—that man called Yesod."

Julian sighed again, this time heavily. "It was thirteen years ago—his first visit," he said. "He must have been barely a man at the time—still a child. And yet, he dared to challenge my father. He didn't win, but he didn't necessarily lose, either. And three months after that, he visited a second time. I don't why, but it was days after that second visit when my father went off to chase him... my mother too. I haven't seen them since.

"And it was a year later...," he continued, frowning deeply, "when *that* happened. It's what people now call the *Mt. Pinnacle Massacre*—an assault of the Longinus Manor. Without my father, we stood no chance against the clan of mercenaries who massacred all forms of life. I was fortunate enough to survive, thanks to the house butler who knocked me unconscious beforehand, hiding me beneath the floor."

Alpheus had teared up, sniffing audibly. In turn, Julian blinked hard to relieve himself of the tears that blurred his vision. Pole seemed to share the grief as well.

"These mercenaries," Reeling said, his back still facing the others. "Were they there for Time-Shifting? Legend has it that it is recorded in a tome. Did they get it?"

"If there's a tome, then I've never seen it," Julian said. "My father taught me without any tomes. And... did the mercenaries get it...? Seeing that no one has made a name with Time-Shifting for the last decade, I would think those mercenaries left with nothing... besides the massacre."

"Then why do you seek him?" Reeling asked. "Yesod—do you think he did it? Do you think your parents are dead?"

Julian shook his head. "I don't know, but that man must know something."

"Why are you asking me? How do you know you can trust me?"

"Perhaps I cannot," Julian admitted. "I don't usually rely on intuition, but it is intuition that tells me that you can help. I've heard things about you, and I've wanted to see you for a long time. I don't know if I can trust you, but I want to trust that you can track that man. I believe you can give me a point at which to begin."

Reeling didn't turn around, apparently not given in by the supposed flattery. "Your circumstances are... grim," he said, spinning back finally to regard Julian. "But my schedule is stacked as it is. And besides, this might be beyond me. I don't know if I can help when—"

"You can!" Julian inserted. "I know you can. So, please...!"

Alpheus glared at Reeling, and that seemed to do the trick as Reeling sighed heavily. "All right, but I cannot promise anything. And I can only investigate when I find the time—which is seldom."

Julian smiled then, looking over to Alpheus, who grinned back.

"Before I forget," Reeling said, narrowing his eyes at Julian, "let me say this: you need to learn to treasure your life. I knew very little of you prior to today, but from what I have seen on this day alone, you do not seem to value your existence. If you are not living for yourself, then you should at least live for the legacy of your family. I do not want to see Time-Shifting die with you."

Julian looked away, perhaps reluctant to accept the criticism.

"Yorke!" Reeling called. The butler had been standing just outside the chambers, and he stepped in now ready to receive orders. "Arrange for Sir Longinus and Sir Pole to be equipped with the necessary items that they would need at the Exchange."

"Understood," Yorke replied, snatching out the two men, leaving only Alpheus behind.

"So," Reeling said, growing suddenly relaxed. "How are you finding your first day?"

Alpheus thought for a moment. "I suppose it was interesting," he admitted finally. "I missed a couple of details, though. First of all, who was that man in the dark red armour... Gale, was it?"

"Would you care to venture a guess?"

"Well, seeing that he bowed down to Quinlan Forredan, I'd assume he works for the man. It looked like some kind of reunion. Could he be a veteran knight who was thought to be dead, but had somehow survived?"

"Almost," Reeling said, nodding with a subtle smile. "Tannon Gale is indeed a veteran knight, a man who had sworn his loyalty to Forredan for over twenty years. Back in his most glorious days, Gale was the commander of an army known as the Salamanders. No one thought he was dead, but metaphorically speaking—for a long time—he was as good as dead, living a miserable life as a peasant—miserable in that it was his means of escaping from a humiliating defeat he thought defined him.

"But although Gale's story is noteworthy, I am only telling you about it so that you can appreciate Forredan's character."

"Forredan?" Alpheus asked. "What about him?"

"The man insisted on keeping Gale as a peasant under his watch, despite his usual ways of *discarding* any men who had fallen from grace. And today, he was finally rewarded. His resourcefulness is extraordinary indeed."

"Twenty years *is* a long investment, I suppose," Alpheus said, glancing at the hourglass. "Anyway," he continued, shaking his head, "the other person I couldn't work out was Nelson. What was he hiding with Victor Breunor?"

"Nelson is his advisor... and his spy," Reeling said. "He's been watching me since they arrived in Zorlia. Espionage is, of course, very common. To succeed—and indeed to even survive on this stage—one must never reveal their true selves. I had Nelson believing what I wanted him to believe, which in turn allowed me to get what I wanted from him."

Reeling brushed a hand over his coat pocket, picking out a parchment, but not flapping it out. "This is my handle against them," he continued. "If this fell in the wrong hands, not only would Breunor be stripped of his powers, but the balance of the powers in the Empire would change as well. There is much at stake."

"What is it?" Alpheus asked, growing suddenly curious.

"Still too early for you to know," Reeling responded, slipping the parchment away, between a couple of books on the shelf. "From now on, I need you to earn your right to accessing confidential information."

* * *

Julian departed Vondra Dawn now with privileges that he had thought might elude him forever. He was now a rightful participant of the Golden Knight Exchange. Though still a soldier by rank, the obsidian pocket watch Yorke had helped him collect was his token to accessing all of the resources that he needed in order to prepare himself. He had even been offered a home in *Stapleton*, which was just outside Vondra Dawn and which was known as the central living area for knights, often colloquially referred to as the *Stables*. It was the greatest of privileges to be provided with a home by the Empire, and yet Julian had refused it, for he already had a place to return to every day in Ramsgate.

He didn't want to admit it, but he had been living with the young boy Oscar and he had enjoyed every day of it. The run-down, abandoned chapel where they had first gotten to know each other was now a place they both called home. And after reworking the chapel little by little, it had become a place they were both fond of.

His bond with Oscar surprised even Julian himself. Oscar was playful, mischievous, and, at times, disobedient. But Julian believed that the boy's demeanour and character was a reflection of what Julian himself would have become if not for the Mt. Pinnacle Massacre. And while initially, it had been more or less a chore, Julian had since grown accustomed to spending his free time mentoring the boy. He had even taught him to defend himself with the sword—he had given the boy a wooden one with which to practice.

Julian cherished the moment now as he watched the boy sleeping peacefully. He had unknowingly started to consider the boy his own little brother, which left him wondering whether he would ever experience the warmth of a true family again.

FOURTEEN

The court of Vondra Dawn

Alpheus found himself finally crossing paths with Christopher Hartland, the *other* scholar who had recently found a home of sorts in Vondra Dawn. Their last meeting had been at the symposium, and Hartland had, on that same day, issued his challenge to Alpheus to emerge as the stand-out scholar of their class.

"What I do, you ask...," Hartland said with a sneer. "I see you have not changed even now that we are in Vondra Dawn. Still ignorant." He paused there, shaking his head. "I work for Lord Morlan, as a squire for Sir John Tristan."

"Ah," Alpheus noted. "The Golden Knight of Cetal."

"Not just any golden knight. Sir Tristan was the first of his generation."

"Good for you," said Alpheus, raising an eyebrow.

Hartland nodded with a grin. "Indeed," he said. "And what of you? I've wondered what you could contribute. I'll be all ears this afternoon."

"This afternoon," Alpheus said, repeating the words in confusion. "What's this afternoon?"

"You really don't know anything, do you?" Hartland said, rolling his eyes. "To think that you work for the Lord Count."

Don't recall him mentioning this, Alpheus thought.

"The monthly court assembly," Hartland said. "Court runs almost every day... to tackle specific issues. Yesterday, for instance, was about the conflicts at the Seniblum frontier. There's a lot that goes on behind how a country is run. And once a month, every facet is conferred, and hopefully, resolved."

Alpheus nodded. Reeling had been telling him quite a lot about seemingly random topics, but the man hadn't said anything about going to court.

The conversation ended there, with Alpheus heading back to Reeling's chambers in the western towers. It had been two weeks since Alpheus had begun working as the Lord Count's assistant—precisely the time frame he had set for himself when he had first agreed to help. Whether he had *done* any work or shared a load of Reeling's troubles was another matter.

In any case, Alpheus had enjoyed his stay, and although he wouldn't admit it, he marvelled at the way Reeling worked. The courtly man was incredible—he could move mountains if he wanted to. Nothing was out of the question if he chose to have a hand in it. The only person Reeling ever consulted was Yorke, who Alpheus had come to learn was an incredibly capable man himself, often resolving problems with great efficiency even when those problems were outside of Zorlia. Despite his abilities, however, Yorke was first to admit that he could never keep up with his liege.

The place itself, Vondra Dawn, also had its positives. It allowed Alpheus to witness how the Empire operated, how the city of Zorlia functioned, and to understand the role of Trubannis on a larger scale.

Of the five countries in the land, Trubannis had long been the largest and the most resourceful. This status had only strengthened after the war against Vinawell of the west and Kraga of the south. King Steele of Vinawell had since signed a peace treaty with Trubannis while King Bardorinoff of Kraga had been usurped by their current leader, King Wandalvic, who had issued a written apology to all countries involved. Even so, the Kragan Dynasty could never be overlooked as long as Milos Rachkoltesz, the draconian strategist credited for igniting the war, remained at his post.

Alpheus had also been learning the *Falling Comet* from Reeling, the skill that had deflected Walford Bors's giant maul at the parlour with only the flick of a die.

Reeling had also urged Alpheus to further his knowledge of sorcery, and it was a request with which Alpheus had gradually been making his peace with. He had tried not to think too much about it, and to accommodate that goal, he had gifted the sapphire ring to Julian, who needed it more than Alpheus himself did. In the process, he had also explained to Julian that he was a sorcerer as well. While Alpheus wasn't sure whether Julian empathised with him on what it meant to suddenly realise a new power, it had been somewhat liberating to share the news with someone who was an actual sorcerer as well as a friend.

"I was told...," Alpheus said now with slight hesitation, "that we're attending an important event this afternoon."

"You could say that," Reeling responded, his eyes firmly focused on his work, showing no interest in elaborating.

It was another hour later when they finally set off. As he tagged behind

Reeling and Yorke, Alpheus thought the citadel more of a maze than he cared for. The narrow alleys, dark passageways, and obscure access between different rooms reminded him of the academy—in particular, its higher floors. Impenetrable and discreet.

They were nearing their destination—the highest point of Vondra Dawn. From the next wide set of spiral stairs, wide enough even for up to five men to pass, imposing voices showered down from above. The reverberations had Alpheus shaking a little. And as they finally pushed open a heavy double door, they stepped foot into the court, where Alpheus was briefly blinded by the abundance of natural light shining through a huge glass window. He rubbed his eyes, blinking away the brightness, and when he looked up again, he gasped to find the space filled with noblemen and other lords—at least more than fifty men.

Alpheus assumed that the spiral stairs were the only way in and out of the court until he noted a door adjacent to the large window. He also regarded a giant hanging bell to the far right of the unspectacular throne that, at this moment at least, wasn't occupied. The emperor hadn't yet arrived. The men continued talking in small groups, but soon the attention was directed his way—though the focus was on Reeling, who was apparently the last to arrive aside from the Lord Emperor.

"Late again, I see," someone commented.

Alpheus looked up to see the portly figure that was Quinlan Forredan. He spared no glance at him or Reeling as he busied himself with trimming his nails, sitting comfortably at one of the few seats there.

"Our Lord Count is quite the self-important man," Forredan added, to which Reeling simply grinned in response.

"I'd worry if he arrived later than the emperor," another man remarked, sitting a couple seats away and speaking with a strong voice that seemed to drown out all of the others.

Alpheus eyed the man from the feet up, noting an imperial garb that stood out even among the many noblemen there. Hanging from the man's broad shoulders was an impressive robe of fine wool with a lavish patch of snowy white fur woven around its collar. It signified authority greater than even that afforded to Forredan. And beneath the attire was a muscular bulk that rendered even Victor Breunor ordinary by comparison.

The seated man shot a grin at Reeling. His hair was a simple flattop, and besides the white fur on his robe, his outfit wasn't at all garish. And yet, effusing out of him was an air of dominance—of eminence—that seemed to keep all of the other men in check.

The Lord Chancellor, Yeremia Schim, Alpheus realised with quiet reverence. *The challenger to the throne.*

Reeling nodded at the Lord Chancellor and then found a seat next to Pierre Morlan, the man who had once been pronounced King of Cetal. Alpheus followed, his eyes never wandering far away from Schim. Morlan sat on the first seat of the east end, opposite them. He stood out even among the many distinguished figures present, with broad shoulders, a strong build, and his stern yet welcoming physiognomy. But, of course, he was without a crown, the one sign of stature that yet eluded him as long as he stayed in Zorlia.

Some men shuffled past Alpheus then, nudging him. Alpheus peered over, and there was Christopher Hartland gazing directly at him. Hartland was with Morlan and Golden Knight Sir Tristan, as expected.

Must say he makes this less scary, Alpheus thought.

Suddenly, a thundering noise rang out across the court from the giant bell hanging to the right of the throne. The emperor was arriving.

This would mark the first time that Alpheus had been in the company of the leader of the country, this man of humble beginnings who had battled his way up to arguably the most enviable position in the land. The noblemen fell silent and they all looked toward the door at the far corner under the bell.

A man stepped out, the platinum crown atop his head signifying his esteemed identity, as too did the maroon-coloured cloak resting on the shoulders that clipped onto near-black armour shaped like claws at the hand and feet. The man's narrow eyes of dark blue glistened in the light, and when he glanced his way, Alpheus felt chills going down his spine.

The emperor's pale skin, almost-colourless lips, and long silvery hair were evidence of his Aizar descent, which had never been a secret. He was striking in appearance, with a slim figure to match. And his charisma seemed to leap out at those around him, rendering the men in subservient postures.

Trailing behind him was yet another distinguished figure donning a gleaming suit of armour of bright, deep gold, Lionel Lachman, widely believed as the strongest of all knights. He was a friendlier person in appearance than such a title would normally afford, and one would assume him to be a man of noble character, almost like Yusuf Seer, but was instead a knight of the highest order.

As he reached the throne, the emperor turned with impressive agility, flipping up the tail of his robe before sinking into the chair. He leaned forward with a hand at his chin, eyeing his men in a way that left people without a doubt about who ruled.

"Let us begin," he said finally.

This was the third month since the arrival of Forredan, Breunor, and Morlan. Today was apparently about them more than anyone else. This was the best forum to outline the progress, purpose, and visions of the tasks that they had been undertaking and how they had contributed to the Empire. The major discussion point on the agenda was the Golden Knight Exchange, which was to commence on the first day of February with five rounds spanning fifteen days.

Breunor was first to speak, and he did so with passion, highlighting his contribution to improving the combat quality of participants with his rigorous training methods.

"Through my interaction with numerous soldiers and knight classes," the military man began, "I am proud to announce that I have increased my roster of candidates to participate in the Exchange to nine men."

Alpheus had learned that Breunor had once been opposed against holding the Exchange, but it appeared now that the man was working the hardest to ensure it was successful.

As the discussion went on, however, Breunor's incentive to do his best became apparent. Much was at stake for him because the performance of the warriors he nominated or developed was to determine whether he would be bestowed with the powerful authority to command *all* the armies under the Empire.

Reeling had exposed Breunor as a somewhat rash leader since his relocation to Zorlia, but Reeling was also the one who had suggested the idea of giving Breunor this utmost authority if he managed to prove his worth. Reeling had argued that, despite the number of impressive armies that were already part of the Truban Empire—which included the Golden Dragon Knights, the Defence Army of Bastion City, the bountiful Cetal Legion, the remnants of the Central Light Army, and the Secondary Light Army—there wasn't a single man who could spearhead all of these armies at once. Victor Breunor might just be the best person for the job.

It was the perfect opportunity for Breunor to step up to the challenge and then reap the benefits. As a former golden knight, Breunor's strength in combat was undeniable. His vast experience, both in personal duels and wars, allowed him the status of a master-class general in training new soldiers.

The court seemed to believe that Breunor simply knew where best to attack and defend, whether the enemy was a solitary target or an entire army.

However, the court still wanted to see Breunor prove his ability to foster the skills of new warriors, and that was despite the credit he had received for developing his very own golden knight vassal in Walford Bors, more commonly known as the *Titan*.

Bors was also in attendance today. But while his sturdy build and impressive raw strength were believed to be the mightiest of all the golden knights, hearsay suggested that Bors lacked the combat strategies expected of golden knights, and that he would fare poorly if matched up against the others in a real battle.

The next to report was Forredan. From his highly successful history as a jeweller, and experience as the State Minister of affluent Whitesand, he had been primarily responsible for maintaining order in the economic activities and trading with foreign countries Vinawell, Aizary, and Seniblum. Management and the control of resources were apparently second nature for him, so while everything reported was in good order, it was expected. The statesman's more interesting contribution, however, was his plan to re-launch the Scorching Salamander Knights emblem as an army under the Truban Empire. In attendance with him were both Claude Lucan and Tannon Gale, the two men he announced now as the commander and second-in-command respectively, of the revived army.

Morlan's report was next, but it wasn't nearly as impressive as those of his peers. By all means, his contributions since giving up sovereignty of Cetal had been phenomenal. Over the past month, the former king had managed to restore Cetal as a state of Trubannis, therefore adding great strength to the Empire in all aspects. After all, Cetal was the third most populous state in Trubannis, and home to the country's second largest army.

In addition to his activity in Cetal, Morlan had toured Pichreuse, Noel, and Cellarsy, in order to strengthen the collective support for the Empire by running campaigns to further spread the popular sense of patriotism across the country. Morlan's downfall, though—at least today—was the shameful confirmation that his daughter had been kidnapped. It underlined the futility of the guards at the Monarchal Castle, and also brought into question just how beneficial Cetal might be as it was merged back as a state of Trubannis.

In defence of both Morlan and the security level of the Monarchal Castle, golden knight John Tristan claimed that the kidnapping was the doing of an 'invincible' group known as the Sail Band. But while he might be right to refer to them as invincible, the thieving crew was nothing more than an urban legend in the eyes of most of the men in the court.

To save Morlan from further embarrassment, Reeling welcomed the spotlight upon himself, and he began speaking about the works he had accomplished in the last month, most of which Alpheus realised he was ignorant of. Apart from the preparation work for the Golden Knight Exchange, Reeling was also responsible for the construction of the osmium mining site in Noel, which was supposedly near to completion.

And on top of those admirable tasks, Reeling had also been working on a thesis at the academy entitled *A Calibration of the Moon Tides*, which aimed to measure the circulation and distribution of the moonlight and moon energy through the interaction of the two moons—the blue Achelois and the red Selene. It was the first time Alpheus had learned about the thesis, and although he immediately recognised that this was the most complicated and taxing of Reeling's tasks, the men at the court were apathetic.

"Your Majesty," Reeling said, regarding the Lord Emperor warily. "To illustrate the importance of continued research, would you first enlighten us on the current balance of powers across the land?"

The emperor nodded. "Since the rise of our Empire, the country has reclaimed the title as the strongest. Second to us would be Kraga, which has continued to invest large amounts on their military."

"And after the Kragans? Who are we wary of?"

The emperor's eyes glinted, seemingly acknowledging the hint Reeling had dropped.

"Aizary's rise to power over the past decade is a concern," Reeling said, turning to the other men. "Despite their small population, Aizary is home to both superior technology and, arguably, the brightest minds. Aizars pride themselves in research. For them, it has been a worthwhile investment. It is regretful to note that our very own academy here in Zorlia has since fallen behind the academies of the Far East. By engaging in research, I am but learning from the best."

Alpheus found himself nodding, realising then why Reeling had asked the emperor. It was no secret that the emperor's ancestors—the Spartamon family—originated from the Far East. The emperor's appearance was conspicuously Aizar, despite never having stepped foot on the island country. Indeed, his ancestors had settled in Trubannis more than three generations ago. Whether the emperor considered his Aizar heritage a part of him was anyone's guess, but Alpheus remembered now a brief conversation he had shared with Yorke just a few days prior. Apparently, it had been the emperor's decision to send Alpheus's sister to Aizary, the country's best scholar behind the retired Grandmaster, as an ambassador to maintain friendly relations. This arrangement had often been called a 'gift' to Aizary.

"Speaking of which," Schim said now, "do we not have a guest from Aizary? A scholar. I heard she impressed at the symposium."

Alpheus perked up, noting that this was Kathryn Trulips.

"Did anyone invite her to court?" Schim continued, peering across the room. "Who's following the case? Lord Count, was it you? Aizary won't be happy about this, that we're not inviting their diplomat."

"I was indeed asked to follow the case," Reeling responded, his head slightly inclined. "And if we were to maintain friendly relations, then it is perhaps imperative that we do something about it."

"Then what are we waiting for?" Forredan asked.

"I have my reservations," Reeling said. "She is undoubtedly a talented scholar, but she's no Charlotte Hindlow. It is not a fair trade."

What are you saying...? Alpheus wondered with a cringe aimed at Reeling.

"I am suspicious of her intentions—Aizary's intentions," Reeling continued. "I have yet to gather the evidence to support my suspicions, but this could be potential infiltration. An emissary, perhaps."

The court fell silent. The postulation was a serious one. Espionage was, of course, common practice, but by casually positing the possibility, Reeling was placing Trulips in real danger.

"No!" Alpheus cried, lurching out from behind Reeling. "She's no emissary! I *know* her. I worked with her. She's not the most agreeable person, but she's a good person. She's working toward good causes. She wants peace throughout the land."

The men glanced around at each other throughout the room, murmuring amongst themselves. Alpheus felt sweat running down from his hair, suddenly very aware that he was at the end of some angry stares from some of the most esteemed men in the country.

"Please, everyone," Reeling said, rising from his seat, settling the men within seconds. "I apologise for the commotion. But I suppose this is a good opportunity to introduce my new assistant. His name is Alpheus, the younger brother of Charlotte Hindlow. He has recently become a State Scholar. I invited him here today to assist me with my tasks."

Breunor snorted. "An idler... and one who clearly doesn't know his place."

"No, Lord Breunor," said Schim with his deep voice. "The court can only benefit from having more people from the academy. State Scholars are granted access to Vondra Dawn for good reason. The Empire is fortunate to have several remarkable war generals here like you, Lord Breunor, and of course the Lord Emperor himself, but a country cannot be run efficiently by only people who can fight wars. We need scholars who can propagate wisdom." Schim paused then, turning to Alpheus with a warm smile. "We expect great things from you."

Alpheus nodded awkwardly in response. "Thank you," he said softly.

"Back to the foreigner," Reeling said. "I suppose I can drop my suspicions for the time being. To better evaluate her, however, I believe it is best to send Kathryn Trulips away... temporarily, perhaps back to Aizary for a time. I shall draft a letter to their king."

Reeling eyed the emperor without actually asking him, who in turn regarded him with caution. The emperor was likely wondering what Reeling was brewing and whether he had chosen to line with Schim. After all, the tug-of-war between the emperor and the chancellor to win Reeling's services was the worst kept secret in Vondra Dawn. Alpheus didn't think that Reeling was supporting anyone in particular, however, noting that an open attack on the emperor on his Aizar heritage was a weak attempt that would achieve nothing.

The emperor leaned in now. "I'll leave it to you," he said. "Make certain that we do not upset Aizary."

"It is ensured," Reeling responded with another slight bow. "Your Majesty," he said, changing his tone. "Many of us have elected contestants to enter the Golden Knight Exchange. But, so far, you have yet to nominate anyone. Can we expect that to change any time soon?"

The emperor twitched a brow. It *did* sound like a little interrogative, but Alpheus thought it was a fair question. As the leader of the former Clan of Light, known for his natural charisma and extraordinary ability to attract skilled men toward him, the emperor should have the least trouble in nominating warriors to enter the Exchange. Schim, who had been second in command back in those days, had nominated over a dozen warriors to contest—most of whom were men who had fought by his side in the past.

Since the war had ended, however, the emperor's closest comrades had mysteriously disappeared, one after another. Rumours had suggested that the emperor had grown paranoid, and that he had started to lose trust in even his closest confidants.

And some said that he had actually murdered those men behind closed doors. But no one had dared bring those rumours up, not even a hint of them. But despite his subtlety, Alpheus realised that Reeling was doing exactly that.

"Lord Count," Lachman said, stepping forward before the throne. "Do I sense interrogation in your question?"

It was well-known that Lionel Lachman had been *the* man to quell all negative rumours swirling about the emperor. He had sworn loyalty to the emperor long ago, as one of the original members of the once humble mercenary clan. Lachman satisfied the role as one of the emperor's closest confidants, and here he was, standing tall and strong and most certainly *alive*.

"I apologise that my words were interpreted as such," Reeling said, shaking his head. "I *can* be lost in my ways sometimes, but no, I wouldn't dare question the Lord Emperor. Please allow me to elaborate."

Lachman glanced over to the emperor, who nodded at him. "Go on," the golden knight said to Reeling.

Reeling smiled. "My recent tasks have led me to the archives of the cellar that houses the documents detailing the role, history, and achievements of the brave soldiers of our country. The archives have been collected since the Sargon Monarchy—and that, of course, means that the Clan of Light is accounted for. It is unfortunate that many of the documents are incomplete or poorly maintained. Stranger yet is an eerie pattern wherein the records of the many men who battled closely alongside the Emperor had disappeared—straight off vanished."

"Is that right...?" Schim inserted with a smirk, clearly enjoying where Reeling seemed to be headed. "Vandalism... and the theft of old archives? Who would do such a thing? It's almost as if someone *wanted* to make sure that no one could find out what happened to those courageous men. If they are truly no longer with us, then I pray that they rest in peace." He paused, then shrugged. "But then, I'm sure no one needs my prayers when those men wouldn't think twice to die for our Lord Emperor."

The hint wasn't so subtle anymore. It was the most direct and daring accusation against the emperor that one could accomplish without actually pointing a finger at the great man. The accusation was consistent with the folk tale of three years ago that had circulated the country. The emperor, however, remained calm and was ready to answer, but only after a disgusted sneer.

"I hope I am correct to assume that you are alluding only to the fact that I could make the Exchange more worthwhile," the emperor began. "And in that case, you are correct. I can call upon more men than you could imagine, but I have opted not to. And why not? —simply put, because it is the task of the vassals. As for that preposterous folk tale and the men who disappeared, it was nothing more than a relief from their duties—retirement. The only way to ensure they could live in peace away from the Empire was to scrap any documents that might point to their actual locations."

Alpheus glanced about the court which had been silenced once again. The emperor's words were powerful indeed, especially behind the confidence he delivered those words. It had apparently been this very quality of his that had won the loyalty of so many of his subjects.

The emperor turned to Reeling now. "I am most impressed with your work ethics. I cannot imagine someone of your stature to be at the hideous cellar full of dust and grime. Your determination and passion in performing your tasks is most admirable.

"However," he continued, his pitch growing shrill. "I advise you spend more time in brighter surroundings. If you become too engaged in the darkness, you may be entrapped within it forever."

The emperor had reversed the roles, hinting back at Reeling. Without raising his voice, his words were spoken in a tone of such contempt that even Alpheus—standing behind Reeling—felt a distressing wave of shuddering cold that had him trembling involuntarily. Matching that tone was his narrowed, chillingly focused eyes, as if he were a predator staking out its prey.

The court dissolved there.

* * *

Alpheus kept quiet until he returned to the chambers with Reeling. He had grown suddenly wary that their words might be listened in on by adversaries with ill intentions.

"Jeffery, you—"

Reeling looked up at him from his desk with disapproval.

Alpheus rolled his eyes. "Lord Count," he said this time. "I don't know what you were trying to achieve, but it's never a good idea to cross the emperor."

"You think I crossed him?"

Alpheus frowned slightly. "Yes."

"It is nothing," Reeling said, dismissing the concern rather casually. "Oh," he then said, pulling out a parchment from beneath his coat. "I have something for you. An invitation from the Imperial Lithia Dominion."

"Vinawell?" Alpheus said as he accepted the parchment. "Invitation to what?"

"The Princess's Purification Ceremony. The girl is turning nineteen come April and they are looking for a prince consort. Invited is a host of young talents across the land. Be proud that you are included among them. But in going, expect your competition to be fierce."

Princess Clarissa Flora Steele, Alpheus sounded out in his head as his vision dulled on the calligraphic text. He knew well what a purification ceremony was: a coming of age celebration for girls, and, in some traditions, also the time to marry off young women.

"She's the crown princess," the courtly man said, meeting Alpheus in the eyes. "And that means she is in position to inherit her father's power and become the first queen regnant in the land. But whether it will turn out that way remains to be seen."

Alpheus turned a wry smile. "And if it does? I'll be the epicurean of a spouse with no influence? One who makes no contribution to any cause?"

"Vinawell is a fine place," Reeling said with a shrug. "And besides, the competition is fierce. I do not expect you to succeed... at least not if you competed as the person you are today."

Alpheus scrunched the sheep skin in a fist. "I never thought to consider it," he said, trying his best to remain calm. "I find it regretful, but two weeks is enough. Vondra Dawn isn't for me. I'm tired of the hypocrisies and the conspiracies. I don't need anyone to arrange my marriage. I don't want to hear about how Lady Trulips might be an emissary. It's too much."

Reeling looked askance at him, regarding him for a long moment. "Very well," he then said with a sigh. "Go if you must. But be sure that this opportunity may never present itself again."

Alpheus shrugged. "So be it."

FIFTEEN

Assassins and sorcerers

Alpheus watched the storm from a window in his estate in Phantom Pond, unable to steady his mind behind the thumping of heavy rain hitting the roof and the façades. The rainstorm was typical of midwinter Zorlia, especially in a year where there was no forecast of snow.

He been waiting anxiously, wondering if his guest for the evening would show up. His guest was, of course, Kathryn Trulips, who had apparently been asked by the court to go for a month-long return trip to Aizary. The offer, which seemed rather forceful, came with the incentive that Trulips would be arranged to be a templar with the Church of the St. Bernard Order, a knight of the Holy Order whose rank was superior even to silver knights. If she had wanted to be part of the Empire, Trulips might not welcome the fact that the tie between the religious faction and the Truban Empire was somewhat loose.

A knock came from the front door then.

Alpheus trotted urgently to the antechamber, hoping that he wouldn't be opening the door to see Reeling or anyone else. To his delight, it was indeed Kathryn Trulips behind the door. The foreigner had sported a heavy straw coat and a conical hat to weather the rain—unspectacular for her standards, but more than enough to impress Alpheus. Indeed, Alpheus had been nervous since sending out the invitation, and he still wasn't able to calm his nerves when he welcomed her at the antechamber now.

It was when Trulips removed her coat and hat that reduced Alpheus to a daze—rendering a delay in his receipt of the guest's garments. The foreigner had *dressed up* and she was simply resplendent. The lavender tent dress revealed and highlighted the shoulders, with matching butterfly sleeves and a band collar tied in a bow. She was like a different person. She was somehow more herself, more exotic, and even more striking than he already knew.

She really is beautiful, Alpheus thought. "Had I known it would rain so hard," he said, "I'd have seen your way here."

Trulips shook her head with a friendly smile. "I appreciate the invite," she said, handing over a tiny book that was smaller than her hands. "A gift for you."

Alpheus flushed slightly as he received it with both hands. "That's too generous," he said before a skim of the title. *Progressivism*, he read silently. *Politics...?*

"I trust that you can find it useful," Trulips said.

"I'm sure I will," Alpheus responded, slipping the tiny gift beneath his robe. "Please, this way," he said, gesturing down the great hall. "The servants have prepared a meal."

Alpheus helped his guest to her seat at the wide dining table, which could seat twenty people, before finding his own seat at the opposite end. They would, of course, be the only ones there. They started on their meals with gentle etiquette, and while the guest appeared to enjoy the meal, she made no remark. She did seem pleased, though.

"Is this where Lady Charlotte used to dine?" Trulips asked.

"Yes," Alpheus said, realising then why his guest was eager about her visit. "That seat you're on—that's the one she preferred."

Trulips beamed, almost like an innocent child, causing Alpheus to wonder if the Aizars had deified his sister.

"How is she?" he asked instead. "My sister. I haven't seen her since she left. She rarely writes. Is she well?"

"I regret that I do not know her personally," Trulips answered. "But in terms of her work, she is certainly doing well. Everyone in Illudia—no, everyone in all of Aizary admires her."

Alpheus looked away with a squint. "She didn't say anything about me? She didn't ask you to bring back any messages?"

Trulips frowned slightly, showing some rare empathy. "No," she said after a moment. "Nothing."

Trulips smiled and then went back to her meal. *What am I doing?* Alpheus thought. *I should talk about the Empire. She likes that.*

"About Zorlia," Trulips then said to break the silence, "it has been a worthwhile experience thus far. Coming here has allowed me to see many things."

Alpheus smiled at her. "Like what...?"

"Zorlia has given me a new perspective on how a country should be governed," she said. "The Truban Empire does a lot of things right." She paused there, hesitating a little. "The Lord Emperor of this country, in particular, is an incredible leader. He is someone we could all learn from."

Alpheus raised a suspicious brow. "Have you heard the hearsay?" he asked. "The Lord Emperor is said to be paranoid—he doesn't trust anyone. And he—"

"Old wives' tales," Trulips inserted, waving a dismissive hand. "Besides, those soldiers' lives belong to him… for without him, they would be dead long ago."

Quite the extremist, Alpheus thought with a glance away.

"How's your work with the Lord Count?" Trulips asked. "I'm sure you've learned more than a few things."

Alpheus fell silent. "The Lord Count," he said with hesitation. "Well, he's… incredible."

"And…? Have you learned anything in particular?"

"I have, indeed," he responded with a smile. "It's called the Falling Comet."

The foreigner raised a curious brow.

"It's a bolt of energy that can be shot out as a weapon," Alpheus said. "The best thing about it is that almost anything can be turned into weapons. But usually, smaller items are preferred—they're easier to flick out. And I—" He trailed off there, realising that this would lead to a conversation about sorcery, which still wasn't something he was comfortable discussing.

"And…?" Trulips said, prodding him for elaboration.

"Ah, no," Alpheus said, scratching his head. "It's meaningless to say more, as I'm only a beginner. My rate of success hovers between two or three in every ten tries."

"When were you going to let me know who you are?"

Alpheus jumped, wondering if he had heard her correctly.

"Have you not accepted your identity just yet?" Trulips added.

"What are you talking about?" Alpheus said with a worried frown, looking away again.

"I can only assume you are one of those rare breeds whose grace was once dormant. The first time I met you, I sensed nothing. But the next time, a small but appreciable amount of grace was burning inside you, as it is now. It was a surprise, especially as Lady Charlotte Hindlow brims with an enormous grace pool."

What? Alpheus thought, suddenly curious.

"It is rare to see your kind," Trulips continued. "And it is rarer that you do not embrace the new found power." She paused, staring down at her glass of wine, a deep violet in colour. "Sorcery can indeed complement one's work as a scholar."

"Could you elaborate on that?" Alpheus asked, no longer able to ignore his curiosity.

"Sorcery is separated into four known categories. It is rare for anyone to master all areas, because each conflict and counteract each other. We have *black magic*, focused on attack and destruction; *white magic*, focused on defence and creation; *green magic*, focused on support; and *blue magic*, focused on replication and mime."

It was the first time that Alpheus learned those groupings, and some of it fell roughly in place with his own research. The tome he had didn't mention the different types of sorcery—at least his translations didn't reveal anything of the sort. Despite his ambivalence in recent times, a part of him still wished that resources on the topic weren't so scarce. The sudden emergence of magic users eight years ago, which coincided with the eschatological 'Awakening' event, meant that sorcerers were associated with cataclysm.

Alpheus appreciated that the attitude toward sorcerers in Aizary was different. People of the island country were educated to believe that sorcery was a natural, and essential part of life. Superstition was rare in the Far East. No one considered sorcerers to be harbingers of misfortune.

Trulips now picked up an inedible leaf used as an ornament on her dining plate. "But what I wanted to tell you is this," she said. With a simple wave of that small leaf, she set it into a wonderful white glow. When she let go of it, the glowing leaf then started floating in mid-air on its own.

"Scholars are tasked with the duty of creation and preservation," she said. "White magic is our choice."

It made sense, and her elegant demonstration helped to convince Alpheus. The idea of creation and how it connected with white magic resonated with him. Even so, Alpheus didn't believe in training in only one area of magic. Any creative ventures were always achieved with the highest level of greatness when the creator was willing to blend and weave together multiple ideas or skills.

Alpheus cleared his throat then. "There's something I want you to know," he said. "And I think I'll have to show you, rather than tell you."

Alpheus led his guest to the second floor of the grand dwelling. His head was warning him that he shouldn't, but he found himself heading there anyway: the atelier. Trulips wavered when Alpheus opened the door. Unlike the rest of the residence, which was meticulously organised, the atelier was a mess. Among the countless painting—stacked in piles or leaning against stands—a number of delicate sculptures sat on the floor. Brushes, palettes, and quill pens lay scattered, and at the centre of the workroom laid the latest artwork Alpheus had been working on. It was incomplete, and it was something that even Alpheus himself couldn't make sense of.

The main subject in the work was a child of apparent Aizar descent, and perhaps that was what had Trulips in quiet contemplation. She was peering at the child and then at the hanged man behind the bleeding sunset. She shivered slightly then, and soon, there were tears streaming down her cheeks.

"I apologise," she said, turning away. "I seem to have lost myself."

Alpheus raised a hand slightly, unsure how to respond.

"Lord Hindlow," the foreigner inserted, stepping toward the exit. "I am scheduled for an early departure in the morning. I should go now."

Alpheus trailed her back down to the ground floor and all the way to the antechamber. He bit his lip as he watched her retrieve and then throw on her raincoat as she prepared to depart. She must have sensed that Alpheus wanted to say something, something more than bidding farewell. But if it was anything to do with his artwork, she probably wasn't interested.

"I want to go to Aizary with you," Alpheus said, the words slipping out, surprising even himself.

Trulips furrowed her brow in confusion. "Is this some kind of farewell jest of this country?"

"This isn't something I'd jest about," Alpheus said, taking some offence. "You must remember that I spoke of my work as an artist. I haven't given up on that. In fact, I won't."

"But...," Trulips said, "what about the Empire? What of the work with the Lord Count?"

"Politics isn't for me," Alpheus said. "It never was. I cannot live my days behind conspiracies—and I'm glad for that. I can now go back to what I'm meant to do. I can even go to Aizary with you. I'll show you what it means to live for yourself. Together, we can—"

Alpheus stopped speaking abruptly as his guest's hand made contact with his cheek with a vicious slap. It stung so much that it was as if his soul had jumped out of his body.

Trulips glared at him, her usually alluring eyes reduced to a furious squint. "Continue that nebulous dream of yours all you want," she said, showing some teeth. "Just don't drag me down with you. Don't even think about it."

"Aren't you overreacting a little?" Alpheus said, refraining from massaging his cheeks that had turned red.

"To succeed is to sacrifice," Trulips said. "Everyone has a role to fulfil. You had the qualities to become something of great value, but instead, you choose to turn to selfish indulgences and foolish ideologies. And to think that I once believed in you."

Trulips pushed open the double door from which a blast of wind and rain crashed in. She stepped outside, hesitating for a moment, and then finally glanced back over her shoulder.

"Pitiful," she said. She then treaded out into the storm, leaving behind a broken Alpheus, lamenting how a pleasant evening had turned sour so quickly.

* * *

Departure was from Dunn Bay, the section of the much longer Dunn River which ran directly to the sea that separated the Far East from the large contiguous land.

Alpheus wasn't sure anymore that it was the best idea to go. He recalled no details of how he got there, but he was at the edge of a long wooden pier now as his pocket watch ticked toward the scheduled departure time. There wasn't a soul around, and there was no ship in sight. The pier—backdropped by the imposing Vondra Dawn—faced the great bay, waves crashing about fiercely. The impact of those crashes screamed out at him as the resulting ripples tingled him with unease.

He removed his glasses, which were now spattered with droplets, seeing no clearer without them as an inordinate amount of water seemed to swarm toward him. The standard set of straw-woven apparel he wore now protected him somewhat from the rain that had continued to fall since the previous night. But it didn't alleviate the pain of Trulips's words. The sky was a gloomy grey that had only further contributed to his misery.

Why am I so bothered? he wondered in frustration. *Is it because... I have feelings for her?*

Alpheus had figured that the foreigner had departed at an earlier time. There was no way any vessel would sail out in such conditions. He cringed now, shaking off some of the rainwater that had drenched his hair and face, collecting that same amount again within seconds. He maintained an intent gaze on the thrashing water, waves roaring at him relentlessly. He closed his eyes then tightly, wedging out a mix of tears and rainwater beneath the lids. He then finally turned away from the bay.

After hours of idle loitering in a city under the storm, Alpheus found himself outside his home again. The rain hadn't stopped, and he simply stood there at the entrance without going inside. Perhaps the sensation of the rainwater crashing down on him could wake him. Perhaps it could help him think about his purpose, or more precisely, the purpose others wanted to impose on him.

The atelier..., Alpheus thought. But he quickly shut his eyes again and shook his head. *No! I cannot hide from this.*

An idea sparked inside him then. Alpheus lurched his way into the mansion. Nothing was lighted inside. Alpheus didn't care, heading toward the library in haste, slowing his step only when he finally got there. He huffed out a breath that slightly warmed his cheeks. He then paced to the shelves on the far wall, collapsing to his knees upon reaching it. He brushed a hand against one of the bookends, which was in the shape of a domestic cat, and turned it counter-clockwise.

A loud clink sounded. Alpheus took a step back, eyeing the carpet beneath the shelves. He huffed out another audible breath and then crouched down to rip the carpet apart, revealing a hidden hatch.

Beneath the hatch was a descending set of stairs that led to a seemingly endless pit of darkness. Alpheus clasped tightly at his double crescent pendant, snatched an oil lamp, and then descended.

* * *

There were only seven more days until the Golden Knight Exchange. The training ground in the south of Vondra Dawn was where many of the contestants sparred. It was also where the competition would be staged. The tiled battle ring, which was elevated several steps from the ground, had been set up only a few days ago. A viewing platform seating a hundred people had also been erected to the north of the ring. The rest of the ground was an open space floored with sand that had hardened from the recent rain.

Julian had spent every day at the training ground since he had been granted entry to compete in the Exchange. It wasn't mandatory to be there—all of the people he knew chose *not* to train there, including Orel Kite, Tannon Gale, and even Percival Pole. But Julian appreciated the opportunity, noting that it might be his last. He had also hoped that, by being there, he would impress the Lord Count, who had made a loose promise to help him track down the man called Yesod.

Julian realised that he was now the most well-known contestant. Not only was he a sorcerer, but he was also the son of the great Royston Longinus. He was indifferent about the sudden fame, however, especially as he was aware that many people wanted to see him fail. He had done well to refrain from calling on his grace in public since his clash against Kite, turning his focus instead on sharpening his skills with the sword. But despite his efforts to maintain a low profile, a host of men had their eyes on him—for reasons that he didn't yet want to guess.

The man he had attracted this afternoon, though, was someone else. It was the Lord Chancellor, Yeremia Schim, whose arrival had everyone at a sudden standstill. After a moment of shocked silence, all of the men there at the training ground fell to one knee, saluting him in turn.

"Rise," Schim said with a gruff voice, grim and demanding.

The men rose to their feet, many of them realising that the great man wasn't there for them. Schim, who had come with only a single vassal, paced toward the battle ring now, eyeing Julian specifically. "Sir... Longinus, was it?"

Julian promptly climbed down from the elevated ring before bowing down like the others. "I haven't been knighted, my Lord," Julian said. "The *Sir* is unnecessary."

Schim raised a curious brow. "And I assume no lords have bid for your services?"

"No," Julian responded, unsure where this was heading.

"Excellent," Schim said. "Let me be your new liege. I promise you a prosperous future."

The other men were listening, and they gawked now, almost refusing to believe that Julian had such luck.

Julian shook his head, however. "I have to... refuse," he said.

Schim regarded him with a grin, expecting an explanation, thinking perhaps that this was some kind of joke. His vassal was less patient, stepping forward with a groan. "You have some nerve," said the man of modest stature, dressed in a noblemen's garb, but looked rather athletic and dark to be of the aristocracy.

"Excuse him," Schim said, holding his vassal back. "Raphael can be sensitive."

Julian eyed the man. *He's Raphael...? One of the three Raiders?*

"Raphael here matches a golden knight," Schim said. "But he's no knight. Being a knight is no more than a status, and it's not something I consider when I appraise a man."

"No, it's not that," Julian said. "The Lord Count has given me the opportunity to compete on this stage, and I have promised myself that I would submit to no one until this is over. I need to confront my past. I need to confront who I am. And the only way to do that is to fight in this Exchange with all I have—for no one but myself."

Schim regarded him for a moment, his expression unreadable. "Bearing the Longinus name is not easy, I suppose," he then said, already turning away. "No matter. I'll ask you again when the Exchange is over."

The chancellor treaded off now without another glance back, receding off into the distance before finally disappearing behind the wall that fenced in the training ground.

Julian sighed, almost as if he didn't realise that he had just been approached by the second most powerful man in the country. He looked above that wall now to the sky that had grown suddenly dark. The sun had hardly emerged behind the thick clouds for the past few days, and it looked like it wouldn't come out today either. The snippets of daylight that lightened the gloom were already fading off into the horizon.

As a sharp gust of wind swept over the men, many of them decided that it was time to go. Sparring in the drizzle could be refreshing, but if the recent weather was anything to go by, then it might soon be pelting down with rain. Still, Julian decided against leaving. He was more comfortable slashing his sword in solitude, with the luxury of a large open space that was far more conducive to training than the cramped hovels he had stayed before.

Julian finally stopped when night fell. The skies had turned out to be kind, too, cooling him with only a sprinkle. While he had the energy to continue, he had a home to return to—the refurbished chapel in Ramsgate that he now shared with Oscar.

The evening walk was rather peaceful with the absence of the day crowds. The rain had stopped, too, and the damp streets shimmered behind lanterns hanging off the terracotta dwellings and the leafless wisteria vines creeping on them. As Julian continued his hike east, the quieter streets coincided with the diminishing amount of artificial light guiding his path. Julian preferred placidity and he didn't mind the long walk to and from Vondra Dawn every day.

Things seem a tad too quiet, though, Julian thought suspiciously, looking further down the path ahead of him. *Strangely quiet.*

Julian blinked and then eyed into a narrow alley on his right. He didn't know what had attracted him to glimpse into that almost pitch black alley, but as he squinted now, he realised there was someone there.

A figure. A person, receding, draped in a cloak that covered its body from head to toe. The stranger paused, perhaps noting Julian's presence. He or she turned back slightly.

"Worry not," Julian said, calling out to the stranger. "I'm no bandit."

The stranger made no response, and from that distance and with the unfortunate lack of light, it was difficult to discern his or her emotions.

Julian shook his head and then turned away, but after taking only a single step, a seething gust blasted at him from behind. A chill sprung up his spine, causing him to puff out a breath before he froze over completely.

What...! he wondered in shock.

He thought that his instincts would call on his grace, but he soon realised that every vein inside of him had shut down, too. On the outside, it was an invisible giant hand that had contained him. The feeling was overwhelming, as if a demon—or a god—were watching over a mere mortal. The immense aura of destructive energy that simmered in the air certainly pointed to that possibility.

Grace? A sorcerer?

"I will not harm you," a voice said. A woman's voice, gentle yet imposing at the same time, emanating as if within his own head. Those words alone were not the assurance Julian wanted, not when he was vulnerable and at the mercy of the stranger.

"Who are you?" Julian dared to ask in return, still barely able to lift a finger, let alone turn back to face his foe. "What do you want?"

"*What is your relationship with Valiant?*" the voice asked in return.

Julian twitched a brow. "I don't know anyone by that name."

"*You have his ring.*"

Julian looked down to his powerless right hand on which the index finger was fitted with the ring from Alpheus. "It was given to me," he confessed. "I don't know where it's from."

"*What about the Humboldtianum Manual?*"

Julian scrunched his forehead and narrowed his eyes in bewilderment this time. "The Hum-Humboldtianum Manual...?! How—how would I know?"

"*I see,*" the stranger said, releasing her invisible grip, at which time Julian stumbled forward from his struggle. "*It is a shame to Royston Longinus to have a son as weak as you.*"

Julian's eyes snapped wide open. The mention of his father's name sparked a quick stream of thoughts rushing through his mind.

He spun now with a burning rage, his grace restored, only to see that the stranger was already taking her leave, pulling away in a supernatural drift that spared her feet from touching the ground. "Where can I find Royston Longinus?" Julian cried, chasing. "Tell me, please!"

The stranger didn't look back, instead taking a giant leap ahead that shot her into the air. The ends of her cloak riffled like stripes of silk—she was flying, or at least gliding, as she seemed to knock about left and right, pushing off the quiet dwellings beneath her to keep her floating body on course.

Julian immediately gushed out his grace, hopping forward and then leaping up to the roofs of the terracotta buildings to chase. Despite already emitting the scarlet glow, which blessed him with superhuman speeds, he looked ahead in awe as he watched the stranger drifting away in at a velocity that seemed even more impressive than what he could manage. Regardless of how dangerous the stranger might be, however, Julian couldn't allow himself to lose grip of her—at least not before he could get some answers out of her.

The pursuit led him all the way to a small forest on the eastern fringe of the city where the stranger finally stopped. She rewarded Julian by finally turning to face him, regarding him with a pair of violet eyes that sparkled enchantingly under the faint hue of Achelois that had penetrated the overcast sky. The blue of the moonlight also accentuated the colour of the stranger's hair, which Julian saw now was a light blue. A young lady, perhaps in her mid-twenties, who also donned a face veil over her nose and mouth.

"Tell me about my father," Julian demanded. "Where can I find him?"

The stranger blinked once, but her expression of indifference didn't change. She said nothing.

Julian scowled, drawing his iron sword and slashing it down fiercely without warning. The stranger, though, evaded the strike with a sly step. In that same motion, she slipped a hand out from her draping cloak, revealing her wrist for less than a moment—though long enough for Julian to note the symbol marked there.

The Endless Knot! Julian recognised, stunned once again.

It was the same symbol that had featured in his dreams for the last ten years, a symbol that was identical to the one marked on the neck of the man called Yesod.

The stranger might not have realised Julian's reaction, but in slipping a hand out, she was reaching at her hips for a... flute, which she whipped out now. When her arm swung out, however, the musical instrument transformed into a full-sized spear. She slashed down the long weapon before Julian could react, cleanly slicing his iron sword into two and ending the battle prematurely.

Stunned, Julian collapsed to his knees as the two halves of his sword crashed down beside him.

The stranger turned now. "*Do not follow me*," she warned, her voice still only channelling inside of Julian's own mind. She leaped away and vanished into the darkness.

A sorcerer, Julian thought, trembling as he stared blankly into the woods. *As strong as the gods.*

* * *

Julian pressed his eyes shut together when he was finally outside his home. He had to calm himself. He wasn't the best caretaker, but he didn't want to bring that anxious face home to a child. He was trying, but in closing his eyes, all he saw was that sorcerer. And the memory alone made him shiver violently.

Julian opened his eyes then to the sound of clanging metal. He jumped and then hurried in desperately, his thoughts muddled, hoping only that the sorcerer hadn't somehow come for Oscar.

She hadn't, fortunately. Oscar was panting, though, holding a sword aloft in the small courtyard. His sparring partner was none other than Percival Pole.

Julian breathed easier, but frowned at the two of them. "You're using real swords...?" he asked in annoyance.

Oscar said nothing, but he hid his weapon behind his back, like a child behaving badly.

"It's all under control," Pole said with a wink. "The boy's learning well. He needs something genuine."

Oscar glanced over to Julian to confirm if it was all right.

"Go take a bath," Julian said, rolling his eyes. "It's late."

The boy nodded, retiring into the back of the chapel that had become their home.

Julian turned to Pole now. "I thought you returned to Bastion City," he said. "Why are you here?"

"We have many capable men in the Defence Army," Pole answered, then waved a hand to dismiss the topic. "Anyway, I came to see you... to see if you knew anything about the sorcerer in Bastion City."

Julian squinted, gaping at him.

"I suppose that means you don't," Pole said.

"Tell me about it," Julian said warily.

Pole sighed. "Well, he—"

"Hold on," Julian interrupted. "He...? A *man*?"

"Yes, a man. A sorcerer's still a man, is he not? You're a sorcerer yourself."

Julian hesitated. "What's... he like?"

"He's been playing hide-and-seek with us, murdering several men since he started lurking about nearly a week ago. Our men have said that he wields a sword of black flames."

"And you're sure it's a man?" Julian asked again.

"A man!" Pole snapped. "We haven't managed to hunt him down yet, but yes, we managed to work out the gender."

Julian flapped his cape up to reveal his broken iron sword. Pole didn't see it initially, but only on a closer look did he note the crevice at the halfway point of the sword. Julian had purposely sealed the two chunks back together with his flames, now holding loosely only so that Oscar wouldn't ask him about it.

"There's more than one of them," Julian said. "I ran into one just now. She was a young lady... or at least that was how she appeared before me. And she was... powerful. I never saw the Apostle, but if the reports were true, this sorcerer is just as terrifying as him."

Pole frowned musingly. "The sorcerer in Bastion City is no pawn, either," he said. "But... I'd think that if we faced off in a fair fight, I'd win. He's not nearly as strong as the Apostle... who was said to be a god... or something of that nature."

SIXTEEN

The angelic spectre

It had been twelve years, but Julian's past continued to haunt him. At the back of his mind, those scenes replayed incessantly. First, it was his father turning his back on him and leaving forever. Then there was the visit of the elusive man Yesod who had spared him no glance. And finally, there were those ruthless murderers reducing his home and all forms of life in it to shreds.

Julian trembled now as he clenched his weapon more tightly. And now as he glanced back out to the rest of the training ground he was sharing with the other contestants as well as a host of noblemen, he thought not of how strong any of them might be, but how utterly weak he himself was. He didn't want to let it bother him, but it did. He had been staring into his own reflection on a new iron sword that had replaced the one that had snapped in two. It had been nearly a week, but the memory was as vivid as ever. The lack of gloss and polish on the new sword was never meant for a mirror, and the vague image that reflected back displayed doubt and fear.

He suspected that even golden knights were no match for the mute sorcerer or anyone of those who seemed to be part of that circle. And yet, here he was to fight for *only* a chance of becoming a golden knight.

"Focus," Pole said now as he joined Julian under the tree. "Sir Patrick isn't someone you can afford to be frivolous with."

Julian looked up, taking a moment to remember he had just been drawn to battle a silver knight called Byron Patrick in the first round, a man loyal to Victor Breunor. It was the first time that all contestants—thirty-two in total—were assembled together as the Empire announced the pairings of the first round matchups.

The Empire had made sure that this opening round was seeded to ensure that the more promising contestants would prevail and move on to at least the second round. The silver knights were seeded highest. Regular knights followed them. Seeded at the bottom were those who weren't knighted, but had proven their strength in way or another—they were termed 'outsiders.'

Julian was grouped as an outsider, and that was why it had been inevitable that his first round opponent was a silver knight. He couldn't bring himself to worry about his competition, though—not when he knew there were sorcerers roaming the land, who were far more powerful than the knights.

"Percival," Julian finally said, still regarding his iron sword. "Let's not discuss this. We are in competition—potentially against each other."

"Just a word of advice, then," Pole said, turning. "A true warrior grows strongest in battle. Remember that."

Julian managed a wry smile, following Pole with his eyes as the silver knight paced out toward the Lord Count, who had arrived only now. A lot of the noblemen flocked to the courtly man. It was as if their tendency to flatter those with more authority than them was intrinsic. After all, anyone who had met Reeling should know that the man didn't entertain sycophants.

When those men dispersed, Julian made his way to see the man himself. "Lord Count, I—" He trailed off abruptly, not knowing how to elaborate.

Reeling regarded him with indifference. "If you have nothing to say, I think—"

"No, please!" Julian spat out, before his brows knitted together again. "I... ran into a sorcerer. It was six days ago." He paused there in hesitation, remembering how he had been overwhelmed. "She had me on my knees after a single blow."

"*She*...?" Reeling asked with a raised brow behind a glint of the monocle. "A... woman?"

"A young lady—or so she appeared," Julian said with a slight shiver. "She spoke not from her mouth, but with a voice that echoed in my head."

"How did it happen?"

Julian reached inside his brigandine, pulling out the sapphire ring he had since taken off his finger. "This ring," Julian said, noting that Reeling had twitched an eyebrow on seeing it. "The sorcerer said it belongs to someone called... Valiant. I can only assume that she was looking for this person. She... also asked about the Humboldtianum Manual. She was probably looking for that, too."

Reeling held a hand to his chin. "What are you suspecting?"

Julian gulped. "Intuition tells me that the sorcerer is related to Yesod."

"Why?"

"The Endless Knot," Julian said. "This sorcerer was marked with that symbol. And so was he."

"The Endless Knot...," Reeling said, musing. "The Apostle was also tied to this knot."

Julian jolted, unable to find the words. *So I really did confront someone of that same caste*, he thought. *A group that are almost gods...*

"This is beyond me," Reeling said, tapping his head with a finger. "I cannot see their purpose. But I would think... at least for now, there is no ill will." He snickered. "And, if there were, there is little we could do."

Julian frowned, unsatisfied. "Incidentally...," he said with more hesitation, "have you had time?"

"For that elusive man, Yesod?" Reeling responded, narrowing his eyes. "He is difficult to track... but I have indeed found some leads." He paused for a moment then with a slight scowl, showing an uncharacteristic hint of anxiety. His succinct words were teasing, and Julian anticipated more to come, yet he was fearful at the same time to receive any information he thought he might not be ready for.

"That man...," Reeling continued with a sense of uneasiness. "He is not what you think he is. And this sorcerer you encountered... It is perhaps best to leave it alone."

"I don't know what you mean," Julian said, shaking his head. "But whatever it takes, I'm prepared for it."

"Your trembling does not convince," Reeling said, looking askance at him. "I suggest you concentrate on what is tangible, and that would be the Exchange. If you are unable to make any impression here, you certainly should not be worrying about people tied to the Endless Knot."

* * *

Julian found himself there again, at the same part of the street where the alley was. The clear evening sky was a change from the upsetting weather of the past week. The full moon of Selene shone with a dazzle—its hue of red covered the stony street and the terracotta buildings from where lanterns of tangerine dangled. More than a few people shared the street with him now, and the company had Julian feeling rather safe. An old couple walked ahead of him, down the same path... living their ordinary lives.

Julian continued his stride, trying his best to forget about that evening and that encounter. *Focus*, he told himself. *The Exchange starts tomorrow.*

A flap in the air.

Julian widened his eyes, looking up to see a figure leaping high above him, dashing its way atop the roofs of the dwellings that were cramped together on the narrow streets. *No,* Julian thought, discerning a slim figure in black dress. *Not her.*

The figure was invisible to an average person. The way it moved above everyone, on top of buildings of about four floors high, was its first advantage. Its slick motion that carried barely a hint of sound was another advantage. If Julian hadn't grown so paranoid, even he wouldn't have sensed this new stranger.

Why…? he thought, looking down. *Why do you keep coming at me? Should I… chase?* It was never really a question. He was already on the run, bolting pass the elderly couple and keeping his eye on the figure who flapped about from above. In taking a quick glance at the moon and then at his own body that had started to emit that crimson red glow, he realised that even he was now almost invisible to the naked eye.

As he continued to trail her, Julian grew more and more suspicious that this new stranger wasn't the sorcerer from last time. This one seemed to be female, too, but she emanated none of those chilling vibes. She *was* a sorcerer, however—grace pulsed with her every step. Since his encounter with the mute sorcerer, Julian had actively worked on the ability to detect grace, which Alpheus had said, according to his research, was an inherent ability of all sorcerers. Although Julian knew he was far from mastering the ability, he thought he was getting better. The sorcerer he was tracing now, however, didn't seem to possess the ability—for she didn't seem to notice that she was being tailed—and that alone meant that she wasn't all that fearful.

The chase lasted about ten minutes, ending when the sorcerer arrived in Phantom Pond, the most affluent neighbourhood of Zorlia. Unlike the dwellings that were packed together in most of the city, each manor here occupied extensive grounds, built with grandeur and extravagance in mind. Still, they didn't compare to the Longinus Manor, otherwise known as the *Castle of the East*. That place was nothing but a distant memory now, part of those memories Julian sometimes couldn't trust.

Julian shook his head then, forcing himself to focus. The sorcerer had prowled her way toward one of the manors, now sitting on a border wall, observing the great house that was unlighted on the inside. Was she just a mere thief?

The sorcerer rose to her feet then, leaping into the garden and dashing toward a window. She held up two fingers that illuminated a soft white glow, which stood out rather clearly in the darkness. The sorcerer rolled her fingers across the window frame that was the size of half a man, nudging it inward slightly afterwards to remove the entire tinted glass.

She entered the building from there.

Julian pounced after her, dropping from the same wall and dashing to the same window. He looked into the house, seeing a hallway, noting that the only source of light drifting inside was indeed the red of Selene from behind him. He also noted the cleanly cut edges of the window frame that the intruder had managed.

Julian hopped into the building with a light step on the window sill. He prowled along the corridor, careful not to make a sound as he navigated. It was several steps later when he turned into another hallway, as he was attracted by a glint of something from there that wasn't moonlight. He crept forward with a hand firm on the grip of his sword, confirming that the wavering of what looked more and more like candlelight originated from an opening on the left, and reflected out to the original corridor by a metal ornament mounted to the wall at the end of this hall.

He followed the flickering and stepped into a room filled with books. A library, perhaps. The artificial source of light came from the ground—more specifically, an open hatch on the ground that led to a set of descending stairs. Quiet crackling flames sounded from beneath. Julian held his breath and then proceeded down the passage whose dark stone walls were installed with oil lamps, all of which were lighted.

Julian took each step with caution, following the path leftward after several steps, only to realise the stairs didn't go down very deep—barely twenty steps in total. A few more steps ahead was an opening into what appeared to be a private cellar where more light shone through. Julian crouched down carefully to peek in, discerning with a shudder a figure standing inside. He hopped back up a couple of steps on instinct, noting that the figure—at least on his quick glance—was hauntingly similar to the mute sorcerer tied to the Endless Knot.

It was her, after all!

A heat surged to the crown of his head then, forming into sweat that rolled down from his scalp. His heart was pounding, and he had to cover his mouth with a hand to ensure that no one heard him huffing out short breaths.

Just what was a sorcerer with such power doing in... *Hold on,* Julian thought then, suddenly wondering why he sensed no grace.

He peeked in again, carefully, seeing the same figure. He squinted then to recognise that the figure was in fact a life-sized sculpture, a confirmation that had him breathe easy again. He finally stepped through the opening into a rather small room, first noting several wooden chests on the ground and then the shelves along the left and right walls, which were stocked with books. Nearly everything was covered in cobwebs and layered with dust. He regarded the statue again behind the lantern that was mounted on the far end.

Clearly, someone had been here not too long ago. Julian stepped closer toward the statue, only to note that someone was indeed here—laying asleep against the foot of the sculpture.

Alpheus, Julian recognised, baffled by why the scholar was here. As he crouched down to regard Alpheus more carefully, he remembered that the scholar had said that he was a sorcerer, too. As a friend, Julian wanted to believe him, but even now, he sensed no grace emanating from Alpheus. *And yet he's still religious*, Julian thought with a shake of his head as he noted the double crescent pendant dangling from the scholar's neck.

"Alpheus?" he whispered.

No response.

"Alpheus," he said again, this time with a pat on his shoulder.

The young scholar jumped, waking with a muffled shriek. He snatched his spectacles from the feet of the statue, throwing them on. When he peered up, Julian had a finger over his lips as a signal for Alpheus to keep it down.

"Julian...?" Alpheus said softly with a wheeze. "What are you doing here?" He shook his head from his blur, holding a hand against it. "And how did you get in here anyway?"

"How did *you* get in here?" Julian asked, throwing the question right back in the same soft volume.

"This is my house!" Alpheus said with a bemused frown.

"Really? Well, someone has broken in. I was trailing the intruder, but I lost her."

"What...?" Alpheus said with a squint.

"We should probably get out of here," Julian suggested.

"Well, *you* should," Alpheus responded. "This cellar is forbidden, especially to people not part of the family."

"What do you mean *especially*?"

"I am not supposed to be here, either," Alpheus said. "The place is a private basement that belonged to my grandfather... who I have never met."

"Then why are you here?"

"I needed some guidance—some direction—and I thought I could find it here. My grandfather was a scholar, too."

Julian nodded slightly, and then peered up once more to the

marble-white statue. The subject was a youthful noblewoman, slim and relatively short, and dressed elegantly in a light robe. Her left hand held a scroll, which was part of the statue design. Her right hand, meanwhile, rested gently over her thorax.

Julian regarded the physiognomy carefully. The eyes *did* look similar to those that belonged to the mute sorcerer, the only difference being that these eyes were colourless and thus carried none of the fearful air of pressure that had overwhelmed him. He then glanced down to the waist of the figure where an item hung from the girdle, recognising a flute—*the* flute.

"Julian!" Alpheus cried suddenly.

Julian spun immediately, but was late to save Alpheus who had been fired at, now wailing, collapsing to the ground. The sorcerer—the one he had chased into the house—was the aggressor, hurling out arrows from what appeared a mechanical device.

Julian swept out his iron sword, drawing a blast of air in the process, and then slashed at the sorcerer who flipped sideways to evade.

The sorcerer—whose figure was certainly female—sported a plain mask of black. She leaped backwards now and summoned a blast of inferno—not at Julian or Alpheus, but at the statue, engulfing it in flames that brightened the entire cellar.

She then sought to escape, dashing up the stairs.

"No!" Alpheus cried, sitting up suddenly and lurching toward the burning statue.

Alpheus swung off his robe, slapping it on the marble to quell the flames. Julian gawked at him, noting that Alpheus had donned a metal plate beneath his white cultured robe. The centre of the plate was the Fenrir symbol of the Truban Empire, and next to it was a dent from where the arrow had struck.

Julian watched him trying to save the statue for a moment longer, to ensure that he was indeed unhurt. "Stay here," Julian finally said, turning to the stairs in pursuit of the fleeing sorcerer.

He raced his way back to the broken window from where both he and the intruder had entered before. But when he got there, Julian stopped and closed his eyes to concentrate. He couldn't rely on his eyes alone if he were to catch the intruder.

Which way...? he wondered, doing his best to collect any waves in the air that resembled grace.

He suddenly snapped his eyes wide open, turning toward the north-west. It was only faint—in fact, he couldn't even be sure if the trace of energy he thought he had detected was grace at all—but Julian started dashing in that direction anyway, even if it meant he was merely trying for luck.

He wasted no time, powering his legs with the glow of crimson red that lifted him to a swift glide. As he continued racing ahead, he felt that the faint pulsing of grace he had initially detected grew stronger and stronger. He was getting closer and closer, and barely moments later, he caught sight of the intruder once again, who seemed to finally notice his pursuit.

The chase eventually brought Julian to the outer woods north-west of the city, but it was over now—the sorcerer had been forced to the edge of a cliff. She hissed at her luck, but then spun to face Julian. She even slid off her mask, as if to reward Julian for his efforts.

At that distance, and under the thick canopies, she was unrecognisable. Julian could tell that she wasn't the mute sorcerer, however—a realisation that had him feel somewhat disappointed and yet relieved at the same time.

Wait... what are you—?! The sorcerer had spread out her arms, letting herself fall over the edge of the cliff. Julian gritted his teeth, dashing forward immediately, almost skidding over the edge himself. He was too late. She was already falling, and from a height from which no one could expect to survive. But Julian widened his eyes then as suddenly the sorcerer began to glow with a hue of white contrasted by dark cloak. The glow coincided with a slowing fall—in fact, a gentle swivel, almost like a feather brushing left and right.

There, at the bottom of the cliff, stood yet another figure draped in a long cloak. That first sorcerer finally landed now, more securely than she could have asked for. She looked up for a few seconds, during which Julian could only quietly concede that he had been outwitted. He grunted as he then watched them disappear into the marshes.

* * *

Alpheus had continued to slap at the marble statue until the last of the flames were quelled. Smoke filled the cellar, and yet the statue seemed undamaged—and indeed, it looked almost polished after some of the dust was brushed off with his robe, which was now discoloured with ash-black edges. Alpheus wasn't sure why he had been so eager to save the sculpture from burning when he had not a clue who the subject was. The stand of the sculpture had been engraved with the name *Rosa*, and even then, Alpheus couldn't recall anyone by that name in the family's history, which he thought he knew quite well.

He took a step back for a better look to see that nothing more was burning. He then circled behind the sculpture, only to learn that parts of the scroll held on the left hand were still smothered in flames. The flames were weak, though, and Alpheus managed to snuff out the remaining fire with only his fingers.

What's this? he thought, feeling something on that scroll. *Another engraving?*

He crouched down to examine it. "The Glider Steps," he read, muttering the words. "Lighten yourself as a petal of the blossom and allow the wind to guide your path. Spread your wings and take flight." Alpheus stood up straight then, wondering what it all meant.

"*Thank you for protecting me*," a voice said suddenly, echoing throughout the cellar.

Alpheus jumped. He looked left and right with urgency, but saw no one. The voice of a woman had echoed inside his head, soft and gentle. "Who... is it?" he dared to ask.

No response.

Alpheus kept still. *Is this... grace?* he wondered, resting a hand on his chest, feeling a surge of heat from within. A tinkle sounded then from behind. He turned to the statue of the noblewoman, which was now enveloped in a faint glow of violet-blue. Alpheus rubbed his eyes. He blinked, but that glow remained. He blinked a second time, only for the glow to grow more vibrant, growing until the blinding light exploded across the cellar. Alpheus stumbled over and hit the floor with his rear end. When he dared open his eyes again, he watched as a *spectre*—a transparent image of that youthful noblewoman—walked *out of* the statue, glowing with a beautiful aura of light blue. Unlike her colourless origin, she had light blue hair, pale skin, and gleaming violet eyes.

Alpheus gaped at the spectacle as a million thoughts raced through his mind.

"*You can feel at ease*," the spectre said, speaking to him without any movement from her lips, her words still echoing through the cellar. Despite the transcendent presentation, the spectre appeared rather affable—angelic, even.

"Are you... a sorcerer?" Alpheus asked.

"*I am what I am*," she answered. "*And you are... something I don't know. But... I like you.*"

Alpheus opened his mouth, but he couldn't find the words to respond.

"*I cannot stay long. Accept this as a parting gift.*" She waved out an arm softly, presenting Alpheus with the scroll that came to life with her. When she loosened her grip on the scroll, it began floating toward Alpheus, who received it in awe with both hands. She nodded at Alpheus as gesture for him to view the scroll. He complied immediately, rolling open the scroll to see a set of illustrations—around twenty in total.

"*This is the Glider Steps*," she said, before offering a hand.

Alpheus hesitated, but decided to take it—a hand that was frosty cold once within his grip. The spectre smiled at him, and then with a *whoosh* she dashed off, taking him with her, circling the cellar with fantastic speed, whirling loose papers into a funnel of wind. Alpheus cried out, unsure whether to be exhilarated or afraid, as he marvelled at the trail of afterimages behind them and the whiffing breeze that enlivened the otherwise dead cellar.

"*Practise this every day for the next week*," the voice echoed. "*You will be forever indebted.*"

When they finally *landed*, Alpheus took a moment to appreciate what had just happened. It was the most memorable journey Alpheus had ever experienced, and that was despite having never even left the cellar. The exhilaration was overwhelming. There were so many questions he wanted to ask as he twitched onto that scroll.

But the spectre had turned away already and was headed to the stairs. "*Farewell*," she said.

"Wait!" Alpheus cried, stretching out an arm, wondering for a moment why she would take the stairs. "Will we meet again?" he asked instead.

"*I cannot say.*"

"Can you tell me your name, then?"

"*Knowing can do more harm than good*," she said, stepping away now, fading from view rather than actually leaving from the stairs. "*Remember that*," her voice echoed back to him, even after she was gone.

It was a few moments later when Julian finally returned. Alpheus had returned to the living area of his home, sitting in the great hall, all of the chandeliers alight.

"Did you manage to catch the intruder?" he asked first.

"She escaped," Julian replied, shaking his head in shame.

Alpheus shrugged. "We'll probably meet her again," he said. "You know, Julian, it's exciting to know there are more sorcerers around."

Julian pondered for a moment. "I'm not sure it is."

SEVENTEEN

Golden Knight Exchange

The format of the Golden Knight Exchange was simple: two knights to battle against one another, with the winner proceeding to the next successive round until the final.

Generally, a contestant would be granted victory by knocking his opponent to the floor and keeping him down, forcing his opponent to surrender, or knocking his opponent out of the elevated battle ring. The primary rule to follow was that all contestants must uphold the gallantry of a knight, which, in fact implied many rules such as the prohibition of concealed weapons and the intentional crippling of an opponent.

The organisers had made it clear that any cause of death—either accidental or intentional—resulted in instant disqualification and perhaps even prosecution.

Traditionally, a golden knight prospect was expected to possess the strength of fifty men. He was also expected to show a knack for warring strategies, so that he could lead armies when necessary. But, more crucially, one had to have the luck and the opportunity to showcase those skills and transform them into results—and therefore, into achievements. An Exchange created specifically to crown capable warriors as golden knights was the first of its kind under any authority that had ruled Trubannis. It was an opportunity for the ages, and the warriors who had signed up looked prepared to give every effort to succeed.

Julian was thankful to learn that his fight was scheduled to be the last of the day. He needed the time to recover from all the drama that had taken place the previous evening. It was all rather inconclusive, but Julian had managed to make his peace with it. Although he had eventually been outdone by the intruder, he rejoiced in the fact that there were sorcerers out there who *were* beatable.

Focus, he urged himself. *Respect the occasion.* He looked up, then, glancing around the battle ring to the other contestants, and then to the five-tier viewing platform, supplemented with tall braziers that warmed the members of the Empire sitting there.

The Lord Emperor was perched at the centre row of the viewing platform, with the Defender of Saffron, Lionel Lachman, in close company. As the event itself celebrated the chivalry of knightly conduct, the five golden knights in attendance had been arranged to assemble in an imposing line of gleaming gold. Claude Lucan was the Defender of Whitesand, John Tristan was the Defender of Cetal, Walford Bors was the Defender of Zenith, and, finally, Paltiel Sagramore, the leader of all the golden knights, hailed as the Defender of all of Trubannis.

Victor Breunor, a retired golden knight, sat behind them next to the Lord Chancellor and Quinlan Forredan. The Lord Count and the former king of Cetal, Pierre Morlan, sat at the highest tier of the platform.

There was no better stage upon which to impress. The contestants, including Julian, sat adjacent to the viewing platform on three rows of humble benches. Of course, the promise to them was the chance to become a golden knight—specifically to become the Defender of Noel. Only a few were anxious to begin with, and the warrior who stepped up to the battle ring now wasn't one of them. He was Tannon Gale, scheduled to fight the first battle of the day.

His armour of dark red was apparently a replica of the armour he had worn during his glory days, when he had led the mighty Salamanders. The man really *was* different from the miserable savage Julian had known in Carrington. At forty-six years of age, however, it was Gale's body that might end up failing him against the competition, who were, on average, more than ten years younger than him.

Gale's opponent was Mayer Northcliff, a silver knight loyal to the chancellor, armed with a colossal bardiche with an axe head forged into the shape of a burning flame. He was younger than Gale, and bigger than him.

Gale was unarmed for now, peering down at the weapons available to him which had been stocked next to the viewing platform for any contestant to use. "The halberd," he hollered out to the soldier standing there. The soldier promptly collected the pole weapon and raced his way up the battle ring.

Gale received it with fervour, slicing it forward, pointing the halberd at his opponent. "I'll outdo you at your own game," he said. "And when I do, your weapon is mine. It suits me more than it does you."

"You talk big," Northcliff responded with a snort, knocking his bardiche forward. "Why don't we just start already?"

Gale spun his weapon in the air and charged forward, slamming down the halberd toward his opponent, who blocked it with the bardiche—the clash thundering out from the battle ring in a circular wave. Gale then spun, his ponytail swinging behind him, using that momentum to slam in another strike.

Northcliff answered again with an expert block, holding out the bardiche with both hands. He grunted this time, though, and his hands shook slightly after absorbing the shock. Neither contestant seemed to have any trouble wielding their large weapons. Indeed, they were putting on an early show with their expert handling of those long polearms.

He moves with purpose and efficiency, Julian acknowledged, watching Gale. *And... Northcliff*, he thought, eyeing the silver knight. *He's good too. Could I beat either of them?*

A hiccup, then. Gale lost his footing after parrying off a strong thrust.

The audience gasped.

Northcliff shot forward at the chance, winding up for a full swing of the bardiche. He slashed down the polearm, drawing nothing but air, for Gale had dove to the side. Northcliff dashed forward again, but he paused suddenly and then looked down with a grumble, realising that Gale was sitting in a crouch now, his polearm extended, its axe blade connected at his right thigh. There was a deep tear in his cuisse and a streak of red streaming out. He screamed, and in his momentary lapse, his bardiche was knocked from his grip altogether.

Gale snatched the weapon in the air, disposing his own polearm off the stage, and then spun in a victory pose. Northcliff hissed, but admitted his defeat.

A roaring round of applause filled the air. And then, pushing aside the brashness that had apparently once defined him, Gale returned promptly to the seating area without provoking anyone. The bardiche he had earned in the battle was enough reward.

Julian peered over to the viewing platform, eyeing Forredan, who looked delighted for his vassal. He watched on as the stout statesman glanced over to the Lord Chancellor as if a friendly taunt.

* * *

Julian's only ally in the Empire, Percival Pole, was scheduled in the seventh match of the day against a knight by the name of Withy. From all the chatter he had overheard on this day alone, this was supposedly a much-anticipated match, but *not* for good reason—not for Pole, anyway.

More than half the people present fancied the potential story of a silver knight falling in defeat at the hands of a regular knight. Julian had been ignorant about it until now, but apparently, Pole was widely rumoured to be the weakest silver knight in history—that rumour most likely owing to Pole's outward flattery of all those men who had more political power than him. That was the other half of the crowd—most of the noblemen and the lords whom Pole had made a friendly acquaintance—probably betting on Pole to triumph, if only to prove that they had an eye for talent.

Julian himself didn't know how strong Pole might be. The only time he had sparred with the silver knight had been during his first years in Zorlia. He had been a child then, and Pole hadn't yet been admitted as a pupil of the great Paltiel Sagramore.

Pole was wearing an exuberant grin now as he stepped onto the battle ring, and even then, Julian wasn't sure whether it was confidence or ignorance behind that expression. He wanted to believe that Pole was one of the stronger contestants in the competition, but the sleek rapier that the silver knight wielded certainly looked inadequate compared to Withy's sturdy bastard sword. Pole's rather slim figure was also a stark contrast to his opponent's, who carried a broad chest and a rugged mass to match.

"A blessing I've been drawn against you," Withy said, staring down at Pole. "You might be a joke of a warrior, but you're still a silver knight. I can be proud to say that I defeated a silver knight."

Pole shot back a wry grin. "Well then, please take it easy on me," he said, slashing out his rapier with a surprisingly quick draw. The power that came with it, however, was rather lean. And the fact that he had slashed at Withy's mighty weapon was almost amusing, winning chuckles from parts of the crowd.

Withy chortled more derisively than anyone, until he suddenly slammed out his double-handed weapon, batting Pole to the far end of the ring. He chased Pole to the edge, thrusting his heavy weapon persistently, limiting the silver knight only to blocking. He dictated the pace of the fight, and he looked to be in complete control, pressing Pole toward a corner now.

Julian glanced over to the viewing platform again, this time eyeing Sagramore, leader of the golden knights, and the man who had trained Pole. Sagramore displayed very little emotion, however, wearing only a grim expression as he watched the battle.

Julian turned back to the battle now as Withy reached for victory with a growl, slamming down the bastard sword with all his might. But somehow Pole managed to block this attack, too, the force causing Withy's arms to blow upwards. In that brief moment, Pole circled behind the larger man, and prodded him out of the ring with a soft push—to his ultimate defeat.

The crowd fell silent to what was a surprising result. Withy widened his eyes upon realising that his knees had hit the ground. He turned back in shock to see Pole scratching his head with an innocent smile.

Pole had made it look like an incredible stroke of luck on his part, but Julian knew better. He recognised that Pole was indeed highly skilled, that his friend had won the fight without having to reveal his true strength. His performance—or lack of it—seemed to have impressed even the golden knights, who were nodding in appreciation.

* * *

Orel Kite hadn't spared him a glance today, but Julian was sure that the man wanted to face off against him somewhere along the way in the Exchange. Julian wanted it, too—to cross swords with the man who was said to have mastered all weapons.

Julian had waited patiently for this fifteenth match of the day, where Kite was going to be featured. Kite was tipped not only to win this battle, but also the entire competition. His opponent was a commoner, a mercenary who had won his credentials for his brief involvement in the Battle for Saffron. Still, this was expected to be a straightforward victory for Kite, who, at only twenty-three years old, was widely believed to be the strongest of all the knights of his class.

Kite carried a sabre with him today, but now even as he stepped onto the ring, he didn't look like he was about to draw his weapon. His opponent—armed with a pair of twin blades—snorted at the lack of respect.

"You damned brat," the mercenary hollered with a growl. "I'll slice you up!" He bolted forward with a vicious swing of his right blade that was aimed directly for the head. That slice, however, was *caught* mid-swing, with only two fingers and a thumb. In his desperation and shock, the mercenary swung out his other blade, but arrived for the same result.

Cheers and applause sounded from the viewing platform. Breunor was clapping, likely very pleased for his most prized asset who might win him much more praise later on.

Kite himself, however, didn't seem to care for his reputation or the cheers. He simply got on with the battle, applying pressure to where he had gripped, and instantly snapping the blades. He then snorted at his opponent who had paled in terror.

"Why you are here baffles me," Kite said in disgust. He then threw a punch out that sent his opponent skidding across the arena.

The difference in the abilities of the two men in battle was clear. The mercenary had picked himself up, but was now kneeling in desolation. He had lost his will to fight, declaring his surrender with a soft utterance. Kite shook his head and then spun a semi-circle to land a reverse roundhouse kick on the mercenary's shoulder, sending him flying off the stage, his armour in shambles.

Julian winced in response to the unnecessary violence, which didn't stop the spectators from cheering the loudest they had thus far. No one seemed interested to call Kite out for violating the rules that said all contestants must uphold the gallantry of a knight. The mercenary was carried away soon enough, presumably to a physician. And though he wailed in pain, he won little sympathy from the crowd, who was only interested in strong warriors on this day.

Kite, who continued to ignore the admiration the crowd had for him, hopped off the battle ring now with a glare over at the contestants' benches, meeting Julian's eyes as well as a few others.

Julian didn't think much of it, however, especially as his name was called now. The sixteenth and final match of the day was here. It was finally his turn to make a mark in the competition. It was his opportunity to impress some of the most esteemed figures of the country, which included the Lord Emperor and the Lord Count.

He stepped onto the battle ring, feeling the ruggedness of the tiled floor as well as a sudden pressure to perform. It wasn't the first time he had been on the arena—having trained there for many days leading up to the competition—but the view from there was different on this day. He knew that many of the spectators present had looked forward to seeing him—many of them were there to see him fail. But if there was anything that he had grown used to since coming to Zorlia, it was the constant need to silent his doubters. There was no better stage to do that than here right in the heart of the city.

Today, he donned the standard soldier's armour with a cape hanging off his shoulders that covered his entire iron sword except the hilt. His opponent was Byron Patrick, a silver knight who was a loyal follower of Breunor as well as one of those who had witnessed Julian wielding the powers of sorcery at the parlour nearly a month prior. The man was the most established warrior in the competition.

At forty-seven years old, Patrick was the oldest contestant, but his achievements were well-merited, having gained a vast wealth of experience over the years, including enlistment with the Golden Dragon Knights army. He was a traditional warrior who paired a broadsword with a shield. He was said to be careful, and he didn't look like he was about to underestimate Julian for any reason.

Julian was first to take initiative, heaving out his chunk of iron from beneath his cape and slashing ahead of him. He aimed for his opponent's helm, but instead thumped onto his shield, the impact resounding with a resilient clunk.

Patrick swung his broadsword out in response, sparking a jangle from another clash of metals. The same sequence repeated itself for a second and third time, with the veteran knight gaining momentum after each strike. Julian realised that Patrick was physically stronger than him, and that the man also seemed to time his attacks with expert precision. Having lacked a good teacher with the sword, Julian's skill with the iron sword was simply negligible on this stage, where the competition was clearly designed for knights who were masters of the sword.

On that thought, Julian leaped back. But surprisingly, his opponent did the same, perhaps in caution of Julian's other ability—sorcery.

"Throw everything you have at me," Patrick said. "This is your only chance."

Julian consented with a squint. "Very well then," he said, waving an arm in a silky motion, which then spawned forth a misty grey steam from his body.

Gasps sounded from the viewing platform then, but Julian had no time to spare any glance elsewhere. "Don't regret getting what you asked for," he said, gritting his teeth with a glare on his opponent, as surges of glowing red static sparked around him.

Julian breathed in then, and the mists spun back into his body like a vortex, and the red static accumulated into a soft aura of crimson red. He wasted no time dashing forward for another slash of his iron sword, which came with fantastic speed, at least multiple times faster than before. Patrick still managed to block the attacks with his shield, but the impact of each clash was highlighted by explosions of crimson red that forced the veteran knight back.

Encouraged by the cheers that he believed was for him, Julian darted away and then immediately in again from another angle to land his first hit that knocked off Patrick's helm—an action that perhaps humiliated the man more than if he had actually been hit. He thought he saw Patrick wince in the blur, but he couldn't be sure, for he had darted off yet again. *From the right next*, Julian decided.

He slashed, aiming for the waist, as far away from the shield as possible. And yet, Patrick managed to swing his shield over, causing Julian to grow suddenly uneasy. Still, he dashed away before Patrick got a better look at him. *From the top this time*, he decided. He raced at the veteran knight head on, leaping up at the final moment and slamming down his iron sword with the added force of gravity.

Blocked again.

Speed alone wasn't going to be enough against the veteran knight, who seemed to rely not only on his primary senses but also on his deep experience, which, after many years, had apparently translated into the ability to read his foes' movements and motives.

Julian moved with a natural flair, but he was expending a whole lot of grace to keep it up. If this turned out to be a battle of endurance and grit, Julian would most likely lose.

But I cannot afford to lose, Julian thought, leaping away now and slowing to a pause.

"What's the matter?" Patrick taunted between breaths.

Julian frowned, regarding the veteran knight for a moment. He relaxed his muscles, which then followed with the evaporation of his crimson red glow.

Patrick scowled at this, but maintained his defensive stance. Julian was sure that the rest of the crowd thought it strange, too, that he had given up his speed advantage.

Julian groaned and then ran forward, feeling it himself that his step had clearly slowed. Still, he whacked his sword at Patrick, who now responded and parried with visible comfort, as he had expected. It must have appeared completely futile to the spectators now as he continued to belt the chunk of iron at Patrick, indeed at the man's shield. He heard jeers in the air, and he also noted that the veteran knight looked to be growing more and more frustrated.

Besides the one instance of losing his helm, Patrick had answered every one of Julian's slash from earlier even behind the blessing of enhanced speed. It must have been insulting to the man now that Julian was throwing at him those same attacks, but without the speed from before.

Just a little more, Julian thought, urging himself on and hoping that his opponent wouldn't see through his strategy.

Patrick growled now, finally slashing out his broadsword and drawing blood immediately, skimming Julian on his sword-wielding arm. "Don't toy with me!" the veteran knight cursed.

Julian ignored his opponent's ire as well as his own wound. Instead, he gripped tightly to his sword to keep up the relentless battering. Patrick was clearly annoyed, but the man continued to limit himself to defending only, perhaps still wary that Julian might suddenly unleash a blazing flame. It was a few moments later when the veteran swung out his sword a second time, drawing only thin air as Julian was quick to hop away.

Julian lifted his iron sword up once again, but instead of dashing forward, he stood his ground and spread out his other hand from a fist. Patrick raised his shield in an immediate response, falling right into Julian's plot.

There it is, Julian thought, not calling on his flames, but instead racing forward toward the veteran knight for the final time. This time, he swept out his most powerful strike yet, and with this, he smashed his sword at Patrick's shield, crushing it into pieces. The truth was that Julian had been channelling his grace into his iron sword, which made for far stronger thrusts than what he could manage with his physical strength alone. He needed none of the garish display of violent flames that he was probably associated with in the minds of most of the crowd. And it was thanks to Pole's earlier showing that somewhat guided Julian to choose such a strategy.

Patrick gaped in visible shock as he watched his shield shatter into rubble, finally recognising then that Julian had been targeting the shield all along. The jeers were no more, the air now filled with stunned silence, and perhaps raised eyebrows—at least until Patrick suddenly whacked out his broadsword at Julian, signalling his intention to continue fighting.

Julian frowned slightly but welcomed the challenge, answering Patrick's attacks far more comfortably than before. Several more sparks of jangles followed as Julian's iron sword clashed with his opponent's smaller broadsword. He noted that his opponent's confidence was wavering, hesitating at almost every clash of metals, at times even looking like he was about to raise his left arm to which no shield was attached. As he had expected, the veteran knight could no longer fight with his accustomed style, which meant that his deep experience was now playing against him. Patrick was too comfortable coordinating his right and left arms for sword and shield, respectively. The battle didn't last much longer, ending when Julian knocked the veteran knight off the ring with his own growing confidence.

Patrick was barely hurt, and yet his expression showed both shock and pity as he had lost on tactics, the one area in which he should have had the obvious advantage. He hissed in Julian's direction and then trotted away from the training ground altogether.

EIGHTEEN

True strength

The second round of the Golden Knight Exchange couldn't have come sooner for almost all of those involved. Some of the spectators had arrived at the training ground earlier than the contestants today, excited about what was to come.

Victor Breunor, the primary person responsible for the organisation of the event, was one of those to arrive early, and he was at this moment enjoying the flattery from the noblemen who lauded him for how successful the event had been up until now. After the court had promised to reward him with the authority to oversee all the armies in the country on the condition that he made the Exchange into a worthwhile event, he had made sure that everything would run without a hiccup.

Apart from translating what had been Reeling's idea into reality, Breunor had also entered nine men to represent him, all of them silver knights. And of those nine, seven had managed to advance to the second round today, which meant that nearly half of the remaining sixteen contestants were loyal to him.

Whether the Exchange was worthwhile or not perhaps didn't depend so much on his vassals' performances, but strong performances would certainly help.

In the past, Breunor had often argued that he had brought out Walford Bors, who had been a golden knight for a decade and hailed as the biggest—the Golden Titan—of all of the greatest warriors. Bors had hardly been guided by Breunor, however—they were of the same generation. They had trained together, and fought alongside one another.

This was the chance to show the court that he could lead, and that he deserved to oversee all the armies in the country. And, finally, it was his chance to finally clear away his poor track record in terms of producing and guiding younger warriors.

The draw three days ago had been kind on him—or on his personal pupil, Kite, for that matter—pairing Kite up against the only regular knight remaining in the competition. That battle was scheduled to be the third of the day. Kite could probably overcome anyone in the competition, but an easy draw was favourable in that it would keep the young knight fresh for the subsequent rounds, which would surely be more challenging.

But the opening matchup of the day was far more intriguing, at least to most other men. Breunor watched with a slight cringe now as one of the first two contestants stepped onto the battle ring. He eyed the young man with disdain—the sorcerer-soldier Julian Longinus—who he continued to hold a grudge against, not only because the boy had dared to give him trouble, but also because he was the child of Royston Longinus, the man who had once handed him a humiliating defeat.

Breunor had wanted one of his own men to avenge him, but as he looked to the young Longinus's opponent then, he sat back with a grin. Tannon Gale, a veteran warrior who belonged in the same generation of prominent knights of the Anaphora era as Breunor himself, could surely bring out a performance to humble the eyesore that was Julian Longinus.

* * *

Julian had thought that the pressure he felt would have lessened the second time around, but the vantage point from the battle ring was still suffocating. He had slipped on the sapphire ring from Alpheus that amplified grace. He needed it. When he was certain that his opponent overpowered him in raw strength and bettered him in battle strategy, his only leverage was sorcery.

Indeed, he regretted not having worn the ring in the first round against Byron Patrick. He didn't allow his naïve inhibitions to hold him back this time. It didn't matter that he used a power that wasn't his own, not when every one of his contestants would most likely do the same if they were offered the opportunity.

He winced now as he watched Gale leap up to join him on the fighting stage. *He was treaded over by a Primal Soldier of Kraga*, Julian thought. *I can hardly picture it. Just how strong are some of these people?*

Gale grunted, slashing forward the bardiche he had won from the first round. If the man was still haunted by his past, his brash grin hid it well, especially as he now thumped the mighty polearm on the platform, which seemed to shake the ground beneath their feet. The man needed no sympathy, and wasn't prepared to give any in return.

"Roland," Gale said, addressing Julian with the name he had first known him by. "Don't think this will be the same as last time."

Julian cocked his head with a smirk. "It *won't* be like last time," he agreed. "Except the result."

As soon as the battle began, Gale was on the offensive, thrashing the bardiche to the left and right. His purposeful prods limited Julian to blocking, drawing first blood early as he sliced Julian across his left shoulder. Gale was aggressive to start, attacking early and often, a stark contrast to Patrick's approach from the first round.

"What's wrong?" Gale called out, pressing Julian about being on the defence. "You won't win if you don't attack."

Julian didn't allow himself to fall for the taunts, but the truth was that he was being given no space to conjure up any meaningful strike. Even as he dashed away now, Gale raced right after him, breathing down his neck.

Damn, he's persistent, Julian thought as he sprinted, glancing down at the sapphire ring on his index finger. He came to a sudden screeching stop, the grind between his feet and the floor sweeping out a puff of smoke. *Come at me!* he thought, ready to unleash his flames.

But Gale was more nimble than Julian had expected. The veteran warrior spun to slow his momentum, and in turn, he drew on his spin to whack out his bardiche.

Julian gritted his teeth, gushing out his grace as his arm wielding sword slashed up with fantastic speed behind a glow of crimson red, parrying Gale in a spectacular block. Julian widened his eyes in surprise as Gale's arms flung up, and then glanced over to the sapphire ring again, which now pulsed with brilliant luminescence.

Amazing, he thought. Julian groaned then, hunching slightly for a brief moment before his entire body suddenly caught in its soft red aura.

The crowd cheered, clearly wanting to see more sorcery that they had last time. Julian granted their wish by setting his iron sword ablaze, slashing it down diagonally with a roaring heatwave, which was surely an amazing spectacle in the eyes of the spectators as well as a welcome air of warmth on this cold winter day. He then erupted against his opponent with a flurry of slashes, meeting Gale's pole weapon with flares splashing about wildly.

The tables had turned, and now Julian was the one pressing while Gale was limited to blocking, struggling to keep up.

Julian maintained a fierce onslaught of slashes behind the amplifying applause from the spectators. He didn't know whether the people were marvelling at the roaring flames, but he himself was certainly impressed by his own powers—or perhaps the power he was lending from the sapphire ring.

He slowed his offence then to bait his opponent into whacking out a counterattack—which Gale did, pushing Julian away with a strong thrust, probably in the mind that he was regaining some momentum.

As he fell away, Julian swung out another slash, this time sending out a giant fireball, blasting at Gale who stooped now in desperation. Gale crossed his arms over his head as the inferno crashed into him, exploding into smothering fumes.

How do you like that? Julian thought with a sneer, before promptly sending out a second, a third, and a fourth fireball, all formed from the tip of his blazing sword.

It was overkill—or at least it seemed that way from Julian's vantage point. Even he wasn't sure what had become of the veteran knight, when half of the arena was enveloped in smoke. And yet, Julian continued to fire away, urged on by the incredible power at his possession.

He finally stopped after a brief glance over to the viewing platform, which was now blanketed by billows of smoke. For a moment then, Julian remembered that any cause of death resulted in instant disqualification. He leaped back from the fumes that had enshrouded his opponent, wishing that Gale survived, and at the same time wondering where that ruthlessness had come from.

But as he worried for Gale, the veteran knight surprised by suddenly emerging from the smoke with a powerful leap. At the end of his bardiche forked an orb of burning molten. Despite being covered in dark ash, he hurled the fireball back at Julian, crashing into him before exploding into another blast of smoke.

His arms, which he had used to shield the rest of his body, were burning intensely—the power of the flames were indeed fearful. But the throbbing pain wasn't what Julian focused on—it was on how Gale had possibly managed to achieve the counterattack in the form of a revived fireball. The veteran knight couldn't possibly be a sorcerer.

Julian emerged from the fumes in both pain and befuddlement, most of him caked in black ash just like his opponent. Resuming the battle from where it had been left off, he slashed out his still blazing sword yet again to send out another fireball. The inferno managed only to smear his opponent, however, who thumped his bardiche down at the molten ball in an effort to stifle its advance. The veteran knight then rooted his weapon into the core of the dying flames, brewing it briefly before heaving it again at Julian with the added force of a whirlwind.

Incredible! Julian thought, batting out his sword to obliterate the ball of fire that exploded this time with a gust that blew up much of the sand around the arena and into his eyes. *Is this what it means to be part of—no, the commander of the Scorching Salamanders?* He could hardly believe it, but Gale was exchanging roaring orbs of fire with him back and forth across the arena for a brilliant yet violent display. For someone who wasn't a sorcerer, Gale was certainly an incredible warrior, having more than proved that he could hold his own even when Julian was giving his best shot and unleashing all of his powers, which had further been boosted by the sapphire ring.

Julian was growing exhausted, especially on top of his burning wounds, but he was sure that his opponent must have been worn out as well. On noting now that he had some space to manoeuvre, he torched his iron sword once more and dashed up at Gale as he looked for ultimate victory. He slashed away with considerably less power than earlier, and yet he still knocked off Gale's polearm.

For a moment, he thought he had won, but he soon noted that the veteran knight's left arm was outstretched as he was falling. And only then did Julian notice his opponent slapping his hand, which in turn, knocked his grip off of the iron sword.

Julian dove for his sword, but Gale was quick to find his feet again, already racing toward him to deny the advantage.

What followed was a battle with gauntlets only, where Julian found himself exchanging blows with Gale, using nothing but their fists. Without the blessing of the crimson glow of red, he knew that it had all come down to a test of willpower and grit.

As everything began to blur now, Julian decided to stake everything on a final strike. And remarkably, his opponent did the same, going in for a jab, meeting at the knuckles.

They froze in that position, their arms shaking. Everything was silent until Julian grunted, as he tried to call on even the small hint of grace that he thought he had left. He looked up then to meet Gale's smirk, wary that the veteran knight had more.

But, in fact, Gale was at his limit. The man's eyelids fell now as he collapsed with a thud, losing all consciousness. Roaring cheers and applause filled the air.

Julian peered up, seeing nothing more than a blur. And soon, everything went blank.

* * *

Julian woke up in the home he shared with Oscar. Next to his bed was a bowl of soup, and when he looked down to inspect his injuries, he saw that he was fully bandaged up. The bitter of the medicine under the swaddles reeked but within that was also the redolence of natural coolants that remedied the burning wounds. He then glanced up at the torn roof where a few stars glistened behind dark clouds.

Just then, Oscar stepped into the hovel. "Do you remember anything at all about what happened?" he asked.

"How long have I been out?" Julian said, turning the question back.

"Well, it was yesterday when you—"

Julian sat up suddenly, grabbing hold of the boy at the shoulders. "It's been that long?!" he asked, realising that round three was on the next day.

The boy brushed off his grip with a scowl. "Didn't know you had that much energy," he complained.

"Oscar," Julian said. "Tell me what happened."

The boy rolled his eyes. "You were sent back by a physician," he said. "He treated your wounds, but he said that it's impossible to have you healed in time for the next round." He paused for a moment. "He said you should give it up."

Julian frowned, looking at his hand and then peering up his arm all the way to the shoulder. *It aches*, he thought. *Every part of me aches. But my grace... it's restored to a safe level.*

"I'm all right," Julian said, glancing to the sapphire ring on his finger. "I still have tonight to rest."

"I thought you'd say that," Oscar said, already heading out. "The soup's for you."

Julian peered over at that bowl of thick soup and the spoon next to it. He lifted the bowl and downed a mouthful. "It's good," he said softly, knowing that no one heard him.

* * *

The Lord Emperor sat silently among the enthusiastic crowd.

The third round was about to begin.

The great man had attended every minute of the Exchange, but had offered little of his opinion. He had made no remarks on how he thought these warriors might be utilised in his empire. Some noblemen thought they had spotted him perk up a few times during the past two rounds when some of the contestants surprised the audience with clever tactics. Most other times, however, the Lord Emperor had been quiet—bored, even. Other than that, he had shared quiet conversations with Lachman, who was incidentally one of the strongest golden knights.

It was always going to be a challenge to engross the Lord Emperor in any competition. After all, the great man had fought on real battlefields and had triumphed as one of the greatest, if not *the* greatest, war tactician in recorded history.

His full name was Kasimir de Spartamon. He had been born as the heir to a family of mercenaries known as the Clan of Light, and with both the honour and responsibility to lead them. He had never been fazed by the immense pressure resting on his shoulders, and had indeed always been the best in everything he had tried to do.

He had been more than a child prodigy. He was a genetic marvel who had succeeded as the Third Leader of the clan at the tender age of sixteen. His personal combat skills would perhaps *only* match the average golden knight, but his leadership abilities and opportunist personality lifted him far above other men. It was his godly sense in seizing the best of opportunities and his expertise in setting up flawless battle tactics that eventually led the clan to be the most feared in the land.

It was a shame that the negative hearsay concerning his alleged tyrannic ways often undermined his achievements. The people tended to forget that he led the Clan of Light from humble mercenaries to arguably the greatest authority that was the Truban Empire of the present day.

Many others—especially in recent years—would argue that the Lord Emperor wouldn't be where he was now without his eternal companion turned rival and nemesis, Yeremia Schim, the current Lord Chancellor of the Empire.

Few people knew that Schim had once been a member of a rival clan. He had been spared only upon offering his loyalty to the Clan of Light after the demise of his own clan. At the time, at the age of about seventeen, Schim had found himself inferior to Spartamon—four years younger than him—in all respects as a mercenary. He had learned that Spartamon had been driven with the ambition to rule his own kingdom, and that had been *before* his succession as the leader of the clan.

Schim had been the only one to believe Spartamon would rule. He had grown to adore him absolutely, the prodigy who had been regarded as a god under a man's disguise. Schim had given his all to help Spartamon to achieve his dream. Schim had worked harder than anyone to make it happen, and he had been instrumental in erasing Spartamon's only flaw which had been the reluctance to entrust his vassals with significant responsibilities. Schim had, of course, been the one to earn that first prominent supporting role, winning his own army to lead.

The clan's rapid expansion of power had begun there, and what had followed had been rather straightforward. They had devoured all other mercenaries in the area. Schim had evolved into an impressive war tactician himself, second only to Spartamon, who had shared his battle strategies only with him. The clan itself, of course, had then established itself as the greatest army in the country until its partial dissolve at the dawn of the new era.

Today, both sat in great honour and dignity at a height that common mercenaries could only dream of. Physically, they were separated by only several seats on the viewing platform, with Schim on a tier higher. But in between that trivial amount of physical space laid a large, invisible void that buried their past camaraderie.

The emperor peered out to the arena now, where the contestants of the first match of this third round had stepped. A loud reception welcomed Orel Kite to the stage. The young knight wielded a sabre today. He had been drawn against Owen Roc, who wielded a claymore. The matchup promised to be an enthralling affair. Both of them donned gleaming silver armour, and they had both been entered in the Exchange by Victor Breunor.

The emperor glanced back at Breunor now, who sat next to Schim. *Cannot have him oversee our armies*, he thought with a squint. He then peered back out from the viewing platform, eyeing the benches on the adjacent where the contestants sat, only six of them remaining minus the two on the battle ring. *A sorcerer*, he thought, regarding the boy who was apparently the child of Royston Longinus. *And a swordsman*, he acknowledged as he peered over to Percival Pole, Sagramore's personal disciple. *This new generation of warriors simply do not measure up.*

* * *

Julian peered out to the battle ring from the contestants' benches, still aching from his previous battle against Gale. He was never going to allow a few injuries to hold him back. Since arriving at the training ground earlier in the morning, he had learned that his opponent today was Percival Pole. While he was still trying to fathom the draw that had paired him up against his only ally of the competition, he had also heard that Pole had apparently won himself many admirers in the previous round with what had been described to be exquisite handling of the rapier.

Their match was scheduled to be the third of four matches, and the mere thought of crossing swords with Pole had Julian in disarray. While there had always been a chance that he would be paired against his ally, the reality of it was still difficult to swallow.

Julian rose to his feet now. He had seen enough of what Orel Kite was capable of. Although the young knight was having a tough time, his slick handles of the sabre would eventually negate his opponent's robust style. Kite was sure to triumph.

Kite uses a slender sword, Julian recognised, as he treaded away and out behind the wall that fenced in the training ground. *And he uses it well, conserving energy while his foe consumes it in chunks wielding that bastard sword. If I am to beat Percival, I'd have to devise a strategy to counter that.*

He reached for the iron sword on his back, brushing his fingers on the grip. Much of his body still throbbed from the burns. He was swathed in bandages, though most of it was hidden beneath his armour.

He sighed.

"I didn't expect you to be nervous," said a voice from behind.

Julian spun, dropping to one knee as soon as he recognised the Lord Chancellor. "My Lord!"

"Are you afraid of your opponent?" asked Schim, his mighty frame more imposing from that angle.

"No, I'm... not afraid," Julian said with hesitation. "But... he... he's like a brother to me. My opponent, that is."

"Is that so?" Schim said before his eyes wandered off to the sky. "I once had a sworn brother myself."

Julian maintained an awkward gaze at Schim, not quite sure what the protocol was in this conversation.

"But brotherhood and knighthood cannot co-exist without sacrifices," Schim continued. "When it comes down to it, one would always choose the best for himself—even if it means betraying those closest to him." The great man looked down to Julian again, staring down at him intently. "Remember this," he said, his tone reverting to his usual grimness. "In the world we live in, it's easier to betray than to be betrayed."

The word, *betray*, echoed in his head. Surely, it wouldn't come to that between him and Pole.

"You seem hesitant," Schim then said. "If you don't give it your all, you'll stand no chance. His execution of the Twin Image Swordplay is superb."

Julian raised a brow, thinking that swordplay a common skill for anyone wielding the slender swords.

"The strength of any technique is dependent on the one using it," Schim added.

Julian stared blankly at Schim, shaking off his blur only when a huge cheer reverberated over the wall enclosing the training ground. Kite had most likely taken the first match, and the cheers marked the end of the second match. The third match of the day was next—the match in which Julian would cross swords with his friend.

"Lord Chancellor," Julian said with a determined glare. "I'll do what I can. And if I manage to impress, you can then consider my recruitment."

Schim shot him a grin. "Go."

Julian turned, pacing back into the training ground. He spared no glance at Hugh Caden, the victorious silver knight who stood atop the battle ring. Julian had his eyes on only one person—Percival Pole—who was still seated at the benches. Julian treaded directly to the battle ring, hopping on despite the second match winner still enjoying his moment of glory.

The crowd jeered at Julian, who didn't care. "Percival!" he shouted at Pole with a beam. "It's our turn! Come on up!"

Pole grinned back in response, stood up from his seat, and leaped onto the battle ring. But unlike Julian, who had ignored Caden, Pole politely asked him to make way, which he did, but only after scowling at the both of them.

"I've finally caught up to you on this stage," Julian said, clenching his fists, trying his best to enjoy the moment.

"Let's make this a battle to remember," Pole replied, whipping out his rapier.

Julian responded with a grunt before breathing a puff of grey fog which coincided with his eyes glowing a crimson red. He swept out his iron sword and torched it ablaze, exciting the spectators who had just now jeered at him.

The battle began at a fast pace. As Julian had expected, it was difficult to handle his sturdy iron sword as sleekly as Pole wielded the rapier. His flames were worthless if he couldn't land a hit.

Pole was prodding his weapon in the Twin Image Swordplay just as the Lord Chancellor had mentioned. And, indeed, his execution was a few levels above anything Julian could accomplish. On appearance, the soft slices of the rapier were powerless, but being at the end of them, Julian realised just how versatile and effective they were. The wielder didn't look to overpower his opponent. Rather, it was a style created to avoid a wrestling match, focused on parrying and countering, all of it in slick motions. On the offensive, it was to be feared for the speed that was so incredible that it created an illusion, a 'twin image' of the wielder's sword.

The technique itself had been developed decades ago during the Anaphora Era, before larger weapons—such as the broadsword and double-handed axe—had become popular. With the introduction of those more destructive weapons, the forging of the slender swords had gradually declined. The Twin Image Swordplay had also become less popular. But judging from Pole's deadly prods, those slender swords might well see a revival.

He's certainly fast, Julian conceded. *As if lashing out with multiple swords.*

But... speed is what I am known for.

After being parried yet again, Julian gushed out some more grace, and soon his entire body effused the soft aura of crimson red. Julian raced toward Pole who had prodded his sword forward, flashing away suddenly just before they would have clashed. As if Pole had seen through his intention, he spun and cut a slice to his left, which was exactly where Julian was aiming—their blades clashing to a sharp jangle that parried away Julian's iron chunk.

Julian recovered almost immediately with his terrific speed, however. He then lured Pole to chase after him, forcing the silver knight to change up his passive battle strategy. Julian then dashed away together with Pole from one end of the arena to the other, trading a blur of slashes and slices that he didn't realise he could manage.

While he had an obvious advantage in speed, Pole held the advantage of superior swordsmanship, expertly blocking and parrying at the same time. On one occasion, Pole managed to throw a counter-slash, only for Julian to flash away at the last moment. Despite the heat of the battle, Julian was beginning to realise that if his own swordsmanship could be cultivated, he would grow far stronger than he was now. Sorcery wasn't everything.

But I only have sorcery to rely on now, Julian thought as he gushed out more and more grace. This was the fastest he had ever moved. He was almost flying. And yet, it wasn't enough—not when Pole stifled his mobility with purposeful slices that felt almost as if he was being played.

Just a little more...! Just a little more and he won't be able to catch up.

He soared toward Pole, searing the arena ablaze, and whacked out his iron sword for the win—his most forceful strike yet behind yet another roaring swing.

Parried again.

How...?! he wondered in shock as he was falling away, noting then that Pole was bolting toward him with a slice of the rapier that he barely managed to defend.

Pole then leaped away to a distance and stepped into a strange stance, one leg lifted up in the air. "It's about time we ended this match," he said.

"I still have plenty in me," Julian claimed, his voice reduced to a wheeze, though the aura effusing from him still glowed brightly. He dashed forward again, winding up that chunk of iron as he prepared to propel for a surprise.

But before he even hacked his weapon out, a vicious slice swept at him, drawing a stream of red on his thigh. He ignored the pain and then drew on all the speed he could, slamming his sword once more at Pole… only for it to be parried off again—like every other time.

Almost like leaves to a breeze, Julian noted as that feeling of being overwhelmed by the mute sorcerer suddenly came rushing back at him. By the time he recovered this time, he was at the mercy of his opponent, a sword pressed at his neck.

Cries of mercy sounded from the viewing platform. And while Pole promptly withdrew his slender sword, returning it to the sheath at his waist, Julian was crushed in defeat.

"You held back?!" he asked, not willing to believe it.

"No," Pole answered. "I fought with all I had from the start, except I didn't use the most efficient stance. The Twin Image Swordplay comprises ten stances, each designed to counter different weapons. The only exception is the first which is a general stance." He paused now, offering Julian a hand. "Anyway, you fought well. Be proud."

Julian took that hand, rising to his feet. He heard cheers—some of them probably for him, but he didn't care for any of it. He thought he saw the Lord Chancellor peeking out from the viewing platform among the crowd there, but he couldn't be sure. He stepped off the arena and headed out. He wasn't going to watch the last match of the round. It didn't matter anymore, and not because it was over for him, but because he was sure Pole would eventually be crowned as the champion.

Julian ignored his injuries and the blood that drizzled from his injured thigh. He no longer thought about Pole or the Exchange. Indeed, Julian thought only about himself, regretting how weak he was.

NINETEEN

An abrupt ending

Reeling had been born a commoner, orphaned at only the age of four, and then adopted by a gentle couple of the noble class, who had later died from an epidemic. His current social status, the reverence and admiration the people had for him, were a result of hard work and persistence in climbing that social hierarchy. Long before he had become the Lord Count of the Truban Empire, he had been rumoured to share a romantic relationship with Charlotte Hindlow. He found it laughable—and indeed, deeper down, he found it frightening just imagining what that would actually involve.

He pushed open the door to his chambers now, widening his eyes at the glimmers of sunset that glared in. The guest who had let himself in was a surprise. Alpheus was seated in one of the two guest chairs, fidgeting with his pocket watch. On his index finger was the sapphire ring that Julian Longinus must have returned to him after his defeat in the Exchange.

"What brings you back?" Reeling said, hiding his delight in seeing the young scholar again as he made his way to his seat.

"Direction," Alpheus said, snapping the watch closed. "I want to confirm my bearings and I trust that you can help me."

Reeling smirked. "And why should I help you?"

"Because I will help you in return. I've decided that the Empire might not be the worst."

"And when things go wrong, will you leave again?"

"I can never be too sure," Alpheus admitted. "*Though*, if I had to leave, I'm sure no one could catch me."

"What is that supposed to mean?"

Alpheus reached under his cultured robe. "This," he said, shooting a scroll across the table. Reeling glanced down at the diagrams, unsure what they represented.

"Watch," Alpheus said with a grin now, rising from his chair. "And don't blink."

Alpheus hopped to his left, and then suddenly, he flashed away, catching fantastic speed in the process. He circled the chamber as if walking on air, sweeping any loose items to swirl about as if caught in a brief wind storm. Twisting and turning at impossible angles, he chased his own afterimages that trailed him along with an air of cool white that dissolved into the invisible atmosphere.

It wasn't the ability that belonged to the Longinus family. It wasn't as fast and possibly not as useful. But it was certainly graceful.

Reeling already noted that the seemingly random pattern in which Alpheus was moving was indeed *Langton's Ant* in physical form. This was a motion skill designed for those who understood what it meant to simulate patterns.

He eventually held up a hand to signal for Alpheus to stop. When he did, Reeling flipped the scroll over to the calligraphy.

"Rosa?" he said, reading the signature.

"Do you... know her?" Alpheus asked, looking hopeful.

Reeling shook his head and picked up the scroll, turning to the window to further inspect it. *This is unprecedented*, he thought, delighted for Alpheus. He paced closer to the wall and slyly snatched a lighted candle mounted there, setting the document on fire—this action causing Alpheus to immediately cry in protest.

With a simple flap of the scroll, the whole thing caught rapid fire, incinerating in seconds. Alpheus gaped at the sight, doing his best to refrain himself from crying out. His glare at Reeling, however, was more powerful than words.

"This manual wasn't meant to be discovered," Reeling said, making little effort to console him. "Let no one else have the fortune." He paused for a moment, finding his way to his seat again. "More importantly, the Empire received a letter from Koren Perfecto—the King of the Far East. Kathryn Trulips is ready to come to Zorlia again. And sharing the journey will be your sister."

Alpheus raised an eyebrow, asking the question without uttering the words, obviously still upset about the destroyed calligraphy.

"For a visit only, I believe," Reeling added.

Alpheus said nothing still, looking more agitated than excited.

"What?" Reeling asked.

"Are you going to apologise?" Alpheus said with a pout.

Reeling simpered. "I do not think—"

"You can make up for it by taking me to Aizary," Alpheus inserted in surprise.

"If time allows. But I would prefer a visit to Vinawell and even Kraga before going to the Far East again."

"Why?" Alpheus asked. "They were our enemies. During the war."

"If we are to discuss this, then you ought to know that Aizary is hardly our allies."

"What are you talking about?" Alpheus shot back. "The ones who slaughtered our people were Vinawell and Kraga. Aizary did nothing."

"Yes, *nothing*," Reeling enunciated. "They did not come to our aid. I do not believe they even considered it."

"Who can blame them when Trubannis was in the mess we were in under the Sargon reign? There was no incentive to work with us."

"And by the same logic, perhaps Vinawell and Kraga did what they did with the intention to *save* the common people of our country—to save them from the corrupted monarch."

Alpheus deepened his frown. "That's absurd. If the—"

"Is it, though?" Reeling challenged. "What is absurd is your bias—your preconceptions, and your refusal to see things from other perspectives."

"What about the evidence, then?" Alpheus said, raising the volume of his voice slightly. "Are you going to ignore all the evidence? It is *well*-documented that the Kragans are barbaric and brutal. They're born that way... most of them, anyway."

"The evidence shows that the Trubans, our fellow countrymen, slaughtered a fair share of men, if not more. So unless you are telling me a Truban life is more precious than a Kragan life, I do not understand your argument."

"But *they* were the ones who started the war," Alpheus argued. "Milos Rachkoltesz instigated everything. It's called the Battle *for* Saffron."

"And that name is recognised only here," Reeling said, rising from his seat once more. "Have you ever wondered what our enemies might call it? It is near-impossible to draw back on all the history and conclude who was initially at fault. On the battlefield, there is no good or evil—only a winner and a loser, because the winner would rewrite history and redefine morality."

Alpheus gaped as a bead of sweat was visibly sliding down his forehead.

"Alpheus," Reeling then said with a cough as he paced again to the wide window above his chair, looking up at the rays of the glaring sun. "You are a scholar first and foremost. You have the duty to disregard your emotions when it is asked of you."

"I'll try," Alpheus responded softly, though Reeling was sure that the young scholar didn't understand what he meant.

* * *

The night was cold. The winds were strong, with patches of rain drenching different parts of the city. It was one of those starless nights where clouds had crept upon the land, hiding even the faintest rays of moonlight.

Alpheus was dressed for the weather, donning a straw raincoat. The stony streets were nearly empty of people. He treaded ahead to the largest, most imposing structure around, the clusters of towering steeples that was Vondra Dawn. The conversation he had shared with Reeling in the afternoon had been inconclusive, and this had bothered him greatly. In fact, Alpheus had felt rather disquieted since. He couldn't recall when it was that he had wanted to appreciate what the man might be thinking and to share a little of the heavy burden often on his shoulders. He hadn't done so yet, but surely, there was more time ahead of them.

And yet, *something* had urged him to throw on that raincoat, to brave the potential storm that was forecasted this evening. Something wasn't right. And Alpheus couldn't be sure what it was. Perhaps it was his intention to visit Aizary. He had gone to see Reeling earlier in the day with his mind set on it, and yet he had seemed to forget about it after only a brief dismissal from the courtly man.

Now, as he paced along the streets of piled stones, he thought about what Reeling meant to him. Next to his faith, the man had been the one he had turned to most in his life. His parents had never been around, passing away when he was only three years of age. His memories of them were vague.

In comparison, he had seen his sister plenty more to remember her clearly, but those memories weren't his fondest. She was thirteen years his senior, now thirty-three. She had told him that his only purpose in life was to be the best scholar he could be. Alpheus didn't hold a grudge, though. He had never hated his sister. He respected her. He was proud of her achievements. And he was sure that it had been difficult on his sister to be like a mother to him even when she pursued her own studies. Perhaps it had been for the best for both of them that she was now based in Aizary.

Reeling was like an elder brother, a father, and a mentor all at once. The man was righteous, unlike his sister, who Alpheus sometimes considered ruthless. Everything that Alpheus had ever been a part of stemmed from Reeling.

Another patch of rain fell now as Alpheus stepped toward the front gate of Vondra Dawn. He pulled out his pocket watch and presented it to the guards. The courtyard was lighted by a number of braziers weatherproofed with cone-shaped metal covers. On confirming his identity, the guards allowed Alpheus to pass.

He headed to the western tower, noting that the wind speed had picked up suddenly, sweeping up vapours of rainwater at the few men on patrol who then cursed into the winds. Alpheus didn't wear a straw hat, and was now forced to use his arm to block the gust and vapour from slamming into his face, keeping only one eye open on the tower that was his destination. Every step grew heavier, and when he thought that the winds might have calmed down a little, a sudden seething gust crashed into him.

Alpheus gasped and almost fell. He hunched, turning slightly, shutting his eyes, until *something* pulsed at him—or, simply, next to him. Alpheus forced an eye open, peering about. A figure had swept past him along with that last gust, now disappearing behind the blur of the strong currents.

Grace? he wondered, suspecting that he might have felt an eerie pulsing. *A sorcerer...?*

Alpheus turned back to the western tower, urging himself to forget about it. He looked up, and when he saw that no one was around, he dashed away with the Glider Steps. It was a turbulent glide, but he had finally made it into the shelter of the isolated western tower, a sanctuary from the brewing storm.

That was grace for sure, Alpheus decided, looking back out to the courtyard, wearing a worried frown. *That had to be a sorcerer. But... what is a sorcerer doing here?*

Alpheus shook his head and moved up the tedious spiral stairs, ascending more than six or seven floors. That journey was bearable, however, now that he could glide his way up, which required less than a fraction of the effort. He would need the rest of the effort to advance through the long corridor, the one he had always dreaded. On this evening, the corridor chilled him to the bones. The winds outside roared ferociously, and the gushes that crashed in through the rather large vents just beneath the ceiling whistled eerily. The sparsely placed oil lamps helped to intensify the darkness and the uncertainty of the night which split open upon each of the sporadic lightning strikes.

Alpheus realised that he should dash forward. But after taking several steps, he slipped on the wet stone floor, crashing to his knees.

He groaned, assuming the rainwater outside had made its way in through those vents. Though when he pushed himself up slightly with his hand, he noted that the liquid on the floor was thicker than water should be.

His heart began to pound as he sat there for a few more seconds until the closest oil lamp flickered at him, confirming his fears. He gasped at his hands, which were now soaked with blood—and he too sitting in a puddle of the terrible red liquid.

Heat surged from within as droplets of cold sweat slid down from his scalp. Alpheus clasped his pendant and peered back toward the stairs, where he now finally made out a dangerous amount of red that trailed him.

Jeffery! Alpheus thought, springing up to his feet. He took a hop and then took off, catching incredible speed. His heart raced like it never had before as he ignored the relentless winds and rain that continued to crash in through the vents and spattering at him. *Please be all right*, Alpheus wished, dashing ahead.

He came to a screeching stop as he reached the end of the corridor, kicking up some water that bounced off the half-open door. No light illuminated from inside. He clenched a fist, trying to calm his breathing and heart rate. The roaring winds outside didn't help him to relax. Another moment later, he found the courage to push open the door completely.

The chamber wasn't lighted after all. The window behind the desk was open, though, with wind crashing in at him. Alpheus stepped inside, unable to discern anything in the darkness, except the loose documents that swooped about in a sibilant whirlwind.

"Jeffery...," Alpheus muttered, not hearing his own voice. "Father of Heaven, please let him be all right!"

He took another step, stopping only when a blinding flash of a lightning bolt crashed down outside, lighting the chamber for a brief second and revealing what Alpheus had feared: the brilliant man smothered in blood, reposed face upward on the desk where he usually worked so proudly. The top hat he always preferred had been blasted to a corner next to his mace, which was broken in two blunt pieces. At the other corner was Yorke, as inanimate as his master, lying in a pool of his own blood.

As if to confirm their deaths, the red of Selene finally emerged from the clouds now, lighting the chambers in a tinge of scarlet red. Alpheus stepped slowly toward the desk. He looked closely at Reeling, whose sternum had erupted with blood, but was otherwise laying there rather peacefully with his eyes closed, as if he was only asleep. Alpheus ran a hand gently across the man's cheeks, feeling his cold, lifeless body.

"No," Alpheus muttered, collapsing to his knees. "This cannot be real."

He shut his eyes and lowered his own head down next to Reeling's, weeping quietly. When he lifted his head again, he looked to the moon. He snatched his pendant, ripping it off his neck and screamed in rage.

* * *

It must have been only a few minutes, but it had felt like an eternity. Alpheus wasn't sure what was trickling down his face—tears, rain, or blood. The thunderstorms outside had yet to subside, and only at the short intervals of silence did he manage to hear something else.

Footsteps. Approaching. And there was more than one set.

"Who's there?!" demanded a deep voice coming from behind the door.

Alpheus wiped away his tears and turned his head slightly. Patrol men—three of them. They had fallen silent, gaping at the terrible murder scene where the Lord Count and his butler lay dead.

"Don't touch anything," Alpheus found himself saying. "Wait for the knights to survey the scene."

No response, at least not verbally. Instead, one of the men pointed a pike at him and cried, "He murdered the Lord Count! Get him!"

Preposterous! Alpheus thought, in the midst of his anguish.

But he was given no chance to explain as a pike was already being prodded at him. Alpheus dashed into the air to dodge, landing behind those men who quickly shook off their shock, hacking toward him again.

"No," Alpheus said, almost pleading. "You're terribly mistaken! I'm *not* the murderer."

"Away with the guise!" one of them snapped. "Do you take us for fools?"

Alpheus cringed, partly for the remark and partly at the man who spoke. While the other two men looked like any average guard, this third man was small, hunched back, and old. In fact, he was hideously wrinkled, with eyes almost bulging out of the sockets.

Alpheus, he urged himself as he dashed away from the chase again. *Focus! You need to get out of this. You cannot afford to be the scapegoat.* Taking advantage of the darkness, Alpheus slipped a hand beneath his raincoat, tearing away a few buttons from inside his robe. He waited for the men to chase him again, and when they came at him, he flicked out those buttons with fantastic power, striking two of three at the chests.

What...?! Alpheus thought in awe, looking down to his index finger, and specifically at the sapphire ring that now pulsed a brilliant blue.

He looked up again to note that two of the guards had collapsed to the ground. He had missed the one he had thought unfit to be a guard, that man fleeing for his life after the brief exchange. Alpheus sighed, turning back to regard the inanimate Reeling.

"I don't know what happened," he said, anguish once again contorting his face. "But I promise you that I'll get to the bottom of it."

He shut his eyes tightly and turned away, dashing his way back out the corridor. *That sorcerer*, Alpheus thought as he glided along. *Was it him? And that puddle of blood next to the stairs... who does it belong to? That sorcerer leaped like a gust of wind. There's no way he could do that if he had lost that much blood.*

That puddle of blood, of course, followed a blood trail, apparently down the spiral stairs and toward wherever that person had fled after that. Unfortunately, with the rain, any trail outside was sure to have disappeared by now. If his sense of time could still be trusted, it had been nearly a half hour since he had arrived at the citadel. The only evidence left was that puddle of blood in the corridor. Alpheus slowed down now as he closed in toward the stairs, but even when he got there, he saw no traces of blood this time.

Why?

That puddle of red was surely too obvious to miss. But the blood trail had disappeared, too. There was no way that the rainwater entering through the vents could sweep out all that blood and not leave even a trace behind. Alpheus snatched an oil lamp off from the wall, refusing to believe that it had vanished. With that small flame, he surveyed back and forth the corridor.

He found nothing.

Alpheus grew colder and more desperate, conscious that precious time was passing him by. He clawed his hands into his scalp, rather uncharacteristically, almost pulling his hair to force out ideas. "Think, Alpheus!" he said to himself, his grief clouding his thoughts. "Think!"

He raced his way down the stairs, spiralling in his confusion and forgetting how to even apply the Glider Steps. And upon reaching the bottom, he found a horde of men marching in. Leading the pack was Victor Breunor, pulling the reins on his warhorse to a slow gait.

The winds had calmed and the heavy rain from before had reduced to a drizzle. The red of Selene had broken further out from the clouds, its fantastic hue now reflecting brilliantly off the drenched ground.

Alpheus paused in the face of what looked like an army before him. And he knew well enough that they were there for his capture. The ugly patrol man was there behind Breunor, his tiny hunched-back body towered over by the impressive brawn of the warhorse.

"You have one chance to explain yourself," Breunor said. Behind a gold-plated helm, his unforgiving scowl showed that he understood the gravity of the situation.

"Jeffery is dead," Alpheus said with brief sob, staring out blankly at the sea of soldiers before him. "Everything's over."

Breunor groaned. "Is that your confession?"

Alpheus looked up, meeting the military man's eyes. "Confession?" he said with a scoff. "No, Lord Breunor. I have nothing to confess."

"He's the murderer!" the ugly patrol man cried, protesting to Breunor. "Not only did he murder the Lord Count. He killed Beggs and Brune too!"

What happened? Alpheus wondered, blocking out the accusations against him, and indeed, everything in front of him. *It was just this afternoon when everything was fine. How did it turn into this?*

Alpheus didn't know when, but on shaking off some of that disarray that clouded him, he found himself forced against a wall with several pikes pointed at him. He glanced to his right, toward the entrance of the tower where four bodies were now carried out in stretchers.

"Jeffery...!" Alpheus muttered, reaching a hand out to the blood-smeared corpse of the great man. *Help me.*

"There are no survivors," a voice reported.

Alpheus perked up, peering out to the other bodies that had been carried out. He grieved upon seeing Yorke, but when he looked over to the two patrol men he had knocked down, his anguish turned to confusion.

"They're alive," Alpheus whispered, certain he hadn't killed them, until he saw blood trickling out from their wounds. "No...!" he cried suddenly, snapping his eyes wide open.

They each had only one wound, for which Alpheus realised he was responsible. But those wounds were punched all the way through, the fissure torn to a point where there was no chance of survival. "No," Alpheus said again, shaking his head. "No, I didn't murder them. I *didn't* murder anyone!"

He peered about, meeting the eyes of some of the soldiers who were all convinced of his guilt. There was grief in their eyes, too—grief for the Lord Count, perhaps. But the stronger emotion was certainly of ire—ire directed at Alpheus.

"It wasn't me!" Alpheus cried, swinging out an arm in rage.

He gritted his teeth in a brief crouch before suddenly rocketing up vertically, to about the height of at least a couple of stories into the air. Heads lifted to follow his astonishing rise, shadowed by the fading afterimages which sprinkled down a glowing white dust. Alpheus then pushed off the tower wall to redirect his course, gliding away with that same motion.

The ring, Alpheus noted. *It's pulsing. It's resonating with the grace inside me.*

It might appear that he was walking on air, or even flying. But Alpheus was, in fact, plummeting—falling to the ground almost as quickly as he had sprung up. The only difference was that he now fell at a steep angle, yet back down toward those soldiers who had become determined to contain him.

An opportunistic soldier was the first to prod his pike up, except he missed Alpheus completely after failing to accurately estimate the speed of his drop. Instead, his intentions allowed Alpheus the opportunity to push off the spearhead and land further away in relative safety.

"Get him!" Breunor cried.

Alpheus snatched up some loose stones and then he was off again, dashing away and leaving only a set of afterimages for those closest to him to slash at fruitlessly. As Alpheus raced about, with men closing on him from every front, he pulled out four stones he had snatched up just now, resting them between his fingers. Without another thought, he shot them out as shining beams, striking five soldiers in quick succession.

That seemed to root some hesitation in those men, stifling their advance slightly. Breunor was quick to bark out orders to rally his men, not allowing Alpheus even a breather. In response, Alpheus dashed here and there, snatching up yet more loose stones. He powered out some of them now, striking another four men.

Breunor probably realised that Alpheus was a sorcerer by now, his gape demonstrating his shock. Even so, Alpheus didn't think he could possibly escape.

"Stop right there!" a voice commanded, echoing powerfully across the courtyard from the opposite side of where Breunor and most of his men were.

Alpheus turned in tandem with every other man there, recognising that the newcomer was Percival Pole. As the silver knight slid out his rapier from afar, the metal in his blade gleamed a wondrous red under the illumination of the moon. Pole didn't wear his usual smug grin, and he hadn't bothered to address Victor Breunor just yet. Alpheus saw that the silver knight had his eyes only on him, with a tearful glare full of wrath.

"Give it up," Pole said, pointing his sword at him.

He's mourning for Jeffery, Alpheus realised, emphasising somewhat. *But he's got it wrong. His grief has blinded him. That idiot!*

Alpheus spun, noting that the soldiers were also pressing into him once again, slowly but surely. *No. I cannot let anyone catch me. Not when the real murderer is out there somewhere!*

He sprung up high again, achieving surprise a second time. He had adjusted his leap slightly on his take-off, and was now bolting off at a curve higher than anyone could possibly reach. The men below shuffled about, racing toward where they predicted he would land. As he began to descend, Alpheus stooped for a brisk plunge that sent him grinding off a distance ahead of where the soldiers had anticipated.

He looked up then, seeing *sanctuary* ahead of him. There were no more obstacles in the way. *I could get out!* Alpheus believed, bouncing off of the floor for another dash forward that left behind more glowing white dust.

"After him!" Breunor cried from behind.

On a brief glance over his shoulder, Alpheus thought he saw Pole standing in the way of the soldiers, and perhaps Breunor chiding the silver knight. He looked ahead again, recognising that the front gate of the citadel was just ahead. He spurred himself to race harder, realising that his legs were feeling almost as if they were independent from the rest of his body.

Almost there. The front gate. The portcullis.

They're all so close now. The path to escape is just over this wall. Just one last turn. If I could—

A sudden pound at the neck from behind thrust Alpheus into a tumultuous swerve, causing him to lose control of his pace and direction all at once, and sending him skidding forward across the ground. As his vision started to blur, Alpheus thought he saw something resembling the scabbard drop to the ground, the rattling ringing in his ears—fading when everything blacked out.

* * *

Alpheus was floating.

Drifting inside a dark void. Dismal and endless.

He had no form. He saw nothing, felt nothing, as if he *were* nothing. He didn't know if he was here or there. Or even if he existed.

A spark of light flashed in the distance, lighting up the undulation of long silvery hair that illuminated a fleck in the otherwise complete black. He reached out to that single speck of light as best he could without any spatial attributes.

He managed to float closer, but before he could grasp onto anything, the glow faded into the indefinite darkness.

Another glow. To his immediate right this time—flashing only briefly before it vanished forever.

That sorcerer, Alpheus thought. *Is this... Vondra Dawn?*

He turned, or at least he tried to turn, unsure if he had succeeded because of the darkness that surrounded him.

That sorcerer knows something. I have to chase.

But there was nothing to chase.

A wicked laughter then, echoing toward him in waves.

Alpheus tried to steer away, but no matter what he did, there was no escape. That laugh only resonated louder.

Help me, please.

The long silver hair appeared again. It was still vague. It was still far away, far beyond his reach. But with its recurrence, the wicked laugh had toned down.

Everything then swept into oblivion on a sudden gust reminiscent of the terrifying chill of reality. Even without a form, Alpheus felt that every part of him was in agony.

No. Please, no.

And sure enough, a roar of thunder followed a vivid lightning bolt that brightened up the black void for an instant. The death image of Jeffery Reeling filled every part of that void.

"No!" Alpheus heard himself scream, finally feeling his arms and legs again, along with a terrible ache at the back of his neck.

He thought his eyes were open now, but the space he found himself in was still a complete black. The added stench of rotten flesh more or less confirmed to him that this was no dream. It didn't take him long to realise his wrists were shackled in metal chains, with even his frailest movements captured by the clanging sound of those chains that echoed eerily and infinitely inside what was clearly a dark, confined space. Backing off against the wall, Alpheus nudged into *something*. When he brushed his hand against it, he realised with a slow dawning horror that it was the head of a dead man.

"Let me out!" he cried, not knowing if anyone could hear him.

TWENTY

On trial

Vondra Dawn was a magnificent fortification. It was situated in the heart of Zorlia, home to arguably the greatest empire in the land. Some of those highest steeples—including the one in which the court was located—oversaw nearly the entire city. It held an impressive supply of artillery, and it tenanted some of the most dignified men of the country—of the land. But deep beneath those glorious steeples was a lesser known dungeon where the most sinful of criminals were locked away.

Each of the ten cells was a completely enclosed space without any source of light, and it was said that the prisoners who ended up there were treated to the psychological torture of absolute nothingness. The idea was that no punishment was worse than the experience of not existing. It was also said that the only means of sustenance the prisoners received were rotting corpses that were dumped in, and the hearsay told that anyone who was sent there killed themselves within days.

The dungeon itself had no formal name, but people referred to it as the *Cells of Hell*. The truth was that this artificial hell was often empty. Only a handful of crimes deserved such abominable treatment. Unfortunately for Alpheus, the crime he had been accused of matched this definition.

On higher grounds, specifically in the south of Vondra Dawn, was where a lot of men now gathered. The fourth round of the Golden Knight Exchange was scheduled for today, but it wasn't to take place. The men there would instead learn about the Lord Count's murder.

It was a shock. It was unbelievable. And it was the source of gloom and grief all around. Julian himself gritted his teeth in anger as he stood beside the viewing platform among all the lords, the noblemen, the knights, and every other contestant of the Exchange. He was clenching his fists so hard that blood was dribbling down from his palms.

The Lord Emperor, whose words had been rare at the Exchange, stood on the battle ring, using the elevated stage to disclose the plight that had fallen upon the Empire. Hanging down under that platinum crown of his was his long, silvery hair, draping over the maroon cloak resting from his shoulders. From his garb to his charisma, he drew attention ever so effortlessly. The man didn't look pleased, however. Indeed, this was the most saturnine many had ever seen him.

"The prime suspect has since been imprisoned," the emperor said, his voice strong, his emotions even stronger.

The crowd, too, reacted with violent passion. "Who?!" some of the men hollered out in anger. "We'll have him slayed a hundred times over!"

"Let us avenge the Lord Count!" others cried.

The emperor raised an arm, quieting the men in seconds. "I have similar ideas," he said before a slight frown. "But we cannot be certain whether the one we have is the murderer."

"Tell us who it is, Lord Emperor!" a nobleman pleaded. "We'll help judge. And if it *is* him, we'll have him regret it!"

The emperor squinted over at that nobleman, nodding at him. "He is of the academy."

The men exchanged looks of surprise and confusion. Some of them had thought it was a sorcerer, perhaps someone like the Apostle, or indeed the Apostle himself.

Julian gulped down a mouthful of saliva in the mix of the crowd. *The academy?* he thought with a squint.

"A State Scholar by the name of Alpheus Hindlow," the emperor announced, inciting raucous protests. "He is to be trialled. And if everything is as we see it, he will be sentenced to capital punishment."

Mumbles amplified suddenly into clamorous hollers. Each man had his own opinion, and while no one seemed to know the truth, everyone was simply too irate to care about the volume of their voices.

"Please!" the emperor cried out, now raising both arms, managing to silent the crowd once again. "Listen to me. The Lord Count has left us. But we must move on. Anyone who has ever come to know the man, Jeffery Reeling, is sure to know he was exceptional. But we *will* find a suitable replacement. If no other man can fill the role, then we will arrange for a *group* to replace him. We cannot let this hurt the Empire more than it already has."

No one said anything in response this time. All of the men seemed to appreciate the gravity of the murder, and they also appreciated what the Lord Count had meant to the Empire. Even the men who might have made an enemy out of him afforded honour for the great man at this moment, with grimaces that said more than words could express.

The emperor turned to Lachman, gesturing for him to speak. The golden knight bowed, and then stepped up onto the battle ring next to his liege.

"Allow me to make another announcement," Lachman said, peering out to the crowd. "Due to the Lord Count's plight, I regret to say that the court has made the decision to discontinue the Golden Knight Exchange—effective as of now."

The men perked up at the information, but many dismissed it with a prompt sneer. No announcement was more shocking than the Lord Count's death.

"Unfortunately, there are much more pressing matters for the Empire to attend to," Lachman continued, heads lifting again to his words. "Those contestants who have impressed, however, are sure to be given prominent roles in the near future."

The men were dismissed there, many of them seemingly leaving with grave feelings on what would become of the Empire, and even of the country. Julian overheard some of it, noting with quiet indifference that the concern many of them seemed to share was the potential waging of war by Kraga.

Julian, too, was aware of the intense talk of potential war four years prior, which had stemmed from the aggression on the southern border where the Truban land met Kraga's. He was aware that that was the time when the emperor's reputation had plunged disastrously following the publication of the book called *The Proud Conqueror*.

Julian was also aware that it had been the Lord Count leading the charge at that time to rebuild morale in the court, which then had the man credited with the honour of having 'saved' Trubannis from potential engagement in war. And yet, Julian didn't believe the Kragans had ever really wanted to wage war in the first place.

The truth was he didn't know enough about the apparent tension Trubannis shared with foreign countries. He simply believed there were more important matters to attend to within Trubannis, especially now after Reeling's sudden death. His first thought hadn't been anything related to Kraga or any other country. It hadn't even been about how he might help to avenge Reeling. Instead, Julian had rather selfishly lamented that the only trail he thought he had to his disappeared parents were effectively severed.

Julian shook his head then in an effort to restrain his selfish thoughts. The Empire had apparently seized Alpheus, who couldn't possibly be the Lord

Count's murderer—at least Julian certainly didn't think so. As the wave of men continued to head out of the training ground, Julian looked for Schim, calling out to the man as soon as he caught sight of him treading away with a group.

As he trotted closer to the group, one of Schim's men stepped in his path to block him off. It took a moment, but Julian eventually recognised Raphael, the former mercenary he had once met. Schim, however, waved a hand for Julian to come forward.

"My Lord," Julian addressed him. "Can you help me to better understand this? The Empire must have got it all wrong. It's ludicrous to call Alpheus Hindlow, a feeble scholar, a murderer."

Schim gazed down at him, looking sympathetic to his desperation. "I have no more information than what was announced," he said. "But the trial is tomorrow. Perhaps we will find out more then."

The great man then turned, already on his way, his men following closely behind. Julian was left there staring blanking at the sandy ground. After another moment of hesitation, he leaped forward, running after the group.

* * *

Alpheus couldn't be sure if he was awake, asleep—or dead. It was all such a nightmare. He didn't know how long he had been there, in a place of complete darkness. He had begun to doubt reality and his own existence. It was all rather ironic, as he found slight comfort in thinking that if reality was delusional, then Reeling might not have died at all.

Father of Heaven, he thought, struggling to maintain his faith. *Where are you? Where are you when I need you?* Still, Alpheus clasped onto the double crescent pendant. Since long ago, he had developed this tendency to reach for his pendant in response to every time he felt a chill. As of late, this instinctive action had occurred more frequently than he would have cared for.

He jumped now—he believed he did, anyway. Footsteps again. The first time he had heard them since being locked in these pits. The sounds came from above.

A rattling sound then. *Keys?*

The sky opened up. *Or was it a ceiling?* A beacon shone overhead, crackling, lighting up his world of darkness in a crackling flame.

A torch, Alpheus recognised, squinting his eyes in the sudden brilliance.

Coughs and retching. But not his own.

"The abomination," a voice said from above, echoing in the hell hole.

"At least *you* don't have to go down there," another voice said in protest.

Standing over him were two guards who eyed him with disgust. At their feet was a square hatch, the only entry and exit from the abyss.

The appalling conditions of the cell had drained Alpheus of almost all his energy. He had trouble keeping his eyes open as his pupils reacted to the growing light.

But after a couple of blinks, he found that one of the guards had landed in the hole, indeed treading a foot onto his thigh. Alpheus didn't care to guess whether it was intentional, letting out only a soft groan, quietly joyful that he wasn't numb yet. That guard then retched again before lunging into Alpheus and grabbing him by the waist, pulling him upright.

"Damn this job!" the guard cursed, before lifting his head up toward his partner. "Hurry it up!"

Alpheus was too weak to flinch, but his eyes managed to wander to that guard's arm, from where he had grasped onto a rugged rope. His own wrists and ankles were still in shackles, and the clanging of those chains resonated relentlessly as he was pulled up. They ascended slowly, stalling occasionally, as the guards too couldn't stand the foul smell of the dungeon. Alpheus, whose head rested forward from the neck, gazed down at the rotten corpses that he had shared a cell with. They were indeed decayed, a couple of them missing limbs, their death image terrifying.

When they finally reached the top, the other guard grabbed Alpheus by his back collar, heaving him up with reckless abandon. Alpheus groaned again as he thumped onto the stone ground. He simply lay there, unable to move, as the guard helped his ally up in a manner much less crude and careless.

Still dark, Alpheus noted, eyeing the dome-like chamber that lacked any windows. *But better than before.*

Something from below clipped onto his ankle, and soon, Alpheus realised he was being dragged along the stone floor—and then rockily up a set of stairs. The only positive was that it looked like he was being carried further away from that dreadful pit. Indeed, there was more to look forward to now as they exited that rotunda of a dungeon, stepping into a space dabbed by sunlight.

If his physical senses could be trusted, the guard must have let go of his ankle, too. He had come to a stop, now lying face-up.

Daylight, Alpheus recognised with a crazed half-smile. It was the sky—the real one, bordered by rather high walls of a dull charcoal.

The little warmth he believed he might have felt was washed away suddenly when a splurge of freezing cold water was thrown down over his head. Alpheus sat up immediately to the stinging cold, clutching his arms in a shuddering cross. But his only reward was another bucket of water that washed over him from the head down.

The guards paced over to him, freeing him from the shackles that bound his wrists and ankles, showing no concern that Alpheus might escape. They then began to strip him naked. Only now did Alpheus realise that he was still in his cultured white robe, which was unsurprisingly stained of blood and grime. On their forceful tear of that last sleeve, Alpheus's arm flung forward, his hand losing grip of the pendant that he had held tightly onto. The specks of ruby and sapphire reflected vividly off the sunlight as it arced across the air.

Alpheus eyed the trajectory all the way, watching it bounce off the ground once before settling to a soft rattle. Despite being almost frozen stiff, he lurched forward madly, stumbling on his rigid step, diving ahead to retrieve that pendant.

"So you *could* move," one of the guards said with a snort. "Yet you lay there like a cripple, like a living corpse."

"The jewellery won't save you," the other guard added in the same bitter tone. "You have sinned, and now you will be punished."

Alpheus made no response to their remarks, now lying there half-naked, still shivering as he held onto that ornament of faith. He twitched slightly again when something else was thrown at him, something softer and warmer.

"Put them on," one of the guards said.

It was a clean set of clothes, dull brown in colour, woven with the poorest quality fabric. It wasn't the kind of garb Alpheus was accustomed to, but he did as he was told. He said nothing, glad to be cleansed of the air of abomination.

The next thing seemingly on offer was a meal. One of the guards was carrying a tray now and walking over to him. It was a substantial meal with an ample amount of meat and a thick soup. But rather than handing it over to Alpheus, the guard dropped the tray on the ground just before Alpheus raised his arms to receive it—all of it crashing to the ground, the soup splashing at his feet, the meat collecting dust and dirt as it clanked on the ground. The rattling sound of the tin tray, bowls, and plates rang thunderously in his ears, causing him to gasp and twitch once again.

"Go on!" the guard taunted, kicking the piece of meat at their prisoner's feet. "Eat up while you still can."

Alpheus didn't have the capacity to understand their motives, and had he tried, he wouldn't then have glared at them, which only resulted in a rough beating. His aggressors used only their feet to kick him, but they were fervent in their assault, not stopping even when their prisoner curled up in humility, kicking him while he was down.

Alpheus only knew to clench hard to his pendant. He did his best not to make a sound, thinking that would only gratify the guards. Besides, the pain of these kicks didn't compare to the wound on his neck that still had him aching. His vision was blurred with tears as he crawled, reaching his arms out with his eyes on only one thing: that piece of meat that was defiled by dirt and dust.

"Pathetic," one of the guards remarked, gazing down at him in disgust and finally relenting in their assault.

Alpheus grabbed the meat and munched on it, consuming it with tremendous speed. He then lurched toward the buckets of cold water, gulping down what was left in there. As he gurgled in that water, the guards chained his wrists and ankles again. They didn't even let him drink the last of it, dragging him by the back collar again.

"Come on," one of them said. "We have to get going."

"Where...?" Alpheus managed to utter, finally speaking now.

The guards exchanged a look of surprise before shooting a glare back. "To the court, of course," one of them said. "To the place where your judgement will be determined."

It was a long walk from the trenches of Vondra Dawn to its highest point where the court was located. The walk was made all the more tedious by the clanging of the metal chains resounding without end along the dark, narrow alleys. It also didn't help that the guards hollered and jostled Alpheus all the way.

Alpheus realised they were close when the grumbles of other men reverberated from above. He remembered those wide arcing set of stairs just beneath the court. The last and only other time he had visited the place had been about a month prior—a rather daunting experience even in his memory.

And only now as he thought back to it, he realised that Reeling's mere presence at the time had managed to considerably appease the intimidation. The stately man had been his guardian angel on that day—and indeed on every other day of his life. Unfortunately, it was now too late to appreciate all that the man had done for him. There was now nothing he could do to atone for his ungratefulness to Reeling. His reluctance to offer any support to him had now become an irreconcilable regret that he would have to live with for the rest of his life—which might indeed end soon depending on the court's decision.

Several steps later, Alpheus arrived at the court that was lighted with a wealth of natural light shining through the enormous glass window behind the throne. Beneath that majestic window were the people, a group of men faceless to Alpheus who would determine whether he would live or die. Even now, he could barely make out what those men were saying, noting only the solemn tone which was enough to send him into a daze.

He was pressed down at the shoulders now and forced to his knees. When he lifted his head and looked forward, he met a set of predatory eyes that belonged to the figure perched in an unspectacular throne—those of the Lord Emperor. Alpheus shivered, turning away and shutting his eyes almost instinctively. He was sure he didn't want to know who else was there.

Among the constant grumbling, however, he could hear that a few men were commenting on his outward appearance—on how he was barely recognisable to them. Alpheus hadn't thought about it until now, but he was without his spectacles. His hair, which he usually wore in a braided ponytail, was now simply unkempt and perhaps fanning out like an old broom. He could imagine that his face was probably pale and haggard. His cheeks, which he could actually feel, meanwhile, were dented inward.

The mutters and grumbled ended then rather suddenly to near complete silence.

"Send for Odo Rittle," a voice said, powerful—but one that didn't belong to the emperor.

Alpheus opened his eyes finally, and there on that modestly elevated platform at the end of the aisle was a knight in golden armour, Lionel Lachman. The knight was speaking for his liege, who simply sat there with a grim look on his face.

Ascending from the stairs at the back of the court now was the patrol man, the primary witness to the murder case—Odo Rittle. He was indeed a tiny, fragile man whose hunchback limited his height to that of a child. His hands were bony and marked with furrows. He was old, and he was ugly, with wrinkled eyes that bulged out from the sockets. Some of the noblemen cringed when they saw him, and Rittle, in turn, stooped further under the attention. Entering behind Rittle was a group of men carrying a pair of stretchers, and lying on those stretchers were the dead bodies of the two guards that Alpheus had inadvertently killed.

Alpheus winced as those bodies were laid out in front of him. He shivered again when Rittle knelt down next to him.

"Speak," Lachman said, regarding the tiny guard.

"I... I was on my typical evening patrol," Rittle began with a stammer. "I was... alongside the West Wing." He paused, taking in a big breath. "It must have been midnight then... when I stumbled into Beggs and Brune. It was then when we heard a scream from the Lord Count's chambers. We... rushed there... and we saw that the Lord Count had already been killed. Alpheus Hindlow sat there next to his corpse. Ah...! And that butler... Yorke... he was dead too."

"Do you attest to that, Alpheus Hindlow?" asked another powerful voice, familiar but unfriendly.

Alpheus lifted his head slightly, glancing at that man only up to the knees, recognising that it was Victor Breunor. "I didn't kill them," Alpheus said softly.

"Then how do you explain the deaths of Beggs and Brune? The guards you killed."

Alpheus said nothing at first, and only when Breunor demanded an answer a second time did he lift his head again. "I cannot," Alpheus said. "I don't know what happened."

Murmurs echoed about now, and Alpheus was convinced that the men there had already decided that he was guilty. They would be making a grave mistake, however—Alpheus knew as much—and a small part of him thought that he should be defending himself. But he simply couldn't gather the motivation to speak up.

"Did you witness the actual murder?" another man questioned, a new voice to the conversation. "The Lord Count's murder, that is."

"Well, no," Rittle said, sounding defensive. "But look, the scholar tried to kill me. He chased me out of the chambers. He—"

"So you didn't see anything," the same voice cut in, his rise in volume finally winning a glance from Alpheus, who recognised it was Lord Morlan, the former king of Cetal.

"I certainly did!" Rittle cried, turning defensive. "I watched him kill Beggs and Brune."

"And can you be certain that Alpheus Hindlow killed them?" Morlan asked with a raised brow. "The last I heard, the boy's feeble. I cannot imagine how he could achieve such a feat—punching stone-sized holes through well-built guards, ending their lives there and then?"

"You weren't there!" Rittle contested. "He—"

"And to say Alpheus Hindlow murdered the Lord Count," Morlan cut in once again, raising his volume still, "a man of supreme strength and wisdom who bested the Apostle? A man to whom Alpheus Hindlow owed his allegiance?" Morlan rose to his feet, spinning to face the Lord Emperor. "Rittle cannot be trusted. I implore you, My Lord, to annul his testimony altogether."

The emperor squinted at the supplication, which had come as a surprise. A lot of the men before him had suddenly started to doubt the witness, too, muttering amongst themselves as they regarded Rittle with suspicion.

"Lord Breunor," Lachman called out, speaking for the emperor. "Why don't you share your accounts of what happened that evening?"

Breunor pondered for a moment. "I don't know if Alpheus Hindlow is the murderer," the military man began finally in a dismal tone. "I cannot even be sure whether he has the power to kill those guards. But I have reason to believe that Alpheus Hindlow is a sorcerer," he continued, the assertion having everyone perk up, including Alpheus himself. "I was surprised, too. That night, he... showed that he's hardly feeble. My men couldn't get a hold of him... he made these incredible leaps—it was almost as if he was flying. It was...,"

He paused there in hesitation, and only when gasps filled the air once again did Alpheus look up to note, firstly, that Julian was present, and secondly, that Breunor was gesturing toward Julian. "He moved like Julian Longinus," Breunor finally finished.

Julian, who stood behind the Lord Chancellor, twitched to the claim. He was one of the few people who shared his secret. Julian appeared befuddled, however, likely because he had always been suspicious of whether Alpheus was really a sorcerer or not. It must have been shocking for him to hear Breunor compare Alpheus's ability with that of his own. Indeed, the comparison sounded silly even to Alpheus.

"Not *exactly* like Longinus," Breunor said. "But similar enough. And that wasn't all. The boy managed to knock down some of my men as well. Only when the skirmish was over, we confirmed that he had flicked out pebbles... with the power of turrets."

"The Falling Comet," Lachman said. "The Lord Count's signature skill. Looks like Alpheus Hindlow has inherited it."

Breunor nodded at him. "Either way, I don't believe he can willfully control his power. And that is why I cannot ascertain whether he could be Reeling's murderer."

"But you would say he has the *potential* to be the murderer now, correct?"

Lachman said.

Breunor eyed Alpheus now. He frowned for a moment, and then nodded.

Morlan sighed, waving an arm of protest. "Potential?" he challenged. "The autopsy has affirmed that the cause of death was *intensive* damage to the organs, particularly the lungs, which were crushed by an extreme blow. Could Alpheus Hindlow amass that kind of power? He could leap and he could shoot out pebbles, but could he crush a person's insides?"

The debate resumed with ferocity from there. A few voices within the barrage of mainly baseless assertions were defensive of him, but the court was unlike the academy in that it was prone to accepting explanations without adequate evidence. The manner in which the trial was being played out seemed to be steering farther and farther away from the truth.

Alpheus coughed, winning himself instant attention. "Allow me...," he said in his weak voice as he looked up to the emperor, "to detail my account of the story."

Lachman who stood to the emperor's right watched his liege for a second. "Go ahead," he then said to Alpheus.

"On my way to Vondra Dawn that evening, I happened by a stranger I believe to be a sorcerer," Alpheus said, his words drawing plenty of suspicion. "In hindsight, I believe he was fleeing. I then found a pool of blood at the top of the spiral stairs, a dangerous amount that would have been a result of a lethal attack. My mind went blank then. I was worried for Jeffery—the Lord Count—and I raced to his chambers. But..." He slowed down now, grief darkening his face. "By the time I got there, he was... already dead."

Alpheus peered about the court, looking to the faces there who now glared back at him, not believing his words. He recognised not faces but the distrust in their expressions. Unfortunately for Alpheus, the assertion that he might be a sorcerer had mightily turned the favour against him. Some of those men might not admit it, or even realise it themselves, but the prejudice they had for the arcane concept wasn't easy to shake off. Indeed, some of those men eyed Julian now as well with quiet suspicion.

"Ludicrous," Forredan said with a scoff, finally speaking for the first time, speaking for most of the men present. "Neither the corridor nor the stairs had any traces of blood when we conducted our investigation. It's obvious enough that he's the culprit. Why are we wasting our time?"

Alpheus closed his eyes again in quiet despair, confirming that his attempt in explanation had always been futile. His accusers' minds had been set to believe that he was Reeling's murderer long before his arrival at the court. It was always difficult to change what others believed, especially when the belief was so strong.

"I hear there's a simple method to test whether a person is a magic user," the statesman continued. "Those heretics are charged with energy pulses many times faster than the average man. Their pulse rates are greatly heightened." Forredan waved an arm at one of his men who trampled his way to Alpheus, snatching his wrist, which Alpheus flung off, the chains rattling again as he did so.

"It's true," Alpheus admitted. "I *am* a sorcerer. But I'm *not* the murderer. I told you... that sorcerer I happened by that evening—he's the one we need to find. I'm not saying he's the murderer, but he must know something."

"Enough of your lies!" Forredan slammed. "Are you saying that the two guards, Beggs and Brune, are not dead? Are you saying there is a pool of blood along the corridor only viewable to you? Are you telling me you didn't purposely hide your sorcerer identity?"

The barrage of accusations had Alpheus dumbstruck, but within that haze of befuddlement triggered an obscure memory. *Quinlan Forredan is the master of court intrigue*, Reeling had once said. And indeed, the statesman seemed pleased to have reduced Morlan to a quiet sulk, at the same time scaring off any other men who dared to challenge his deduction, which was more forceful than convincing.

Alpheus held his head now as it felt like it was about to burst open. He clenched a fist, glaring out at the men. "Imprison me for as long as you want," he said. "I don't even care, but the real murderer is out there and I beg of you—*someone*... please avenge Jeffery for me."

Perhaps his plea was hopeless. Perhaps it wouldn't resonate with anyone, at least not from Alpheus who was being branded a murderer as well as a liar now. In any case, the trial was over. If no evidence would come to light in the coming days, Alpheus was as good as dead.

TWENTY-ONE

Mourn and grieve

Agnes lined up next to her fellow scholars as part of a blockade at the entrance of the academy. Neither she nor the rest of the Villa of Enlightenment had been given a chance to mourn Jeffery Reeling. No one had even managed to get a breather when there were men, women, and even children amassed at their doorstep—all of them shouting accusations at the academy for developing an educated rogue in Alpheus.

Worse yet was the fact that the academy was without a leader. Yusuf Seer was away on an expedition in Farella. The Grandmaster, meanwhile, remained in seclusion, seemingly without a care to uphold the academy's reputation. The scholars who were left behind could only defend the academy by forming a human barricade to deny the fuming protestors the chance to ravage their place of training.

But despite being there physically, Agnes's mind was drifting elsewhere. The truth was that she was only at the academy to meet Christopher Hartland, whom she had compelled to come see her, to share with her everything he knew about the murder case. And now, as Hartland shuffled in through the protestors, Agnes spared not a second thought in abandoning the blockade, stepping away as she waved Hartland into the foyer.

Hartland shook his head with a frown, and then pushed through to join her. "I'm not sure you want to know," he said, keeping an eye on the conflict raging outside.

Agnes winced. "Why do you think I asked?" she said. "Tell me!"

"Execution is due to take place in ten days," he said with a grim face. "It will be on the streets for public viewing."

"No...," Agnes uttered as she then stumbled to the floor. She stared blankly at the marble floor, ignoring all the dissonance streaming in from outside.

"I'm sorry," Hartland said, offering a hand.

Agnes lifted her head, reaching a hand up, but then she suddenly leaped to her feet. "No," she said again. "I won't allow it to happen! I'll save him."

She was prepared to do anything, including breaking into the prison by herself. And she was already treading away, but Hartland pulled her back and delivered an audible slap to her face. "Don't be so impulsive!" he chided with plenty of volume, drawing attention from their fellow scholars and even some of the protestors closest to the entrance. "You can change nothing!"

The slap was a surprise despite feeling none of the sting that should have come with it—perhaps drowned out by the ringing in her ears. Either way, none of it helped to clear her mind.

"Come," Hartland demanded then, snatching her by the wrist.

He pulled her deeper into the foyer, stopping next to one of the impressive columns that held up the next floor. Hartland looked ready to berate her more, but when he met her eyes again, he seemed to be taken aback. Perhaps it was because he saw her tears. Apparently, men were clueless on how to act when they saw tears.

"You'd be going against the Empire," he said with a toned-down voice.

"Then so be it!" Agnes snapped, her ire surprising even herself. "Just... please do not stand in my way."

"Allow me to warn you, then...," Hartland said, "that you are by yourself. Don't expect any help... not from me or anyone else, not even from Alpheus who no longer wants to live. He's not ready to be helped." He turned away then. "One more thing," he added. "Alpheus was moved to the general prison. For whatever good that will do you."

* * *

Julian sat a lonesome figure at Rogers. The tavern was quiet this evening, with fewer than a dozen customers present in a venue that could potentially host over a hundred.

The streets were almost near empty as well, a stark contrast to the day when they had been filled with the furious protestors. Those same protestors were apparently still together now, but gathered in peace and silence at the Luxuriant Gardens just outside of Vondra Dawn. Every one of them were said to have a white ribbon tied at their necks, the symbol that was said to guide the departed to heaven. Each held onto a lighted candle to create what would have been a glorious display, bringing a replication of thousands of stars to the gardens, the place that the Lord Count had frequented. They were paying their final respects to the stately man.

"Well?" the stout tavern master said. "Aren't you going?"

Julian peered up to him, out from his dark hair that shrouded his vision.

"No," he answered, downing the small remainder of his mead.

Dock sighed, wiping clean an empty glass, the squeaks making Julian grow irate. "A lot of people should be there now," he said. "The Lord Count is a special man—*was*... a special man. He managed to do what the Lord Emperor has failed to, to win over the hearts of the common people." Dock then paused with a chortle. "And yet, we never even knew how he did it."

"One more," Julian said, pointing to the keg of mead behind the bar.

Dock shook his head, but went on to fill another glass. "You know, Julian," the stout man said, pressing on the subject, "it's a good gesture that the Empire allowed the common people to attend the death ceremony. I don't think it has ever happened this way."

Dock thumped down a new glass of mead in front of Julian, who could hardly find the motivation to look the tavern master in the eyes. "I have nothing to say," Julian finally uttered, regarding the brimming froth.

What good is a funeral? he thought with a grimace. *The man's dead. Everything's over. Alpheus is accused the murderer. And me... I'm here drinking away.*

Useless.

It had only been a day since the common people had learned about the Lord Count's departure. And while their grief for the man seemed genuine, many people apparently dreaded that the Empire might not ever fill that void. The talk of a possible Kragan invasion had consequently caught fire, and the fear that had spread across the city in only a single day was distinct. It was real.

Julian couldn't make any sense of it, and he wasn't about to delve into the discussions. The enticement of sorcerers was something else, however. The talk of beings with the same powers as him was difficult to ignore. The prospect of encountering these people stirred the grace inside of him—it had him burning from within. The problem was that he didn't know how or where to unleash that rage.

While the noblemen and other lords had eyed him with suspicion during the trial, Julian's thoughts had been elsewhere. He had imagined, with guilty pleasure, the Lord Count slain at the feet of the one known as the Marvel Mage—the divine man he was chasing.

No, he thought, shaking his head. *This is wrong.*

Alpheus! I must focus on saving him.

But... how? What can I achieve alone?

Unless..., he thought again, as a mental image of Percival Pole flashed in him. *No, what am I thinking? He was the one who seized him.*

And... what was all that talk about Alpheus leaping about... shooting out pebbles with the power of turrets?

Julian groaned, hanging his head.

It was a while later when he perked up at the startled cries of the few customers present. Julian turned to the entrance where a familiar face appeared, the man donning his signature breastplate of blazing dark red and armed with an imposing bardiche which he had no intention of hiding.

As Julian had assumed he would, Tannon Gale treaded over to him, settling onto the empty stool next to him. The veteran warrior leaned his polearm against the wooden bar table and waved Dock over. "I'll have the same as him," he said.

"Sure," Dock said with a raised brow.

Julian remembered his battle with Gale now, which had been a test of endurance. He recognised that he had managed to win only because of the veteran knight's obvious lack of stamina that was a result of his long absence from training. Even so, it didn't matter anymore. Julian had lost in the following round, and now the Exchange had been discontinued altogether.

"What do you want?" Julian asked, turning back to the mead.

Gale said nothing as he watched the tavern master serve him. He then guzzled down the glassful in seconds as Dock retreated. "Just wanted to make sure you had nothing to do with it," Gale finally said now in a soft utter, also without looking at Julian. "You may be a sorcerer, but you don't have it in you to slay Reeling. You're far too weak."

Julian rolled his eyes.

"Sorcerers are on the rise," Gale then mumbled, the remark instantly catching Julian's attention. "In Zorlia, at least. There's a fair share more capable than Alpheus Hindlow."

Julian squinted. "What are you talking about?"

"Since facing you in the Exchange," Gale said in elaboration, "I've developed a rather troublesome ability... to sense your kind."

"*What...?*"

"Yes," he said, leaning closer into Julian, "and I also sense that you're about to do something stupid."

Julian winced and then dismissed it, as even he didn't know what he wanted to do.

"Don't go to the prison," Gale whispered before leaning away. "It's suicide. You still have your entire life ahead of you. And besides, you still need to learn the Fire-Wind Wheel."

Julian widened his eyes this time as he finally regarded Gale. "You're...," he said carefully, "offering to teach me?"

"It's been talked about," the veteran said. "The Lord Chancellor has approached my liege. At first, it was a joke to me. But I have since thought about it." He sighed. "I am well past my prime. Someone must carry on my legacy. I cannot let the Wheel die off with my own decline."

"But why—"

"You play with fire," Gale cut in with a wry smile. "Nothing more."

The Lord Chancellor, Julian thought. *To think he would do that.*

And... Tannon Gale, is this a real offer?

Julian pulled himself to his feet then, retrieving the iron sword he had placed on the bar table. "I have something I must do," he said, stepping away. "I'll survive as I always have. And when I return, I'll be ready to learn all your skills."

Gale responded with a smug grin as Julian exited the tavern.

The streets were indeed empty, peaceful. Julian looked up to the night sky, letting the soft breeze invigorate him. Few evenings of late had been as clear as this one. It was the thirteenth day of February, close to the middle of an even-numbered month, otherwise marked as the time for one of the most beautiful natural phenomena to occur: the eclipse of Achelois and Selene.

The cobalt blue of the waxing Achelois lined up below the waning scarlet red of Selene, the congregation of the celestial bodies at its most divine, as if serenading for Jeffery Reeling himself. It was as the Ionian faith depicted the moons on their symbol, and it was the only time Julian didn't mind it. The blend of the colours resonated through the city, dabbing it gently in a wondrous luminescence, embellishing the basic lanterns hanging off the dwellings along the curving stone path.

"Goodbye, Lord Count," Julian whispered with a sigh. "You'll be missed."

* * *

Julian arrived home to the sound of the swishing of a sword. Oscar was hacking against a metal plate nailed onto the trunk of the only tree there, not realising that Julian was watching from behind.

To be fair to Oscar, Julian had grown to become quite a prowler, avoiding detection against even the most vigilant of foes. He wasn't about to sneak up on the boy, however. Instead, he continued to watch him, with nostalgia.

When Julian had been that age, his home had been ransacked, every person in the household slaughtered. He still remembered the servants, the mayhem that had been caused while he had been hidden. Although it didn't happen often, every now and then, that horrendous episode sparked anew inside of him. An intense wrath would then feed into his conscience, sending him into a terrible frenzy. Sometimes, Julian wondered if he was mad. The only thing he could be sure of was that he hated himself. He hated that he was still so far from where he needed to be.

Julian groaned now, treading toward the boy, who jumped at his sudden approach. He seized the miniature sword with a simple swipe, the action startling Oscar into a stumble.

"You call this training?" Julian chided. "There was no power! No substance! And for all that time, you didn't even realise someone was standing behind you!"

Oscar gaped. Covered in sweat and panting from the hard work he had put in all evening, he looked like he was trying his best not to cry. But his vision was already blurred by tears, and within a moment, they came rushing out.

Julian turned away with a hiss.

"You're crazy!" Oscar cried, pushing himself to his feet again before storming back into the hovel and slamming the door behind him.

What am I doing? Julian thought, dropping the tiny weapon to the ground with a clang. He stepped into his own room—merely partitioned from the rest of the hovel with a simple drape hanging from the ceiling—peering at its near emptiness for a moment. He then went on to collect everything he had of monetary value, shoving the items into a knitted bag.

He carried the bag, small as it was, back out into the courtyard. He sighed and then left that bag of valuables at the doorstep before heading out again, with one last glance over his shoulder at what he now already regarded his old home.

* * *

Behind the thick shade sails that flapped out overhead—even nullifying the evening moonlight—the place appeared to be fraught with danger. It was the first time Agnes had visited anywhere like it. But she had no time to worry about any immediate threats that might be lurking in these dark alleyways. Urging herself on, she reminded herself that Alpheus was in a much direr situation than her, that Alpheus needed her.

It had been two days since she had learned that Alpheus was due for execution. The Empire had yet to announce anything to the public. And while Agnes also had yet to conjure up any plan that would free Alpheus, she had instead discovered a conspiracy that revealed that someone by the name of Neal wanted Alpheus dead even sooner than the scheduled execution.

Indeed, there was allegedly a plan in place to assassinate Alpheus *in* prison. Agnes couldn't confirm if any of it were actually true. But if it *were* true, her idea wasn't only to prevent it from happening, but also to see for herself how this man called Neal planned to infiltrate the prison, which would then provide her with some potential ideas about how she could manage the deed herself.

This was such a time to apply her skills in inquiry to good use. The potential danger ahead, though, was an unknown.

Her sources had led her here to a neighbourhood not too far from Vondra Dawn. It was a place with worn-down buildings cramped together, a notorious gathering place for outlaws, known by some as the *Felon Square*. Agnes wasn't usually one to roam the city, especially at night. She could hardly imagine herself here, alone. It was dangerous for anyone, and to avoid attention, she had come donning a dark coloured mantle complete with a hood.

And if need be, she thought, feeling the grip of the sabre under her mantle, *I might have to use this.*

Alpheus never wanted me to learn swordplay, but today, I might not have a choice.

She paused suddenly, noting footsteps trailing her. The neighbourhood was small, and though she had only just stepped into the area, it had been strangely quiet. *Keep going*, she urged herself, picking up the pace again. *Act like you belong.*

But she didn't belong. And a few more steps later, she found herself surrounded by four figures in dark robes, closing in on her from all directions.

She didn't look up, but had reached for her hidden sword, ready to slash it out on provocation.

"Who are you?" one of the men asked in a croaky voice.

Agnes hesitated. "Just a passerby," she said. "I seem to have lost my way."

"Is that so?" another said. "Show your face and let us decide."

"There's no need for that," Agnes said. "If you'll excuse me, I'll be—"

She stopped speaking abruptly when one of the men from behind pounced toward her. Agnes, though, countered with a reverse slash of her sheathed sword, the strike battering away the crook, sending him to the ground. The others jumped at her, forcing her to pound at them in the same way. It was barely a moment later when all of them were at her feet. The hood that covered her eyes had flapped off from her quick turns though, and now her hair of medium length was conspicuous.

"A woman?!"

"Not just a woman," Agnes said, sliding out the blade with a pair of deadly eyes that glared out. "I can be a murderer if you force me to be. But I have no intention to hurt you. I am here to see Neal. Take me to him."

The men scrambled together, frowning. "How do you know that name?"

"I have my sources."

The sound of hands clapping together drifted out from one of the buildings. A younger man stepped out through the doorway. He sported a robe similar to the ones worn by the men Agnes had defeated, but judging from their grimaces, this newcomer wasn't their ally. Indeed, the four men scrambled away altogether now.

"Your bravery is commendable," the stranger said after the others had left. "But I suggest that you leave now. Otherwise, no one will be able to save you."

"You must be mistaken," Agnes said, turning to the man who seemed more willing to talk than those other robed men from before. "I am not here to be saved. I am here for information."

"You won't get what you want. And, certainly, you will not leave with it."

"Enough talk!" Agnes snapped, reaching for her sword again. "If you refuse to speak, I'll force it out of you."

"A stubborn one," the man remarked with a grin, reaching for his own weapon hidden at his belt, a short sword which he swiped out suddenly.

Agnes managed to block the impetuous attack, but the stranger promptly followed with a poke, gashing open her left sleeve, as if a warning before she slashed into her skin.

He's tough! Agnes acknowledged. She didn't give in, though, slashing back at the man with everything she had. *This is a part of me you don't know*, she thought, continuing to strike. *I suppose we all have our secrets.*

Agnes was never very strong to begin with. She worked on her swordplay from time to time, but when matched up against an opponent with real training, she knew that her flaws would be immediately exposed. She wasn't sure if her opponent was holding back now, and she didn't have the time to wonder. All she could do was to keep fighting. If she couldn't even get past this, there was no hope of saving Alpheus.

Hold on, Alfie, she thought, gritting her teeth, *I'm coming for you*. Her momentum exploded then as she thrust her opponent into the wall. She sliced diagonally at his thighs, drawing first blood. When the man swung his short sword with a growl, Agnes parried it from his grip altogether with another strong thrust. But as Agnes thought the battle was about to end, the man whipped out an arm, spraying out a white powder that blinded her.

Agnes screamed, her hands clawing at her burning eyes. Her opponent showed no mercy, connecting a forceful kick to her stomach that sent her sliding across the floor. Her abdomen throbbed, but it was nothing compared to her eyes, which stung with a terrible pain.

Agnes picked herself up and forced her eyes open, making out a dark blob amid the darkness. *I still have my sword*, she realised, looking to her hand which she could barely see. *I cannot afford to fall now. Alpheus needs me.* It wasn't looking good, though, when that dark blob—the sordid foe—was still approaching.

What do I do? Father of Heaven, please help me.

A zigzag stroke flashed before her suddenly—a brilliant angular shape that illuminated her world for a second. Then the dark blob collapsed to the floor.

Another stranger had arrived.

TWENTY-TWO

Infiltration of the Prison

Vondra Dawn shared the bay with the Luxuriant Gardens on the west and a small hill to the east across the stream. A strip of stalls were carved into the foot of that hill. Sitting on top of the hill was a block-shaped structure the size of a typical chapel, a dull grey in colour similar to the imposing citadel.

That structure was, of course, a prison. More accurately, it was the entrance to the prison, which was itself a subterranean construction that housed criminals destined for execution. The thirty cells' expanse was lighted by oil lamps, a clear contrast to the complete darkness of the dungeon beneath Vondra Dawn. Ironically, this was the same place Alpheus had once joked about Hartland being an occupant, and yet he was the one held captive there now.

In this prison, the convicted were often quiet, for anyone who caused a ruckus was beaten without mercy. The authorities who would beat them, however, hid behind stone masks, doing so on the superstition that the executed returned to haunt the living, and that the first ones they would visit were the ones they last saw.

But while some of the prisoners fantasised about afterlife, Alpheus had put no thought toward the idea. He had been nesting at a corner of his cell in dejection, clasping onto his pendant and letting it dangle in front of him, watching it wave left and right.

He didn't mind anymore that he was due for execution in four days' time. In fact, he wished it would come sooner. Every time he had dozed off, scenes of that stormy evening had come rushing back to him. Adding to that was his own reproach on how he hadn't done more to prevent Reeling's death in the first place. He blamed himself for not having lent a helping hand to the great man when he had asked for it. He tagged himself as the most selfish person in the land. Had he applied himself more at Vondra Dawn, had he been better alerted of the dangers Reeling had faced, and had he been more wary rather than curious about sorcerers, things might not have ended this way.

Alpheus curled up on the ground, weeping quietly.

He didn't know how much time had passed before his tears dried out, only annoyed that his stomach was grumbling of hunger when he simply wanted to die. As if the guards had heard his stomach, they now began distributing rations. Alpheus tied his pendant on his wrist before slipping it under a sleeve. He then crawled his way to the bars to receive his meal, lingering on his bowl of slop, examining it rather than eating it, remembering how on previous days it had been tasteless, disgusting.

When did I become so pathetic? he thought as he stared blankly at the unsightly meal.

A half hour later, a guard came to collect the empty bowls. Sitting with his knees up and his arms wrapped around them, Alpheus leaned his back against the bars and stared blankly at the stone wall. He hadn't eaten his share.

"Are you going to eat this?" the guard asked, his voice an echo from behind the stone mask.

"I've lost my appetite," Alpheus said softly, without turning.

"I need you to eat this," the guard said, nudging the bowl into Alpheus's backbone. "You'll need it. Tonight will be a long night. Do you understand me?"

Alpheus perked up. The voice was unrecognisable, but the tone was familiar. He turned to the guard, who sported the same garb as every other guard there—a mail shirt of interlocking loops of metal and an olive-green stone mask. He peered down across to the guard's left arm, which was banded with a unique prison guard tag that allowed those guards to identify each other.

Alpheus squinted with suspicion. "Are you...?" he said in a whisper.

The guard leaned in with a nod. "Listen," he said, the sibilance of his whisper shrouded in the crackling flames of the oil lamps. "There are five guards here including me and the warden. Another ten guards patrol the top. Every one of them has a horn attached to their belts, a horn that can call for an army. We need to move fast if we want any chance of escape."

"Julian...!" Alpheus shot out in a mumble, almost ignoring all the other information and focusing only on the fact that his friend had come for him.

The guard behind the mask said nothing, only breathing a deep sigh. "I hear you can take giant leaps," he then said. "When I clear a path, I'll race you out of here."

It was Julian indeed, and although that last remark was unlike him, that sombre tone of his was unmistakeable. Of course, he also emanated the air of grace that was unique to sorcerers.

"The warden has the keys," Julian said. "He's sitting at the exit end of the corridor. When I get—"

"Wait...!" Alpheus said, holding Julian's arm.

Julian cocked his head.

"Leave me be," Alpheus said, almost pleading, seeing his friend's glare glistening out from the pair of tiny holes of the stone mask. "I don't want another crime listed next to my name."

* * *

Julian regarded Alpheus for a moment longer, recognising that look, that feeling of hopelessness. He thought back to how he had spent days spying on the prison guard from whom he had thieved the unique outfit, giving his best efforts to learn the guard's routine, demeanour, and behaviour—only to give himself the best chance of saving Alpheus.

Although the process had gone more smoothly than he could have wished for—almost as if someone or something had helped pave the way for him—it really was disheartening to see that the one he was trying to save didn't seem interested in freedom. And regardless of how straightforward it had been to infiltrate the prison, the exploit was still an enormous risk that even Tannon Gale had urged him not to take.

He shrugged off the scholar's grip finally, rising to his feet. "I'm getting you out," he said, already treading away.

As he stomped toward the warden, Julian had eyes only for the chain clipped at the man's belt where the set of keys hung. Like the guards, the warden was masked, though his was of a darker shade. He boasted an imposing physique despite his sitting position, and instead of the arming swords that the others carried, the warden clutched onto his broad chest a thick handle to which a dangerous ball of spiked metal larger than a human head hung off a sturdy chain.

And yet... *he's asleep?* Julian realised in surprise.

The dreary lighting and the mask made for the perfect place to doze off. But who would have thought the primary man responsible for the security of the prison would sleep while on duty. He was snoring aloud, not at a volume that resonated across the subterranean prison, but loud enough for Julian to confirm that the man was asleep.

In any case, it worked for Julian who prowled closer to him now. He swiped an agile hand out to snatch the keys, managing to do so without waking the warden.

When he turned, however, Julian found himself confronted with one of the other guards who had stepped in from behind him. "Hey!" the guard cried. "What do you—"

Almost by instinct, Julian dealt the poor guard a fierce punch in the face, cracking open a part of his stone mask. He eyed the horn attached at the waist opposite a sheathed arming sword, snatching the weapon and using it to pierce through that potentially troublesome horn. He then discarded the weapon, stomping his way over the guard and racing his way back to free Alpheus.

The prisoners closest to the brief exchange jolted to their feet with wide, lop-sided grins, their eyes crazed and lost, perhaps hopeful for some final entertainment before their looming deaths. The other couple of guards perched at the opposite *dead*-end of the corridor jumped to their feet immediately.

"Stop," Alpheus pleaded, not calling Julian by name. "You don't have to do this. You can still run."

"Save your breath," Julian said, crouching down low, now trying the third of nearly ten keys in the set. "You'll need it later."

Julian afforded a smile no one saw, when a cluck sounded behind the lock. He then pushed open the barred door immediately and climbed into the cell. He slashed down at Alpheus, cleaving off in a powerful crash the metal chain that bound the scholar's hands and feet.

"Behind you!" Alpheus cried suddenly.

Julian paused, realising all too late that there was a sword at his neck.

"Remove your mask now!" the guard demanded from behind, pointing that sword from above. "Or I'll take your head with it!"

Julian raised a hand carefully up to his face. But before reaching it, he flung out the chain of keys—a distraction that won himself a second to draw his own weapon, an identical arming sword at his belt, which he slashed upwards to clang the startled guard back several steps and out of the cell.

The guard cursed, holding a tighter grip to his weapon. Two others rushed to join him, including the one who had been smashed in the face, easily distinguished by the noticeable crack in the stone mask at the nose. "Identify yourself!" one of them cried.

Nearly all of the prisoners were on their feet now, poking their heads out from the bars. Some of them howled like animals.

Julian stepped out of the cell, pointing his arming sword forward, a weapon that he wasn't used to handling. He eyed the horns attached at the waists of two of the three guards.

If I could just get those, I can let them live, he thought. Julian paused then, looking back out toward the exit where the warden looked to be still in his slumber—bewildering, but certainly welcoming.

Julian hissed, turning his attention back to the three guards in front of him. He slashed ahead at thin air, daring his foes to charge at him. When they did, Julian gushed out grace, blessing himself with unbelievable speed, pushing the guards forcefully to the back end of the corridor with quick slashes that they simply couldn't keep up with.

The rapid clanging of metal incited the prisoners to cry louder, some of them cheering for reasons they probably didn't even understand. Julian slashed the middle guard at the thigh, drawing first blood. Before that guard could recover, Julian swept out again, but only to detach the other two horns on the second and third guard, collecting those devices on his sweep back. He continued by promptly gashing out crosses to disfigure the horns.

"Lord Pylon!" one of the guards cried, his voice resonating across the cells to the warden. "Blow the horn!"

Julian grew suddenly desperate, gritting his teeth, dealing that babbler a threshing cut on his sword wielding arm. He threw out another couple of slices that caused blood to spray forth. When those guards fell to their knees, Julian jumped at them, elbowing their heads in quick succession with the intention to knock them out.

Managed to not kill them, Julian thought as they fell to the floor. *But... that warden.*

He turned. The warden had finally woken up, and he looked far more formidable now that he was on his feet. The man didn't blow onto the horn to call for support. Instead, he simply clutched onto his dangerous looking weapon with his arms crossed, the spiked metal ball hanging off the handle.

By standing at the stairs, which was the only exit out of the prison, the warden was clearly challenging Julian to fight him. From his vantage point, this final foe within the prison seemed magnificent, dwarfing him by a head.

Alpheus, meanwhile, had scrambled to the far corner of his cell, trembling against the stone wall. The spraying of blood had likely reminded him of that stormy evening when he had discovered Reeling's body. The other prisoners were also backed up against the walls of their respective cells now, reduced to almost complete silence in the fear that they might be Julian's next victim.

Julian looked up at the warden, who gazed down behind that stone mask of pine green with what Julian could sense was ill intentions.

"Be gone or be dead," Julian warned with a snarl, grasping tightly onto his sword.

The warden snorted in response. He then slowly raised his weapon wielding arm, stopping as it extended out horizontally, the spiked metal ball hanging off like an exotic pendulum off from the handle, swinging gently back and forth.

Julian found himself following that rocking motion with his eyes, and when the metal ball came to a stop, the warden slammed it out.

Julian lifted his arming sword just in time to deflect the dangerous ball away with a deafening clang, noting the incredible speed and strength behind the strike.

The warden smiled, or at least that was what Julian thought he saw behind that line of a hole in the stone mask for the mouth. He didn't have time to be sure, though, for the metal ball came crashing toward him again, this time edging closer to him than before.

Julian swept out his weapon to smash away the deadly ball once again, this time with his sword having been enhanced with a glow of crimson red. His instincts had helped him gush out much more grace than he had needed against the guards, and he realised now that he would have to call on even more if he was to triumph against this latest foe.

The same pattern followed for a third, fourth, and fifth time—with Julian pushed further back each time. The heavy collisions had sparked off brilliant radiances while sending waves of low thudding echoes that stunned the other prisoners still confined to their cells.

The metal ball was hurled at him once again, and although Julian managed to block, the impact sent him crashing into the metal bars of the cell behind him. The prisoner inside gasped.

Julian looked up in desperation. "Who *are* you...?!"

The warden chortled. "How is that important?" he asked. "We are only numbers in this game. Like you, I am comfortable behind a mask."

The battle resumed, with the warden dictating the momentum as Julian was sent crashing against the cells. It was never easy to break someone out of prison, but for Julian, the worry had been for the potential army he would face—not a damned warden *within* the prison.

As Julian peered back out to the stairs now, he realised how close the escape path was. And yet so far. He looked up at the warden, pressing at him, realising that he was stuck fighting for his own survival.

This was certainly *not* how he had planned it.

I need an opening, Julian thought. *A chance... I'll have to kill him!*

Julian didn't know how long he had defended for, only that he had been given no opportunity to call on his signature flames. It was then that he finally saw the opening he had been watching for.

Now!

Julian gushed out all the grace he could manage, the crimson red in his body roaring out behind a blur of a slash that he made with the sword.

I didn't actually want to kill you, Julian thought at that split second, seeing a twinkle in his opponent's eyes. But he had been sorry too early. The warden not only evaded the roaring attack with a simple hop, but the man had in turn dealt a counterattack that smashed Julian's sword into pieces.

No..., Julian thought, his eyes wide as an image of that mute sorcerer sparked in him. As if time had slowed down, he watched his weapon shattering. Piece by piece, the metal exploded as an overture to what would inevitably, it seemed then, result in his sound defeat.

The warden still pressed on. But when the man heaved out the metal ball again, looking for a kill, a spark of light whizzed by, knocking the weapon itself from his grip. Both the warden and Julian peered down to the ground where the projectile dropped with a tick and a tack.

A small stone.

The warden was first to turn his head, looking out to the stairs. And by the time Julian followed suit, Alpheus had dashed at him, grabbed him by the arm, and spun to dash away up the stairs.

My god, Julian thought as he watched the cool vapour of air trailing behind them. *Those steps, that breeze. When did he learn something like that?*

Alpheus slowed down after nearly a hundred steps behind those fading afterimages and glowing white dust. Though he was puffed out, his efforts were rewarded upon reaching the block-shaped building at the top.

Julian shook off his daze, before pulling open one side of the double door to an evening where lunar light was notably lacking behind heavy overcasts. At lower elevations, things were even hazier. Indeed, the thick mists that swirled about now shrouded over the entire hill.

I cannot see anything! Julian cursed to himself, taking a step out. *But neither can the guards.*

Julian was without a sword, and when he took a cautious second step, a flock of bats swooped by, the fluttering of their wings reverberating miserably in his ears. Alpheus gasped and stumbled at the doorway, while Julian thrashed his arms about to swipe away the winged beasts, sweeping up whiffs of mist in the process.

When the bats finally cleared, the guards he had expected treaded in behind the fog. They sported that same shirt mail of interlocking loops of metal, but they wore no masks. They waved their arms about to clear to haze, which obviously bothered them as well.

"What have we here?" one of them said with a grin as his allies joined him, forming a barrier to surround the double door.

"Go," Alpheus said wearily, sitting with his legs stretched out.

Julian paused.

"They don't know who you are," Alpheus said. "Not behind that mask. They won't catch you."

"They won't catch you, either," Julian responded without glancing back. "Follow my lead and we'll—"

"No," Alpheus said, cutting in, huffing out a tired sigh. "I'm all drained of energy."

"What are you saying?!" Julian questioned, raising his voice. "Why do you think—" He turned to rebuke him, but paused on seeing Alpheus, who had closed his eyes and was now weeping in remorse.

"No one's going anywhere," one of the guards said with a scoff. "You there, impostor!" he said to Julian, pointing a sword at him and leading the other guards to do the same. "How did you smuggle your way in… and out?"

Julian ignored them, still regarding Alpheus with pity, recognising that Reeling's death had indeed overwhelmed the young scholar.

"I'm talking to you!" the guard cried, losing patience.

The guard waited no longer, swinging an arm forward, signalling his team to seize both prisoner and the guard impostor. Julian spun finally—drawing momentum from the whirling motion—to smash away that first foe with a punch that sent him flying in the other direction. The other guards paused briefly, and just when one of them reached for his sword, Julian dashed forward, knocking the man down and snatching the weapon away for himself.

With no plan yet, Julian darted toward a couple of guards to his right, prodding the arming sword out and piercing the horns at their belts. He followed with a customary slash at their thighs to take the attention away from the horns. The guards hollered in pain, and the distraction had left another three almost frozen in place. Julian darted toward them, piercing and slashing in the same pattern, destroying more horns.

That's five. I can do this.

Julian eyed the guard who he had first knocked down, that man now reaching for his horn, perhaps having seen through his scheme. Julian crouched down, ready to dart at him, squinting out as if staking out prey. That guard started shaking, and his hand wavered slowly away from the horn. Though, strangely, his eyes weren't on Julian, but behind him.

Julian frowned, turning back slowly to the dull grey entrance of the prison, cold sweat building up on his forehead.

Despite the haze, there was no mistake that the warden had stomped his way out, too, and was now standing over Alpheus. The imposing man glared out to Julian as if to say that their battle wasn't yet over.

Julian trembled, his knees going weak. *This feeling... of being completely overwhelmed.*

Just like that time.

And yet, he is no sorcerer.

"You're the warden?" one of the unscathed guards dared to question, treading toward the dangerous man. "How did you let this happen? How did you—"

The warden grunted, staring down at that clueless guard. "Get lost!" he said, his voice more coarse now under the open sky.

"What...?" the guard said with a raised brow. "You'll be begging at—"

The warden had flung his flail out before the sentence was finished, blasting off the guard's head. Blood immediately sprouted up from his exposed neck. The other guards cried out in horror while Alpheus passed out altogether after an audible gasp. Every one of them scrambled to their feet and raced down the hill, running for their lives. And sure enough, as soon as they disappeared into the mists, a noisy low hum resonated back. Those few who still had horns had finally blown into them.

The warden cocked his head, glancing down at the unconscious Alpheus. The man chortled, clawing Alpheus by the head before heaving him out onto the grass, the scholar crashing down several steps in front of Julian.

Julian hissed, raising his sword, reminded that his previous one had been shattered only moments ago.

The enemy lurched forward again, hurling out the deadly ball of metal *not* at Julian, but at Alpheus. Julian hissed, slamming his sword out for another thunderous clash with the spiked metal ball, a nebulous cloud of crimson red roaring out with his swing that sent the warden stumbling back.

The enemy, however, let out a chuckle as he steadied his footing almost immediately.

"To hell with you!" Julian cried, charging forward, again with the spectacular speed of Time-Shifting, slashing out a blazing sword of flames.

But it wasn't enough.

The warden, despite his size, was deceptively agile. He had of course already demonstrated how nimble he was. Even against Julian's lightning quick motion, the hefty man retained control of the battle with the help of his much more efficient motility. Indeed, the warden had again limited Julian to blocking alone, wearing out the blazing arming sword by the second. It was no contest.

"Perhaps you need more motivation," the warden said, before suddenly withdrawing and leaping instead toward Alpheus.

Julian growled, rushing after him, dashing to Alpheus first and then unleashing a roaring fireball as he spun back. *Dodge that!* he thought.

The other man slammed his weapon forward, nullifying the fireball into a deafening explosion that flared out, penetrating the mist for a few brief seconds. The sudden brightness transformed into clouds of smoke. And when Julian swallowed away the excessive saliva in his mouth to ready himself for the next engagement, the warden emerged from the clouds, thrusting that flail forward yet again.

"Damn you!" Julian cursed, caught in a wrestle of heavy weapons, fighting for his life.

The mists shrouded everything beneath the elevated hill, but an army *was* on its way, Julian knew. And as soon as they arrived, there would be zero chance of escape.

Julian looked up, still pushing. *Won't escape even it was just him*, he thought. He had called on all the strength and powers that he had at his disposal, and was now almost spent. He soon found himself thrust away by the enemy's overpowering force again, this time snapping his sword in the process, stunning Julian and causing him to stumble backwards into an awkward fall.

By the time Julian had pushed himself back up again, the warden had taken another giant leap toward Alpheus. And this time, Julian was too far away to do anything.

"No, no, no!" Julian cried, raising an arm in futility.

He could barely see through the mists, but the horrid sound of flesh being cut through was crisp and clear. The scream that followed, however, didn't belong to Alpheus—a deeper voice. Julian peered out hopefully, noting that the warden had stopped a few steps away from Alpheus.

He's alive! Julian noted. *Just barely.* The warden, though, was turning his head about as if searching for someone or something.

The victim of that gash was one of the guards who had earlier fled the scene. And as Julian eyed that man now, he recognised him as the one he had punched, but now with a severed right leg which he held while screaming. Another five—more than half of his team—stood a short distance away.

Julian couldn't understand why they had snuck back up, but he was sure that the warden hadn't been the one to deliver that ruthless blow.

The poor guard coughed up blood and sweat as more blood was spurting out from his ruptured leg. He cursed up into the gloomy night sky, his scream echoing in the clouds. He dared his attacker to show himself, and he got his wish almost immediately.

Following a flap above him, a figure of black dropped down in a glide, sliding a slender sword across the guard's throat to end his misery.

His killer—a phantom of a man—then flipped into the air before performing a graceful landing several feet away from the warden.

This newcomer, too, hid behind a stone mask, black-coloured with two white stripes on either side of the cheek—like some kind of beast. He donned a common soldier's armour, but his outfit was entirely black, unlike the standard wheat-colour. At his waist were twin rapiers and hanging at his shoulders was a black cape that fell all the way to his feet. Compared to the warden, the newcomer was rather slender, standing at about the same height as Julian. His alignment and his purpose, meanwhile, was anyone's guess.

He leaped back into the air now, flapping that tremendous cape in a slick motion and disappearing from view completely. Everyone there—including even the warden—peered through the mists and high up toward the stars, searching for any trace of him. And when that phantom finally emerged again, he had already slashed at another three guards, drawing dangerous amounts of blood as he tore through their chests.

Before the last surviving guard even considered running, the phantom leaped up high into the night sky again. With his black cape flapping out like wings behind the soft illumination of the eclipse, he looked almost like a giant vulture. The ruthless man wasted no time, swishing down at his final victim, slashing his twin swords at him, drawing another eruption of blood. And on that last guard's stumble, the team that had returned was defeated.

Annihilated.

The three men left standing formed a precarious triangle now. They were all masked, hiding for one reason or another. The warden didn't seem to care about Julian anymore. And the newcomer, too, swivelled smoothly away from Julian and toward the warden.

The warden, with his impressive brawn, was first to strike, throwing out that dreadful ball of metal at a speed and strength beyond what he had demonstrated earlier, perhaps in desperation. Even so, the hefty man would soon find himself at a slight disadvantage. The phantom—who had used his dark cape to blend in and out of sight—continued to surprise with every exchange, expertly prodding out his twin swords.

Another one, Julian thought in shock. *So much stronger than me. Who are they?*

Julian perked up now as the phantom of a man managed to parry away the much larger warden, and in turn, land a roundhouse kick that sent the warden screeching across the grass.

Julian shivered, regarding the phantom. *Friend or foe?* he wanted to ask. But he could not find his voice.

"Go," the man said, his voice distorted through the mask.

It took Julian a moment, but when he shook off his daze, he realised that the cavalries were approaching from just beneath the hill. The warden—who had picked himself up—was gazing down at the slanting of the hill as well. He must have known what was coming, too, but rather than rejoicing, he shot a cold hard stare at the phantom soldier.

"So this is the modern day warrior," he said. He then turned, heading back into the prison.

Julian dropped his guard even against the phantom, who had urged him to leave. *But how?* Julian thought. *We're surrounded!*

The phantom shared none of the indecision, dashing now at Alpheus. He collected the scholar by the waist and threw him over his shoulder like a heavy sack.

"No!" Julian cried. "What are—"

But he was too late. The phantom had begun sprinting down the hill. And when Julian thought to give chase, the phantom flapped his cape over Alpheus and himself, flashing away and vanishing altogether.

Julian gaped and then gritted his teeth in anger. He shook his head then, recognising the silhouettes of horsemen trampling up, dangerously close to emerging from the mists. He glanced back at the dead bodies and then dashed toward one who had donned a dark cape. Julian tore it off, wrapping himself in it just like the phantom had.

He took a deep breath. *I have to go for it*, he decided, taking off in a flash with clouds of crimson red roaring behind him. Julian soon stormed into the cavalries rushing up. Betting on his blurring speed and the mists that hazed the landscape, he hurtled on, knocking into more than a few stallions and some footmen.

He continued to dash forward even after escaping the hill, charging away through the city without looking back, passing buildings he didn't have time to recognise. He only started to slow down upon realising that he had almost reached the eastern outskirts of Zorlia, before finally finding refuge in a quiet alley concealed by the dark of the evening.

Julian removed the stone mask, huffing out a visible breath of stress and fatigue. He quietly admitted that it was his good fortune to have escaped this evening in one piece. At the same time, he rued the fact that he couldn't confirm whether or not Alpheus was safe.

TWENTY-THREE

Farwell, Jeffery

Alpheus woke thrashing his legs against a pressure he had always dreaded. He waved his arms madly, his instincts urging him to spring up from his submerged position as he gurgled in mouthfuls of water.

The bay? Or the sea?

Alpheus was frantic, unable to see anything through the murk. He had developed a fear of water long ago following an accident in which he had almost drowned. Given the fact that he couldn't swim, it was impressive now that he was actually rising toward the surface. When he thought that there was a vague dab of illumination from above, he kicked harder.

He failed to reach the top, however, for a hand plunged in at him, grasping his cranium and forcing him down.

Alpheus kicked desperately against the hydraulic pressure, desperately gasping for air, and instead forming a surge of bubbles that soared up into a huge mass above him. He drew on the tiny amount of energy he had left, throwing his arms up for a tight grip on the wrist of his opponent.

I don't want to die! he thought, close to suffocation. *Father of Heaven, help me.*

And finally, he emerged, spattering out of the water for a much needed gasp of breath. *It let go,* he realised, barely making out anything around him. *The hand.*

He was still struggling, though, slapping at the water and coughing up water and saliva. In his haze, he thought he saw a hand coming at him again, and indeed, he was snatched up by his shoulder and heaved up until he thumped back down onto hard earth.

His back throbbed, but the pain was worth it as long as he was on land. He lay there in a sprawl on the wet ground, drenched, wheezing without much care anymore for who was there with him. A dismal night sky greeted him from above, but emerging behind the greyness were the moons, in an eclipse.

Alpheus sat up slowly, noting a wall of reeds on one side of him and a body of murky water on the other. Directly in front of him was a man in black, relatively slender, donning a soldier's uniform with a long cape hanging off the shoulders. The man wore a stone mask, also black in colour, scarred with white stripes at the cheeks.

"You are...?" Alpheus asked.

"You don't know me," the man said, his voice gruff.

He's not Julian, Alpheus thought. *Julian's friend, perhaps? Or...!*

"Jeffery...!" Alpheus exclaimed. "Did Jeffery send you?"

The man in black snorted. "A dead man cannot send for anyone."

A dead man. Those words were more difficult to hear than Alpheus had imagined, and they had him immediately grieving once again.

"The Lord Count is no longer with us," the man said, this time with a hint of empathy. "Accept that. He had faith in you, and he asked me to share that faith."

Alpheus shook his head. "Faith in me? I don't know where this—"

"Here," the man said, cutting Alpheus short as he offered a creased parchment.

Alpheus received it and flapped it out hopefully, but a prompt scan told him that it wasn't a message from the beyond. It *was* from Reeling, but not penned by the man himself. It was the invitation to the Vinan Princess's Purification Ceremony. Alpheus remembered that he was the one who had crumpled it up.

"He asked me to hand this to you if anything were to happen to him," the man in black said.

"You want me to go to Vinawell? To do what? And why?"

"There's nothing *I* want you to do. You are responsible to fork out your own path. What I can do for you, I have already done."

Alpheus perked up suddenly, turning his head left and right, looking over the reeds. "What happened to Julian?!" he asked. "Where are we?"

"We are in the marshes in the southwest of the city," the man said in the same cold tone. "As for your friend... I would assume he's safe."

"You... *saved* me?" Alpheus asked, narrowing his eyes in suspicion. "Do I... really not know you?"

"Know that I am not your enemy," he said, stepping away now into the tall reeds. "But do not think me your friend, either."

"Hold on!" Alpheus cried, reaching out a hand. "Are you just going to leave me here?"

The man snorted. "I'm not someone you can or should rely on. You're a fortunate one, though. If I am not wrong, an ally of yours is on her way."

The man spared not a second more on Alpheus, flapping his cape out, and then vanishing into the reeds.

Alpheus furrowed his brow in confusion. He thought that he should be grateful for the mysterious man's arrival, but he simply couldn't bring himself to admit it, not even now after the man had left. Alpheus looked down at his hand that held the parchment, his double crescent pendant beneath it tied at his wrist.

He rubbed his hands as he exhaled a puff of breath visible in the cold air. Alpheus stepped back out to the edge of the murky water which was, in fact, a swamp. He held his breath, looking down at the reflection of a figure that was barely recognisable. From the blood-smeared rags of a prisoner to the strips of tangled hair that drooped over his dreary eyes, it was as if he had aged ten years since that fateful night when he had discovered Reeling dead.

What has become of me?

Alpheus jumped as the reeds waved behind him. The clattering of hooves followed, further unnerving him.

"Alfie!" a voice cried out in quiet sibilance. "Alfie! Are you here?"

Alpheus recognised the voice. "Agnes? Agnes! I'm here!"

Breaking out from those dense reeds was a sizeable horse, and riding on it was indeed Agnes, who leaped down now from the animal, racing toward him. "You're safe!" she cried, holding him in a tight embrace.

Alpheus reciprocated the affection by brushing her hair with his fingers. Her warmth was inviting, and at that moment, he didn't want to let go. It had been so long, it felt to him then, that someone had greeted him warmly. When he finally did release her, he held her by the shoulders, leaning back to have a good look at her—but to his horror.

"Your eyes...!" Alpheus remarked, noting they were glazed over and wandering like a blind person. "What happened?!"

"Things are a little blurry," she said, shaking her head, sounding as if it wasn't much of a bother. "But I can still see."

Alpheus had no words, his own eyes wandering as he contemplated a world without the gift of vision. He also realised now that Agnes was more than warm—she was burning hot, and gasping for breath.

"We had better get going," she said then between breaths. "Master Seer is waiting for us."

"What...? Master Seer...?"

"He's in Marshallville. We'll talk when we get there. And Alpheus, perhaps you should take the reins."

Alpheus regarded her for a moment, fretting for her wellbeing. He then helped her to the saddle before climbing up behind her, laying her in his arms as he grasped onto the straps. "Sit tight," he said, pulling hard on the reins.

As they raced to the west, Alpheus found it impossible to ignore his troubled thoughts. Everything that had happened in the past week since Reeling's death had yet to sink in. A part of him had hoped that it was all a nightmare from which he would soon wake. But the sensation of the wind slapping at him now was too real to dismiss. The stars above were real. The eclipse was real. Agnes and the heat she was emitting were real.

Everything that had happened was real, too.

Nearly an hour later, they arrived in Marshallville, a village sitting on the western border of state Saffron. It was well past midnight, and none of the humble dwellings located there were lighted. Alpheus didn't have to navigate blindly, however, for Seer had expected them and was already treading toward them now.

Alpheus almost didn't recognise the scholarly man who now sported a simple robe, most likely to avoid attention. And when he was about to greet him, Seer raised a hand in urgency. "Attend to Agnes first," Seer said softly with his usual stern tone.

Alpheus nodded, stepping down from the horse with Agnes, who had fallen unconscious during the ride.

"Follow me," Seer then said, as Alpheus carried his childhood friend on his back.

They entered a small home, lighted from the inside. None of that light spilled outside, though, for Alpheus was quick to realise that all the windows had been shut off completely with thick drapes. He closed the door behind him and Seer trotted through the modest living area, into a room with a simple bed.

"Lay her down," Seer instructed.

Alpheus did as he was told, noting that Agnes was burning hotter and hotter.

Seer regarded his disciple-patient with a concerned expression on his face. He then pressed a thumb down at her sternum, gently gliding an index finger along her arms, applying pressure at certain points which caused Agnes to jerk in reflex. Seer swept her forehead with a palm, an action that seemed to cool her down from the dangerous heat, as illustrated by the thin wave of smoke billowing from her body.

It was Seer the physician at work. His healing ability was renowned as the greatest within the academy, but this was only the first time Alpheus had been fortunate enough to bear witness to it. Seer ended the treatment by slipping a tiny tablet in Agnes's mouth, swiping down slickly from the forehead to her chin to help the medicine stream in.

"Let her rest," he said finally with a deep sigh.

The two men retired to the living area together. Alpheus had yet to speak even a word, but when he looked up, the scholarly man who had been lauded as Reeling's equal wore a solemn scowl that was once again too real for a dream.

"It is obviously not a good time for the academy," Seer began. "To learn that Reeling has passed away, that you are the accused, and that Agnes has been blinded, I feel such incredible remorse."

Alpheus grew more anxious now, but he kept silent as if to spur the man to offer more information.

"It was four days ago when I received a letter from her, begging for my help. I was on an expedition in Farella. Indeed, our team is still there now. She asked that I lend my power for your cause—that if I advocated for you, there was a chance to avoid execution. By the time I rushed my way back to Saffron, it was too late... for her, anyway."

Alpheus frowned, shaking his head in confusion. He opened his mouth but no words came out.

"While you were sitting in prison, she was prying around in the city in search of a group that wanted you dead even before your scheduled execution."

Alpheus cringed, a cold sweat breaking out across his body.

"The world is fraught with danger," Seer said. "For her efforts, she managed to track down the group in the place they call Felon Square. But it came at a cost." He paused for a sigh. "The only consolation is that she is still living. And for that, we have the phantom to thank."

"The phantom?"

"I do not know who he is," Seer claimed. "But the man came to her aid when I could not. He then got you out of prison as well. Regardless of who he is, I am grateful for him."

Alpheus shook his head. "Her eyes," he said. "Is there a way to heal them?"

Seer regarded him for a moment. "The powder that was thrown into her eyes was pernicious... made of ashes, flour, and a poisonous substance that I cannot even identify. Although she has not yet completely lost her vision, her condition will only worsen with time. When that time comes, she will never see again."

"Never... see again...," Alpheus muttered, stunned.

Seer rose to his feet, turning away. "Get some rest," he said. "Your bath is drawn."

Alpheus closed his eyes for a moment before rising and then retiring into the lavatory which barely fit the round wooden bath that it contained.

The water was tempting, heated to a murky white with a few bubbles surging to the surface. Alpheus wasted no time, undressing and then climbing in—to a blissful sensation. That warmth and that luxury had once been so simple, but right now, he wanted to be nowhere else. He submerged himself up to the eyes, brewing in that fine vessel that tingled every part of him with relief and pleasure, feeling that he was being cleansed from all the sin, the bloodshed, and the vice that seemed to have chased after him for such a long time—when in fact, it had only been a week or so.

* * *

The sun had yet to rise when Alpheus stepped out from inside the simple home. He didn't think to stroll about in a village he didn't know. Instead, he settled just outside the house on a patch of grass. It seemed so long ago that he had last slept on a bed, and yet he couldn't enjoy it. Sleep had evaded him ever since that stormy evening. The accumulated fatigue hadn't helped him kick into slumber even now that he had escaped Zorlia.

Seer had assured him that he was safe. And in the past few hours, Alpheus had tried to do his part to become a renewed person. He had groomed himself, trimming off the stubble that he had found discomforting. He didn't fix his hair into his customary braided ponytail, instead letting it fall in tresses to mid spine. He fitted into a new set of clothes, a modest top that fell to the knees with a pair of matching pants. They weren't woven with the quality fabrics he was used to, but Alpheus was grateful as he held a hand to his chest now, brushing the simple linen which did its job in keeping him warm—one of the many functions missing from his prisoners' rags that had been grimed with smut and blood.

Blood, he thought. *I can still smell it.*

Alpheus found it ironic that the only possession he had on him now was the double crescent pendant tied to his wrist. He continued looking up to the sky now, where the stars were gradually fading away in the light of the rising sun. The moons had been in an eclipse only last night, at a position that closely resembled the central symbol of the Ionian faith. And perhaps there *had* been a miracle—his escape and survival—only, it had come too late.

Reeling was dead. There was no denying that. The ambivalence was a struggle. His faith had been a significant part of who he was. Without it, he was a stranger to himself.

His identity as a scholar was at risk, too. The pocket watch that was a mark of his State Scholar status had long been gone, perhaps taken by an opportunistic guard during his incarceration. His spectacles were gone, too, though Seer had presented a new pair to him on the previous evening—apparently, Agnes had been meticulous enough to have prepared a pair before his escape. Alpheus didn't wear them now, though. He didn't want to be reminded of who he had once been—a helpless young man. For the same reason, he didn't tie his hair in a braided ponytail either, instead letting it fan out and fall naturally at his shoulders.

The ring, Alpheus thought, as an image of the sapphire solitaire flashed into his mind. *Where is it? That night was the last time I saw it.*

And this power, this grace, flowing inside of me, he thought as he studied his hands. *The text talked about unbearable pain, that it could ignite one's grace. But if this was what it took, I'd rather never hold this power.*

"Alpheus," a voice said.

Alpheus turned. "Master Seer," he said, unable to find the motivation to stand.

Seer had seemed to wait for that, but instead, he sat down now on the patch of grass next to Alpheus. "What are your plans?" he asked.

"I don't know," Alpheus said, pulling his knees up and resting his head in between.

"Do you have—" Seer said, stopping mid-sentence when Alpheus lunged at him, holding onto him as he wept.

"I miss him," Alpheus said between sobs as he rubbed his face and tears on the scholarly man's arms. "I miss him so much. Why? Just why did he have to die? He was a good person. He was the best. Just who would do such a thing?"

Seer shared his grief, stroking Alpheus by the head. "I miss him, too," he said. "We all do." Seer patted him again and then nudged him upright. "But, Alpheus, this is not the time to grieve. It is the time to make a difference. You have talent. You have an existence. If you want to honour Reeling, know that you have a heavy burden rested on your shoulders."

Alpheus rubbed a hand across his eyes, sniffing. "But I don't know what to do. Where to start."

"Nothing?" Seer asked. "Think. Did he leave you any clues? Knowing him, he must have planned for the worst."

"Clues?" Alpheus said, cocking his head before emitting a sudden gasp. "Yes!" he then said, springing up to his feet. "It's inside!"

Alpheus led the way back into the house, snatching up the creased parchment the man in black had given him, offering it now to Seer.

"A Purification Ceremony...," Seer said, skimming the text.

"For the princess of Vinawell," Alpheus added. "He wanted me to go... though, I don't know how the invitation ended up in Jeffery's hands in the first place."

Seer nodded. "Fleeing the country is the easy way out," he said, putting a hand to his chin. "But is that it?"

"Then...," Alpheus said hesitantly. "Should I go?"

"You should," Seer said, handing the parchment back. "I can never be certain of his intentions. But this *does* seem like something he had left behind with a purpose. You can be sure that he always had your best interests at heart."

A cough sounded then from the bedroom. Alpheus was the first to rush inside, urgently attending to Agnes, who had finally woken up. Even under the faint rays of sunlight, her colourless eyes reminded him that she was soon going to lose her vision completely.

"Did I hear something about Vinawell?" she asked with a weak voice.

Alpheus glanced over at Seer, who said nothing in response. "There's a Purification Ceremony for the Vinan Princess," Alpheus said, turning back to Agnes and helping her to sit up. "But don't get the wrong idea. I'm not interested in some princess in a foreign land—and even if I were, who's to say she would pick me among the myriad of candidates."

Agnes coughed again. "What are you so anxious about?" she said with a faint smile, her eyes still glazed over. "I think it's a wonderful idea. If Alfie, you were to become the Prince Consort, you could—"

"I wouldn't dream of it," Alpheus said, cutting her short.

"No, Alfie," she said, "you have to—"

"I want to be with you," Alpheus said, speaking over her again, those words seemingly lifting her heavy eyelids and restoring a temporary gleam in her pupils. "I wasn't sure what you meant to me in the past. But now I know—I know all about what you have done for me. I'm going to Vinawell, and I'm taking you with me. Agnes, let me take care of you."

Agnes gaped for a second, and then finally relaxed. "I appreciate it, Alfie."

Seer cleared his throat at the door. "Let us end the idle talk here," he said. "There are more important things to discuss. Agnes, will you join us?"

The young lady nodded gently, raising a hand for Alpheus to support. They staggered out of the room and settled at the simple table. Alpheus helped his childhood friend, nudging her to lean forward against the table. When he made his way to his own seat adjacent to Agnes, he spotted a collection of papers that Seer had brought with him. Alpheus couldn't help but notice that one of them was penned by Reeling, something he knew the man had been writing—an incomplete thesis entitled *A Calibration of the Moon Tides I*.

"It's difficult to believe he had time to write this," Alpheus said as he picked out the paper.

"He always made time for what was important," Seer said. "This paper, however, diverges from what one would expect of him—or of any top scholars for that matter."

Alpheus gulped at that. "Is it... bad?"

"No, not at all. Despite its incompletion, it is fascinating, vibrant—indeed, a work of genius. Contrary to his usual style, the thesis employs frequent use of conjectures that allow for an unworldly perspective for the otherwise incomprehensible questions at hand. Its arguments which initially seem arbitrary are supported substantially with insightful theories. Rather than an individual thesis which deals with independent issues, this paper can be a profound and immense foundation to further our enlightenment for decades to come."

Alpheus nodded slowly and began flipping through the pages, skimming its contents. It was indeed unlike any of Reeling's previous work. The man had been well known for his empirical and practical approach as he collected, sorted, and classified information. This thesis, though, spoke about ideas which were only at initial theoretical stages, but the ideas were daring and, perhaps, more importantly, tackled the many sensitive issues of society that most scholars would avoid. It was, as Seer had described it, a work of genius.

Jeffery was amazing, Alpheus thought as he read on. *I've been praised, admired, envied since the first day at the academy. Others have expected me to become one of the greatest scholars, and for a long time, I believed that to be true. But... these ideas, these theories... they're far beyond what I could ever dream up.*

He didn't realise he was crying until a couple drops of tears splattered onto the paper, at which time he clumsily rubbed it with his sleeve, only to smudge the solution more against the text.

"The Grandmaster has once said that, among his many disciples, there are two who stand out," Seer said, unbothered by Alpheus's clumsiness. "Reeling is one of them. I never approved of his decision to pursue life on the political stage, but I must admit with reluctance that he was excellent as the Lord Count. It was his destiny.

"As for you, Alpheus, you need to find your own destiny. It is futile to linger on the past. In this land, there are many people who play different roles, all with unique powers. There are knights, scholars, and even sorcerers—and beyond those are many, many more. Until you can identify these people and how their roles might complement you and your world, you cannot expect to achieve what Reeling failed to accomplish. And to begin, you will need to define where you belong inside this complex chain of beings."

"Alfie's headed for Vinawell," Agnes said. "That's a start."

Seer looked over to her. "Perhaps."

"About the other disciple who stands out," Alpheus said, returning to the earlier topic. "Is it my sister?"

"Indeed," Seer said with a grin. "I would add that Charlotte Hindlow has the potential to eclipse even the Grandmaster in ability."

Alpheus said nothing. He had been told how great his sister was ever since he could remember, but all he wondered about now was whether his sister had learned about what happened and whether she would spare much thought to any of it.

"Let us get back on topic, Alpheus," Seer said. "When will you depart?"

"Any time, really," Alpheus said. "I just need to inform Julian... eh, Julian Longinus... I need to let him know that I'm safe. After all, he bet on his life for me."

"Write him a letter," Seer suggested. "I will deliver it. That way, you can leave sooner."

"How soon?" Agnes said, reacting first.

Alpheus rested a hand on her shoulder. "I'm sorry," he said. "I'm sorry that you have to follow a suspected criminal. But I promise that I won't let anything happen to you."

Agnes breathed a sigh. "No, it's not that," she said. "I was just thinking that I need to at least say something to my housekeeper, and perhaps settle a few other things."

"Oh, of course!" Alpheus said, holding his head. "But it's nearly two hours from here. Would you be all right travelling that distance?"

"She has my company," Seer said, to which Agnes nodded.

Alpheus retired to the cramped room in which he had tried to sleep in last night. With no desk present, he resorted to writing on the bed.

It was a half hour later when he returned to the living area. Alpheus entrusted his letter to Seer, who was all ready to return to Zorlia with Agnes.

"I'll be back before dusk," Agnes said. "We can head off then."

"Be careful," Alpheus said. "Cling tight onto Master Seer."

"I will."

Alpheus eyed Seer then. "And...," he said hesitantly. "The thesis. Jeffery's thesis. May I please have it? It's the only thing I have left that is his."

Seer nodded, offering a rare smile. He picked the paper out from his shoulder bag, offering it to Alpheus. "I hope you can find some use for it," Seer said. "Farwell, Alpheus. The next time we meet, I expect you to be fully revitalised."

Seer stepped out of the house, leaving Agnes behind for a more private goodbye. She reached out for Alpheus's hands and held onto them tightly before gently brushing her hand across and down his face, as if to help her remember what he looked like. Finally, she fell into him for an embrace.

"Take care, Alfie," Agnes said in a whisper.

* * *

It was noon when someone knocked on the wooden door of the humble house. Alpheus was startled at first, but upon hearing the voice of a woman, he managed to relax. "Open up, please," the voice said, loud yet gentle.

Alpheus proceeded to the door, opening it to an unsuspecting woman in her mid-forties, rather plump in size, but with a smile as amiable as her voice. She clung onto the tiny hand of a young girl about six years of age. The girl had big round eyes that sparkled in the light. Her amber hair was unusual to see in a Truban. Even at her tender age, she was pretty, and that was despite wearing clothes common to lower class families.

"Can I... help you?" Alpheus asked, suddenly awkward.

"You can, indeed," the woman said, before nodding down at the girl who then handed a parchment over to Alpheus that was much smaller than the one he had penned only hours earlier.

"The young lady who was with you asked me to pass this to you," the woman said. "Oh! Almost forgot. Call me Mother March. That's how everyone else addresses me."

"Nice to meet you," Alpheus said, receiving the parchment. "My name is Al... Albert."

"I'm Thelma," the girl responded with a crispy voice and a wide grin.

"Nice to meet you too, Thelma," Alpheus said, patting the girl on the head.

Mother March then presented Alpheus two gold coins. "Your friend left this for us," she said, nudging the coins into Alpheus's hands. "She's too generous. Will you give it back to her?"

Alpheus hesitated. It wasn't surprising that Agnes could write despite the condition of her eyes. She must be so used to extensive writing that her poor vision wasn't enough of an obstacle to prevent her from penning a letter. It would have taken a little more time and effort than usual, though.

But why had Agnes written to him? What could she not say in person?

"Thank you," Alpheus finally said, accepting the letter and the coins. When March and Thelma left, Alpheus slowly unfolded it and began to read.

My dearest Alfie,

Please forgive me, for I cannot journey with you.

You need to rise up again and become the person I have always admired. Please do what you need to. You can entrust me to investigate the murder and clear your name.

I hereby pray for your safety and happiness.

Agnes

Alpheus stared blankly at the handwriting for a long while. This time, he managed to hold in his tears. The letter had clearly been difficult to write, and upon seeing the words, he finally came to fully appreciate what Agnes really meant to him. Everything she had done had been for him—even this decision now to not travel with him. And for that, Alpheus *loved* her, but like a sister. Like family.

He breathed out a long sigh, folding the parchment closed once more. "Wait for me," he said softly to himself, as if speaking to her over the great distance between them. "I'll come back, and I'll find the best physician there is to heal your eyes."

He then peered over to the table where he had left Reeling's incomplete thesis. "And you too, Jeffery. I promise to honour you. But for now... farewell."

EPILOGUE

Julian stood on the court without a twitch behind the Lord Chancellor. He was secretly glad for Alpheus, having since learned from Yusuf Seer in a brief, private meeting that the young scholar was headed for Vinawell. He had made sure to leave no evidence behind, burning the parchment immediately after he had read it. He still wondered, however, as he peered out about the court now, who the phantom was and why he had helped. But no one seemed suspicious of having worked with the use of a disguise.

It had been the second morning since that evening at the prison, and now, as a scribe had reported, six guards had been confirmed dead, seven injured, and one missing. The missing prison guard had of course been the victim to Julian's theft. Not only had Julian taken his outfit, but the guard had also been shipped off to another state, along with a herd of sheep.

Julian had since discarded that outfit. He couldn't be sure whether anyone knew about his involvement, but he had been surprised to learn that the warden was apparently also an impostor, just like him. Still, Julian realised how fortunate he was to have escaped the prison with nothing more than a few bruises. No one around seemed to be suspecting him, and he believed it had helped to be standing by the Lord Chancellor, who had once again invited him along to the court today.

The discussion in the court now was heated. The Lord Emperor was in the middle of it all, furious that a prisoner had broken out under their watchful eye and that there were no leads on where Alpheus might have gone.

"Lord Breunor!" the emperor called out, causing the military man to jump. "Will you explain this?"

Julian could hardly suppress his grin now as Breunor stepped out onto the aisle, opening his mouth but with little to say. "I...," Breunor said with a stutter, glancing back at his retinue. "The cavalries... they..."

"Your Majesty!" Bors said, stepping out next to his liege. "It was *my* responsibility! I was late in letting Lord Breunor know. It was *I* who delayed our team of cavalries. If we must find someone to take the blame, let it be me."

The emperor narrowed his eyes. "Do you think that to be a sufficient explanation?"

"If I may," Morlan inserted from the seat on the emperor's left. "Your Majesty, it was reported that the prison hill was clouded in thick mists that night—so oddly thick, in fact, that one could hardly see past an arm's reach. A few years back, I would say it was witchcraft, but if you ask me now, I would say it is sorcery."

Julian squinted, suspecting the same thing. The mists that night *had* been rather thick. And had they not been so, he might not have managed to flee.

"We have mists here almost every day," Forredan said then with a smirk, waving a dismissive hand. "To say that the mist was created by sorcerers is absurd."

Morlan regarded the stout statesman. "To break out of the prison is no simple feat," he asserted. "And to do it without a trace of evidence left behind is nearly impossible. Could we open our minds to the possibility that a being of the Apostle's stature was behind it?"

Forredan applauded with derision this time. "Excellent!" he remarked. "It is *indeed* convenient to blame something that no one knows about. Now that I think about it, could it also be the Apostle who kidnapped Lord Morlan's daughter?"

Parts of the court laughed at the former king's expense, while Morlan himself flushed. "Do you have a better explanation, then?" Morlan challenged.

"I don't," Forredan said. "But I would ask Alpheus Hindlow."

Morlan smirked in return. "And that's your answer?"

"My answer is his *capture*," Forredan said. "As the greatest Empire in the land, I trust that we'll manage to hunt the boy down. At such time, the riddle will be solved."

"I concur with Lord Forredan!" Breunor said, finally finding some of his ego. "I'll arrange for thorough inspections at every checkpoint across the country. I won't allow the boy to escape a second time."

Breunor seemed determined enough for redemption. But the emperor said nothing. No one wanted to guess what the proud conqueror was thinking—not when he wore such an unforgiving expression.

"Your Majesty," Schim said with a spiteful grin. "A decision needs to be made. The longer we contemplate, the further the truth will drift away from reach."

The Lord Emperor shot him an irate glare, lifting his chin in defiance.

"Lord Schim," he addressed him. "Did I miss something? Or do I sense that you think this to be a trivial matter?"

Schim shook his head. "I think this to be a waste of time," he said. "The damage has been done. And here we are on a second day of discussions, still contending on who is to blame, mocking one another. If the Lord Count was still with us, he would have steered us to a solution by now."

"It is a pity that he's *not* still with us, then...," the emperor responded, his voice growing shrill as he spoke. "But we still have *you*, Lord Schim. What do you propose?"

"Order the capture of Alpheus Hindlow," Schim said, echoing Forredan's words. "Do everything in our power to seize him. The suggestion has been pitched more than a few times... only that *someone* has continued to refuse acknowledging."

"Lord Chancellor!" Lachman warned, stomping a foot behind the throne.

The emperor held up a hand to halt the golden knight. "Very well then, Lord Schim," he said. "Let us put the case on hold until we find the criminal." He then turned back to Breunor. "Lord Breunor," he said, "I will entrust you to the task. Do not disappoint me."

The military man bowed in acceptance. "Aye, Your Majesty."

"Now," the emperor said, "if there is nothing else to report, let us end—"

"Hold it there," Schim cut in. "I have an announcement to make." He smiled, turning from his seat to his retinue behind him—indeed, specifically eyeing Julian. "Step forward," he said.

Julian frowned slightly in suspicion but he did as asked, treading out to the aisle with all eyes on him. "On one knee," Schim then said, standing up as Julian abided again. "Let it be known that Julian Longinus will be Silver Knight, as of this moment," he announced, his strong voice resonating clearly across the court.

Julian gaped in surprise as murmurs suddenly filled the court. He knew that he had become well-known ever since his performance at the Exchange. He also had his fair share of enemies, but none of them was about to do anything to stop the inevitable now. To make it official, Schim clicked for a servant to bring out a set of polished silver armour, carrying it on a sizeable tray.

"You have proven your ability to fill this role," Schim said to Julian as he handed him a silver helm from the tray. "This would have happened sooner, but for the Lord Count's untimely and unfortunate death. I trust your ability to aid me and the Empire."

Julian accepted the helm without a word. He wasn't least bothered by what others might have thought. He thought not of the lucrative income that would follow, and not of bringing glory back to the Longinus name. The Endless Knot and all those tied to it was all he mused about, and the authority he received now would surely aid him in his upcoming quest.

"Lord Chancellor," Julian said with his head inclined. "I shall give it my all."

* * *

Julian would only meet his new liege a few times in the following week, spending almost all his time at the training ground in Vondra Dawn, where he had previously competed and made a name for himself. Sharing the battle ring with him was Tannon Gale, his instructor for the week.

Julian had first learned about the opportunity when Gale sought him out at Rogers. He had doubted that it would actually happen then, and it was still hard to believe even now that he was learning the Fire-Wind Wheel. It was one of the most outstanding techniques demonstrated in the Exchange, and the one that had allowed Gale to trade molten balls of fire with him, torching the arena in a spectacular display. And now, Julian was on his way to managing that display all by himself.

Julian had spared little thought about how the Lord Chancellor had managed to arrange for it. Instead, he simply accepted the favour, doing the best he could to learn what Gale had to offer him. There was a time constraint, after all—one week. That was the amount of time that Forredan had agreed to release Gale. And today was the final day of that window.

Julian was never going to master the technique in only seven days, but having worked through all the foundations, he believed he was on track to master it on his own without further guidance. He had also come to appreciate the fact that Gale was indeed a seasoned warrior. And while he didn't think the veteran knight was the best instructor, it was clear that they both wanted this to work.

I chose you because you play with fire, Gale had said when he first flirted with the idea. But now that they were to part ways, the veteran knight regarded Julian with a grave expression as if to say that his legacy was in Julian's hands. Julian had an urge to assure his master of a week, even if it were a lie. But at the end, he was unable to promise anything.

"Thank you," was all Julian managed as he watched Gale disappear behind the gate under the tangerine of the falling sun. *I owe you.*

Julian swung his iron sword on his back, the sword that had grown black from the intense burning. He had opted to wield this same dreary weapon, despite the new gleaming silver armour he now donned. In fact, he preferred the simple sturdy leather and light metal faulds of a soldier, which he believed was more practical. He admitted, though, that this armour of silver certainly provided enhanced protection. One day, he might need it.

He happened by the southern atrium now, which seemed rather crowded for this time of the day. His armour of precious metal had attracted a group of noblemen who now flocked toward him. In his eyes, these were the sycophants of the Empire—of the land—men who acted solely for personal gain.

"Congratulations, Sir Longinus!" one of them said with the fake smile that Julian had come to recognise. "I always knew you were going to make it. You know, I was rooting for you during the Exchange. It was just bad luck that you couldn't win—no, no, indeed, no one won! It all ended before a winner was named."

Julian gazed at him with a squint. He didn't recognise that face—a middle-aged lord with a thick beard draped in a red robe of silk.

"Come on now, Lord Dawson," another said, shoving his way forward. "You're stammering. Sir Longinus here doesn't need praise. He *knows* we all love him."

This one was younger. He wore a round hat over long tresses of hair that swept over his shoulders. But perhaps they all looked the same.

"Sir Longinus," that man by the name of Dawson said, with a grin and a nudge on his arm. "You know, I recently secured a piece of land not too far from Mt. Pinnacle. If you want it, you know, for a place near your hometown, just say the word."

This is new, Julian thought as he nodded along with a smirk. *I've had this before. Status... is what they call it.* He went on to convince himself that none of these people, now five of them gathered around him, were genuine. But Julian didn't think about exposing their hypocrisy. Instead, he pitied them.

A familiar voice echoed out from a larger cluster of men to his left.

Julian glanced across the sea of people, making out... Percival Pole. His old friend was swarmed by noblemen, more than a dozen of them, who were all singing his praises. "You're the most deserving to be golden knight," one of them remarked.

"Absolutely," another agreed. "*And* you were the one to take down Alpheus Hindlow, when even Lord Breunor struggled. They should give you

Noel already."

Pole wore a big grin, clearly enjoying the flattery. "But I wouldn't go to Noel," he said. "Not without all of you!"

The group shared a raucous laugh, the sight of it all causing Julian to wince. "If you would excuse me," Julian said to the men around him.

He withdrew from them and kept his glare focused on Pole until he finally noticed him. Julian nodded at him from afar. And soon, Pole excused himself from the nobles as well.

"Julian," he said with that same fake smile. "Come."

They retired briefly from the crowds, ascending to a small balcony that oversaw the atrium. This was the first time they had shared a word since they crossed swords at the Exchange. Julian reminded himself that he wasn't mad because Pole had proved a superior swordsman. He was mad at him for other reasons.

"Why are you not in Bastion City?" Julian started.

"Hey, hey...," Pole said with a raised brow. "What's with the tone? And to think I was about to congratulate you on your promotion."

"Why are you here? Did Sir Sagramore approve of this?"

Pole breathed a sigh and then looked up to the last glimmers of daylight with a sense of pride that Julian had never seen before. "I don't need that anymore," he said. "I'd admit I owe much to my teacher. But my future lies beyond what the Defence Army can provide. These men," he said, peering down and gesturing toward them. "*They* are my future. With their support, I can be much more than just a knight. I can be a lord. I will have my own title. I will have land, gold, and women. I will have *power*."

"These men?" Julian said with a sneer. "They're simply following the ebb and flow of the tides. If you were ever to fall from grace, they will be the first to abandon you."

Pole smirked with a shrug. "And that's why I'll never allow myself to fall. Instead of dampening the mood, why don't you smile for a bit and enjoy what we have?"

Julian glanced at the hand Pole had rested on his shoulder, shoving it off now. "I'll only ask you once," he said with a wistful frown. "I understand it's the duty of a knight to do what you did that night—to seize Alpheus. But I'm not convinced that you, Percival Pole, someone who knew him, would believe him to be a murderer. Tell me, did you do it for—"

"Like you said," Pole said, cutting in. "My duty was to seize him. He was a suspected murderer and now he's a runaway prisoner. I have done no wrong."

Julian clenched a fist. "You'd betray a friend...?!"

"You must be mistaken. He is *your* friend, not mine."

Julian grunted, and then let out a growl that echoed out over the men below. "What happened to you? Have you been completely blinded by vanity?!"

The noblemen beneath them fell silent for a brief moment. But soon enough, they carried on as if they hadn't heard a thing. Julian continued to glare at Pole, looking to find even a glimmer of guilt or shame. Instead, all he saw was indifference.

"Well then, Sir Longinus," Pole said, turning sour now. "If you don't believe he did it, then why not investigate yourself? Complaining to me changes nothing. In any case, our conversation should end here. It's not looking good in front of the lords."

"I will leave. Don't you worry. But...," he said, hesitating. "There is something I want to ask you."

"Oh?"

"A man who uses the flail," Julian said. "Do you know him?"

Pole turned his head slightly, clearly intrigued.

"He who can crush a person with a simple swing of his weapon," Julian added. "Do you know of such a man? Also, a man who dresses in a soldier's uniform, wraps himself in a black cape, and can blend into the darkness at will."

Pole chortled then. "Are you really asking me?" he scoffed. "Why would I know men with such strange descriptions? And besides, anything I say and whatever I suspect will be met with your contempt. It is best I say nothing at all."

Julian shook his head in disappointment. "I want to punch you," he said softly. "Maybe beat some sense into you."

"Don't," Pole said, treading away now and waving a hand behind him. "I would crush you. And then what would you have? Nothing."

ACKNOWLEDGEMENTS

Writing is indeed a lonely journey, gruelling in many ways, but also incredibly rewarding. While it's easy to quote the saying that the journey matters more than the destination, this hardly applies to writing.

The destination matters. Until the manuscript is edited over a thousand times and then finally published, a writer really has nothing to show for. And it's this harsh reality that many aspiring writers never overcome, and hence never manage to bring their words to see the light of the day.

I am both delighted and relieved that I have come this far. And hopefully, this is only the beginning.

Along the way, however, I have found that I am not alone. In terms of writing with better clarity, from the sentence level to the bigger picture, there is no one I owe more to than my excellent editor, Richard Larson. In the art department, I am grateful to Shovel for her patience and willingness to work with me to ensure that all the artwork fit in, or in some cases, enrich my original concepts.

Finally, I must thank my family for the continuing love and support they have given me—even if not directly related to my writing venture, then certainly to me as a dear member of the family.

FINAL WORD

Thank you for reading *A Serenade for Selene*. It really is very much appreciated. If you enjoyed it, I'd be grateful if you could leave a short review on Amazon or Goodreads.

Please note that the second book in the *Memories from Oblivion* series, entitled *A Revolutionary Ballad*, is due to be released in the third quarter of 2018. Meanwhile, you can find out more about the series on:

www.atlas-hill.com

If you had wanted to learn about me, unfortunately, I would have to disappoint you, for I wish to keep my personal life separate from my alter ego as a writer. At least for now.

Thanks again for reading.